First Witches Club

OTHER TITLES BY MAISEY YATES

Happy After All

Cruel Summer

The Lost and Found Girl

Outlaw Lake

Cowboy, It's Cold Outside

Dallas

A NOVEL

MAISEY YATES

This is a work of fiction. Names, characters, organizations, places, events, and incidents are either products of the author's imagination or are used fictitiously. Otherwise, any resemblance to actual persons, living or dead, is purely coincidental.

Published by Montlake, Seattle

www.apub.com

EU product safety contact:
Amazon Media EU S. à r.l.
38, avenue John F. Kennedy, L-1855 Luxembourg
amazonpublishing-gpsr@amazon.com

ISBN-13: 9781662535451 (paperback)
ISBN-13: 9781662535444 (digital)

Cover design by Letitia Hasser
Cover image: © Abscent84, © FScottMattern, © Mangata, © Sensvector, © Svetlana Ievleva / Getty

Printed in the United States of America

For everyone who needs to find their magic.

A PLAYLIST FOR SPELLS AND MAGIC

"Practical Magic" – Alan Silvestri

"The Lost Words Blessing" – Spell Songs

"Like a Prayer (Epic Version)" – Axel Avix

"Crystal" – Stevie Nicks

"The Prophecy" – Taylor Swift

"If You Ever Did Believe" – Stevie Nicks

"Like a Prayer (Choir Version)" – I'll Take You There Choir

"Season of the Witch" – Lana Del Rey

"Addicted to Love" – Florence + the Machine

"labour" – Paris Paloma

"Little Girl Gone" – CHINCHILLA

"Cassandra" – Taylor Swift

"Mother's Daughter" – Miley Cyrus

"My Kink Is Karma" – Chappell Roan

"as good a reason" – Paris Paloma

"Who's Afraid of Little Old Me?" – Taylor Swift

"Silver Springs" – Fleetwood Mac

I call my power back to me.

I call my energy back to me.

I call my magic back to me.

I am shielded from anything that would take my power from me.

Nothing can harm me or take my light.

I am safe. I am protected.

I am powerful.

And so it is.

—A spell for trying times

Chapter One

Nora

If your life is going to fall apart over a man, he should be hotter.

Like your husband?

The swift comeback from Nora's subconscious made her grimace as she stood in front of her neighbor's hospital room door, flowers clutched tightly in her hand.

Her life hadn't fallen apart. She and Ben were just separated.

She stared at the whiteboard by the door. *Alexandra Stone.*

Alexandra was the most organized, pulled-together, formidable woman in Hemlock, Oregon. She and Christopher were a power couple. Though Nora had always thought Christopher was getting the better end of the deal.

Nora lived across the street from Alexandra and Christopher, and Nora worked with her on community art and writing classes for kids in foster care, but when Christopher's affair had come out, Alexandra, who spearheaded more committees than Nora could readily list, had quit everything.

She'd started staying out late. Going to the casino two hours up the freeway and gambling. Drinking. She'd been unraveling.

And two days ago she'd gotten in a car crash on her way home from the casino, and now she was hovering between life and death.

All because she'd been betrayed by a man with the round, smooth face of a gallon milk jug. A man who was essentially a pair of sentient khakis wandering around the car lot he owned like it was a kingdom, and he its very king.

That's not me.

Nora blew out a breath.

"For God's sake, Nora," she muttered as she raised her hand to knock on the door.

Which then opened before her hand could make contact.

"Nora!"

Her fist was hovering right above Daisy McNamara's face. She lowered her hand quickly. "Hi."

"I was just dropping off a bouquet."

She looked behind Daisy and saw a gorgeous array of flowers that made her own look a little sad.

"Same." She lifted her vase slightly.

Daisy was dressed all in green, from her green skirt to her green cardigan, and green, thick-rimmed glasses.

"Come in," Daisy said. "Not that I'm . . . Madison stepped out for a vape break."

Madison was Alexandra's adult daughter.

"Ah. Vaping. The deeply less cool way to compromise your lungs." Nora stepped into the hospital room and looked around.

"Our cigarette era was much cooler," Daisy said.

She and Daisy had been friends in high school but had lost touch in that way you did. She didn't avoid Daisy in the produce aisle. Whenever she and Daisy ran into each other, they would talk for fifteen minutes, at least, and promise to do something sometime, which never happened because they were both busy, and that was fine.

She meant it when she told Daisy they should have lunch. She was sure Daisy meant it too. It had just never occurred.

It wasn't like Daisy had stolen Nora's boyfriend or worn the same dress to prom or spit in her iced coffee. There hadn't been a dramatic friendship breakup. Their friendship had been a victim of the relentless continuation of space and time that carried them away from the people they'd been in high school. They'd gone to different colleges and done life on different timelines. Daisy and her husband, Jonathan, had gotten married very quickly after school and had started having kids.

Nora was mildly embarrassed that she didn't know the name of Daisy's third kid. The first one was Avery. The second one was Wren.

What was the third one?

It was a boy. Nora was reasonably sure it was a boy.

"Which florist did you get yours at?" Nora asked, because the flowers were stunning, and small talk was all she had. She deliberately avoided looking at Alexandra's bed, the soft beeping of all the machinery reminding her of exactly where she was.

"Oh, I made it."

Of course she had. Daisy was one of those women who did everything. Not unlike Alexandra, really.

Nora kept her focus on the flowers for as long as possible. There must have been fifty bouquets. She took a step toward an arrangement of sunflowers in a rusted water pot, tied with a burlap bow. She touched the card and turned it over.

God Bless!
Xx Soraya Nichols

Oh, Soraya. She'd barely seen her since high school, and apparently today was a near miss.

She glanced up at Daisy and was about to say something dry about Soraya, but the expression on Daisy's face, which was suddenly so bleak, stopped her.

Finally, she looked at Alexandra.

Oh God, Alexandra would hate for people to see her like this. With her dyed red hair half bandaged—likely shaved—and tangled on her pillow. With bandages on her arms and no makeup on her face.

"I've never seen her without lipstick."

Daisy let out a short, shocked laugh. "You know . . . neither have I."

They both stood there for a moment.

"Nice to . . . see you," Daisy said. "Even if it's . . ."

"I didn't know you knew Alexandra."

"Yeah. I do. In the way that everybody knows her. But I've been back and forth between my house and YMTO rehearsals and the hospital a lot because my grandma is getting PT before she can go home, and my mom isn't doing so well, so she and my dad are dealing with . . . Anyway, I was here." Daisy tucked some of her rigidly straight light-brown hair behind her ear, her blunt bob in perfect order, as she always was.

"Oh. Sorry about your grandma. And your mom." Nora had no idea what was happening with her own mom or grandma, but she imagined at this stage of life there was a strange sort of freedom in that.

Now Daisy had to care for the people who had cared for her. Nora was free because her family had never cared for her at all.

"Jonathan knows Alexandra," Daisy continued. "He's been on the city council for a couple of years. It's good for him. With the construction company. You know, he gets a lot of information on zoning changes and things like that. It gives him some influence."

Nora frowned. "That's not a conflict of interest?"

"It's hard to find someone who doesn't have a conflict of interest here. This town has like ten thousand people," Daisy said, and Nora huffed a laugh.

"Indeed, it does."

All they had talked about when they were younger was wanting to leave. Because as beautiful as Hemlock was, nestled in the mountains of Southern Oregon and only a few miles from the California border, it was boring for teenagers.

Nora had never asked Daisy how she had ended up back here.

Of course, Daisy had never asked Nora how she had ended up back here either.

"We should get lunch," Daisy said.

"Yeah," Nora replied, meaning it just like she did every time. "We should."

Daisy shook her head. "No. Not sometime. Let's have lunch, Nora. *Today.*"

If this moment was a reminder of anything, it was that life was mean and took unexpected turns off the road.

You couldn't keep putting the deep, important things off until a tomorrow you might not have.

"Yes. Let's have lunch."

Too late, Nora realized that might mean talking about her personal life. Which might mean bringing up the subject of Ben and the separation.

Would that be so bad?

Yes, it felt potentially fatal, actually.

Proving Ben's point.

Wasn't that what he'd said? That she clung to the past in unhealthy ways and resisted healing and kept her walls up?

But what was the alternative?

She looked back at Alexandra. That was the alternative. Being so vulnerable, caring so much, that when someone left you, all the pieces of yourself fell away.

Nora was sad about the separation, but she was okay. She also had every confidence they'd get back together. They'd made vows. They were a team, a partnership. Friends. He needed to go and deal with his issues, which was fine. She was strong enough to let him go away and do what he needed to do. *They* were strong enough.

"I hope you . . ." she started to say to Alexandra, but the words died on her lips. "The community might fall apart without you," she said instead. "I mean, who's going to organize the Christmas parade? The tree lighting. Community trick or treat. The Arts Club won't be able to function without you. We'll all be lost without you." Nora cleared her throat. "Okay. I'm ready."

Daisy nodded wordlessly, her lips closed in a way that suggested she might cry if she tried to speak. They walked out of the room and down the hall.

It was quiet in the elevator, and Nora felt like she didn't know what to say. She looked down at her purse. Ben had given this purse to her for Christmas just last year.

The perfect purse. Black with the cycles of the moon embroidered on it in gold. It went with everything she owned, and it felt like *her*, and of course he'd known that.

Had he found the purse in a cute little boutique, bought it, and carried it back to his car thinking, *In eight months, I'll tell her I haven't been happy for years*?

That would be insane.

Yet now she was stuck on it, her hand on the purse feeling like it was on fire. Feeling like Ben was right about her.

No.

When the elevator doors opened, she could breathe again.

She wasn't the worst.

She did have friends.

They walked through the lobby area and past the gift shop, which was when she caught a glimpse of her.

Soraya Nichols.

Sunflower Soraya.

She had been one of the most obnoxious girls in high school. Every so often Nora hate-scrolled Soraya's Facebook feed, just to check and see if she was still deserving of Nora's rage. She was.

She would look at photos of Soraya's sparkling white kitchen, photos of her wearing dresses that seemed like they belonged on a prairie somewhere as she made glorious loaves of sourdough, her blond hair still up in a big messy bun like she was fifteen years old, or down in bouncy Instagram curls. *Happy, happy. So blessed so blessed. Hashtag boy mom.*

She made Nora's teeth ache.

But right now Soraya was not standing in her kitchen looking thinner, prettier, and better than Nora. She was currently standing in front of a shelf of crystal angels crying. Not pretty crying. Ugly crying. Her shoulders were shaking, and people were just walking by her. It was a hospital.

Given that, it wasn't weird that Soraya was crying. It made it seem reasonable to walk by her.

Nora wanted lunch.

"Oh God," Daisy whispered. "Is she okay?"

Of course.

The problem was, Daisy was a good person. Nora had never claimed to be nice. She tried to be kind, she supposed, but there were limits.

"I don't know. She's probably sad. Because it's a hospital. Seeing Alexandra was really upsetting."

"We should see if she's okay."

Just like that, Nora could feel the third invitation to lunch hovering in Daisy's spirit. She was that kind of person.

Daisy's kindness was how they had ended up hanging out with Soraya occasionally in high school. On field trips and in certain classes when her youth group friends weren't around. Most of Soraya's friends had been part of the homeschool clique in town, and so sometimes at school events she hadn't had anyone, and Daisy had always been the one who wanted to collect people like they were wounded birds.

Nora was okay with being the worst person right now, actually. But it seemed like Daisy was intent on being the bigger and better one, taking off toward Soraya without giving Nora another glance. Nora looked down at her purse and decided she really didn't want to be alone this afternoon. She followed Daisy to the corner where Soraya was standing, inconsolable.

"Hey," Daisy said. "Are you okay?"

Soraya looked up at them, glassy eyed. "I . . . No."

She seemed surprised by the answer that came out of her mouth. Shocked that she was in fact not okay.

That was what had always irritated Nora about Soraya. Well, it was one of the things. But the relentless toxic positivity was a lot. One of the times Nora's mom had come back into town and pretended, yet again, they might have a shot at reunification, only to leave Nora devastated by her (predictable) defection instead, Soraya had said God would show Nora something good through this betrayal, that it would be a lesson.

Nora had told Soraya exactly where she thought God could shove his lesson.

Soraya had taken exception to the mention of God's holy asshole.

It really wasn't a mystery why they weren't friends.

Unfortunately, Nora was no longer sixteen. So as much as she would like to give Soraya a half-hearted wave and leave with a snarky *Praying for you*, she wouldn't do that.

"I saw that you brought Alexandra flowers," Daisy said, like she was talking to a frightened animal, all soft and soothing. "I didn't realize you and she were so close."

"We work at the food pantry together." Soraya looked helpless and lost and very sad. "It's . . . it's awful, isn't it? She's one of those people who seemed like she had a blessed life, and then he—her husband—left her, and now she's in the hospital and . . . and . . ." She hiccuped. She managed to do it prettily.

Daisy gave Nora a long look. Nora let the left corner of her mouth twitch upward slightly, the most enthusiastic consent Daisy would get from her.

Daisy turned back to Soraya. "We were going to go have lunch. Do you want to come?"

Soraya glanced between the two of them. "Really?"

"Yes. I'm hungry." Nora tried to smile. "And you seem like you need something. A drink?"

"I don't drink."

"Of course you don't. How about a lemonade?"

Soraya's expression was so hopeful, Nora had a hard time being spiteful. "I *would* like a lemonade."

"Great," said Nora.

Soraya turned away from the angels and pressed her palms against her cheeks, aggressively pushing her tears away. "*Great*, let's go."

Soraya was even lovely after a crying jag.

They started to walk out of the gift shop when Daisy stopped mid-step. "Nooo." She grabbed both Nora's and Soraya's arms and jerked them back behind a tower of pastel teddy bears and Mylar balloons. "Look! But don't *look* look. It's Christopher and *her*."

Both Nora and Soraya gasped and peered around the tower, just in time to see khaki-wearing Christopher Stone walk by, hand in hand with a blond who was young enough to be his daughter.

"How dare he?" Soraya whispered at the same time Nora said, "Bastard."

"I can't believe he's bringing her to his . . . not-even-ex-wife's bedside," Daisy hissed.

"Maybe he's meeting his daughter here," Soraya said. But it was obvious not even she believed that best-case scenario she'd cooked up in her fluffy, optimist brain.

"He's probably standing over her, gloating." Nora's tone was far more acerbic than she'd intended it to be.

They disappeared into the elevator, and Nora could only stand there and marvel at the audacity.

The three of them stood in silent judgment for a few more moments until Soraya sighed. "So. Lunch?"

Nora wasn't sure if she felt hungry now, but she could always eat.

The hospital wasn't far from the main town square, where there were eclectic clothing boutiques, a yarn store, several restaurants, and a British pub, for some reason.

It was all part of the quirky charm of Hemlock.

They let the sound of the traffic on the street stand in for small talk as they walked toward the square. "Brickroom?" Daisy asked.

"It's too millennial gray," Nora said. "Half the menu is avocado toast. Last time I was there, I think the server got mustache wax on my water glass."

"*We're* millennials," Soraya pointed out.

"That doesn't mean I have to surrender to every dish having microgreens and pickled onions on it."

"Louie's?" Daisy asked.

"Sure," Nora and Soraya said together.

They walked through the alley that led to the entrance of the restaurant, up the stairs to the dining room, and stood in the entry waiting to be seated.

"I'll probably get a salad," Soraya said.

Nora clenched her teeth together but didn't say what she was thinking, which was growth, really.

She was already feeling crushed by the weight of how mundane the conversation was going to be, and she couldn't even be mad about it because she was going to be part of that mundanity.

She would rather drill a new hole in her skull than discuss the state of her life presently.

It didn't take long for them to get seated at a four-person table by an upstairs window that overlooked town.

The square had a small clock tower in the center, with flyers tacked to every inch of surface that could be reached.

There were also drinking fountains, one with fresh water, and one with the sulfuric water that came out of the local springs. It was a time-honored tradition to trick your children into trying the sulfur water without warning them.

It was little wonder Nora had trust issues. Though, to be fair, it wasn't from surprise sulfur water.

You were right. You were right about the world and love and everything. Hooray.

She couldn't order that drink fast enough.

They were greeted by a waiter and handed menus. She was going to order a hamburger now, just because Soraya was getting a salad.

When the waiter returned, Nora ordered a beer, while Daisy got a white wine.

"I might actually like a glass of the zin," Soraya remarked, smiling.

"I thought you didn't drink," Nora said.

"It's white wine. It's not really drinking."

She couldn't tell if Soraya was kidding or not.

She decided to let that one go.

"How old are your kids, Daisy?" Soraya asked, and the familiarity in Soraya's tone made Nora wonder if Daisy and Soraya had been hanging out without her. That would normally be fine, wouldn't bother her at all, except right now she was feeling a little bit raw, and if she found out that Daisy had made time for lunch with Soraya but had never managed to make time for Nora, she might cry.

Maybe.

"They're nine, seven, and five."

"Oh wow. So they're all in school."

"Yes." Daisy twisted the ring on her left hand. "Yeah. All in school. All day. Which is nice, but it's definitely different."

"Well. My boys don't have any time for me anymore. They're seventeen and fifteen."

Seventeen and *fifteen*. Nora felt closer to being a teenager than not. It blew her mind that somebody her age had nearly full-adult humans. But then, Soraya had gotten married one month after their high school graduation. Like a lot of those church girls tended to do.

That was what happened when you weren't allowed to touch underneath the clothes until marriage. The timeline had to be accelerated.

"You must have a lot of free time," Daisy said.

Soraya looked like she didn't quite know what to say to that. "I make a lot of sourdough."

"Oh," Daisy and Nora said at the same time.

Soraya turned to Nora. "You still don't have kids, Nora?"

Nora was *quite* certain Soraya knew she didn't have kids.

"No." She let that be a complete sentence.

The drinks came, and they put their order in for food. They ordered salad, a burger, and a chicken Caesar wrap. It seemed somehow very Daisy that her order was a middle ground between Nora's and Soraya's.

Soraya took a sip of her wine. Nora watched her closely to see what her reaction was. Did she actually drink? Or was she about to have her first taste of alcohol in the middle of the day on a Friday?

Soraya started to tear up, setting the glass down, her hands shaking. "I . . . I do have a lot of free time," she said, her lower lip trembling. "Because I . . . I kicked David out."

Chapter Two

Nora

When you're in need, ask the divine power in the universe. It will provide.

—Rules for Witches

Nora could only stare at Soraya, her mouth dropped open. "What?"

"You kicked David out?" Daisy asked.

"Yes. I did. Two weeks ago. He's staying in a house his real estate company was selling, with our boys, and they just want to live with their dad because he's better than me, apparently." She blinked back tears as she took a sip of wine.

"What happened?" Nora asked.

Soraya was the perfect tradwife. The kind who deferred to her husband in everything, or at least that was what Nora had assumed based on knowing her in high school, plus what she posted on social media. She couldn't fathom Soraya throwing her husband out.

Not without a very good reason. Nora didn't know what even counted as a good reason to a woman like her.

Soraya set her wineglass on the table, her hand trembling slightly. "We were . . . We were at church. We were at church, and he went into the bathroom during the sermon, and I was sitting there, and my phone vibrated. I thought I should check it, even though you're not really supposed to have your phone on during the sermon, but I always think it might be one of the kids, so I pulled my phone out to check, and it was a picture of . . ." She looked around and lowered her voice to a near-imperceptible whisper. *"Of his penis."*

"What?" Nora gasped. "You kicked your husband out because he sent you dick pics during a sermon?"

"*No.* If he'd wanted to send me . . . I . . . If he wanted to do that, then I'd have been okay with it." Soraya didn't look okay—she looked perturbed—but Nora didn't comment. "It's that it was a penis photo that wasn't meant for me."

"How did you know it wasn't for you?" Nora asked.

"Because he's just never done anything like that before, and there's something to be said for trying new things, but usually you don't try new sexual things during the Lord's Prayer."

"Everyone has kinks," Nora pointed out.

"Well, not David. Or at least I didn't think so."

Daisy put her hands flat on the table as if bracing herself. "Your husband misdirected a picture of his—"

"His cock."

"Thank you, Nora," Daisy said dryly. "He sent *that* to you from the church bathroom?"

"Yes." Soraya spun her wineglass in a circle. "I don't . . . I don't know what I'm supposed to do now. I've never had a job. I've never had a job, and he's not supporting me. The kids won't talk to me, and they're my whole life."

"Why won't they talk to you?" Daisy asked.

"I'm the bad guy," she whispered. "I'm the one who kicked him out and broke up our family."

"How did *you* break up the marriage?" Nora asked.

Soraya looked down at her hands. "I'm supposed to forgive him. It's supposed to be not that big of a deal. Our pastor said because David repented, I . . . I need to forgive him. He was supposed to install some software on the computer to keep him from going to websites he shouldn't be on. I don't want software to keep my husband from looking at other women or trying to hook up with other women. I just think it's wrong. Shouldn't it be enough that I don't want him to?"

Silence fell around the table. Nora took a sip of her beer.

Daisy looked like she was about to vibrate apart. "Jonathan left."

Soraya and Nora turned to her. *"What?"* they said at the same time.

Daisy nodded. "Just . . . just like that. My high school sweetheart. Suddenly it's . . . *You don't know me, not really. We haven't been happy for the last ten years. Who* hasn't been happy for the last ten years? I've been perfectly happy. I . . . I thought we had everything. He said he needs more, that people aren't meant to just meet someone and settle when they're as young as we were, and he met her and found out he wanted all these different things."

"Her?"

"He moved into a new house with his new girlfriend." Daisy picked her fork up and set it back down, then did it again, like she was trying to find the perfect place for it on the table where it might help ease her nerves.

"Hold on." Nora pinched the bridge of her nose. "I haven't heard rumors about *any* of this. About either of you."

"Alexandra's divorce and accident have been enough for the rumor mill," Daisy said. "No one's that interested in me."

"We've still been going to church together as a family," Soraya mumbled.

"Oh, Soraya." Nora groaned.

"I'm an Enneagram Type Two."

"I don't know what that is," Nora said.

"It's—"

"Oh, I'm not asking." Nora turned her focus to Daisy. "Why didn't you tell me? Why haven't you told anyone?"

Daisy's eyes glistened. "Jonathan doesn't want his mom to know yet, so he's been really careful, because I think he wants to make it seem like Amberly was someone he met after we split up. But I know she's living in that house with him."

"Amberly?" Nora asked. "Is she a shih tzu? An *infant*?"

"Not canine. And she's twenty-five." Daisy blinked her tears back, her tone hard and bitter now. "Which makes sense, you know, since the last time Jonathan was happy, we were twenty-five. So I guess he had to find a twenty-five-year-old who didn't have stretch marks from bearing his children in order to be happy again." Daisy looked down at her hands. "He murdered our life. We had this really good life, and he just walked in one day and . . . blew it up. For himself. Nothing I said made any difference to him. I told him I didn't want it. I told him I wanted to work on it, that I didn't care he slept with someone else."

Nora's stomach twisted. "How can you not care about that?"

"Because I just wanted him to stop . . . saying those things. I just wanted it to go back to how it was. Before he said that. Before I knew it's . . ."

"It really is like having your life murdered," Soraya said, her tone soft. "No warning and no way to defend yourself, and when you know, you can't go back and *not* know."

"I'm sorry," Nora said. "That's awful. I can't even imagine it."

It was a stupid thing to say. Who wanted to hear that their life was so shitty you couldn't even begin to imagine what they were living? Nora knew better than that. It was the kind of thing people used to say to her when she'd been a kid living in foster care.

I can't imagine not having a family!

Good for you.

"I just mean," she tried again, "I don't want to be dismissive of what a big deal that is."

"It's fine." Daisy took a deep breath. "So, how are you and Ben?"

The question Nora had dreaded didn't seem so dreadful now.

"Fine," she said, not sure why she wasn't being totally honest.

But it was different from all this. It wasn't church-bathroom dick pics and affairs with twenty-five-year-olds. He just needed a little bit of space. He was just finding himself.

Ben's decisions had been more unilateral than she would have liked, but he hadn't told her he'd had ten years of unhappiness, and he hadn't left her for another woman. *It was different.*

"Fine?" Daisy pressed.

"Yes. Just . . . fine. I mean, you know how things are. They move in waves. Marriage is complicated. But you know, we've only been married for five years. There's just not . . ." They were both looking at her like they could see through her. "I mean . . . we are a little bit separated right now."

"You're *separated*," Daisy said.

"But you're *fine*," Soraya added.

"He needed some space."

"Oh, space?" Daisy said. "That always means they're sleeping with someone else."

She didn't have to spread her bitterness over to Nora.

"He's not." She did her best to affect a neutral expression. "What happened to you guys is terrible, and I'm really sorry about it. What happened to Alexandra is *awful*. I hate that everything unraveled for her when Christopher cheated, but it's not the same. He needs to go be by himself and deal with some things. I love him, and he's going to . . . find himself."

"When did he *lose* himself?" Soraya asked. Yet again, Nora couldn't tell if she was being funny or tragically sincere.

"I just think . . ."

Suddenly she *heard* herself. Sitting there at this table with two other women whose marriages had come unglued, having come from the hospital room of a woman who had gone through a heinous separation.

She did sound naive. She did sound silly.

But they didn't know Ben. Ben was fun and funny, and there was a reason he'd been voted Hemlock's Favorite Dentist three years in a row. He wasn't like a regular dentist; he was a cool dentist.

He had a twenty-sided die tattooed on his arm, and he liked to tell jokes with kids, and . . . and . . .

She knew him. He'd talked to her. She hadn't liked everything he'd had to say, but they'd talked.

"It's not ideal," she finished.

“I’m Jonathan’s bookkeeper,” Daisy said. “That’s my job. I do all the financial stuff for the construction company. But I do more than that too. I collect the payments, and I organize everything. I make sure all his accounts are balanced and he isn’t going to overdraw. I’m still working for him.”

“That’s not okay,” Nora said. “Unless he pays really well.”

“We just share all the money.” Daisy’s lip trembled. “Or at least we did. I don’t know what to do. I hold his whole life together. Plus, if I don’t keep the job, I won’t have enough money to maintain the mortgage. There aren’t any divorce papers; he just left. I don’t have a timeline. I don’t know how much child support I’m going to get.”

“I’m a freelance writer and artist,” Nora reminded her, and herself at the same time.

She’d never faced the potential reality of what life would look like without Ben’s dentist salary, but it suddenly felt very heavy.

Ben had left for his solo trip to South America three weeks ago, to stay at a wellness retreat in Chile, and she’d let it stop there in her mind. He was going to sort himself out. He’d been working for years—doing school, establishing his practice—and he needed time to himself. It had seemed reasonable.

She suddenly realized all the practicalities she hadn’t considered.

Like if he decided he didn’t want to come home.

Where would that leave her?

She wouldn’t be able to afford their mortgage, and if he decided to not pay it . . .

The anger she felt at herself right then was swift and judgmental.

She’d been like a frog, boiled slowly in the promise of Ben, and she’d lost her cynicism.

She’d done the right things.

She’d gone to school. She had a degree; she’d majored in English and minored in art. She could teach at a school if she wanted to, but she’d never done that. They’d lived modestly, and then Ben had finished dental school and graduated without loans, thanks to his parents. They’d almost immediately started making a decent income, and Nora, who'd always had to be independent and protect herself fiercely, had never had to worry about anything since being with him.

Somehow along the way she'd convinced herself she was taken care of.

She had a career, sure.

But that career wasn't a steady paycheck. Her unstable childhood should have served as a warning. She *should* have known better than this all along. Hadn't her own mother taught her anything?

"There's no way I'll be able to keep the house," Soraya said. "I don't know what I'm going to do. I . . ."

"We'll think of something," Nora said.

Her irritation with Soraya suddenly felt petty.

Daisy and Soraya had been totally screwed over by the men who were supposed to care about them more than anything else.

As for Nora, she wasn't as secure as she'd thought.

On that they were united, even if there were a lot of other things that divided them.

"Thank you." Soraya finished the rest of her wine. She had barely taken a bite of her salad. "I don't have an appetite right now."

"Can't relate," Nora said, polishing off the last of her fries.

"I just want to eat my feelings," Daisy said.

"I can't," Soraya said. "My feelings sit in my stomach like a giant ball of lead. I was a good wife."

They were all quiet for a moment. Because the truth was, they had all been good wives. Nora was sure of that.

She'd been a good wife to Ben. Or maybe she hadn't been.

Maybe she'd been a human ice sculpture lying in bed next to him. That was how he made it sound. That was why he'd said he had to reevaluate.

"We're going to be okay," Nora said, her tone way more determined than she felt.

"We are?" Soraya asked.

"Yes," Nora said. "We're going to be okay. We're resourceful women. We're going to find everything we need to navigate whatever is coming."

"I'm going to need a job," Daisy said. "One that's flexible, because of my kids."

"I'll need a job other than my baking. I'm starting to sell loaves of sourdough at different stores, but I'm one person, and there's no way I can support myself on bread alone."

"Jesus said that," Nora pointed out.

"That's not quite what Jesus said." Soraya took a breath. "But someone will have to take a thirty-five-year-old woman with no job experience."

"You have skills," Nora said.

"You never think it will be you." Soraya scrunched her eyes up, like she was trying to hold her tears back. "This happened to one of my mom's friends, and everyone ostracized her. She couldn't get work because no one wanted to hire a woman with no education and no experience, and I judged her like everyone else. Now I am her."

"We'll be okay." Daisy reached across the table and put her hand over Soraya's.

Nora settled her hand on Daisy's shoulder. "We will."

Soraya looked down. "Okay. We will."

Goose bumps rose on Nora's arms, a chill coming through the front door of the restaurant as it opened.

"Ready?" she asked, suddenly feeling restless.

The other two nodded, and Nora signaled to their waitress. They split the check three ways, then walked downstairs and back out onto the street.

"I'm parked up that way," Soraya said.

Nora jerked her chin the same direction. "I'm that way too."

They began to walk toward the park, when Nora noticed a store she hadn't seen before. "What's that?"

A building wedged between the yarn store and a brewery had its lights on, when it had been dim and empty for months.

There were really only two kinds of businesses in town. The kind that came and went in less than a year, run by people who had fantasies about cute, cozy stores but were unable to handle the reality of the harsh churn of doing business in a town where crowds ebbed and flowed with the seasons.

Or businesses that had been there for thirty years or more. Fixtures that never seemed to go away. This storefront was one that often rotated, and it had gotten to the point where she didn't really notice when it changed hands. She often didn't bother going inside. Why get attached?

But this one stopped her.

There were brooms in the windows and hanging herbs. A large wooden sign read Lady's Mantle Apothecary.

"Oh, you didn't know about this?" Soraya asked. "It's *occultic*."

"What?" Nora asked.

"It's . . . it's *satanic*," Soraya whispered, like she was concerned people would think she was being rude saying the store was satanic, though saying it anyway.

"Satan? Sounds fun." Nora grinned.

Soraya gave her a look that took Nora right back to high school.

"Why do you know about the store?" Daisy asked Soraya.

"Oh, Pastor John mentioned it in church last week. When he found out it was opening, he wanted to make sure everyone in the church knew so they could guard their . . ." She seemed to realize she was saying too much to an audience who hadn't even wanted to hear half of it. "Whatever."

That was some growth for Soraya, Nora had to admit.

"I want to check it out. So if you want to stay away from the occult, you can keep going, I guess," Nora said.

"I want to see it." Daisy was already walking toward the front door.

"I can't." Soraya took a step back.

"You can't go into the store?" Nora asked, incredulous.

"No. We're supposed to stay away from even the appearance of evil."

"I wonder what category dick pics in the church bathroom fall into. Pictures that you were supposed to be fine with, I might add," Nora said.

Soraya's face turned pink. "Okay, I can stop in for a second."

Nora smirked at Daisy, who gave her a hard look. This interaction was oddly cheering, because it reminded her of a time when she didn't feel so desperately jaded and out of hope.

She pushed the door open, and a bell jingled above the door. The room was dim and cool, soothing music playing over the speakers. A table sat in the center of the room with a sign in the middle that proclaimed tarot readings were available. There was a shelf next to that with boxes of tarot cards on display. Beyond that was a large counter, and behind it were shelves of dried herbs and jars of tea.

Across from that were bookcases filled with books about the metaphysical and the divine feminine. Then there were bins of crystals with cards attached to the front that spoke to the purpose of each one.

For the first time in weeks, Nora felt like she could take a full breath. She walked over to the counter and admired the large jar filled with dried yellow flowers. A small handwritten card was placed just in front of it.

Lady's Mantle: the patron herb of alchemy, often used in love spells.

"There's not even anyone here," Soraya said, still standing at the door. "Let's go."

"No." Nora touched the lady's mantle card and then moved farther into the shop. "I want to look at some of the stuff."

She'd always been interested in the idea of magic—what little girl with no control or power in her life wasn't?—and of course her gothic aesthetic had frequently led her into witchy shops, where she liked looking at crystals and bundles of herbs, but that was all it was. A vague interest. Whenever she picked up a deck of tarot cards and considered buying them, her more practical self told her it was nonsense, and she ended up putting them back.

Everything felt like it was off kilter, which made her feel like maybe this time she would buy a deck of cards. Or some crystals. It couldn't *hurt* anything.

There was a shuffling sound, a fabric curtain hung over a doorway opened, and a very small woman with long white hair came out and stepped behind the counter. "Good afternoon," she said. "Welcome in."

Nora waved awkwardly. "Hi, thank you."

Daisy walked deeper into the room. "This is great."

"Is there anything that you're looking for in particular?" the woman asked.

"Just looking," Nora said. "We were walking by and saw the store and thought we should check it out."

"I'm so glad." The woman smiled, the skin by her eyes crinkling.

"What's . . . an apothecary?" Daisy asked.

"I'm not sure what all the other ones are," the woman said, "but this one has medicinal herbs, teas, spells. I want to do tea parties and tarot readings, tea leaf readings, though I won't have my full menu of services ready until I get some employees. I need a bookkeeper and a baker, and I really need someone to run the front counter."

The same goose bumps that had risen on Nora's arms earlier rose again now.

We'll be okay.

"A bookkeeper?" Daisy asked.

"Yes," the woman said. "I can't do that for myself. I'm not good with numbers."

"What . . . kind of baking?" That question came from Soraya, who was almost pressed against the door, like she was afraid Satan himself was going to pop out from behind one of the shelves.

"I'm open. When I find the right baker, I'll defer to her skill."

Nora moved over to the tarot cards and touched one of the boxes.

"Do you read tarot?" the woman asked.

"No," Nora said. "I don't. I've always been interested."

The woman nodded. "You have to wait until a deck speaks to you."

"I guess that's my problem. No deck has spoken to me yet." Nora released her hold on the box and walked back to the counter.

"Do you have questions?"

Nora looked up at the older woman, at her faded blue eyes surrounded by innumerable wrinkles. She wanted to have questions. She wanted to ask her those questions. Get some of the wisdom of the elders she'd been told existed but had never actually experienced. Her grandmother hadn't contained wisdom. Only bitterness.

"I don't," Nora said.

"I'd like to pull a card for you," the woman said. "For all of you. Since you're among my first customers, I can give you an idea of what I do here."

"Oh." Soraya looked nervous. "I can't—"

"You don't have to receive it," the woman said.

Receive it.

The words lingered inside Nora like a cloud of mist.

"I'd like a card," Daisy said, in that calming, peacekeeping way of hers. Obviously trying to undo the rudeness of Soraya's response.

The woman reached beneath the counter and pulled out a stack of cards. They were gilded on the edges, with midnight blue on the back and large yellow moons. She shuffled them quickly, her crooked hands moving deftly as she did so. She spread the deck out in front of her and looked at Daisy with a steely-eyed gaze. Then she carefully took a card from the deck fanned out before her and turned it over.

The image on the card was a tower, on fire, with people either falling or jumping from the crumbling structure to the ground below.

"I *thought* there was big energy here." She looked at Daisy. "That's a significant card. It feels like things are falling apart, doesn't it?"

Daisy stood still, but Nora could see tears gathering in her eyes. She nodded slowly.

"The Tower can feel brutal. It's destructive, and it's painful. But the secret of the Tower is that what falls away doesn't need to be."

"But those people are going to hit the ground and . . . die," Daisy pointed out.

"They won't die. That doesn't mean they won't be *hurt*. But being down there is better than being where they never belonged."

Nora's heart started to beat faster. It was so . . . apt. Too spot-on, in fact.

The older woman looked at Soraya next and pulled out a card. She turned it over so its face was showing, but Soraya didn't move any closer.

"The Hierophant." The woman pointed at the card, which had an image of a man in robes, who looked like a priest or cardinal or something. "Structures and systems are very important to you. Maybe even religious systems. But sometimes those systems that once served you can hinder your growth."

Soraya opened the door to the shop and slipped outside without saying a word.

"Sorry about her," Nora said. "She—"

The woman didn't seem bothered at all. Instead, she turned her startling eyes to Nora. She flipped a card over, and a soft smile crossed her lips. "The Moon. It's a complicated card, the Moon. The moon is light, but it's darkness too. It moves in cycles. It changes the tide. Though it may not seem clear now, it will in time."

Without thinking, Nora touched her purse, her fingers skimming across the embroidered moon.

"This is just where you are right now," the woman said. "It's the energy you brought into the store with you. When it comes to matters of tarot, nothing is fixed. Everything, life and the future, is on a continuum."

Nora swallowed hard. "Right. Well. My present continuum blows."

The woman laughed, a deep, hearty sound that came from low in her belly. "It can certainly be like that. For a while. The universe has a way of taking away what isn't needed and providing what is."

Platitudes. Good guesses. She probably did this for everyone who walked in. Daisy was the walking embodiment of someone going through a crisis, and Soraya looked like she'd stepped straight out of an LDS influencer's Instagram, so guessing that religious structure was part of her life wasn't really difficult.

As for Nora . . . things being unclear but becoming clear could apply to anyone.

"Well. Thank you."

"Of course," the woman said, then turned away. "If you know of anyone who needs a job . . ."

"I might . . ." Daisy stopped. "I'll let you know if I hear of anyone."

"Thank you," Nora said.

"Of course." The woman fixed her gaze on Daisy. She didn't say anything, but Nora felt like something significant passed between them.

"Bye." Daisy turned away, and Nora followed behind her, out the door and onto the street.

Soraya was standing as far away from the store as possible without falling off the sidewalk, her arms crossed tight. "No surprise she said weird stuff about religion," she muttered.

"It's just a little bit of tarot," Nora said. "It's harmless."

"It's how the devil gets a foothold," Soraya responded.

Nora scoffed. "Is that how the devil got a foothold in your husband? Tarot?"

Soraya narrowed her eyes. "No."

"It seems to me he was able to get a pretty good hold on him at church."

"Well, there's no use tempting bad things to happen."

"She's hiring. And you need a job." Of course, Soraya had probably just made the worst first impression in history.

It was a coincidence of the highest order, one that was almost too good to be true, and definitely too good to pass up.

"I don't have any experience working in a store."

"But you bake," Nora said.

"I . . . I don't know."

"No one from your church would know. Anyway, if they did, they would have to admit they walked into the store," Daisy pointed out.

Soraya seemed to consider that.

"She needs a bookkeeper, Daisy," Nora said.

Daisy sighed heavily. "Yes. She does. But if I'm going to take a new job, I have to quit my current job, and that's . . . complicated."

"I once played with a Ouija board at a slumber party," Nora lied.

She hadn't been to slumber parties. But she *had* gotten a Ouija board at a yard sale when she was twelve, and she'd played with it one evening, until her foster mom had found it and thrown it out. Because of the devil. The devil was a big concern around these parts.

"You did?" Soraya asked.

"Yes," Nora continued seriously. "The devil came out and said if I gave him my soul, he'd give me something shiny."

"Nora . . ." Soraya looked both frightened and annoyed.

"It was bullshit," she finished. "Satan wasn't in the Ouija board, just like he isn't in the apothecary, Soraya, because nothing but herbs are in the apothecary. She's probably a very intuitive person who does card tricks. The end. But she has books that need keeping and bread that needs baking, and it sounds like it would be perfect for the two of you."

"What about you?" Daisy asked.

"Ben will be home in three weeks." Maybe. He hadn't exactly given a definitive time frame. And she didn't know what he'd decide when he did come back.

"There's no harm in taking a job until he comes back," Daisy pointed out. "Just in case."

It wasn't a mean thing to say. She was trying to keep Nora safe, and Nora knew that, but it felt like being stabbed, even if shallowly.

Why *would* Daisy think Ben would come back? Her own situation was so dire, she was projecting onto Nora.

But Nora also knew there was merit in protecting herself.

"It's been a very long, sad day," Soraya said. "I'm tired. I need to go home, and I'm never going back there."

Nora sighed. "Fine. I was kind of thinking we really received some divine intervention there."

"You just said it was all bullshit," Daisy said.

"I said the Ouija board was bullshit. Not *every* spiritual thing."

Daisy's phone buzzed, and she looked down at it, then growled. "Oh, shoot. I have to go get Alden. He threw up."

Alden. *Alden.* His name was Alden, and he was a boy, so Nora wasn't the worst person ever.

"I have to run, but we need to make sure we all have each other's numbers," Daisy said. "Whatever happens . . . we're not going to be Alexandra. I just keep thinking about how she withdrew from everything and everyone, and was so exhausted and under so much stress . . . And who was there for her?"

"No one," Soraya said sadly.

It was what they'd all been feeling all day. It was clear then. If Alexandra, a woman who had so much in her life, could be so undone by her divorce, then anyone could.

"We're not going to be Alexandra," Nora repeated.

Soraya nodded.

Before they headed to their cars, they started a group chat.

Discarded Wives Club.

It was a little depressing. But also a little funny.

It had been that kind of day.

"We're not going to be Alexandra," Nora whispered as she got into her car.

It was strange, but it felt more than a little bit like a spell.

Chapter Three

Soraya

All is never lost—unless you give it away.

—Rules for Witches

Today had been weird, and she hadn't been herself, honestly. She shouldn't have gone into that store. She shouldn't have gotten wine drunk in public and spilled her guts to Nora and Daisy.

Nora didn't even like her. She never had.

Which was fine. She and Nora were just . . . too different. Soraya had tried being nice to her, but Nora had been such a hot mess in high school, it had been hard. She couldn't be okay with Nora smoking cigarettes in an alley. It was bad for her. So of course she said something about it, and Nora got mad.

Nora was always mad.

Now so are you.

Ouch. She didn't like that. She'd tried so hard all her life to be happy. Filled with joy. The light she was supposed to be in the world. A beacon on a hill.

Now she was alone in her kitchen, everything far too quiet while she kneaded her sourdough loaf and listened to nothing, a black hole of darkness shut away, which wasn't a commission in any ideology.

Usually, she put on a Bible-study podcast or some worship music, but she felt empty, and for the first time didn't want to be filled by anything. Not someone else's thoughts or opinions on what she should do or how she should feel.

Her whole life was about receiving instruction and listening to it.

Maybe that was part of why Nora had always felt tricky.

She didn't listen to anyone, and Soraya had to listen. Always.

It was so quiet that the knock on her front door followed by the ring of the doorbell just about sent her straight to heaven.

"Probably hell," she muttered. She stepped away from the counter and wiped her hands on her apron as she made her way to the foyer. "Since I went into Satan's lair today."

She peeked out the side window and frowned. Kristi, her Bible study leader, was at the door. She had missed the last two weeks.

She felt a little bit guilty about that, but at the moment, she felt weird and bad and guilty about everything, so nothing really galvanized her into action like it used to.

It was a tangle she couldn't sort through.

She jerked the door open and smiled. She hadn't even forced the smile, it was compulsory. Her church smile. The everything-is-fine smile. Glory-to-God smile. Hallelujah.

"Kristi," she said. "What an unexpected surprise." Well, that was both redundant and obvious.

"Can I come in?"

"Sure. I was just . . . I'm about to put a loaf of bread in the oven."

"Oh. Lovely."

Kristi came in and stood there in the vast entryway, her smile competing with Soraya's for brightest. And most fake.

Anxiety hooked itself around Soraya's stomach. She thought of the missed Bible studies. She was definitely getting a check-in. A *Hey, girlie, let's have coffee* without the preceding message.

An ambush.

At least the house was clean. She didn't have anything else to do. Nothing but keep it clean, bake the bread, and worry. Worry that the entire place was going to crumble around her. That everything she had lived for, created, would fall apart. That she would be crushed beneath the weight of it.

But she kept smiling. "Come in. I'll make you a cup of coffee."

"Tea for me, thank you," Kristi said. For some reason, that felt like a rejection.

"Of course."

Kristi had been to her house a number of times, so Soraya didn't have to lead her to the kitchen but did anyway, wringing her hands as she did.

She put a kettle of water on the stove. Kristi sat down at the small table by the window. Soraya found she couldn't join her, so she stood next to the stove, waiting for the kettle.

"We've been worried about you."

She didn't have to ask who. The women's Bible study. Kristi was here representing the group, clearly.

"I appreciate it. But . . . there's no need to worry about me."

"We've been praying for you."

Which meant talking out loud to God about her, as they sat in a circle listening intently to glean all the possible details of why she so desperately needed prayer.

They would never gossip, of course.

Soraya clenched her back teeth together.

"Thank you." Even though her smile was wide, she could hear the tension in her voice.

"David texted me," Kristi said.

Did he text you his penis?

Somehow she didn't ask that question. Somehow. But it felt like the floor had fallen away, and the frightening thing was she actually had no idea what he had texted Kristi, because she didn't know him.

The husband she thought she had would never have sent photos of his naked body to anyone else. Never. But David had. He wasn't the man she knew.

He could have sent Kristi anything.

A photo of his penis, a shared location halfway around the world, because maybe he had decided to leave everything behind. A selfie with a person he had just murdered. Genuinely, it could be anything.

"He texted me," Kristi repeated, and Soraya realized she had just been sitting there with a smile frozen on her face and hadn't responded at all.

She wasn't going to. Because Kristi had come here. She was the one who knew what she wanted. Who knew why she was here, and what David had texted. Why should Soraya have to play a part in a performance she hadn't agreed to be cast in?

"He wanted me to talk to you about the separation." Kristi sighed, like she was talking to a child. "Soraya, you have to go back to him. He's your husband. He made a mistake."

"He did make a mistake," Soraya said, her lips barely moving. Maybe she was still smiling. Maybe she was snarling. She had lost feeling in her face, so she couldn't really say. "He directed a text intended for someone else to me. Then I found out who he really is."

Kristi tilted her head to the side, the faux compassion on her face so apparent to Soraya it nearly choked her. "That's not who he is. He's a good father, a good husband. He volunteers on the sound team at church, he is so good. He was tempted. Satan comes after people who are doing the Lord's work."

Soraya was about to say something—anything—to stop this recitation of her husband's supposed virtues, but Kristi pressed on. "Think about the internet. It's filled with women trying to tempt good men to sin. There has never been a point in human history where men faced greater temptation. Now, with the push of a button, they can be in easy contact with someone looking to fulfill their fantasies."

Soraya blinked. "But you have to *look* for it."

For a moment, Kristi's eyes went blank. Soraya could see she'd said something Kristi didn't have an instant response for in the preplanned script she'd come with.

Then Kristi's eyes lit up, as if a flash of inspiration had just hit her.

"If a man is looking for it, it means he's missing something." Kristi stared at her meaningfully. "It's up to you to fulfill your husband's fantasies."

Soraya huffed. "I can't do that if he doesn't share them."

They had sex at least three times a week. That was a lot, she was pretty sure. Not that she sat down and compared notes with anyone, but it seemed like a reasonable quantity of sex.

He never asked what her fantasies were.

An uncomfortable feeling began to bloom in the pit of her stomach.

She didn't know what her fantasies were.

She didn't know what his fantasies were.

They didn't talk about sex. They just had it. Since he seemed to like having it, she'd never had reason to believe it wasn't satisfying for him.

She'd never considered if it was satisfying for her. It was often fine, and she really didn't mind it. They did pretty good, she'd thought, all things considered.

They had gone from kissing chastely to their wedding night, which had been like going from walking slowly down a country road to getting into a speeding car and careening around corners at a hundred miles per hour.

Anything she knew about sex she had learned from him. And neither of them knew anything. Because they weren't supposed to know anything about sex before they got married. Because they were *supposed* to keep their thoughts pure. So she had gone from very much keeping her thoughts on whatever was pure to having to figure out what to do with a naked man, and that was a difficult thing to do.

How could it be *her* failing?

How could it be her failing when they had been in the exact same position? Why did he know more about what he wanted? It meant he wasn't doing what they'd been commanded to. It meant that he was . . . If he had information she didn't, then he had come by it during their marriage. He had come by it keeping secrets.

Alone at night in her bed, her thoughts spun around in circles, eating their own tails. Alone at night, she blamed herself. Of course she did. She wondered why she wasn't pretty enough. She wondered why her life hadn't divinely worked out the way she'd been sure it was ordained to, since she had done everything right. Had done everything to earn blessings. A perfect, easy marriage, because she'd had that good godly sexuality with her husband. Because she had given herself to him—after marriage and only to him—just like she was supposed to.

But with Kristi staring at her like this, she could not accept the blame. Watching another woman verbally absolve David of any wrongdoing. Hearing what she'd said to Nora parroted back to her . . .

It didn't sound so reasonable when she wasn't the one saying it.

In fact, it felt entirely unfair.

"As wives, we need to be in tune with our husbands," Kristi said.

"It sounds to me like you're in tune with my husband," Soraya returned. "Does your husband know he was texting you? Because texting David is a risk."

"Soraya." Kristi's cheeks turned red. "I'm satisfied in my marriage. My husband is satisfied with me. He has nothing to worry about."

"That's what I thought too. Until recently."

She was feeding into this, and she knew it. By continuing to go to church with him. She wasn't making a definitive enough stand. He had asked for her back, but he'd never admitted wrongdoing. It was all defensiveness. It was all this: *I was tempted.* The undertone of it all was: *You aren't enough.*

No. He was going to have to actually repent. It couldn't simply be excuses wrapped up in blame. She was going to stand firm on that.

If that was a sin, then . . .

Maybe she didn't know God as well as she thought. Or maybe they didn't. Because suddenly there were all these endless excuses being made when a man did something that was expressly forbidden.

She didn't think she was the one who was wrong.

She just didn't.

"You don't have a job, Soraya. David has been a good husband. A provider. He made a mistake. But he's the one who takes care of you. He takes care of your boys. What are you going to do without him?"

The words sounded like a threat. A prophecy.

You're nothing, and he's everything. What will you have left if you leave him?

"I'm going to get a job," she said, in defiance of both Kristi and the voice in her head that called her nothing.

She thought of that store, the one she'd been scared to stand in earlier. Suddenly, she wanted to go back to it. Suddenly, she wanted to be there. She wanted to do something no one would expect.

Because apparently David could have virtual affairs, and she was expected to forgive him just because it wasn't physical. Just because . . . because he was a man? Because she was expected to be endlessly understanding of the temptations men faced?

Because she didn't have a choice.

She was going to show them that she did, in fact, have choices.

"Soraya," Kristi said slowly. "We all prayed for you at the church staff meeting earlier."

Oh, there was the truth. They were talking about her. All of them.

"Pastor John prayed that you'll see what a good man you married, that God will show you how to forgive and be gracious, and that's really why I'm here today. I hope you can hear the words I have for you. I know everything seems difficult right now. But you know God won't give you something you can't handle. As long as you continue to honor him."

A faint memory began to scratch at the back of her mind. Her telling Nora that her mother leaving her was some kind of test from God. That he was trying to show her his goodness through trial.

She remembered very clearly what Nora had said in response.

At the time, she had been horrendously offended. Not only because what Nora said was sacrilegious, but because she hadn't been able to understand that God didn't make mistakes. That any trial she was experiencing had to be for her own edification.

What a . . . a *bitch* Soraya had been.

What a bitch Kristi was being now.

"Don't blame my husband's mistakes on God." The teakettle whistled. "Wow. Too bad that took so long, and now you have to leave."

Chapter Four

Nora

When the light goes out, make your own.

—Rules for Witches

The pictures Ben sent from Chile were pretty. Mountains, him standing on the edge of one of the mountains, him with his group of people all out there searching for . . . themselves.

She and Ben were still in contact, because they were *only separated*. Not that it wasn't painful. His comments about how she'd created distance between them with her issues and prickly attitude had been hurtful. But after he'd told her about his retreat, she'd started texting him, and he was keeping in contact.

She liked it. It made her feel like there was a bridge that still connected her to him.

She didn't know exactly when he was coming back, but that was part of the separation. There was a little bit of contact, not total contact. This was about him and his journey. She could accept that.

She didn't need to be possessive. She didn't need to be desperate and feral about it. One of the things he'd said before he left was that she was both emotionally unavailable and insecure. It hurt to hear, but it wasn't really untrue. She had a lot of baggage about abandonment, and she was sure it came out in her interactions with him. She had completely melted down initially when he told her he needed a separation. Like he was leaving forever. Because, for her, that's all it meant.

Of course. There had never been a reunification with her mother.

But he wasn't her mom.

He'd reminded her of that when he left. She knew it was true. Which was why she made sure to respond to the photos he sent with genuine enthusiasm, so he could see she was supportive of him doing this.

She was supposed to be finishing up some copy for a corporate website she did work for, but she was having trouble focusing, and she was mainly looking at tarot decks online and making her third cup of herbal tea. Maybe she should have bought some at Lady's Mantle. She could have given herself a reading while drinking a brew for concentration.

Or maybe she'd abandon copy for the night. She could write an article called "My Husband Went to Chile to Find Himself, and I'm the One Who's Lost." Or maybe "Everything in My Life Seemed Perfect, but It Turns Out I'm Sad like Everyone Else."

"Blah blah blah," she muttered, standing from her desk and stretching her stagnant body.

Her tea had gone cold, so she decided to go throw it in the microwave. She opened the door, closed it, hit the minute button, and then "Start."

And all the lights went out.

"Shit."

The electricity in this house was finicky at best. Her best friend, Sam, said it was practically negligence, especially considering what the house itself had cost. She didn't disagree with him. If she'd had her way, they would've used Sam when they did the build, but Ben said that Jonathan McNamara, who had been their contractor, would work only with specific subcontractors, and Sam wasn't on the list, and it would cause delays and issues.

I do fine. I don't need to do your house.

But of course, he'd done nothing but criticize the electrical work on her house. Well. After all the problems.

She went to the electrical box, because generally the finicky fuses would trip themselves, and she just had to reset them.

None of the levers were in the wrong position.

She flipped them back and forth, and nothing happened.

She was going to have to ask for help. She really didn't want to ask for help.

She opened her texts and started a message to Sam.

I'm flipping the switches, and the lights still won't come back on.

It only took thirty seconds for three dots to appear at the bottom of the screen.

Context would be good

you know the context already. It's my terrible electricity, and Ben is gone.

She hadn't gone into a whole lot of detail with Sam on what was happening in her marriage. Okay, she'd gone into no detail. All Sam knew was that Ben was in Chile. He'd made a joke about Aaron Rodgers that she'd only vaguely understood.

Is he that football player who does the ayahuasca sweat-lodge thing?

Yeah.

What does that have to do with Ben?

Nothing, I'm sure.

She always had the feeling Sam didn't like Ben. Of course, that seemed to be a mutual thing.

In Ben's case, it was less about Sam and more about his worry she was hanging on to elements of her dysfunctional childhood. She could understand why he'd think that, but it wasn't fair.

Sam had never felt like a component of the dysfunctionality. In many ways, he was part of the only stability and sanity she'd ever had. He was certainly the only person from her years in the system who kept in touch with her.

He's like a brother.

She had always told Ben that. It was true. Probably. It wasn't like she had a real brother to compare it to.

I'll come and look at it. Bet you blew a fuse.

You don't have to come over.

Except if he didn't, she was going to be stuck without electricity all night.

Don't.

She sat there and stared at the single-word message, wondering what he was telling her not to do exactly, hoping he was on his way.

Five minutes later, she got her answer. The firm knock on her door was most definitely Sam. As she went to let him in, she had the vague wish that she'd put a bra on, but she was wearing a hoodie. Also, it was Sam. He'd seen her looking far worse.

Hell, he'd seen her hunched over the Ouija board all those years ago.

The Ouija board had not been her finest hour.

With that in mind, she pulled the door open and looked up at him with her most grateful and pleading expression. "Thank you."

He sighed heavily, lifting one large hand and rubbing it over his jaw. His whiskers scraped against his palm. He was wearing a green baseball hat pushed high up on his head, a hoodie he probably hadn't looked twice at before putting on, and a pair of jeans with holes in the knees that were splattered with paint and other various pieces of evidence from construction sites. The way Sam didn't give a shit about what he wore was nearly admirable. Of course, when you were over six feet tall and devastatingly handsome, you didn't need your clothes to do any work for you. Not that she went out of her way to ponder Sam's looks. They had known each other for far too long.

Other women were welcome to his capable hands, blue eyes, and perfect smile.

She just wanted his electrical skills.

"Yep. I was hardly going to leave you here trapped in the dark."

"Considering you did this kind of thing all day . . ."

"This is not a big deal."

"What were you doing today?"

"Wiring. At that new complex that's going in next to HomeGoods."

"Oh. Neat."

"You don't have to pretend to be interested in my job for me to fix your blown fuse. It's literally going to take less than five minutes."

"Thank you," she said again.

"Yeah. It's just too bad that . . ."

"What?"

"Nothing. It bothers you when I bring it up."

"Oh. The slander of the electrician who did the house?"

"Yes. The slander of the electrician who did the house. Because he did a piss-poor job, which is one of my issues with Jonathan McNamara as a contractor."

"Yeah. Well. I think your issues are likely founded in truth, since it turns out he cuts a lot of corners in his personal life too."

She felt a little bit bad gossiping about Daisy when they'd had a pretty genuine conversation earlier. But Sam wasn't going to tell anybody. Plus, it would feed his contractor beef, which seemed like great payment for services rendered.

"Oh yeah?"

"Yeah. I visited Alexandra in the hospital today."

"That's nice of you."

"Not really. She's my neighbor, and she's a huge part of the Creative Kids program."

"True."

"Daisy McNamara was there. We went to lunch afterward. She told me that Jonathan left her and moved into a new house with his twenty-five-year-old girlfriend."

"Jesus Christ," he muttered as he opened the fuse box.

"He told her they were done. No discussion. It was all about him having to find himself—" She winced because it sounded close to what Ben had said, but it wasn't quite. "And of course finding himself meant finding himself in another woman's bed. He just left her with three kids."

"That sounds about right, based on the kind of work he does. No commitment. Sloppy. Lazy. Plus, I'm willing to bet he overcharged you. Because this electrical work is cheap shit."

"As far as I know, nothing about this house was cheap."

"I'm sure it wasn't."

She didn't really know, because the person with the money was Ben. A realization that made her uncomfortable all over again.

It had felt like it all belonged to them. Because they had gone through college together, and built this life together, and . . .

It was his.

What was going to happen if he came back and decided he didn't want to get back together?

That won't happen.

But it could.

But there is no one else. It's not like Daisy. It's not like Soraya.

Sam pulled a fuse out of his pocket, popped one out of its space, and slipped the new one in. Then he shut the door decisively and turned to her. "Are you going to tell me what's going on with you?"

"No," she said. "I mean . . ." *Bastard.* He'd surprised her. "There's nothing going on with me."

"Why is your husband on a random extended trip to Chile?"

"Because it was a bucket-list thing."

"When is he coming back?"

She sucked breath between her teeth, rocking back on her heels. "You got me there. I don't know."

"You guys having problems?"

"No. He's having . . . something. I don't know if it's a problem. I don't know what it is. He's having a moment. He's looking for himself."

"Oh, for God's sake. That is rich-guy shit."

"*Excuse* me?"

"I have work to do. I don't sit around wondering if I misplaced myself."

She rolled her eyes. "You're an electrician. You're hardly scraping pennies together."

"I'm not a dentist."

"Well, fine. So he can afford to take some mental health time. That's not a bad thing."

He arched a brow. "You used to make fun of that stuff."

Sometimes, having known Sam for so long was a burden. He was relentless in his knowledge of her. Who she was, who she'd been before, and who she wanted to be. He was just a lot sometimes, so no wonder she hadn't told him about the separation.

"Okay, sure," she said. "There was a time when I had never been to therapy. Now I have."

"It seems to have really helped," he said, deadpan. She couldn't tell if he meant it or not.

"You should go sometime."

"I'm good."

"Are you?"

"Are *you*? You're the one who just told me your husband is off on some journey to find himself."

"Yeah. He is. It doesn't have anything to do with me. That's called being in a mature relationship, Sam. Everything he does isn't about me."

"Yeah. Well. I've never been married, so forgive me . . . but I kind of thought the point of marriage was that everything you do is about your spouse, actually."

"No. I think that's codependency."

"Well. Neither of us would know anything about that."

That made her smile. One of Sam's ex-girlfriends had accused the two of them of being codependent. Which was funny, because neither of them had ever been able to afford to be codependent on anyone or anything. They were connected, sure. But that wasn't the same.

She could see back to that afternoon when they had sat down with the Ouija board. She'd bought it at a yard sale for twenty-five cents, and they had taken it out back at their foster parents' place and sat cross-legged in the barn, the summer heat oppressive, the air thick around them. He had put his hands on one side of the divining tool, and she had put hers on the other.

They had messed around with a few questions, but nothing had happened. She'd felt embarrassed and a little vulnerable asking what she really wanted to know with Sam, intense and very Sam, sitting across from her.

She'd gotten the board because she wanted . . .

This was one of the better foster homes she'd ever lived in. Sam was the best foster brother—she'd been in the same household with him a couple of times. It was a small town, and the kids like them shot around like pinballs, sometimes landing in the same place together more than once.

She liked him. She liked this place. It was a ranch, and there was a lot of open space. She could breathe here and think. Mark and Tabitha were nice people who seemed to care about the kids they took in. They didn't proselytize to them, and they weren't crazy strict. If she could have picked a family, it might have been something like this.

It made her wonder if she'd ever have one.

"Will I ever find love?"

It moved then. Y. E. S.

"You're moving it," she said, her heart hammering hard.

"No, I'm not," he said.

She was suddenly angry. Which happened more than she'd like. She'd be fine, totally fine, and then her whole face and body would get hot, and she'd lose control of her heart, her hands, her mouth. She leaned forward and punched Sam on the shoulder.

"Sam, don't mess around with me. Don't mess with this."

"I'm not. I don't give a fuck if anybody ever loves you, Nora." He stood up and brushed his jeans off. "You're too big of a pain in the ass anyway."

He kicked the board and walked away.

She could still see it. She'd been sure she and Sam wouldn't be friends after that. But they were. They stayed in that same house for six more months, and they'd been friends for twenty years since.

But she'd been pissed off at him for a week after that.

They could say anything to each other, though. That was what this many years of friendship got you. That and an on-call electrician.

"So, when he gets back, everything is going to be like it was?"

"I don't know," she said.

She didn't even like to admit it to herself.

But he'd asked, and she found she couldn't keep putting on that same brave face.

"You weren't having any other problems?"

"I don't want to talk about it. I just . . . When I can talk to him, then I can talk about it, but I'm not going to talk about it with you."

He tilted his chin upward, his jaw tight. "Okay. I was just asking. Because I'm your friend."

"I know."

He was. Always. But he wasn't her friend in the way the board-game friends were. The people who came over, couples, who had dinner with them at their house. He was distinctly her friend, and not Ben's.

"Good night, Nora."

"Sam, I'm sorry. This is . . . It has been a hard few weeks."

"Yeah. It sounds like it. I wish you would've told me."

"I told you tonight. Because it was when I could."

That softened his face, but only slightly.

Life had carved that man out of rock. He had to be, or he wouldn't have survived.

"Good night," he said.

"Good night."

He went out the front door, and she closed it behind him, securing it. Locking everything up.

Did she really think everything would go back to the way it had always been?

Did she?

She was smarter than that. This house was Ben's.

He was the one with the money. She wouldn't be able to afford much of anything if she was left with only her writing salary.

She wanted her marriage to work. She wanted to get back together with him.

That was what she wanted.

But she'd been through too much and knew too much about the cost of depending on people to let go of that nagging doubt inside her.

To let go of her survival instincts. Well, she had done that. She'd let herself get complacent. She had been lulled into a sense of security.

Because she had thought she'd found love, just like the Ouija board had promised. Which was dumb.

That whole day had been dumb, and she had known it then, but somehow, later, she had turned it into something meaningful. Had held it up against herself like a talisman.

Like it was a beacon of hope.

She had let it make her stupid.

Maybe she should take the job.

God knew having a little bit of extra money would be helpful.

She felt depressed, though. It felt like giving up. It felt like quitting. It felt like losing faith in him. In them. She had never wanted to be divorced. She didn't want to be part of a broken family. She was already part of a broken family. People who split up and left each other and didn't even bother to . . .

She went upstairs to her bedroom, which felt alarmingly empty. When she looked around the house and actually saw it, instead of letting the familiarity make it nearly invisible, she realized how little of it was hers.

It looked like his dentist's office. Bright white with a plethora of neutrals. Her office was like a little goblin horde. Her corner desk had lots of plants, a Himalayan salt lamp, lavender bunches hanging from the wall. She had paints in the corner, and paintings in various stages of completion.

She liked knickknacks. She liked color.

But it was only in her corner of the house.

Like a playroom.

It hadn't felt that way until now. Until he wasn't here. Until he didn't occupy the space with her.

Now, the room might as well be a hotel room.

Just with a lot of her stuff in it.

She lay down across the bed, sideways, not bothering to get under the covers. She didn't realize she had drifted off until she felt pressure on her chest. Her neck. She felt like she couldn't breathe.

She couldn't breathe.

An image of Alexandra in the car minutes before her accident passed through her mind.

She sat up, feeling like she had just run a marathon.

No. She wasn't Alexandra.

She wasn't Alexandra.

She wasn't Alexandra.

Chapter Five

Daisy

Magic doesn't make itself.

—Rules for Witches

So. What time are we all heading down to the shop today?

Daisy looked over at the text that had come through on her phone. Thank God it wasn't Jonathan. Every other text today had been. After last night's explosion, that seemed about right. *This* one was from the Discarded Wives Club, sent by Nora.

I'm already at the coffee shop across the street.

For real? Nora asked.

Yes. Come down to the coffee shop.

Mix? Because I'm on my way.

Yes.

Soraya didn't contribute. Maybe she wouldn't. That store had really freaked her out. Daisy couldn't help but feel sorry for her.

She was . . . She was nice. She was just . . . When Daisy looked at Soraya, she swore she saw ropes tied all around her. Like she was bound up. In herself, and the expectations of everyone else.

Daisy stared down into the remains of her cup of coffee. She wasn't any different, she supposed. It was just that her expectations didn't come from a church community, and Soraya's did.

It had taken a hell of a lot to get her to do something decisive about Jonathan.

Last night's discovery had been *a hell of a lot.*

Was he actually going to marry that *child*? He was still married to *her*.

She sighed and looked at the clock. Lady's Mantle was opening in twenty minutes. She intended to be over there asking about that bookkeeper position as quickly as possible.

There was a flurry of movement in the coffee shop—a line that stretched to the door, people grabbing small bags of pastries from one end of the bar and coffee from another. Given there was so much activity, she had no idea why this particular blur of movement caught the edge of her eye and made her turn.

It was her bad luck that her gaze didn't glance off the subject that had grabbed her attention. No. Her eyes went right to his. And held.

Zach.

Great.

He probably knew the answer to the question she had. The one that had caused last night's implosion and explosion, which resulted in her quitting before she'd actually lined up a new job.

He was her husband's best friend and business partner.

Zach had come to town about five years ago after retiring from acting. He'd created a buzz in the community that had yet to fully die down. She could hear whispers rise and fall as he walked through the coffee shop, and she was sure he could too.

He didn't seem to notice, or care.

Zach Woods had been one of the main crushes for any teenager who liked boys back in the early 2000s. The frosted tips and bad-boy pout had been too much for mere mortal teen girls to resist. Including her.

She'd been obsessed with his show *Second Chance City*, where he'd played a troubled youth who'd fallen for the equally troubled daughter of a state senator. Very Romeo and Juliet. When he'd first come to Hemlock, she'd been certain she was hallucinating.

Then Jonathan had gotten a job building a custom house for him, and they'd hit it off and started planning to expand the business.

Then Daisy had gotten to know him. Or, rather, tried to. He was inaccessible in a way she couldn't put her finger on. Not unfriendly, necessarily, but she just never seemed to get any closer to him than she had the day they met.

Not that she needed to be close to him.

Zach legally owned half the business—and technically probably more than half the assets—though he didn't have anything to do with the day-to-day operations.

He was at quarterly meetings, and sometimes even the company Christmas party, but he wasn't around all the time.

He was handsome. Not a normal kind of handsome. Not the kind of handsome you expected to see when you looked up in a coffee shop in a small town.

The trouble was, even though he'd left Hollywood behind, he hadn't transformed into a mortal man. He was still too good looking, too impactful every time he walked into a room. There were rumors, whispers, that he was fantastic in bed and rotated women through that bed with the frequency of a man who was still on top of his game.

He was well liked in town, but she knew a few women who worried when their husbands took up a friendship with him. Surely his life seemed more attractive than the average man living in suburban drudgery.

It had proven to be true. Not that she *blamed* Zach for Jonathan's infidelity. Jonathan deserved 100 percent of that blame. She didn't even want to cast any blame on Amberly, who was young and hadn't been married to Daisy.

Jonathan was the one who'd been obligated to her. No one else.

Sometimes she wondered, though, how much Zach's lifestyle acted as dream fuel.

"Hi, Daisy." The expression on his face let her know he was well aware she would have rather avoided locking eyes with him.

"Morning," she said.

"I heard you quit," he said.

It was weird that all she had exchanged about her resignation with her husband was a few texts. She was actually talking to *Zach* about it in person.

"Yeah. I did."

"Good."

He grabbed his coffee off the counter, removed the lid, and looked at it. Then he blew across the top of it, the steam cascading over the side. He put the lid back on and raised his cup to her. Without another word, he walked out of the coffee shop. She had forgotten to ask him what she'd wanted to.

Good? Was that all he had to say about that? Good. Was it good?

It was good. It was good because she couldn't keep doing everything for Jonathan. It was good because she needed to have a little bit more dignity. It was bad because she had serious concerns about his business imploding if he didn't find somebody competent enough to do his books. After all, her kids were dependent on their dad having that business . . .

She grabbed her own coffee, which had now gone cold. The way Zach said *good* made it seem almost like—

The door opened, and it wasn't Nora who came in, but Soraya, her blond hair up in the same sort of bun she'd been wearing yesterday in the hospital, the scarf wrapped around her neck almost comedically large. She was wearing big sunglasses and did not remove them when she came inside. She was looking out of sorts, to put it mildly.

She lowered the glasses slightly and saw Daisy and moved quickly across the room. "I'm going to order," she said.

Then she fluttered to the end of the line and stood there, antsy and bouncing lightly on the balls of her feet.

A couple minutes later, the door opened again, and Nora walked in.

It was fascinating to Daisy the way Nora had kept her high school look and evolved it. Like a latter-day goth who had realized that eventually she would have to style herself to get a job. Her hair was still a shade or two darker than her natural color, long and straight, her bangs as blunt as her manner. She had a nose ring and rings on every finger, her nails painted a dark-cherry color. In high school, she'd had a sticker on one of her binders that said: I'M ONLY WEARING BLACK UNTIL THEY MAKE A DARKER COLOR.

She seemed to adhere to the same philosophy now.

The style seemed intrinsic to her, and Daisy had always admired that. How Nora bent rules around her to suit her had been one of the first things Daisy had found appealing about her. They were different. Daisy's family was close knit and happy, mostly. Nora's family was dysfunctional, her living situation very often subpar.

She had never been sweet. Acerbic, yes, and terribly funny.

Daisy hadn't needed Nora to be sweet. She had none of Daisy's people-pleasing tendencies, and Daisy had found that fascinating and liberating.

In many ways, Nora was who she wanted to be when she grew up. Even still.

She glanced back at Soraya, who had two people in line between herself and Nora, and realized Soraya was leaving her sunglasses on so no one would accidentally make eye contact with her. Daisy took a look around the coffee shop. *Really* took a look.

No less than three people were sitting at tables with a Bible.

Hemlock Christian Fellowship was the biggest church in the area. With over five thousand members, people drove long distances to hear Pastor John speak. It was an oddity, a church that popular in a town so small, and Soraya was deeply entrenched in that community. Daisy wouldn't be surprised if she knew every single person in here with a Bible.

When she completed her order, she scuttled quickly to the table, taking the seat that faced the back wall. Only then did she lower her sunglasses.

"You look like you're fleeing the law."

"Kind of. I'm fleeing my Bible study."

"Fair enough. Are you actually going to ask for a job?" Daisy asked.

"Yes. She said she was thinking about having somebody bake. Well, I can do that. I can . . . I can do that." She suddenly looked wobbly.

Nora popped over to the table right after.

"You didn't text," she said to Soraya.

Soraya seemed to fold in on herself slightly. "I didn't want to text because I was afraid if I did, I would talk myself out of it. Or misdirect the text. You know, I have recent trauma with misdirected texts."

Nora laughed, then shut her mouth quickly. "Was that not supposed to be funny?"

Soraya frowned, her eyes round. "Oh no, it was."

"It was." Nora picked her laugh up where she left off, seeming relieved.

"So, what was your breaking point?" Daisy asked Nora.

"My friend Sam asked me what I was going to do if Ben didn't want to get together when he came back. I'm embarrassed to admit that's the first time I really let myself consider that."

"Lavender latte."

Soraya put her sunglasses back on, then stood up and went to the end of the bar to collect her coffee, then returned a moment later, taking them back off.

"I think you look like you even with the sunglasses," Nora pointed out.

Soraya frowned. "Then maybe that means no one is talking to me because I'm excommunicated."

"Oh, don't be silly." Nora patted Soraya's shoulder. "They won't excommunicate you. If they did, how would they shame you?" Soraya frowned and opened her mouth, but Nora forged onward. "Anyway. I thought I could use a little bit of income supplement."

"Yeah," Soraya said.

"What about you?" Daisy asked Soraya.

"I had a visit from my Bible study leader." She clutched her coffee cup with both hands and looked around the room like she was afraid someone might overhear. "She thinks I should get back with David because he's such a good man."

Nora made a loud scoffing sound, then got up when her drink was announced and returned to the table a moment later.

"I'm not taking him back," Soraya said. "That is, of course, going to be a financial problem, but I can't let go of the infidelity, even if it isn't physical. It feels like a betrayal."

"Yeah, you kind of made vows about that," Nora said.

"Thank you." Soraya reached across the table and grabbed Nora's arm. "*Thank you* for saying that, Nora. Because that's how I feel, and no one seems sufficiently upset about it."

"I'm sorry." Daisy realized it was her turn, but she wasn't particularly in the mood to talk about it. "I quit. The construction company. I'm not working for him anymore."

Nora's eyebrows lifted. "What happened that made you quit?"

Daisy looked away for a second, trying to . . . ground herself. Suddenly the room didn't feel real. "I think he might be marrying her. I saw a big purchase from a jewelry store on his business account."

"That's so screwed up in so many ways," Nora said.

"I know. And I think this is how he was telling me. I couldn't stand it, not anymore. Ever since he walked out, everything has been his decision. Everything. He decided we were done, that he was moving out and moving on, he decided— *Not* this. I decided this."

"Good for you," Soraya said.

Daisy wasn't sure it was good for her. She might make way less money at the apothecary, and it was definitely not going to be as flexible, and it might lead to the collapse of her husband's business and therefore her children's legacy. That was *fine*.

"So now I just have to take a day job where I don't get to be home and balance that with the Youth Musical Theater of Oregon and the big production we have coming up and, oh—he was going to build sets."

"Don't worry about that," Nora said.

"I am worried. We don't have a big budget, and the kids are doing so well with rehearsal, but we can't do this if we don't have sets."

"Black-box theater?"

"*Seven Brides for Seven Brothers* isn't black-box-theater appropriate," Daisy said. "And I have my mom and my grandma and the kids and . . . What did I just do? How am I going to live?"

"Daisy." Soraya stared at her with uncharacteristic focus. "How are you going to live if you don't get a real, decent settlement from him? How are either of us going to live? Everything is really messed up whether you keep working at his construction company or not. At least you have your pride."

"Do I?" Daisy laughed. "Because my high school sweetheart left me, broke my heart, and looked at me like I meant nothing. I don't feel like I have pride." It had been the most lowering moment of her life. He'd told her he was leaving, and she'd had to vomit. He'd acted like nothing had happened, like she hadn't been sick because of him. Like she wasn't broken because of him.

She'd seen people give more empathy to total strangers than Jonathan had given her after he'd dropped that bomb.

Nora put her hand on Daisy's. "You have us now."

Soraya looked like she might cry. "I haven't felt like I've had anyone. All of my friends, my mother, everyone just thinks I'm stupid for kicking him out. For staying apart."

"I don't think that," Nora said. "I think what you want matters."

Soraya covered her mouth to stifle a giggle. "I'm not familiar with that concept."

"This is so . . . It's so ridiculous," Daisy said. "Your husband sent a picture of his penis to another woman at church. My husband left me and is already buying major jewelry for the twenty-five-year-old he's shacking up with, and we have all these . . . worries and fears and pain because of them, and they don't even care."

"You're not sociopaths," Nora pointed out.

"Neither is Jonathan. He's doing a great impression of one right now, but he's not one. I don't think my whole life was a lie. Whatever he's telling himself right now, though . . . I don't know. And it's killing me. I hate that. I hate it for all of us."

Nora would deflect and say Ben wasn't really gone. Maybe he wasn't. Daisy's trust in men was at an all-time low.

"The store is open." Nora looked down at her phone.

"Yes."

But she found she couldn't move now that she had made this decision.

"Come on," Nora said. "We're all going together."

So Daisy let herself be collected like she was a child and dragged out of the coffee shop.

She startled slightly when she saw Zach standing out on the sidewalk next to the outdoor tables, talking to someone else. She turned away quickly.

Nora craned her neck past her. "Isn't that—"

"Yes. My husband's business partner."

"Yeah, but he's *also* famous," Nora said.

"Zachary Woods." Soraya's words sounded reverent.

Both Daisy and Nora looked at her. Soraya shrugged. "We pray for him a lot."

Nora snorted. "I'm sorry, what do you pray for him for?"

"For his eternal soul. You know, after we discuss what we assume are the details of his personal life."

"Is that how you excuse gossiping?" Daisy asked.

"Absolutely," Soraya confirmed.

It was the first time Daisy felt like she could relate to Soraya. Maybe Soraya was a human like the rest of them, with flaws and feelings she had to keep buried deep or risk being rejected.

"That man is so hot," Nora said. "I think if I look directly at him for too long, I'll spontaneously combust."

"I've never looked very long, of course." Soraya sniffed piously, but the corners of her lips turned upward slightly.

"He's arrogant." Daisy walked ahead of everyone else as they moved quickly down the sidewalk toward Lady's Mantle.

"Even better!" said Nora.

That was funny. She wouldn't have necessarily thought Nora would like that.

Daisy didn't think Nora's husband could be called arrogant. Smug, maybe. Or at least that's how she'd always perceived him. He wasn't her dentist, but she did see a different dentist in the office, and she'd had glancing contact with Dr. Ben Clarke and his waxed mustache. Where Nora was simply cool, Ben seemed like he cared very much about being cool, to the point where he had convinced himself he was the coolest person in the room. Which was an odd look on a man in his mid-thirties.

Of course, Daisy's husband in his mid-thirties had decided to cliché his way into a twenty-five-year-old's bed, so maybe she needed to be less judgmental.

Either way, Zach was arrogant but not smug. She would make a two-column list later regarding the differences between those two things.

"It's not *better*," she said. "Anyway, I don't know him that well. He mainly hangs out with Jonathan."

"Oh, bummer." Nora looked performatively glum. "Then we have to hate him."

"Yes. We do," Daisy agreed resolutely.

They stood in front of the door, and she could see their reflections in it. Three women framed by the painted floral carving in the wood frame. Three women who looked like they were about to walk into a fire.

But life had felt like that recently. For all of them.

"Well," said Nora. "Let's do this."

Chapter Six

Nora

I release the past,
I embrace the road ahead,
I gather sisters for the journey,
I embrace the power in us,
Maiden, Mother, Crone,
Every part of me is magic,
I walk forward without fear,
And so it is.

—A spell for moving on

Nora pushed the door open and found herself enveloped by the quiet store, the only sound the bell above the door as she, Daisy, and Soraya walked into the dimly lit space.

"The bell is so you don't bring any evil spirits in with you," came the sweet, clear voice behind the counter.

The same woman from yesterday, who did not look surprised to see them at all.

"You're back." She beamed at them.

Daisy stepped forward, like they were back in school and she was answering a question. Nora was almost surprised she didn't raise her hand.

"Yes. I'm a bookkeeper," Daisy said. "Though I don't have a job anymore, so I thought I would see if you still needed someone."

"Strangely enough," the older woman said, "no other bookkeepers have shown themselves to me since yesterday. What happened to your job?"

"She *was* doing the books for her ex-husband," Nora said.

Daisy shot her a glance. "He's not exactly my ex-husband yet. But we are separated."

"I take it not happily," the older woman said.

"I'm not the one who left."

The older woman stared at Daisy for a long time. "I'm sorry." Then she turned her attention to Soraya. "I thought you were afraid of my store."

"I am." Soraya's honesty had annoyed Nora in high school. Not that it wasn't a little annoying now, but she had to respect her owning up to being afraid like that.

"But you came back."

"You said something about needing a baker. I bake all the time. I take orders for my bread, and I sell some from my house and some from stores. I'm very good in the kitchen. I've never had a job before in my life, and I don't know how to ask for one. But I need help. I can't ask the people I would normally ask because they don't think I'm doing the right thing. If they already don't think I'm doing the right thing, then what's the point of trying anymore?"

"I do hope you keep trying. Especially if you're going to bake bread and other sweet treats for me."

Soraya cleared her throat and looked away. "I assume that running out of the store wasn't the best way to impress you."

"I was never asking to be impressed. Of course, men are welcome in my store, people of all genders and walks of life are welcome here, but I do have a particular desire to help women. You three walked in, and I knew you needed help."

"I don't have any special skills." Nora could feel the angry, rejected foster kid inside her bristling, coming right to the front, and she had no idea why the hell that bitch was being so assertive. *You know why. You feel rejected.* "It's been a while since I've worked retail."

The older woman's gaze was direct. "I have a feeling you have skill enough."

A sense of calm came over Nora. A sense of comfort.

"I hope so," Nora said.

"Can you start today?" the older woman asked.

"Yes," said Nora. "But then I'm a childless cat lady."

"You don't have a cat, do you?" Daisy asked.

"Colloquially," Nora said.

"My . . . Jonathan is picking my kids up today, so I can," Daisy said. "But I have a lot of obligations. I'm working on a theater production right now three nights a week that my kids are in."

"I think we can work with that."

Soraya frowned. "I'm free. My kids are in high school. They're not really speaking to me. So."

The older woman slowly walked out from behind the counter and over to Soraya. She reached out and took her hand. Soraya flinched, but only for a moment. "I'm so sorry about your children," the older woman said.

Soraya seemed confused and conflicted by the comfort she was receiving from this woman she'd been afraid of just yesterday.

"I'll show you around. This counter over here"—she gestured to an area across from the main register—"is where there will be coffee and baked goods. I do have an oven here, but of course, my dear, if you want to bake at home and bring your treats in—"

"Doesn't my kitchen need to be certified?"

"It will all work out either way. What's your name?"

"Soraya."

"I'm Aggie Green. I had a young lady come in and ask about a barista job. She'll make most of the drinks. But you can help her. I'll have *you* work here. Behind the main counter. You can help her." She directed that at Nora. "Now I need names for the two of you."

"Nora." Nora gestured to herself first. "And Daisy."

"Wonderful. Now that I have help, I can focus on my readings. Tea leaves, tarot, and, of course, a bit of spellwork."

"Spellwork?" Nora asked.

"Yes. I have some pre-blessed spell bags. I find it most useful, though, to have someone come in and manifest the spell with me, so I can infuse their energy into it."

"Oh." Soraya looked a bit ill.

Nora had no issues with this kind of thing, but listening to someone talk about readings and spellwork so matter-of-factly was a little odd even to her.

"But I've been so busy with appointments that I have difficulty manning the counter."

"Where did you come from?" Nora asked.

Aggie waved her hand. "Here and there. I imagine that's where I will continue to be from. But for now, this is a good place to rest my bones. Are you all getting divorced?"

"No," Nora said quickly, needing very much to clarify that even though she was with Soraya and Daisy, and supported them completely, her situation wasn't exactly the same. "I'm separated from my husband. But it's just while he figures out what he wants next."

"Everyone has to do that from time to time, I suppose," Aggie said.

"It's *reasonable.*" Nora could hear the desperate justification in her own voice.

"Ah. I don't have a training manual," Aggie said as she rounded behind the counter, "but I would like it if you all spent some time with this." She took a big leather-bound book from beneath the counter and set it on the glossy wood surface. "It's my grimoire, which I've spent years working on. It has all of my tea blends and what they're for. Crystals, tarot. Oracle. I would ask that you know just enough to help any traveler who wanders in off the street looking for something. Eventually, you'll learn to recognize what they need before they tell you."

A shiver went down Nora's spine, because she couldn't help but wonder if that was what had happened with Aggie.

Had she looked at them and just *known*?

That she had mentioned needing a bookkeeper had seemed odd at the time, and even odder now. That she'd somehow known they might need work.

Miraculous in a way, though Nora had stopped believing in miracles a long time ago. She might not believe in this stuff like she had when she was a teenage girl, but she thought it was harmless, unlike Soraya, who appeared to be dying a thousand deaths in the corner.

Though, she hadn't run away this time.

The bell jingled above the door, and two young women came in, probably in their early twenties, looking excited.

"Yeah," one said. "We have an appointment for a reading."

"Of course." Aggie gestured to the corner, where there were fluffy floor pillows designed for sitting and a low, round table with cards at the center. "This is where I'll be for most of the day. I trust that I'm leaving the running of the shop to your capable hands."

She practically floated over to the reading area, and whatever she was saying to the girls was drowned out by the music playing over the speakers.

"We're going to hell," Soraya muttered.

"Promise?" Nora asked. "Because it sounds like a good party."

Soraya wasn't listening. "*I'm* going to hell. I'm *going to hell.* I've left my husband, and I'm dabbling in the occult."

Nora sighed. "*Soraya.* If you thought this was going to send you to hell, you wouldn't be here. You just don't want anybody from church to see you."

Soraya huffed, opened her mouth, closed it again, and then huffed one more time. "Well, that matters to me because if they saw me here, they would think I was falling away."

Whatever Nora thought about that, it was important to Soraya, and there was no use telling her that something she cared about was dumb.

That realization was growth, Nora was pretty sure.

"Right, I get that. But they already think that's true," Nora said.

Soraya was quiet for a moment. "I'm sorry." She looked at Nora. "For what I said in high school. The time when your mother was supposed to come, and she didn't. I didn't understand then why you were so angry. I get it now."

That was unexpected.

"Thank you." Nora inclined her head.

"It was a little offensive what you said about God, though," Soraya added.

"I'm resolutely not sorry about that," Nora said.

"I'm *trying* to connect with you." Soraya sounded petulant.

"Does God need me to say sorry? Because it seems to me God should be tough enough to handle what a surly teenager says about them."

Soraya wrinkled her nose. "I guess that's true."

Daisy was slowly flipping through the grimoire pages from where she stood behind the counter. Soraya stayed glued to the back wall, and Nora couldn't help but watch Aggie, who was turning cards over with certainty and speaking to both women with all her focus directed resolutely on them.

Did Aggie actually believe in this stuff?

Was she just good at reading people?

"You aren't that much more comfortable with this than I am," Soraya whispered.

Nora glanced at her out of the corner of her eye. "It's not the same. I'm trying to decide if this is a grift. You're scared of it."

Soraya huffed and looked away. Nora pushed off from the wall and went over to where Daisy was standing peering at the grimoire. "Spells?"

"I'm reading through the Witch's Code of Conduct."

Nora snorted. "Seriously? I would have thought the point of being a witch was that you didn't have to obey the rules."

"Oh no." Daisy's tone was grave. "You really have to obey the rules. Karma and all that."

They both looked at Soraya. She peeled herself off the wall and started to walk toward them. "I don't consider it karma. But the golden rule, of course, is that you do unto others as you would have them do unto you. The Bible also says . . . what you sow, you will also reap. Which I think is a pretty similar concept."

"Kind of." Nora didn't really think it was.

Soraya was still keeping her distance from the evil book of spells. Nora watched her for a long moment and experienced the first stirring of true sympathy for her. Whatever Nora thought about Soraya's beliefs, Soraya was genuine. She was afraid. And she was on the verge of losing her entire support network.

Nora had been raised by wolves, basically, so she hadn't had a lifelong network of support. But Soraya did. Now, because she was doing what she had to do to keep her sanity, to respect herself, they were all on the verge of turning their backs on her.

That must feel lonely. The girl who had told Nora things happened for a reason back in high school was a girl who hadn't been through hard things yet.

Though Nora's lifetime of previous disappointments hadn't prepared her for the one she was currently experiencing. For the clawing despair and uncertainty that hit her when she imagined how it might be if Ben didn't come home. If he didn't want to be with her.

Daisy turned the page in the grimoire. "Spellwork," she whispered. "Love spells. Spells for revenge. Spells for prosperity. Manifesting."

"None of that is real," Nora said. Both Daisy and Soraya looked at her. "Well, I just don't think it is." But something in her wanted to believe it. Something in her that had always wanted to discover that she was a secret princess or a secret fairy or, of course, a secret witch.

What teenage girl didn't want to have secret magical powers?

She had needed those fantasies, those hopes, when she was young and hadn't felt like she had any control in her life. She didn't need it now.

Except . . .

She felt like she was standing on the edge of that chasm again. Maybe she did need it now.

A steady stream of people came into the apothecary for readings. It surprised Nora. She hadn't imagined there was that much of a demand for an old lady to tell you about your life. But then, she supposed she kind of needed it. Why shouldn't everybody else?

Soraya learned how to refill the loose-leaf tea jars and how to make individual portions, then started going through recipes for drinks. Nora worked the cash register, and Daisy began to peruse the financial records for the business.

All in all, the day went relatively quickly. It was definitely a business mostly supported by Aggie's readings, but Nora wondered if that would change once there were food and beverages on offer.

When it was time for the store to close and the streetlights outside had come on, Aggie walked to the door and turned the sign. "I think today went well," she said.

"How do people find out about your readings?" Nora was curious.

"The people who need me find me."

Nora wanted to roll her eyes. She also wanted to believe in something.

Not that belief seemed to be giving Soraya any peace in this moment. Nora was half surprised Soraya hadn't bolted out the door as soon as the sign was turned.

Daisy picked the grimoire up off the counter and held it to her chest. "And you do spells for people."

"Yes," Aggie said. "Though not as often. At least, not yet."

"Do you teach people to do their own spells?" Nora asked.

"Oh yes," Aggie replied. "In fact, I am going to begin hosting spell and tarot nights. For people to learn how to do their own readings and to cast their own spells. To tap into their own magic."

"Everyone?" Nora could think of half a dozen people off the top of her head who were definitely not even a little magic. So she doubted this point of view.

Aggie nodded. "Everyone is magic. But we forget about it as we grow older, so we have to look back and dig deep, find our young self, and find our magic again."

"I was definitely not magic when I was younger."

"Something took it from you. Not the magic itself, but your belief in it. It can happen when you're very small. Something makes you afraid, or it makes you think you have no control. It makes you think your intuition is wrong or that it can't be trusted. But everyone has magic. They just have to relearn it."

Nora felt a lot like she had when she'd found that Ouija board. When she had really, really wanted to make it work. To get it to tell her that things would be okay. To get some assurance that her whole life wasn't going to be as a driftless foster kid who didn't have anyone.

Then Sam had made her feel embarrassed. Because he had been standing there looking at her, and she had been talking about love and . . .

"What if I wanted to learn to do a spell?"

Daisy and Soraya were staring at her now. "I still think it might be bullshit," Nora said. "But there's no harm in trying."

Soraya looked like she really wanted to say that there was harm in trying. Hellfire and all of that, but she held it in.

"I'm afraid you will have to have a bit more intention than that to tap into your magic," Aggie said.

"What is this, like a faith healing?" Nora asked. "Where it only fails if I don't believe enough?"

"No. But the power has to come from inside of you. If you can't believe in it, you won't be able to feel it. You won't be able to guide it. That said, this isn't a bad place to start." Aggie looked at all of them. "In fact, it would be good for the three of you to learn a spell. Just a small one."

"Oh no. No. I am not doing spells." Soraya took a deep breath and moved away from the group. "I don't want to do spells. I can bake. And I can be here, but I can't do . . . that."

"What do you think spells are, Soraya?" Aggie asked.

"It's . . . asking the universe or . . . Satan to do things for you that you can only ask God for."

Aggie looked thoughtful. "It *can* be those things, I suppose. It can also be you asking your higher power for something."

"I do that all the time," Soraya said.

"Right," Aggie said. "Mind you, I like to put some crystals with my intentions. What is it that you're afraid of?"

"I'm not supposed to do this." Soraya looked away, fidgeting.

"And why is that?"

"Because I . . . It's wrong. You aren't supposed to look to your own power. Doing this means turning away from what I believe."

Aggie shook her head. "You don't have to abandon your faith. What I believe doesn't ask you to do that. I believe in the divine in all its forms, including the form that you recognize. It's your belief that would require me to give up mine. It's your belief that says mine can't exist. I believe you can hold your faith and this power together."

"I don't do spells. I pray."

Aggie arched one white eyebrow. "What are spells but prayers men don't like?"

Soraya laughed, then looked conflicted. "I . . . It's fine. You can all do it."

"And you'll judge us," Nora said.

"I won't!" Soraya cleared her throat and lowered her voice. "I won't. I know I'm tired of being judged. Having people not understand why I made the decisions I did. I'm not judging, I just . . ."

"All of you think about what worries you most right now," Aggie commanded. "You don't have to, Soraya."

"Well, I'm *worried*," she said. "A lot, and I'm thinking about it."

"Capture it." Aggie went behind the counter, took out two leaves, and handed them to Nora and Daisy. "Write what you need on the bay leaf. Something small."

"I'm worried about the sets for the play I'm working on," Daisy said. "Something like that?"

Aggie nodded. "Anything, but that works to start."

Nora stared at the leaf. She could use an art commission or a new article job, but she put herself out there for those. She didn't expect to get spontaneous offers. She wrote: *New art commission.*

"When you go home, you can either hang on to these or burn them to set your intention. It's up to you."

"That's it?" Soraya asked.

"Yes," said Aggie. "Do you have a vision board, by any chance?"

Soraya blinked. "Yeeesss." She drew the word out slowly.

"For you, you could write what you need and put it on your board. That's where you set your intentions, right?"

Soraya looked conflicted. "Yes."

"It comes from you. Whether you see it as a goal or magic or manifestation. It all comes from you."

Soraya cleared her throat. "Okay. I'll take a leaf."

Aggie smiled and handed one to Soraya, who wrote on it quickly and then put the leaf into her purse.

Nora would have rolled her eyes at Soraya, except now she didn't feel like she was as different from Soraya as she'd always thought.

They were all products of their upbringing. Nora didn't trust easily. Soraya trusted people in certain positions of authority. It was a learned behavior. And right in that moment, Nora could see how they were both just reactions. She wasn't better than Soraya because she was a skeptic. She was a skeptic because of the shape of her life.

Everything had worked for Soraya. Up until now. Why wouldn't she put faith in an institution that had always been there for her?

It was only now that Soraya was getting a taste of what Nora had always known.

Aggie showed them how to close down the shop. Cleaning up any dishes that had been used, refilling all the bins of dried tea. Aggie lit a bundle of sage and cleared the room of negative energy before turning the lights off and ushering them outside.

"It was a good first day." Aggie smiled at all of them. "Your help is exactly what I needed."

"I think it's what we needed," Daisy said.

"We need each other. That's the most beautiful thing about life. I'll see you all tomorrow." With a wave of her hand, Aggie turned and left them all standing there.

Nora stared after her. "She's a funny woman."

"Well, she's a witch," Soraya said. Daisy and Nora looked at Soraya. "I mean that in a nonderogatory way."

"*Do* you?" Nora asked.

"I'm trying to." Soraya let out a long breath. "I don't know. I don't know anything. And I feel overwhelmed by that. Sorry. I don't know who I can trust. I don't know what to believe in half the time. I'm just trying."

"We're all trying together." Daisy sighed. "I have rehearsal tomorrow night, and then Jonathan is going to take the kids. I hate being alone in the house."

"Let's have dinner," Nora said. "After your rehearsal."

"It'll be kind of late."

Soraya shrugged. "That's fine."

Daisy looked relieved by the offer. "Thank you."

"What time is the rehearsal over?" Nora asked. "I can bring something by your place."

"We'll probably get out around seven thirty."

"Sounds great."

It actually did. There was a kind of magic about the fact that anything could sound great right now. Nora had hoped to hear from Ben, but she didn't.

But before she fell asleep, she had texts from Sam and the Discarded Wives Club. Even in the middle of all this darkness, there was some light.

Chapter Seven

Daisy

When you ask, the universe provides.

—Rules for Witches

"Nathaniel," Daisy said, "when you sing, you need to be projecting toward the audience."

"But I'm singing to *her*." He gestured toward the leading lady.

"I know. But that's where you have to learn a technique called cheating out. You don't want to be facing totally to the side, or the audience can't see you." Daisy moved from where she was standing in the auditorium of the old theater, up to the stage. "You want to stand like this, so when you sing to her, you *are* singing to her, but you're also singing to the audience."

She started to climb offstage, half folded up, her jeans about cutting her in half. She put a hand over her muffin top as she stepped down to the floor, just as she heard a familiar voice.

"Good direction."

She looked up and startled. *Zach.*

Who had probably just gotten a great view of her muffin top. Fantastic.

She straightened and tried not to look flustered. There was no reason on earth she should be flustered. "Thank you. What are you doing here?"

"I'm on the board. We were just having a meeting about the summer schedule."

The old Holly Theater was a historic building that had been on the brink of being demolished or reconfigured for years, until it had gotten a substantial injection of cash a few years ago and had been restored. Since then, they'd hosted ballet companies, musical acts, and traveling theater companies, plus it had given a new, better home to the Youth Musical Theater, which Daisy had been involved with since childhood. She wasn't good enough to be a professional actor by any stretch of the imagination, and she was too self-conscious to actually act or sing in front of anyone anymore, but directing kids was fun.

Suddenly, she wondered where the money for the theater had come from. And if maybe Zach . . .

"This looks great," he said.

"Thanks. I don't know . . . I don't know. We have about two weeks until we open, and I'm having some logistical issues."

"Such as?"

She sighed. "It isn't your problem."

"Daisy, I asked. Which means I'm open to making it my problem."

"Jonathan was going to make the sets. But I don't feel comfortable working with him on that. Not at this point."

"Fair. I can handle that."

"What?"

"Either acting as a go-between or just facilitating the building another way. I'm pretty handy. And I know about sets, though I don't know that I would trust myself to be the one to do all the building if you want them to stay standing."

She had a feeling that was a lie. He had *knight in shining armor* written all over him, and it was hard for her to imagine that anything he did could fail. It was such a strange feeling, in the middle of the cynicism that had been choking her since Jonathan had walked out.

It was stunning that this man who barely knew her would offer this when her own husband hadn't even picked her up when she'd fallen to the floor after he'd told her he was leaving.

Something in her had felt so broken since that day, and now a very small piece of it had mended. Maybe it had been mending since she had linked up with Nora in Alexandra's hospital room.

She could remember now, Nora looking at her and saying everything would be okay. It was after that they'd gone into the apothecary. And now Zach was here and . . .

She thought about the bay leaf. It had to be a coincidence. It couldn't actually be . . .

"You really don't have to do this." She wanted him to, because it felt so nice. Nice to be thought of, nice to be near him. But she also felt obligated to at least try to let him off the hook.

"I want to." He waved a hand over her protestations. "These programs mean a lot to me."

Of course. The *program*.

"That is just extremely generous of you."

"It's really not," he said. "It's a small thing. I have your number."

"Oh. Yeah, feel free to . . . text."

"I might even call you."

A strange rush went through her body. Was this flirting? No. She was not flirting with Zach. And he was definitely not flirting with her.

But what a completely disorienting and exhilarating realization. She could. She hadn't chosen for Jonathan to walk out the door, but now that he had, she was free to imagine a life that looked however she wanted it to. She could flirt with Zach. Or the next guy who walked in. And maybe things would be okay. Maybe she and the other discarded wives had actually done something. Something magic.

Was it normal to be euphoric in the middle of your life falling apart? She suddenly felt like she might be. This was an ending. One she never would've chosen. One she and her kids were suffering for. It was like she'd gone bungee jumping and someone had cut the cord. There was an exhilaration in the free fall. Though that was just what you thought before you hit the ground and died.

She couldn't discount that.

Psychosis was a real possibility here.

"I'll let you get back to it." Zach gestured at the stage.

"Yeah. Thanks," she said.

The rest of rehearsal went well, with only one forgotten-line meltdown by one of the kids, and she watched from inside the theater as her children went into the lobby, peering through the window as Jonathan greeted them. She just . . . She didn't want to have to face him unnecessarily.

It was better to keep him far away. Through a window, if possible. It wasn't always. Of course not. He was the father of her kids.

And a stranger. And the man she had loved since she was sixteen.

All those things.

She waited until everyone had cleared out and then picked up the multiple bags she carried all the time and walked out to her car, feeling empty-handed despite them, because the kids weren't with her. She was so glad she wasn't going home to an empty house. During any other time in her life, she would've said she craved being alone. Now it just felt sad, her rattling around with her thoughts.

It was atrocious, truly.

"Nora sent a message: *Daisy, I need to know what you want.*"

The text popped up on Daisy's car system, the message from Nora read to her in a robotic voice as she pulled out of the parking lot.

"Nora sent a message: *Teriyaki chicken?*"

Daisy responded. "Is that a question?"

"Nora sent a message: *I don't know. Is there something better that I should be getting?*"

"Soraya sent a message: *I'm getting teriyaki noodles.*"

"Not salad?" Daisy asked.

"Nora sent a message: *I asked the same thing.*"

Soraya and Nora must be together, which was strange and hilarious, because Daisy would have said the two of them would never, ever willingly hang out alone.

There was a saying about strange times and strange bedfellows. It had never felt more apt than it did now. But as she listened to robot versions of Soraya and Nora banter in text, Daisy experienced a riotous sense of relief. Like everything might actually be okay. Or at the very least, tonight would be.

It was a short drive back to her house, and she pulled in and unlocked the door, then went inside and did a cursory cleanup of the kids' trinkets strewn all over the house.

There was more of her own detritus than usual too—likely a reflection of her mental state.

But she didn't have it in her to be hard on herself right now. Everything felt hard.

She made a quick call and checked in with her mother, then made another to her grandma, and that was when Soraya and Nora knocked on the door.

Daisy opened the door to let them in and had the strangest realization that it had been years since she'd had friends over.

Having friends over had been a staple of her life growing up. It was for most kids. Hanging out, spending the night. It was the most exciting thing, and she just didn't do it anymore. She met people for coffee, went out to dinner sometimes, but this felt like the kind of slumber party she hadn't had since she was a teenager.

"I have the craziest news," Nora announced, sweeping into the entry. She was burdened with take-out bags, and Soraya was holding one small one.

"Pork rolls." Soraya brandished the bag.

"We ended up ordering the entire left side of the menu." Nora raised each bag up as an example. "Soraya has found an appetite."

"I'm glad to hear that. But what *happened*?" Daisy asked, trying to corral the conversation back to where it had been.

"Oh." Nora closed the front door behind them. "I got commissioned to do a mural for the Holly."

"The Holly Theater?"

"Yes. *Your* Holly Theater. The one that you're doing *Seven Brides* in."

"That's . . . incredible. You haven't done a mural since you did the gym in high school."

"No. I haven't. And that isn't in my portfolio for a reason."

"I liked it," Soraya said.

"Really? I think all the basketball players have arms that are about four inches too long. But, anyway, the woman who runs the committee for the theater saw the community painting I did for the art center, and she loved it. She wants me to do a bigger version, with symbols that are important to Hemlock. And it pays well. So not only do I now have money coming in from being at Lady's Mantle, I have this payment for the mural."

"That's amazing. I . . ." Daisy snagged the takeout from Nora's hand and gestured for her friends to move into the living room. She had put plates and forks in there earlier and now set the takeout on the coffee table. She was glad she'd decided they should eat in here, because it added to the slumber-party feel. "Zach came by today. Zach Woods."

"I knew exactly which Zach it was before you clarified," Nora said. "Because there is a reverence with which you speak his name."

Daisy huffed. "I think we all do?"

"Who can blame us?" Nora tore into the food and put forks into the containers of noodles, rice, meat, and rolls.

"Who could?" Daisy agreed as she started to fill her plate. "Also"—she licked some teriyaki off her thumb—"he offered to build sets. Or at least facilitate it. He's on the board for the theater."

"That's amazing!" Nora said.

Soraya sat on the floor in front of her full plate, frowning. She started to fiddle with her bun, pushing it higher, then tightening it.

"What?" Daisy asked.

"I got more orders for bread today through my Instagram than I've ever had before. They're not all from one place. It's like a bunch of people spontaneously woke up and ordered loaves of bread from me. I've been working on it all day. I'll have to spend days getting through all of them. I . . . It's going to help so much. He's still paying the bills right now, but there's just nothing coming in for me to live on. And now there is."

"Because of your spell." Nora grinned, obviously picking up a conversation they'd started earlier.

"It wasn't a *spell*," Soraya said. "I added it to my vision board."

Nora made a loud grunting sound. "Oh, Jesus Christ, Soraya. It's the same thing! How do you not see that? When you do that, you're trying to *manifest* something. That's what a spell is. It's not communing with the devil, it's just wishful thinking."

"I just . . . There's no way it . . ."

"Maybe it's a coincidence." Nora was never one to try and assuage someone else's feelings, so Daisy didn't think she was hesitating on the magic now for Soraya's benefit. Something about it clearly bothered *her*.

Daisy wouldn't normally jump on the magic-is-real train so immediately, but how could it happen like this? This quickly, this decisively, for all of them, without any mystical influence?

"Do you really think it could be?" Daisy countered. "We all got what we asked for today."

"I don't know," Nora said, then she laughed. "It's silly. Right?"

"Is it?" Daisy asked. "We sat at lunch together, and you said everything was going to be okay. That we would get what we needed. Then it was like the apothecary was just there. And we walked in and . . ."

"It's a blessing." Soraya looked a little pious as she said that, but Daisy chose not to be offended.

Daisy chose to agree, because why let word choice be a barrier? "It is. I don't care what we call it. I think . . . I think we were meant to find each other. I think that us being together, being friends, is doing something."

"Divine intervention," Soraya added.

"Exactly," said Daisy.

"Real talk." Nora turned toward Soraya. "How is an enneagram not Christian Girl astrology?"

"What?" Soraya asked.

"I'm serious. Vision boards, enneagrams. It's like the same thing with different branding. Spells and manifestation, prayers and your enneagram number."

"Oh, now you know enneagrams?" Soraya asked.

"I don't *know* them. I'm aware they're a personality test and you get a number type, but I don't know what they're supposed to mean. But you and so many other girlies I went to school with talk about them like they're something we should all know and like they're some intrinsic part of you. Most especially you church girls. So I ask, how is that different from your astrology sign? The idea that you have these immutable characteristics and can glean whatever you need to from categorizing it."

"Well . . ." Soraya blinked. "You take a test. You don't just enter your birth date and act like the stars are deciding everything for you."

"If God made the stars, couldn't he assign meaning to them and the time that you were born?"

Soraya made an exasperated sound. "He could do whatever he wanted. So, sure."

"Listening to you two really is like being back in high school," Daisy said.

"No, it isn't," Nora said. "I would've made her cry by now. She's a lot hardier these days."

"Oh, I'm untouchable. Nothing will ever match the crashing horror of finding out my husband . . . well, you know, and there's only so many times I can say it."

Nora made a disgusted sound in the back of her throat. "That's awful. Genuinely awful. What is he even doing right now?"

"Pretending to be father of the year and acting like he's the victim. He's coaching the kids' baseball games, and because they're so into sports, and he's all involved in that, they're living with him and . . ."

"When is the first game?"

"In a few days."

"Are you going?" Nora asked.

"Of course I'm going. I'm going to end up sitting by myself and hoping the kids talk to me." Soraya looked so glum, and Daisy had to be thankful that whatever other nonsense Jonathan had done, he hadn't turned the kids against her.

He wouldn't want to take care of them all the time.

"No, you're not going by yourself," Nora said. "We're going with you. I love sports."

"You really love sports?" Daisy asked.

"No. I don't at all. But you know what I do love? Unsettling men. I would like it if we sat there and stared at him and made him feel like just *maybe* we might put a hex on him."

Soraya winced. "Oh, I don't really want to generate hex rumors."

"Why not? They probably already exist. In fact, if he knows you work at the apothecary, he's probably told everybody at the church by now that you're a witch."

Soraya examined her noodles. "Well, yeah, he did. I left him. There is no greater sin than leaving a man who has been labeled good, even when he's done nothing to demonstrate his goodness. I guess it doesn't matter if they think I'm a witch, in practice, since they already do because I stood up for myself."

"What are you supposed to do? Lay down and let him wipe his feet on you?" Nora asked.

Soraya blinked. "Yeah."

"Absolutely not." Nora wrapped her arm around Soraya and jostled her. "You're going to keep manifesting, bitch!"

"Hell yes!" Daisy stood up, the euphoria from earlier gripping her again. "You know what? Yes. We are . . . we are going to keep growing and getting stronger." She lifted her soda from the coffee table. "Here's to getting what we want."

"To getting what we need." Soraya lifted her water cup.

"To getting everything." Nora held her drink up.

As they all brought them together in a toast, Daisy thought that if today was any indication, that might actually happen. If nothing else, she almost felt like things would be okay.

It was the first time in a while she'd felt like that.

Chapter Eight

Nora

A coincidence is one of life's common forms of magic.

—Rules for Witches

Two days later, Nora was set up to begin the mural on the Holly Theater. She had made arrangements with Aggie to adjust her hours around her painting time, and it was nice to have an excuse to just never be at home. Her communication with Ben was perfunctory, and it was costing her not to dig into that.

She felt like she was hovering in space in a small glass box. She had to stay there and not push too far forward, not push too deep, be careful not to shatter it.

She'd had that feeling quite a bit in foster care, like it would only take one wrong move for her to get booted out of the house she was in and sent somewhere else. It was the same every time she'd gone to stay with her grandmother too. One wrong move and she'd be right back in the system, which had happened a couple of times. God. How had it come to this with her husband? Where she was afraid to question him on when exactly he was coming back? What he was actually doing?

It was like she'd been put in time-out. Like she was being tested.

That wasn't how marriage should work. Unilateral decisions cut across the other person when your life was built together.

She did her best not to dwell on that while she painted. Writing had been difficult for her since Ben had left because her mind was continually wandering, and it was almost impossible to bring it back to focus. While she painted, she liked letting her mind wander free. It was one way that the painting supported the writing. Usually, she used it to brainstorm new ideas, to think about the story she might write eventually and try to sell to a major publisher. The novel she had always intended to get to someday, but that felt too big and too lofty for her.

Now, though, she wasn't loving her free-range thoughts, roaming around and picking at poison berries, tormenting her with an unknown future.

Bullshit.

She had been so sure she was past uncertainty.

There were just so many potential consequences to this. So many potential dreams and versions of her future that could be destroyed.

Like kids. She and Ben weren't sure if they wanted them. They'd decided to wait. She'd been good with that, because she was the product of young, stupid parents who hadn't been ready to have kids, and really, never got ready to. She was a casualty of people who had procreated without giving it any thought, and she'd always imagined if she did become a mother, it would be when her life was settled and she'd really honed her writing, or her art, and his practice was solid. When everything was financially in order.

Now she was thirty-five, staring down the reality of sundowning fertility and . . . What if she had to start over?

She was rescued from her own thought process when the side door to the Holly opened, and Sam walked past her ladder.

"Sam," she called down to him.

He stopped and looked up, shielding his face from the sun. She could have jumped down and kissed him. Genuinely. It was just such a relief to see him. Because he made her feel sane. Because he made her feel grounded.

"What are you doing up there?"

"I'm painting a mural," she said.

"That's incredible. Back in high school, you would've been doing graffiti."

"I never *graffitied* anything."

"Untrue. I believe you spray-painted the building of one of the local political parties in protest one year."

"Yeah, that was a *protest*, not vandalism. I have the courage of my convictions."

"That you do."

"What are you doing here?" she asked.

"I'm doing the electrical for the stage."

"Oh. Did Daisy hire you?"

He shook his head. "No. Zach Woods."

"Is he here?"

Sam shot her a long-suffering stare. "No. Sorry. You can't thirst on him. I've never actually met him. But he shot me a text about doing some of the electrical on the set and also getting everything set up for the lighting. I'm putting in a whole new system. It's going to be for all the shows."

"That's cool."

"Yeah. It's nice. Usually, the big jobs go to . . . well. You already know my beef."

"I know. With Daisy's husband. That's funny that Zach isn't supporting Jonathan, though, isn't it?"

"Not really," Sam said. "He's a tool."

"But Zach is in business with him."

"Yeah, true, but honestly, I'd believe it if he didn't show his true colors to Zach either. Guys like that are pretty good at gauging who would call them out on their bullshit. They hide it. But once you catch a glimpse of it, you can't unsee it."

"Yeah." She frowned and ignored the strange feeling sitting in her stomach.

"How are you?" he asked.

"Ah. I'm good. I have this mural."

"What exactly is the mural of?"

"Trees and berries and shit," she said.

"Nora," he mock-scolded. "There are kids in there. Watch your language."

"Okay, but seriously, a whole scene. The mountains will stretch along here." She gestured across the upper part of the building. "And trees in the foreground will be growing up and out of the space. There will be big blossoms framing it around the front and bottom. The Logtown rose, fritillaria, and then blackberry bushes, obviously, because those are everywhere."

He gripped the bottom of the ladder, leaning into it. She felt a warmth in the familiarity and safety of him. And something else altogether. "They picked the best. It's going to be amazing."

"Thank you," she said.

He let go of the ladder and turned away from her, and she was left wondering if anyone else had ever expressed that level of confidence in her.

When she finished her session for the day, she packed up all her art supplies and headed back toward her house, where she was meeting the Discarded Witches Club. She'd changed the group text a couple of days earlier to that name, which Soraya did not find funny. But she hadn't changed it back either.

They were going to bundle herbs at Nora's tonight, part of Aggie's eminent flexibility with them. Daisy had the grimoire to help them, and every bundle would be assigned a spell card. Soraya and Daisy would do most of the bundling, while Nora designed some spell cards, drew them by hand, then scanned them in and printed them on nice paper.

When she pulled up to the house, Soraya and Daisy were already there with containers of Chinese takeout.

"Blessed be." She aimed that directly at Soraya.

"Jesus loves you," she said.

Nora laughed. "Thank you. Because everyone else thinks I'm an asshole."

They trooped up to the front door, and Nora unlocked it. The bins of herbs were sitting in her kitchen, the scent sweet and strong. The first order of business was food. Nora was starving. She'd painted through when she should have had lunch, but once she got rolling on it, she hadn't wanted to stop.

After she'd taken the edge off her hunger, she looked at her friends. "How were your days?"

"I got more sourdough orders," Soraya said. "I'm having trouble keeping up."

"You?" Nora asked Daisy.

"Sam came by the theater to talk to me about what we need for electrical. He's donating his time to my set, which is just incredible. I thanked him today, but please thank him again and again and again for me."

"Zach arranged it," Nora said. "I talked to Sam today."

"Well, he's amazing." Daisy's face glowed.

Nora experienced a twinge of discomfort over Daisy's effusiveness about Sam. Nora *knew* he was amazing. She had known it for years. But the amazingness of Sam felt like a lovely secret that was only hers, and it felt strange to share it.

"And how are you?" Daisy asked.

"Great. I spent the afternoon boiling in the sun while I painted blackberries and pondered my dwindling fertility."

"Wow," Daisy said. "That's . . . a lot."

"It is. It's another thing I didn't think about when he left, because I just wanted him to come back. Like the house, and how I'm going to live. But if he wants a divorce, there are so many things it affects. I was fine with not having kids yet. I'm still not sure that I want them. But I also don't *not* want them. I'm thirty-five, and if I have to meet someone else, and assuming I go through a bunch of wrong guys first, then meet another one, I'll realistically be forty before I remarry, and then who knows if I'll be able to get pregnant if I want to. I hate this feeling that he's taking choices from me. Decisions we were supposed to make together."

"Yeah, I get *that*," Daisy muttered.

"I'm scared to talk to him about it. I'm scared of what he'll say. I'm scared of what all this means."

"It's not fair of him to leave you in limbo like this. What David did was horrendous, but it was also definitive. It's something I can't get over. I'm not going to get over it. I'm not going to be able to be with him. I—I have to divorce him." Soraya's eyes filled with tears. "I can't forgive it. More than that, I don't want to. But at least I know what I want."

Nora looked at Daisy. Daisy took her empty plate to the sink and returned to the table, then unwound a section of twine and began to bundle together some rosemary, sage, and basil. "I just don't think I can ever trust him again. It's not even the affair. It's that he could look at me, devastate me in that way, and have absolutely no emotional response to it. It's almost better that he cheated. At least I can tell people that. It's quick, it's easy. I can use it as this simple way to explain that he betrayed me, but the biggest betrayal was him walking past me when I was crumpled up on the floor crying because he told me he wasn't happy with me. That he was leaving me. I will never be able to get that image out of my head. I will never be able to forget that he could do that. It was cruel. I've always known Jonathan to have flaws, but he's never been cruel. But I've seen his capacity for cruelty now. I can't unsee it."

It was a weird thing to have these women feel sorry for *her*, because what they'd both gone through was so hideous.

Nora's marriage wasn't over.

But they were right. She was left suspended. Ben hadn't given her a timeline or a plan or anything. He wasn't giving her something to work on about herself. Something to work on about them. Except her emotional availability, she supposed.

"That's exactly what it is," Soraya said. "Even when David did things I didn't like, repeatedly, when we would have the same fights over and over again, I told myself it was okay because he was a good man. A good man I loved, and so I would use that as my compass to find my way back to being content with him. But that's just gone now. I can't look at him the same way. But all the people around us still do. All our friends from church. The kids. I feel exposed, I feel embarrassed,

I feel like I'm the one who did the wrong thing. I wish he could share even a percentage of my humiliation. Just the tiniest bit. That's what I want. I want him to be humiliated."

"You should write it on a bay leaf." Nora smiled slyly at her.

Soraya shot her a withering glare. "Embarrassing your ex isn't a *goal*."

"Disagree," Nora said.

"I can't put that on a vision board."

"Your magical manifestation board?" Nora affected an innocent expression.

"*Regardless.* I can't put it on there."

Daisy held up the herb bundle. "This is sage, basil, and rosemary. There are properties of protection, cleansing, and healing. Also joy, transformation, manifestation, and growth. Which I think we could all use. Especially ahead of the baseball game."

"I just don't—"

"Aren't you curious if it'll do anything? Because you are actually going to have to see him tomorrow," Daisy said. Usually not the antagonist, Nora was fascinated that Daisy was pushing now. "All these wins happened after we did our little bay leaf spells. And even before that. All the victories lined up after we found each other. At this point, it could be a series of coincidences."

Goose bumps rose on Nora's arm. She rubbed at them. "I'm in. I could use some joy. Manifestation. Clarity."

"We can add horehound for that, Nora, which seems right up your alley."

"Some boys used to call me that in high school."

Daisy laughed. Soraya looked like she wasn't sure if she was supposed to laugh or not.

"Can you get a bowl?" Daisy asked.

Nora grabbed a silver bowl out of the pantry and set it in front of Daisy. Daisy reached into her purse and took out a lighter.

"What do you have a lighter for?" Nora asked.

"Definitely not the occasional random cigarette since my husband left." Daisy laughed. "I haven't had one in about a week. I'm just hanging on to it for witchcraft now."

She lit the end of the herb bundle, and sweet-smelling smoke filled the air. Daisy looked down at the grimoire.

"I bind the energy around me, which threatens my light. I cast it far away, and I draw all that is good toward me. I myself am sacred. Whatever harm has been meant for me, turn it back to the one who sent it. And so it is."

If Nora could give that much credit to spiritual things, she'd have sworn she felt a wind blow through the room.

Daisy looked up, and Soraya had her hands pinned squarely to her chest. "Maybe it's nothing."

"Maybe," said Daisy. "We'll have to wait for the game tomorrow."

Chapter Nine

Soraya

Let the foolish,
The selfish,
The small and the weak,
Shine through,
So that I see him as he is,
And not as what I hoped.
Let the silly things topple the proud.

—A spell for falling out of love

Soraya thought she was going to vibrate out of her skin. She had her leggings on, her T-shirt for her sons' high school, a baseball hat that said *boy mom*, and absolutely no confidence that her boys were going to be remotely happy to see her.

She held on to her Stanley cup as she got out of the car and walked slowly across the lot toward the bleachers, and briefly sighed in relief when she saw Daisy and Nora standing on the sidelines whispering to each other. How weird to find Nora's presence comforting. Only recently she would have crossed the street to avoid talking to Nora, as long as she was sure she hadn't seen her.

But now she and Daisy were the two most important people in her life, and Soraya needed them. Even when they were doing things that freaked her out and making fun of enneagrams and vision boards. At least they listened to her. Believed her. It was more than she could say for anyone else in her life.

"Yay, sports!" Nora did a mock cheer as Soraya approached. "Can't wait."

She ignored Nora's sarcasm, which she'd begun to realize was her love language. "Thank you for being here."

One set of bleachers was already full, with parents she knew mainly from church, and she hesitated. She didn't want awkward questions; she didn't want to deal with anyone giving her the side-eye.

Nora charged ahead. She sat right in front, and Daisy followed, then Soraya sat beside Daisy. Nora glanced behind them, but Soraya didn't because she didn't want to see people whispering or any of their speculative glances. She couldn't bear it.

She looked through the fence and saw David standing on the third-base line, chewing sunflower seeds, spitting them into a paper cup he was holding and clapping against his wrist, doing his coach *Go Team!* routine.

Then their eyes caught, and she wanted to crawl underneath the bleachers and hide from him. Up until she'd gotten the job at the apothecary, grown a spine, and gotten some good friends, she'd been going to church with him. But just a week and a half without seeing him made this feel weird.

He lifted his chin, like a weird, hostile greeting.

She frowned and did not wave or lift her chin.

She looked over at Nora, and Nora sputtered a laugh.

"What?" Soraya asked.

"Your face. You look like you just saw a mouse."

"Mice are cute," Soraya muttered. "I feel more like I saw a cockroach."

When the teams filed into the dugout, she turned her focus to the kids.

"All right, ladies," David shouted. "Let's see some hustle!"

"Ladies," Nora scoffed. "God, is he the coach in a '90s sports movie?"

"For the villains," Daisy said.

"Close," Soraya said.

When he turned away from the boys, one straggler came careening out of the dugout and ran smack into David and into the spittle/sunflower seed cup, which crushed against his chest.

A dark streak leaked from the bottom of the cup onto his white shirt.

His expression was furious as he scowled at the kid he clearly wanted to yell at but couldn't because his parents were sitting in the stands.

"Oh noooo," Soraya whispered, putting her hand over her mouth so she didn't laugh.

"Deserved," Nora said, and Daisy nodded in agreement.

There were a few uncomfortable giggles around them, so she wasn't the only one who found it funny.

David recovered, then moved back into position on the third-base line as their first batter went up and stood in the box. She looked down at his shirt stain again and then looked down farther and noticed his shoelace was untied.

"Strike!" The umpire's call was loud and decisive.

David didn't like it. "Are you blind!? That ball was so high, it practically hit a seagull!"

He stepped forward like he was about to go and argue with the ump toe to toe, when his cleat caught that loose shoelace and he tripped, the whole crowd gasping as he fell into the side of the dugout, clinging to the chain fence to keep himself from sprawling onto the dirt.

He straightened up, his face red. He was not a clumsy man. He was proud of his athleticism—and all the high school baseball that never translated into anything more but was a whole box bursting full of potential that he liked to talk about endlessly, even though the potential was long since squandered.

But he *could've been someone.*

She could feel all that and more coming off him in waves, anger a shimmering aura around him.

His anger wasn't her problem.

That thought almost made her smile.

The next pitch was wild, but the batter swung anyway and tipped the ball right off the end of the bat, sending it flying. It went right toward David, and to avoid it, he had to duck and dive, this time tripping and falling into the dust as he did.

Daisy and Nora both looked at Soraya, who was sitting there with her mouth dropped open.

"Oh my God." Nora stared at Soraya, her eyes wide. "You transferred your humiliation to him. The harm that he *meant for you*."

"No," Soraya said. "That's not . . . possible."

"This is amazing." Nora smiled. "It's amazing."

Everything David touched turned to disaster the whole evening. It was like God had reached down and had his finger hovering right over his head. Not quite set to "smite" but, still, between outbursts, collisions with his own players, and mustard and sunflower seed spittle spilled on his shirt, his pride was probably charred.

"I'll admit it." Nora leaned over and elbowed Soraya. "This is more fun than I thought it would be."

Soraya bit the inside of her cheek and turned her focus back to the game.

It was her son Levi's turn at bat, and her chest seized up, because she did *not* want him to be embarrassed.

"Go, Levi!" she shouted, and she didn't care if people stared at her. She was here for her son. They could judge her or whisper about her all they wanted.

He hit the ball and sent it soaring, and Soraya jumped up to cheer, with Daisy and Nora cheering beside her. The team was on fire after that, with her son making it home, and three more hits loading the bases. There were two outs, and this was it.

It was make it or break it.

The batter had a strike one.

Then a ball. Another ball. Then strike two. Another ball.

Full count.

She held on to Daisy's shoulder and braced herself.

When the last pitch was thrown, it was wild, and the call from the umpire was egregious. "Strike three."

"What?" David shouted from the sideline, then he walked forward, hand out, gesturing wildly at the umpire, deriding the bad call. When he normally would've stopped, he just kept going.

His face was red, his cheeks puffed out as he strode toward the official. It was like all his self-control had evaporated. It was the very worst of him, a temper he usually only saved for Soraya or the boys, on display for a stadium of spectators.

"You're gone!" the umpire yelled. "Two games!" He held his fingers up, his face red. "Two-game suspension."

"You can't do that to me!" David shouted. "I sponsor the field! I own Nichols Realty."

Soraya felt a slow, curling sensation of horror at the center of her chest, secondhand horror he didn't feel for himself.

It was official. She was embarrassed *for* him. She had the ick, as her boys would say.

Deep down to her soul, she had the ick now when she looked at that man.

That posturing, ridiculous man with a spit stain on the front of his shirt, trying to pretend he was special, that his business name on the field meant he *mattered.*

But he was just a man who had to send pictures of his penis to women on the internet to feel something.

Nora was laughing almost helplessly, her hand over her mouth as she tried to regain some composure, and Daisy was staring in open-mouthed wonder.

Soraya put her hands on her face, her cheeks burning. "This is . . ."

"Just and fair," Daisy said.

"Magic," Nora added.

Magic.

The feeling burned in her chest.

She was thrilled with David making a spectacle of himself in front of everyone, but her boys had to be dying of embarrassment, and she couldn't enjoy that.

"I'll be right back." She stood and walked down the bleachers, heading quickly to the dugout.

Levi was in the doorway, staring out at his dad, who was having a total meltdown, and Jaden was deep in the dugout, probably hiding.

When Levi saw her, his whole face lit up for just a moment. Like when he'd been a little boy. Like when he wasn't angry at her.

Her heart clenched tight.

Then his expression dulled.

She moved closer to the fence. "Good game."

"We lost." He looked down.

"You did great, though."

"You came," he said.

She took a sharp breath, words gathering low in her throat and getting caught there. Why would he ever think she wouldn't? That had something to do with David, she was sure. But this wasn't the time or the place to ask. "Of course I did." Her throat was tight, her words hushed. "I wouldn't miss it, sweetie. I love watching you play."

"I'm . . . I'm glad you're here." But he didn't come closer, and she knew there were a hundred potential reasons for that.

Him being mad at her. Him not wanting David to see him talking to her. Him not wanting his bros to see him talking to her—which honestly would have been true before the separation, so she didn't push.

But she did wave at Jaden in the dugout and take the win when she got a chin tilt in response.

It was, in fact, almost normal.

It wasn't good enough, though, because they weren't coming home with her afterward. Why was this the choice? Hanging on to her self-respect, trying to make a better future. She could sacrifice herself for her sons, but she couldn't sacrifice them on the altar of public perfection.

She didn't want them to grow up to treat women this way. She didn't want this narrative—about how she didn't matter apart from David—to be the thing they believed, and she was already part of why they believed it.

Because she had, for so many years.

All she could do now was try to fix it.

Without embarrassing them. Without shouting that she loved them in front of all their friends or making anything worse because their dad had just given the slapstick silent-film performance of a lifetime in front of the whole team.

Part of her clung to that. To the hope they would see him more clearly now.

She walked away from the dugout, and Nora and Daisy fell into step beside her.

"I fear," Daisy said, "we're witches."

The word hit Soraya funny in her chest. And yet, she felt powerful. She felt in control.

She wasn't sure if she'd ever experienced that before.

Strength and power were wonderful, but being able to laugh at David like the ridiculous man-child he was . . . that was gold.

Because she wasn't the one who should be embarrassed. He was the one who had sent that picture of his penis in a church bathroom. Hadn't even been able to wait until he got home. Who sat there and listened to a sermon and got horny?

She put her hand over her mouth.

"What?" Daisy asked.

"He's so ridiculous and sad." She wiped tears from her cheeks. From laughter or sadness, she wasn't sure. "An existential threat to my health and happiness, but sad."

"Yeah," Daisy agreed. "He is."

"The saddest," Nora said.

The public humiliation of David Nichols was something she could really get used to. She'd always been told not to embrace that part of herself. But all the softness, all the sweetness and light and whatever else she had tried to portray for all these years, hadn't kept her safe. It hadn't made her more important to anyone than David was by virtue of the fact he was a man. So, for the first time in her entire life, she took that little ball of anger in her chest and kept it there. She was going to nurture it. Hold it close. It made her feel powerful.

In the midst of her pain, it was a bright, beautiful beacon.

And she could honestly say she'd never experienced that before.

Chapter Ten

Nora

Even when you don't feel powerful,
your magic is.

—Rules for Witches

Nora had messages from Ben when she woke up in the morning. She smiled at the screen and unlocked the phone. There were pictures of the views from the hike he and his group had gone on the day before. She hit the phone icon and dialed out.

He answered.

"Hi," she said. "I just really miss you. I miss your voice. Tell me about everything."

"Nora, hi."

She heard him shifting something, and she tried to imagine what he was doing. He didn't sound all that happy to hear from her. "I wanted to touch base."

"I don't think it's a great idea for us to talk right now."

The words stunned her. "What?"

"There's a reason I've been sticking to text," he said.

"I know, with the time difference and everything, it's kind of tricky." Except they were only three hours ahead. But there was a little bit involved in that.

"I left so I could have space. I didn't want to ghost you or anything, and I like messaging with you. But . . . I really need this time to myself."

Words got jumbled up inside her, and she couldn't sort through them, couldn't figure out what to say to that. What about what *she* needed?

She cleared her throat to buy herself a second. "You made it sound like you needed time to think."

"I do."

"About yourself."

"About us too," he said. "I'm not happy. Our relationship is a big part of that."

His words were like a bullet ripping through her chest. "What?"

"I think if you recall our conversation before I left, I said that to you."

"You didn't. Not really." Yes, there had been some criticisms of her, but he'd made it clear he needed some time away, and it had to do with him and where he was in his life. She was sure of that. Almost.

The maddening calm in his voice just about shattered her.

"Your mural looks great. Thanks for sending the pictures of your progress. I can't wait to see it when I get back."

It was like whiplash. How could he say something like that? Like they would see each other and everything would be normal, after he said that.

"I have to go. We're about to sit down to lunch."

"Yeah. Sure." God. What was wrong with her? She did *not* go quietly into any good night, and here she was, letting his comment defeat her.

She felt like a zombie all the way to the apothecary, and when she got there, Daisy was telling Aggie about the spells, with a solemn-looking Soraya standing there. The spells hadn't done anything for Nora. She felt more than humiliated. She felt stupid. She had really been taking the separation as something that was about Ben and his need to find himself. There were things about her that made connection hard, and it had hurt that he'd said that. But he hadn't said their relationship was the problem.

"They *worked*," Daisy said.

"I'm completely unsurprised," said Aggie. "I told you. Everyone has magic. But some have a little bit more than others."

"How do you know?" Daisy asked. "Who has more or what will work or . . . anything?"

Aggie smiled. "Intuition."

Intuition. Did Nora have any of that? A pet rock probably had more intuition than she did.

The day ticked by slowly. Nora sold ten smudge sticks, several herb spell bundles, four tarot decks, and three tarot journals. Soraya stayed busy on the baking side, while Daisy talked to a few women who came in asking for advice on spells. Nora watched as Daisy flipped through them and grew more confident. Was it real? It felt like it sometimes, but then everything else around her seemed distinctly not magic. Her life felt like the furthest thing from a manifested dream, so how could it be?

Just another Ouija board. Her wanting to feel hope in something and being an idiot.

When they closed for the night, Nora could see that Aggie had something on her mind. "Daisy said you had success with your spells," Aggie said to Nora.

"I don't know if that's true."

"Don't you?"

It really wasn't fair. The baseball game had been like a comedy of errors. If there had been a single cloud in the sky, it would've gone directly over David's head and rained buckets on him alone. She'd asked for a sign, and now she felt reluctant to take it. But if there was a divine plan in the world, why was her life such a shit show from childhood to now? That didn't make sense to her.

"What's wrong?" Aggie asked.

"Nothing." She was silent for a long moment. "I always wanted to believe in magic. But when you're a kid with no hope for anything better, you can't. There's nothing out there in the universe big enough, or powerful enough, to come down and save you. If there is, that's almost worse, because nothing did. The idea I could have fixed my situation by putting herbs into a bundle or praying harder or turning in a circle three times while chanting in Latin just kills me."

Aggie shifted closer to her. "Magic doesn't take the darkness out of the world, Nora."

Nora laughed, almost hysterically, certainly not with humor. "Is this where you tell me we need darkness to see the stars or some shit?"

Aggie shook her head. "No. The darkness isn't there to help the stars shine. The stars shine to spite the darkness." She put her hand on Nora's. "The magic lives inside you in spite of it all."

Her words touched a hidden, bruised place in Nora, and she didn't want them to. She was tired of all this. Of living without a guarantee of anything. Of having to shine through the darkness while the darkness got thicker, heavier.

"I talked to Ben earlier. It's just . . ." She stared down at her hands. "He said our relationship is part of why he's unhappy. And he doesn't think we should talk while he's gone. Not on the phone."

"Oh." Soraya pressed her hand to her chest, like Nora's pain hurt her.

"I'm sorry," Aggie said.

"It's just a rough patch," Nora said. And she despised that she said that. She wasn't an optimist. She wasn't naive. But this marriage had made her want to be. It made her want to believe in a love she never had.

Was she the stars? Shining in spite of it all?

It didn't feel quite as glorious as that. She didn't feel like stars. She felt like what she was: a thirty-five-year-old woman who'd been hoping—secretly, shamefully, for so long—and now had that hope crushed.

"Come. Sit down." Aggie beckoned Nora over to a low table at the center of the room. Daisy and Soraya followed, though as Nora, Daisy, and Aggie sat down, Soraya stayed back. A small pouch, rose petals, and crystals were spread out on the table.

"When I feel hopeless, I do a spell. We can't control everything, or everyone. But we can make our intentions into actions. It's better than sitting in sadness, I find."

"Do you have any love spells?" Nora asked, trying to laugh again. Trying not to seem as sad and hopeful as she was. That was the really sad part. She wanted the hope to be drained from her, beaten out of her by all the shit that had happened to her, but it just never was. It kept on, relentless and painful, a new opportunity to be devastated every single day.

"Soraya, can you get some selenite out of the bin?" Aggie asked.

Nora was fascinated that Soraya didn't balk but went to grab the pale-white stone.

Aggie pushed the selenite, rose petals, and a piece of paper toward her.

God, this was hideous. Was she actually going to put a love spell on her own husband? Almost as hideous as having to show faith in the idea of magic and miracles. If only she could be half as cynical as she pretended.

You've seen it. You've seen it all come together since you met Daisy and Soraya at the hospital.

Why not try this?

An image of Sam filtered through her mind. Of the embarrassment she felt the last time she'd tried to appeal to the divine for answers.

I just want someone to love me.

She despised that she felt this way. That Ben had *made* her feel this way. She still wanted him back. She wanted their life back.

"Write your desires down on the paper."

Aggie passed a short pencil to Nora, and Nora sat there, holding the pencil in her hand, poised over the paper. "I just write what I want?"

"Yes."

"How? I mean, isn't there a formula to this?"

"Some people like to write out a spell as if their desire is something they have already. Some like to make requests. Some prefer poetry. If you want to get really dramatic, you can turn in a circle three times and speak in Latin. This is all about *your* magic, Nora."

Her magic. She wanted to believe in it.

She wanted to believe in *anything* right now, so she'd have some sign that she might be okay.

She lowered her head and looked at the paper. "I just write it."

"Three times," Aggie said.

I have the love I deserve.

She paused and studied the sentence. She hadn't been aware that was what she was going to write. She imagined Sam again, looking at her, watching her do this. She felt hot, flustered like she had all those years ago, angry, and filled with a deep yearning she couldn't quite put a name to. Then she pushed that away and thought about Ben. About their wedding. Their marriage. Their life.

He would want to come back to it. He would have to.

I have the love I deserve.

I have the love I deserve.

Aggie struck a match and lit a wide candle at the center of the table. It sparked, and then the fire burned to life. "Seal your intentions with flame, and put the ashes into the bag with the selenite and the rose petals. Then put it under your pillow."

Nora lifted the paper, her hand shaking, and touched the corner to the fire.

It went up in a flash, before turning to shimmering ashes.

Chapter Eleven

Soraya

A witch is simply a woman who
listens to her intuition.

—Rules for Witches

Soraya was watching Nora's spell burn, the ashes settling in a dish on the table, her heart pounding hard. This seemed . . . wrong, and yet she couldn't tear her gaze away.

Her phone buzzed, and she felt like the text had interrupted something sacred.

She took her phone out of her pocket and saw a very long text from David.

There was a joke in there somewhere about *length* regarding previous items he'd sent via text.

She stared at the words, having difficulty making sense of them.

Since you won't see reason.

Out of the house within the week.

Go to church with me on Sunday.

Try to restore our family.

She blinked.

The words were all out of order in her head, jumbled.

He was actually threatening her. Threatening to take the house away.

Just yesterday he'd . . . imploded on a baseball field in front of the whole community, and he had the audacity to act like he was . . . so lofty? So far above her?

He'd been staying in one of their unoccupied rentals, and now some new tenants were going to move in, and he wanted her out. Or she was going to have to take him back, because he wouldn't sleep in the guest bedroom at his own house, and he would not be denied access to his wife.

Access?

None of this was about missing her. It was about getting what he wanted. Saving face. It was about his pride. But she wasn't the one who had caused this. She wasn't the one who had done it. She didn't have any power. She didn't have . . . anything. He was making sure she knew it. That she felt it.

The boys want their mother back.

Oh, of all the lies. Of all the diabolical lies he had told, this was the worst. The only reason the boys didn't have her was because he had made them angry at her. Somehow all of this had been twisted around and turned into her fault. No one could see it. *No one could see it.*

They *had* her.

She was the one being punished. Who was being kept away from them, by her husband's brainwashing nonsense.

"I need them to see it," she said.

She hadn't meant to say the last part out loud.

"Did you find a spell, Soraya?" Aggie asked.

What are spells but prayers men don't like?

She nodded and took a step closer to the table.

Maybe Aggie was right. Maybe she didn't have to abandon who she was. In fact, that was the problem with all of this. Soraya felt like she was being herself. Like she was being the woman she had been taught to be. The person she was supposed to be.

The Christian chorus line was behaving like she was in the wrong. She felt like everything she'd ever believed had been turned and twisted, and no one seemed to notice except her.

They all thought saying God's name cavalierly was taking it in vain, but what was this? Using God's name to try to manipulate her, to try to force her back into a home where she wasn't respected. Where she was lied to and betrayed.

They were all saying she was the one who couldn't see. That she was deceived in some way.

It was *them*.

Aggie slid a piece of paper to the center of the table. Soraya sat down on the low cushions very slowly, then she reached out, grabbed a pencil, and began to write a piece from memory.

For all that is secret will eventually be brought into the open. And everything that is concealed will be brought to light and made known to all.

Everything that is concealed will be brought to light and made known to all.

She was saying the words out loud, over and over again. A prayer, an incantation. Both things. Everything. It came from deep inside her. She wanted her kids back. She didn't want to lose her house. She didn't want to lose all her friends.

You will have to lose something.

That voice, that certainty, was still and small inside her.

She was going to lose something. But she would be absolved of this thing.

That was a promise. It was in the Bible. All of David's secrets would be brought to light.

It would be more than petty embarrassment, more than the revelation of how fragile his pride was.

She wrote the scripture out three times, and before she could stop herself, she lifted the paper and touched it to the flame. As it was consumed and turned to ash, she whispered, "Amen."

"Amen," said Nora.

Aggie nodded slowly. "And so it is."

"Daisy?" Nora questioned. "Do you have a spell?"

"I don't want Jonathan back," she said. "I don't want to get revenge on him."

Soraya felt scolded by that, like she'd been petty in contrast to Daisy's graciousness. "I'm not trying to get revenge. I want everyone to see who the villain is. I want everyone to know. Because right now, they're all blaming me. My kids, my parents, everyone from church," she whispered. "He's letting me suffer. He wants me to."

"I know, Soraya, and it's terrible. David deserves it."

"Why don't you want the same for Jonathan? He betrayed you."

Daisy looked uncertain. "That seems reasonable. *Karma.* Nothing more, nothing less. Just so he gets what he deserves. He left me, and he didn't keep his commitment about the play and . . ." She opened the grimoire and set it on the table. "I saw a spell for that in here."

She skimmed the pages, then stood up and walked over to the bins of crystals and dried herbs. She returned with a collection of items. Of course, it was very Daisy for her to begin trying to do more complicated spells and readings on her own, and to have done all the studying necessary for it to happen.

"What goes around, comes around. What you sow, you will reap. Your intentions will come back to you. And so it is." Daisy wrote the spell onto paper, cast it into the fire, and collected the ashes. Then she put the herbs, flowers, and ashes into the bag. "Now what?"

"You have to put it with the person you think deserves their karma," Aggie said.

"I'll put it in his work truck when I go pick up the kids. His truck is a mess. He'll never notice if I throw it under the seat." Daisy paused for a moment and let out a breath. "This is silly." She laughed. "I am *not* putting a spell on my husband. I . . . It's one thing to ask for what we need, and I think . . . Soraya, I think your husband deserves the worst outcome, but I'm not . . ." She dropped the package back on the table. "I'm not . . . It wouldn't . . . I'm not doing that."

Aggie nodded slowly. "You have to follow your own arrow, Daisy. If this doesn't feel right to you, don't dabble in magic that isn't yours. We'll clear the energy, and it will be like it didn't happen."

Aggie went behind the counter and set out a cauldron. An actual witch's cauldron. It was small, but large enough for her to put the bag that Daisy had created inside.

Then she took out a small white candle and lit it with the wick from the blaze on their table. She dipped it into the cauldron, and a flame that burned blue and green ignited—bright, hot, and fast.

"Into the smoke, I release all the energy that no longer serves me," Aggie said.

Soraya looked at Daisy, who was staring into the flame, even as it sputtered and died down.

"So it is," Soraya whispered.

Soraya hadn't made a bag or a talisman. She didn't feel like she needed one. Maybe she would at another time.

Maybe.

Cold fear settled over her. She might actually lose her house.

If she didn't go back to him, she might lose her house. And yes, she had gotten this job, but that wasn't going to pay the rent. It wouldn't get a roof over her head.

"Are you okay?" Nora asked. It took Soraya a moment to realize she was talking to her.

"David texted me." She stared at the ashes on the table in front of her. "I have a week to take him back, or he's going to throw me out of the house."

"Oh, fuck him," Nora said. "Fuck *that.*"

Soraya flinched at the harsh language and realized the irony of that, since she was sitting in an occult shop having just possibly cast a spell, but was still grimacing at the f-word. If any moment in time required it, she supposed it was this one. She definitely thought David deserved it. She would let Nora handle it, though. She wasn't there yet.

Yet? No. She would never be there. But . . . she didn't want to be the one kicked out of her house. She didn't want to be kicked out of her church.

You're going to have to lose something.

Daisy wrung her hands together. "I have my house, if you need a place to stay—"

"I have a whole week." She felt numb and floaty. Lightheaded.

"You don't need a week." Aggie's tone was much sharper than normal. David had even managed to make her angry. "You can move into the apartment above the apothecary."

She felt so torn. If she moved above the apothecary, it would feel like she was really saying she was done with David.

He was the father of her children. He wasn't perfect. He had a temper about petty things sometimes, and he yelled, but he'd never hurt her. She'd never been afraid of him. He could be sweet and romantic, buying her flowers just because.

It was hard for her to remember good things with him sometimes. She almost didn't want to because it *hurt*.

If he had come to her genuinely contrite, maybe it would be a different story. They had kids together. She did love him.

She *had* loved him. She wasn't sure she did now, because she didn't feel grieved at being separated from him. She was just mad about the circumstances. About how she was being treated. By him, by her kids, by her supposed friends. If he really felt bad, he wouldn't be sending her threats. He wouldn't be acting like her inability to forgive this was strange or difficult. If he truly was repentant, then he would be behaving differently.

Aggie was right. She didn't need a week because she wouldn't be changing her mind. She thought of her house. Her beautiful white kitchen.

All the times she had stood in it and baked bread and thought that she was so blessed, but none of it had really been hers.

David didn't see her as an equal. She was just another thing that belonged to him, like that house. He didn't care about her happiness. Maybe he loved her in a way that he understood, but it was a possessive love.

Manipulative.

"Thank you," she whispered. "I . . . I really need your help. I need this apartment. I . . . Oh, but I don't have enough money to pay rent."

Aggie put her hand on Soraya's shoulder. "Remember, you were concerned about the commercial kitchen. The kitchen upstairs is certified. You can bake there. It's all working itself out. And it will continue to."

It didn't feel like it, and yet it did. All the right doors were opening for her, she supposed. Even if it felt strange and wrong in some ways.

She'd never felt like this before. Right and wrong had always been clear and totally reinforced by her community. Right had been comfortable. She'd done good and received good in return. Now she was . . . flailing uncomfortably, and she was being cared for, but it wasn't comfortable. It was scary and challenging, and she didn't think she liked it at all.

Everything that is concealed will be brought to light and made known.

It was the one hopeful refrain inside her.

Chapter Twelve

Daisy

Even witches have to know their limits.

—Rules for Witches

"Daisy, do you have a moment?"

Daisy had just put her purse over her shoulder and was about to leave Lady's Mantle for the night, but Aggie's soft voice stopped her. Soraya and Nora had just left, and she'd stayed an extra hour doing the books and making up for the other nights she'd left early for rehearsal.

She almost wondered if she was in trouble for not doing the spell earlier. It was silly, maybe, but Aggie had gone to all that trouble, and then Daisy had rejected it.

"Of course." Daisy turned toward the older woman.

"I wanted to give you something."

"Oh, Aggie, you've given me plenty."

Aggie shook her head. "No, I haven't given you quite what you need yet." She reached beneath the counter, took out a box of cards, and passed it to Daisy. Daisy looked at the box, cream colored with holographic beams of light surrounding art deco–style imagery.

"This is beautiful," she said.

"You have very deep intuition, but I think it is best served with the framework of the cards to help give it shape."

Daisy laughed. "Are you saying even my intuition needs to be organized?"

"There's nothing wrong with that. It can make it easier to latch on to. Soraya's power is in what she makes—in the herbs, the flour, the magic she puts into her food. Nora's is big, profound, creative energy. Angry, sometimes, and pulls from the moon itself. Yours . . ." Aggie tapped the cards. "You already know, don't you? You're the one who's been reading most from the grimoire."

"I like to learn everything I can learn," Daisy said. "Not very magical."

"It's extremely magical. It just informs the elements you work with best." Aggie looked at her. "Go ahead, open the deck."

Daisy slipped the lid off the box and picked up the deck, going through the cards and looking at the artwork.

"Every reader works with cards differently. Some feel the energy in the cards. Some look for symbolism in the art and read intuitively. Others extrapolate the meaning more closely to the traditional. Some read reversals, others don't. Some see reversals as opposite energy to the upright, and others see it as a shadow side, or blocked energy. There might be rules and a framework, but it's your own intuition that brings it to life."

Daisy shuffled the cards in her hand. "I'm not sure I can trust myself. I feel . . . like I don't know who I am. I know who I am when it comes to other people. I'm a mom, and a daughter, a granddaughter, a soon-to-be ex-wife who wasn't enough for her husband."

"That is not who you are, Daisy. You are all the magic that's existed inside you since you were a little girl. You used to spin in wild circles and howl at the moon. When did you stop? That girl, that's who you are."

She swallowed hard, trying to hold back tears. She hadn't been that girl for a long, long time.

"What bothers you most right now?" Aggie asked.

An image of Jonathan came to mind, and Daisy pulled a card from the center of the deck, then flipped it over on the counter.

She laughed. "The Fool. My own personal fool is giving me lots of problems."

"There are layers to that," Aggie said. "As the Fool is clearly a person. Also the new beginning you've been forced into."

"Hmm." Daisy picked the cards up and put them back into the box, the Fool on top. She watched him vanish as she closed the lid over him. "Thank you, Aggie. I'll work with these."

"You have it all, my dear. It's just learning to see it."

The words sat heavy in her chest as she drove home.

She stuck her key in the lock of her front door and turned it, laughing gently. Learning magic. She really wasn't sure how she felt about any of it. Sure, she liked the idea. Not enough to go out and howl at the moon. Not enough to try to curse the father of her children.

Though it had been tempting. Even as she'd balked at it even being a possibility.

If pressed, she supposed she would say she was someone of *a* little faith, if not *little* faith. When she thought about what would happen when her grandmother finally slipped past life, she couldn't believe there was absolutely nothing waiting for her. But she also wasn't sure what form any of that took.

Soraya believed in *all* of it, that much was clear. She seemed genuinely afraid of witchcraft, like it had the ability to take control of her life and her eternal soul and send her straight to hell.

But once her husband had threatened to kick her out of the house . . .

Daisy shut her front door behind her and looked around the dark entryway of her own house. Jonathan could've taken the house from her. He *still* could. She wasn't going to be able to afford to pay for it on her own. He could afford to pay for both houses. He could afford to pay for two women. Maybe that was where she had made the mistake. A man who could afford two lives . . .

He's really just living the one.

She took a breath and flicked the lights on. The kids couldn't come home to a place looking like a mausoleum where the remains of her old life were trapped for all eternity.

She also wasn't entirely in the mood to see her ex. She felt complicated about him right now. Today, when she'd been faced with the thought of cursing him, giving him his just deserts, her old feelings for him held her back, and it had her mixed up.

Anyway, it wasn't like he would know she had opted not to curse him, and he wouldn't thank her if he did know.

If she asked Jonathan, he would absolutely say magic wasn't real. He didn't like to entertain the idea that Bigfoot might exist (*Where are the bones, Daisy?*) or that intelligent life might be out there (*Who cares? Even if there is, maybe they don't know about us either*) or that the B&B they stayed at on their fifth anniversary felt haunted (*It's an old house; it was creaky*). It had always annoyed her, mainly because it just felt arrogant.

Jonathan McNamara, always with the answer. Always logical.

Not that Daisy considered herself overly whimsical. But she wasn't . . . Jonathan. Jonathan liked what he could see. What he could touch with his hands.

Including other women, it turned out.

She resented that whenever she thought of him, she thought of *her*. Of the betrayal. Their relationship didn't and couldn't stand on its own. They'd had so many years where he hadn't had affairs and—

Had they? That insidious thought burrowed deep into her brain and wouldn't let up.

He was her high school sweetheart. The love of her life. She'd thought she was his.

What did she actually know about him at all? What did she know about her own life? It was such a humiliating thought. She didn't have time to marinate on it, though, because almost the moment it occurred to her, she heard tires in the driveway. She pasted a smile on her face, turned around, and put her hand on the doorknob.

"Someone, *something*, give me strength." Then she pulled the door open, attempting to smile as brightly as the sun. Her smile faltered, only a little bit, when she saw Amberly sitting in the passenger seat looking perky from her smile to her boobs.

Daisy locked her back teeth together and tried to come up with a mantra. She liked a mantra. She didn't like feeling out of control.

I can't control anyone but myself. I can't control anyone but myself.

Jonathan got out, and thankfully Amberly stayed put even as she waved wildly.

She was just . . . obvious, that woman. Like it didn't seem to occur to her that Daisy might not want to be besties with her—not that they'd ever spoken alone. But she had once commented very sincerely that she took the role of *bonus mom* very seriously, and Daisy'd had to stop herself from saying something heinous.

Even so, Daisy couldn't help but wave back, then lowered her hand like it had betrayed her, as the kids tumbled out of the pickup one by one.

Maybe *tumbled* was the wrong word. They practically levitated. The kind of energy that spoke to sugar and Red 40 vibrating their tiny bodies straight from the truck into the house.

"Dad got a VR!" Avery shouted on his way past her.

"I played it." Wren hopped over the threshold and kicked her mismatched rain boots off (it wasn't raining).

"I don't feel good." Alden staggered after his siblings, clutching his stomach in an overdramatic fashion.

"Hello to you too," she said. "I hope you had a good day."

"The best." Alden grinned, suddenly just fine, the red ring around his lips confirming what she had thought. Sugared up. And returned home. Definitely responsible for whatever tummy ache he was currently stricken with.

Then Alden disappeared around the corner after his siblings, leaving her with their dad.

She peered past the kids, at Jonathan, who was standing there with his hands in his pockets, looking so familiar and handsome it made the back of her throat ache.

But just behind him in the car, staring at her phone, was the woman he had chosen instead of her. Instead of their life.

She was . . . taking a selfie, her head pressed to the back of the passenger window as she pursed her lips into a pout and held her phone up at an angle.

Daisy gazed back at Jonathan.

How could it still hurt this bad to look at him when *Amberly* was sitting right there?

Why did she still love him?

Daisy blinked and hoped he didn't see any of the emotion in her eyes.

I can only control myself.

"They had a good day?" she asked.

"Yeah. Monsters." He shook his head, the affectionate smile on his face so . . . him. "I think they ate an entire bag of Swedish fish in like an hour."

"So I can expect for them to be very hungry for dinner."

He shrugged. "I don't know what time you do dinner these days." There it was. A touch of unearned defensiveness and just a little bit of resentment, breaking right on through his affable, lovable-dad thing.

She touched her tongue to the roof of her mouth and let it hold back the words that rose inside her. He said nothing. Like he was daring her. Challenging her.

"Why is that?" Her tongue didn't hold. Neither did the words.

"You know what I mean," he said, light and easy like he hadn't started something on purpose.

I can only control myself.

"No, Jonathan, I don't know what you mean." She smiled. "I don't gatekeep that information from you. You could have it if you wanted to. You could live in this house if you wanted to."

"Is that right?" There was an edge to his voice now, and it scraped her raw.

"Not under the current circumstances. But nobody made you leave."

He leveled his gaze at her. "You did, actually."

Oh, she'd made a mistake. She'd set this up wrong.

"Let me revise that. Nobody made you *cheat*."

"Daisy," he said, in the low, conciliatory way he had always said her name when she was mad at him. It was so intimate, so familiar. It spoke of years and years of knowing just how to calm her down, just how to make her melt. She hated that he still had that knowledge. That he knew how to placate her. That he knew how to kiss her. Touch her. That he knew what she looked like naked. That she knew what he looked like naked, and he was the only man she had ever seen . . .

She had been holding off a breakdown.

But she had *quit* the job, finally. She had really taken steps to separate herself from him, and here he was, standing there looking like her husband, when he just wasn't. Wasn't the man she had married. Wasn't the man she had thought he was.

"It doesn't have to be like this," he said.

"What, exactly?"

"Like *this*. It doesn't have to be . . . toxic."

"Toxic." The word echoed inside her.

"You didn't need to quit."

"This is about me quitting as your bookkeeper?"

"Yes. I mean, no. It's about our family. It's about our kids. But no. I don't want you to quit. I need you. It's ours, Daisy."

It's ours. That was . . . She just couldn't do this. She couldn't take the lying. She couldn't take him standing there all handsome and being this much of a liar. She just couldn't. He didn't see it as theirs; everything was his. Including her. That was why he was bringing this up.

No matter how much he stood there, nonconfrontational and smiling, he was mad. Furious at her for leaving.

"You *need* me. You need me to do math for you. You need me to tell you what time I feed your children dinner. You need me to balance the checkbook that you use to buy her jewelry."

"Hey." He looked back at the truck. "Leave her out of this."

"I can't, Jonathan. You brought her into it. You brought her into our life."

"Relationships end, Daisy. I don't know what you want me to do."

I don't either. Because I don't want you back, because I could never take you back, not after that, not after her. But I just want to go back to the way things were before. She couldn't say any of that, because it was too sad.

All of this was so sad. She felt . . .

I didn't curse you earlier. And maybe I should have.

Because God, it was like none of this touched him. He was looking at her like *she* was the bad guy. Like *she* was the villain.

"You cheated on me," she said.

"I don't really want to have this conversation with you in the driveway. The kids are right in the house."

There he was again, pretending to be the voice of reason. Pretending to be reasonable. Like she was the one who was unreasonable. Like she was the one who had caused this, when he'd said *he hadn't been happy for ten years*. She had never considered him a manipulative man. She had never thought he was pulling the strings on her, like a puppet.

She'd loved him since she was sixteen years old.

She just didn't know anymore if he had ever been the boy she thought she knew or if it had always been a lie. He made her feel guilty. He made her feel like she was causing this. Made her feel like she was the one ripping them apart when he was the one who had slept with somebody else. Who had left her for somebody else. Who was buying that woman rings and . . .

"I'm going to need you to have some perspective," he said. "Because when Amberly and I get married—"

She'd suspected it. But . . .

She looked back at the truck, where Amberly was now playing with her hair during the selfie, and saw a ring sparkling on her finger. She looked down at her own left hand.

She still had her ring on.

"You're marrying her?"

"Yeah."

"We aren't divorced yet."

"That isn't going to take long, is it?"

"You haven't told your *mother*, Jonathan." Her heart was pounding so hard she thought she might throw it up. "What are you thinking? You can tell her you left me on a Friday and marry Amberly on a Sunday?"

"I'm waiting for the right time."

So many angry words boiled inside her, and she wanted to just let them all spill over. Screw control. Screw him.

"Why . . . why do you even want to get married to her?" It wasn't the zinger she would have liked to get out. But why? This was a new level of humiliation. Because it was one thing if he wanted to go out and sleep around—that was insulting and unendurable, and she'd never have stayed with him—but at least that felt like it was about him.

It didn't mean he was in love.

Him loving her, wanting to marry her, that . . .

That hurt.

"She wants to get married."

"What . . . what does marriage even mean to you, Jonathan? Because our vows meant nothing."

"That isn't fair. We were married for twelve years, and I kept my vows for a long time. Don't act like you didn't have anything to do with the state of our marriage."

"What was the state of our marriage? Enlighten me. *Communicate* with me. Because that's one thing you never did, Jonathan. You never told me what was going on with you. I thought everything was fine," she said, her voice breaking. "If I didn't . . . cook for you enough, or clean for you enough, or fuck you enough, I would never have known because you didn't tell me."

He turned his head away, like even he couldn't bear looking her in the eye now. "Don't play the victim."

"I *am* the victim. I am the victim of your endless bullshit. You can . . . you can go. We don't need to talk. We don't need to rehash this. You're marrying her. *Great.* You don't know the name of your kids' pediatrician or their teachers. You don't know what time they eat dinner. You won't be here to tuck them in every night. You sugared them up like a fun uncle instead of their dad and dropped them off with me. I quit." She looked him dead in the face. "*Everything.* I quit, and I hope you get everything you deserve."

She turned on her heel and went back into the house, slamming the door behind her. She turned the lock, and when she heard him knock once behind her, she realized he still had a key. She braced herself for him to use it. Part of her wished she had stayed outside and fought with him just to see if she could tempt him into it. To see if she could entice him into a screaming match, because God knew it would be fun. Because he always tried to pretend he was the reasonable one. He always tried to act like he was the one holding everything together and she was the one letting their life fall apart like he hadn't torn down their marriage. Like that hadn't been everything.

It would be fun to see if she could make it so he couldn't pretend to be rational anymore.

He didn't use the key. He didn't knock again. That was Jonathan all over. He just didn't care enough. He never would.

He was never going to give her what she wanted. What she needed. He was never going to love her like she'd loved him. That was the bottom line. He didn't love their life.

"I hope you get everything you deserve," she whispered.

She thought about the spell bag she had burned, that she had committed to ash. She was going to do that spell again, but this time, she meant it, in every dark way possible.

She reached into her purse and took out her tarot cards, taking the lid off and revealing the Fool.

A man, walking, heedless of the world around him, careless, unconcerned.

She picked the card up and looked at the image, not breaking her focus.

"Jonathan McNamara," she said in the silence of the room. "What you have sown, that will you also reap."

Chapter Thirteen

Nora

By the light of the truth, may the
shadow of deceit be unveiled.

—A spell for exposing lies

Do you want to go out?

Nora looked down at her phone just as she sat down on the couch. She didn't really want to go out. She wanted to curl up at home. She felt foolish and drained and, genuinely, dealing with Sam on the heels of giving in to doing that love spell felt a little bit . . . eh.

She was afraid he would be able to see it on her. Her foolish hope.

He was the only person who really knew her. Who really knew how sad her life was. Who really knew all the dark truths she tried to keep tucked away.

He knew about her disastrous hope. Her optimism in the face of everything, and the real issue was he was the only one who knew how silly it was.

So did she want to see Sam? Absolutely. Because the alternative was staying in her empty house, and she didn't really want to do that either.

"Hey," she said, opting to pick up the phone and call him.

"I'm at Trigger's."

"You got started drinking without me and you need a designated driver?"

"I'm not drinking. I was going to order a cheeseburger, and I was hoping that maybe you would be off work and you can tell me about your new job."

"Yeah. I can do that."

Trigger's was only a five-minute drive from her house, though she felt persecuted putting pants with a firm waistband and shoes back on to get in the car again. The theater company hadn't opened for the season yet—when it did, it would be busy in town most nights—but until then, it would remain relatively quiet. It was a Wednesday night, so there would be some church traffic at the restaurants, but of course not at the bars.

She thought of Soraya and her blazing anger as she had cast that spell on her husband. Witchcraft! Soraya!

Biblically based witchcraft, somehow. But still.

She should feel satisfied that it turned out Soraya was kind of a hypocrite. Except it didn't really feel all that hypocritical to Nora, as much as she wished it could.

The hurt Soraya was experiencing was real. What a shitty thing for her husband to do. Cheating on her, and then throwing her out of their house?

Nora parked on the side street near the bar and got out.

If Ben ever did anything like that . . .

Well, he doesn't want to talk to you right now. How is that better?

She cut that thought off as she crossed the street to the narrow strip of buildings and slipped into the alleyway, opening the door and heading up the stairs to Trigger's. It was fairly quiet inside, the old country-western bar not really coming alive until later. There was a barrel in the corner that used to have peanuts for the patrons to eat and throw shells on the floor, but they didn't do that anymore because it was a liability, and also messy.

In a few hours, it would be filled with people looking to get drunk, line dance, and hook up. She and Sam would miss the rush.

But this suited her just fine.

She spotted Sam as soon as she walked in. He was seated in the corner at a booth, facing away from her. Broad shouldered, a baseball cap on his head, his red T-shirt stretched tight across his back, his muscles visible through the thin fabric. That was a weird thing to focus on. Her best friend's back muscles.

She walked across the room, maybe more loudly than strictly necessary, and took a seat across from him. "Did you order already?"

"Just a drink," he said.

"Good. I'm starving."

It didn't take long for the waiter to come over and take their identical orders of a cheeseburger and fries, and Nora added a Coke to her order. She would've liked a drink, but she would start when she got home. Drinking alone when she was sad seemed like a great idea.

"How was the witchcraft?" he asked.

"Fine." It made her uncomfortable that he zeroed right in on that. Like he knew she had cast a spell. Like he could see the sad hope burning at the center of her chest. Those blue eyes had always been far too keen at seeing beneath her defenses. She didn't like it, but she loved him. It had always been a problem.

"Do you think you're going to like it?"

"I think at the very least I'll get a lot to write about."

"You finally going to write a book?"

She scoffed. "I'm not going to write a book. You have to have money to self-publish and connections to traditionally publish, and look at me, I have none of that."

"I think they call that self-rejection, Nora."

"Maybe if everything was secure with Ben. Being a writer is a lot more practical when you have a dentist husband as your patron."

"Yet, you didn't write a book while things were good with him."

She wanted to punch him in his handsome face. "I'm a serviceable writer. I can do copy and articles that entertain people for a minute. I don't think I have enough in me to write a whole book."

"That is bullshit."

"I don't have enough in me I want to write about."

"Because then you'd have to deal with your issues?"

"Shut up." She tried to laugh like this was friendly banter and not something a lot deeper and more uncomfortable. "I'm the one who went to therapy." She cleared her throat. "Soraya's husband is kicking her out of her house, and we're going to help her move."

She needed the subject change, and badly.

He lifted a brow. "Are you asking me to help?"

"Yes," she said slowly. "I mean, you're helping Daisy with her set. Might as well help my other friend with her divorce drama."

"True," he said.

She was about to say that she needed a man's help, and since Ben wasn't here, she had to recruit him.

The truth was, Sam was the person she would've asked even if Ben had been home. Ben would've been too busy. If they moved over the weekend, it would be his day off, and he caught up on his gaming and stuff on his days off. He worked really hard and . . .

Sam also works really hard.

The plain, matter-of-fact thought hit her hard.

Sam would always help if somebody was in need. Not because he was sweet or anything like that. Sam really wasn't sweet. Sam knew what it was like to have nothing. He hated injustice. He was the kind of person who had a tendency to grudgingly rally around anyone who needed it. He might not crave community, but he also knew community was necessary.

"I appreciate it," she said.

"I didn't agree."

"I know you didn't. But you will. Because she's a woman who has nothing because her husband is a douchebag."

"Yeah. Well, I'm sorry about that." He took a sip of his soda. "I don't really remember who she is."

"*Soraya.* She was a Bible-thumper. So it's not like we hung out with her."

"No. They tended to run the other way from me. Missionaries know a lost cause when they see one." He smiled, and she wrinkled her nose.

"In my experience, they don't, but how nice that you figured out the code to being left alone."

His smile lifted higher, just on the left side, and her stomach lifted slightly in response. "Maybe they think I'm holy."

"Somehow, I doubt it."

The waiter appeared and set Nora's drink, a basket of fries, and a basket with burgers in front of them. She just about pounced on the fries.

"Have you heard from anyone in your family lately?" he asked.

"Hell no," she said, nearly choking on her fries. "What made you think of that?"

"I don't know. I feel like I don't know what the hell is up with you right now. For all I know, you could have had a tearful reunion with your mother."

"Ha! No. Unless you think she'd cry because I punched her."

She chose not to ask herself if she actually wanted to punch her mother, or if thinking about her made her want to cry.

"Just . . ." He looked behind her. "It's weird you didn't tell me that Ben left you."

Her mouth dropped open. "He didn't leave me. I told you that."

"He left, and you're separated."

"Yeah. I don't want to talk about it."

"Why not?"

"Because I was surrounded by the divorce brigade today, and I've had enough of the relationship doom talk. I'm not getting divorced. We're separated because he's having a midlife crisis. You're right, doing that in Chile is rich-guy nonsense, and we absolutely would've made fun of him way back when. I still kind of want to make fun of him, but he's my husband, and if he's feeling like he isn't happy, then . . ."

"Maybe he should figure it out with you?" Sam finished.

"Because you're an expert on marriage, Sam? You've never even let a woman have a toothbrush at your house."

"I barely had time to have a toothbrush at the houses I lived in when I was a kid. I find that one begets the other."

She tilted her head and stared him down. "I was in the same situation. I got married."

He gazed back at her. "Yeah. Well. You always wanted that."

She felt scalded again. "Do you think you're better than me because you didn't want stability? You didn't want a normal life?"

"Is that what you wanted? Stability? I thought you wanted love."

"I do. I did. But I mean . . . I wanted to be normal. Why is that so hard to understand?"

"It's not. I guess I just figured it was a little bit late for normal."

"You're normal," she said.

Except even as she said that, it felt like such a wan, insipid descriptor for him. He was *something* all right. He was big and handsome. Protective. He was rough, and obnoxious. And loyal down to his core. So whatever his issues were with romantic relationships, they didn't extend to friendship.

"I know you wanted to be normal. I've always known that," he added as he took a french fry out of the basket in front of him. "I certainly never wanted to get in the way of that."

"How could you ever get in the way of that?"

He looked at her for a little longer than was strictly necessary. She sat there and did her best not to turn that over. Not too many times, anyway.

"He thinks that I upset you," Sam said.

"I know he does. But he just . . . He's protective."

"About your own past? Because that's stupid."

Okay. He had a point about that. It seemed silly that Ben would try to protect her from things she'd experienced. But it was true that sometimes she went out with Sam, and they would start trading stories about foster life, and she would come home broody.

Ben just didn't like that.

He doesn't accept that part of you.

Well, no, he didn't. Why should he? It was sad, and it wasn't good the way that she had been treated. So there was no accepting it. Not really.

She sure didn't accept it.

It was shit.

"Sorry, you were talking to him while he's gone?"

"Yes." She wasn't going to tell him about Ben's request she not call anymore. "He's been sending me pictures. It's really not like we're having a conflict. That's not what it's about."

"Ah. I get it. So he's in some big tour group?"

"Yes."

"Are there group photos somewhere?"

"I don't know. I just look at what he's sending me."

"Interesting. I would want to know who my husband was traveling with."

"If you had a husband, then you could worry about that."

"You know what I mean," he said, picking up the cheeseburger, which looked comedically small in his large hand. He took a bite and nearly demolished half the sandwich. It brought back memories of him being a lanky teenage boy who was clearly not getting enough food. The family they'd lived with had been about the nicest ones Nora had ever lived with, and they'd tried to keep up with feeding growing teenage boys. Even though it was expensive and difficult to do.

There had been an endless pot of rice and beans for him to carb-load on. She smiled, just a little bit. Those memories were painful, but also, sometimes they felt warm. Sometimes it was nice to sit with someone who did know. Someone who didn't need her to pretend to be anything other than what she was.

Not that Ben needed her to pretend. That wasn't right. It was just that they had different lives, and he didn't see the point of going over and over her past.

That was the point of her escaping it, after all.

"Do you miss him?"

"What kind of question is that?" She picked up a french fry and stabbed it into a puddle of ketchup before taking a bite.

"I'm just wondering if you miss him."

"Of course I do. I . . . I miss him. I wish that I had any idea what he was planning to do next, and I . . ."

"You keep playing it down, but I feel like you're actually worried."

"Of course I'm worried, Sam," she snapped. "I'm trying to be mature. I'm trying to understand. I'm trying to figure out why he couldn't talk to me. I think it's my fault. I think it's because I don't know how to talk to anybody. Not really. Because of the way we grew up. I mean, you and I have shared my issues with him. But you and I know how the dynamic in our marriage is. I love this about Ben, I love it for him. He's had it easy. I think sometimes when he tries to share his struggles with me, I'm not that sympathetic. I've had to worry about where I was going to sleep at night, and his primary concern in high school was getting the grade point average he needed to go to the college he wanted to go to. Which he didn't get into. I think that was a big deal for him. I kind of ruined him being able to confide in me, because he can tell I don't really see that as a problem. So I tried. I try really hard. I tried to be the wife that he needs me to be."

He let out a slow breath. "I'm going to be honest with you, Nora. He's a shithead. He always has been."

"He's my *husband*."

"And I don't like him. I never have, not from the minute you married him."

"Is that why you didn't go to my wedding?"

They didn't talk about this. They hadn't actually kept in great contact for a couple of years after she married Ben. They hadn't spoken about why. He had acted like it was so not a big deal that he didn't come to the wedding, but it had felt like such a big deal to her.

He gave her a half-savage-looking grin, then took another bite of the cheeseburger. "Not exactly."

She needed to shift this conversation. "I feel bad. I feel like maybe I haven't been what he needs. I don't know how to be that."

"Here's my perspective as your best friend. As your best, single friend who clearly doesn't know anything about love. Hell, I'm a stray. Feral, really. But it seems to me that if you marry somebody, and you have problems, you figure them out together. You don't go off to find yourself in South America, or anywhere, and leave your partner sitting at home by themselves wondering what the hell they did wrong. That's the problem I have with it. Because, yes, he played the whole game where he tried to tell you that it's all him and he has to find himself. But he also made you feel bad. He said just enough about you to make you feel like it might actually be you, and I have an issue with that, Nora."

It did spark a little bit of anger in her chest. Because he was making sense. What he was saying sounded reasonable. It sounded genuinely like it might be the correct take, and she didn't think that was just because she was hungry for something, anything other than the recriminations she had been heaping on herself.

"When he gets back, I'm going to talk to him about it. Because, yeah, you're right. It is . . . wrong. He doesn't accept my past, so that makes all of it hard. So maybe I do make him feel like his problems aren't valid, but he makes me feel like I have to be ashamed of parts of myself." She thought about their pristine house, her goblincore office. "I just really don't want my life to fall apart." She laughed. "Of course I don't. But you know, it happened enough times growing up."

He nodded slowly. "I don't want that for you." This was the kind of evening they would've had during normal times. While Ben was at home gaming or something. Yet it felt so different knowing Ben wasn't at home waiting for her. For just a moment, she was captivated by Sam. By the way he was listening to her. By the way that he looked. By the memory of the back muscles she had noticed, even though she hadn't wanted to.

Sam.

She cleared her throat and stuffed the rest of her fries into her face before tearing into the burger. "What's going on with your job?" she asked, talking around a mouthful of cheeseburger.

"Do you want me to talk electricity to you?"

Lord, no, she didn't want to think about electricity. Not when she'd also recently pondered his back muscles. This wasn't her. She was on the fritz because she was so . . . angry. She was angry at Ben for doing this to her. It was abandonment. Just like her mom, and he did know. He knew. Maybe it wasn't totally unreasonable for him to want to go away and do some work on himself, but given everything she'd been through, the way that people would leave and not come back, it . . . it was a whole lot less fair than she had told herself it was.

Sam had pulled his phone out of his pocket and was looking at it.

"Are you on Tinder while we're out to dinner?"

"And if I was?" He looked up at her, his electric-blue eyes particularly bright.

Her mouth went dry. "I would judge you."

He stared at her blandly. "Oh no. Not the harsh judgment of my childhood friend."

"You're a jerk."

"I'm also not on Tinder. Right now. Do you follow your husband on Instagram?"

"Yes. Are you on Instagram?"

"Yes."

"Let me guess, you DM women in bikinis."

"They DM me, Nora. But the reason I ask is that I found his tour group. There are a lot of . . . group photos."

She hated herself for this. For being curious and interested. She grabbed his phone before she even gave herself permission to do it and saw a group picture with a bunch of tagged names. One of them was Ben. It was a big group. Lots of men and women. She wondered if they had all left a spouse back at home.

"Yeah. That's about how I thought it would look."

"Looks like fun." He scrolled from the group picture to the next photo, where they were cooking over an open fire at a campsite.

"They're climbing mountains."

"Right. It's just, that's what he's doing while you're sitting here worrying about your relationship. I think that sucks, and I think you should be treated better than that."

She huffed a laugh. "Based on what?"

"You're you. What other reason does there need to be for you to be treated better than this?"

His words hit her with the impact of a car accident. Except . . . what did that even mean? She was her. She was an inconvenient, abandoned girl who had grown into an even more inconvenient, abandoned wife. There was nothing inherently special about her. Nothing that required any sort of deference or elevated thing she deserved. It was sweet of him to say so. But he was just saying so.

"You don't deserve to spend the rest of your life alone," she said softly.

"I'm not alone, idiot." He took his phone back. "I might open Tinder, though."

"I would rather you didn't."

He grinned unrepentantly, and whether or not he looked at Tinder at any point during the evening wasn't something he shared.

"Where you parked?" he asked when they walked out of the bar.

"Oh, just up by the store. I . . ." It suddenly felt imperative that he not walk her back. It suddenly felt important that she get some distance. Right now. "I'm exhausted. It's time to go home."

"Okay," he said, his expression carefully neutral.

"I'll call you if my lights go out or anything."

"Yeah. You do that."

She went back to the car and drove home without thinking. She just let it all wash over her. She just let the music sweep through her soul and distract her from everything that was happening.

When she got back inside, she dropped her black moon purse onto the floor. The purse that Ben had bought her. When he had probably already known he wanted to separate.

She stared at it and opened Instagram on her phone. She went back to the tour-group page Sam had shown her. She zoomed in on the picture of the group. Ben was smiling. He looked almost like a different person. Wild, free. Happy.

Something she didn't see in him when they were together. Not in their life.

There was a woman standing next to him. Blond and smiling. She clicked on her. On the tag on the photo. She was suddenly on an Instagram filled with her ass. Because she was apparently double-cheeked up in the Andes Mountains, swimming in streams.

She flicked through a carousel of photos, and then her heart sank. There was one of her in a stream, standing underneath a waterfall. There was a man holding on to her. His hand was pressed against her hip, a smile on his face that had never once been directed at Nora.

Beaming. Unencumbered. Unburdened.

Her husband.

It was like the room tilted. She pressed her hand against the wall, like it might keep her from collapsing.

I have the love I deserve.

"You motherfucker."

Chapter Fourteen

Soraya

Sometimes a witch needs some hot hex.

—Rules for Witches

She had been sitting in the mostly dark, empty room for longer than she would ever want to admit to anyone. Aggie had taken her upstairs after work to show her the apartment space, and Soraya had asked her permission to linger. She hadn't left yet. She was afraid that if she did, she would have to face that all this was really happening. But as long as she sat upstairs, on the floor in front of an old coffee table—the only piece of furniture in the room—with a few candles set on top and a matchbook to their side, then she wouldn't have to face this.

David was really throwing her out. Levi and Jaden weren't speaking to her. She squeezed her eyes shut, tears pushing against them. Her kids were too old for her to make them engage. She texted them, and they didn't respond. Because he'd done it. He had succeeded in making everyone think she was the one who was bad.

She was helpless. Screaming into a void she'd once called *friends*. But they'd closed ranks. They didn't listen. She knew exactly why. They'd been warned about her. She might lead them astray! She might make them dissatisfied with their marriages or grind their bones to make her new sourdough starter.

She could remember, years ago, a man at their church had been coming without his wife, and when asked where she was, he'd said, "She's just kind of doing her own thing right now."

He hadn't vilified her in so many words, but it had been a powerfully cutting statement in the right crowd. A crowd where they'd been taught that their *own thing* was only ever wicked and sinful. Her *own thing* wasn't at church, and he was.

Was that what David would say?

She's doing her own thing.

Like he'd had nothing to do with it. Like she'd just decided to go off in a fit of selfishness because she'd woken up one morning and gotten tired of her life, and not like he'd betrayed their vows or anything.

She hadn't questioned it when that man had said those words to her. No one would question it about her either. No one would demand accountability from David. She, Soraya Nichols, was a cautionary tale because she'd pushed back against her husband's infidelity, and she just felt . . .

She had never felt so powerless.

Her phone screen lit up. It was the Discarded Witches Club chat.

He *is* cheating on me.

Soraya unlocked the screen and stared at the message. There were three dots at the bottom, and she waited for Nora to continue.

I found pictures of him on Instagram, this other woman's Instagram.

He's touching her.

A screenshot came through, and Soraya grimaced. There he was, clinging to a mostly naked woman. Soraya would have lost it if it were her husband. But there was some plausible deniability, she supposed. It could be . . . friendly.

She took a breath, then started to type. It's not his penis. It could be worse.

It can't be worse.

A message from Daisy popped up next. What is happening tonight? Is it a full moon?

Are full moons significant? Soraya typed out.

Sweet baby. That was from Nora.

Jonnathan tojld me he's marrying her. Ambgerly.

Soraya imagined Daisy typing that with unsteady fingers.

Soraya let out a hard breath, the back of her head hitting the wall. The truth was, she had only ever casually been friends with Daisy, and Nora never had been her friend. But she hurt for them. Really. Genuinely.

I don't suppose you guys want to come over to my sad, empty apartment.

Daisy's response was quick. My mother-in-law said she would watch my kids.

Why are you sitting in a sad, empty apartment? That was from Nora.

Because I came up here to look and I can't bring myself to leave.

I'll be there in five minutes, said Nora.

I'll be there in ten.

Soraya scrubbed at her eyes and set her phone down. Then she stood up and paced the length of the room. This old place should give her the creeps.

Being above Lady's Mantle, first of all, when the store seemed evil to her initially, should have set off a lot of spiritual alarm bells. But by the end of the day today, the store hadn't given her the creeps. Not after everything that had happened. Not after she had done the spell. She had waited for guilt to hit her about that. But it hadn't. She didn't feel bad, because he deserved to have his sin find him out.

She walked out of the living room for the first time, traipsing all the way down the hall and into a bedroom. There was a bed in there, and a nightstand. The dark, empty room did make her feel just a tiny bit creeped out. She flicked a light on and touched the bedspread, then walked to the side and looked at the end table. She opened the drawer and saw a deck of cards inside.

Tarot cards.

Goose bumps rose on her arm, a strange prickling sensation on the back of her neck. She touched the top of the box. Then she drew her hand away.

Suddenly, she just felt tired of herself. Tired of everything. Why was she so afraid? All this fear hadn't served her at all. It hadn't guided her toward anything. She didn't blame God. She didn't blame faith, the church, or the steeple. It was all the people. They made her afraid to stand up for herself. To have any of her own opinions. She didn't know who she was. All these people were trying to tell her who that was supposed to be, but she knew they were wrong.

She picked up the deck of cards and walked slowly back into the living room. Shortly after, there was a knock at the door. She let out a breath, walked over, and opened it. It was Nora. She had never seen Nora look sad. Angry, yes. Like she wanted to get into a fistfight with the world, sure. But sad? Not like this. Not like she had been crying until she couldn't breathe.

With the tarot card deck still in her hands, she folded Nora in for a hug. "I'm sorry."

She had always felt like she was better than Nora. Truthfully. Here they were in the exact same place. All of Soraya's good decisions hadn't protected her. All of Nora's realism hadn't spared her. They had both been betrayed by the men who were supposed to love them.

"You're not going to tell me there's a godly reason for all this, are you?"

Soraya barked a watery laugh, wiping at the tears that had fallen down onto her cheeks. "I surely am not."

"Good."

Nora stepped inside, and Soraya heard more footsteps in the hallway. "I'm here," called Daisy, who came into view.

She hadn't been crying, but she looked wrung out. "I was just telling my mother-in-law that her son is a coward who doesn't want to tell her we are getting divorced. I just realized that I did that for him too. I didn't mean to. I wasn't doing it to do him a favor, I just thought she needed to know."

"Oh, Daisy," Nora said, dragging her inside.

Nora's phone rang, and she pulled it out of her purse, the cheerful, mustached face of her husband clearly visible on the screen. Nora looked at the phone like it might bite her, and then clicked the answer button, and a shaky, darkened video and the sound of sex filled the room.

A look of horror crossed Nora's face. "Oh my God," she said. "Oh my . . ." She held the phone out toward Soraya and Daisy. "Is this . . . is this happening to me right now?"

Soraya felt like she was back in that church bathroom, getting a misdirected picture of her husband's dick. She hated this for Nora.

The camera wasn't showing anything, but the sounds were unambiguous.

"Yes, Dr. Ben!"

"Jesus!" Nora dropped the phone onto the floor with a clatter, and Soraya wasn't even mad about the blasphemy.

"Oh no," Daisy said, covering her mouth. "Oh . . . oh no."

The absolute worst-sounding porn dialogue continued to come through the phone speaker. "Examine meeeee."

"I'm dead." Nora put her hands over her face. "I'm dead, and this is hell. You were right all along, Soraya, I was hell bound and this is it."

There were moans and grunts, and Soraya scrambled for the phone to end the call like she was performing a lifesaving procedure.

"Thank you." Nora's breathing was sharp and short. "Thank you. I knew . . . I knew it. Because Sam showed me his Instagram tonight, but this . . . He *ass-dialed* me while he was having sex with her."

The digital age made it so much easier for men to cheat, but also so much harder, and they just . . . did it anyway. Flinging their penises around cyberspace.

Nora wiped her hand over her cheeks and looked surprised that her hand came away dry. She wasn't crying. She just looked defeated. "You know, I used to make fun of him for how careless he is. He butt-dials, he leaves receipts for presents lying around. He's just not sneaky. He's sloppy. It's insulting. He . . . he didn't even bother to make sure his phone wasn't in his pocket so this couldn't happen."

"Well, if he looks at his phone after he's done, he'll know there was an outgoing call," Daisy pointed out.

Nora huffed. "I mean, that would again require observation. *Thought.* He . . . he only thinks about himself. They *all* only think about themselves."

The defeat began to turn to anger, Soraya could see it, while her own anger turned quivery in her stomach, her hands shaking.

Soraya gestured around them, absurdity guiding the moment. "Welcome to my home."

Then she burst into tears.

None of them spoke for a few minutes while Soraya gathered herself—great, gulping sobs interspersed with laughing. Nora was the one who'd just gotten the horrible confirmation her husband was just like Jonathan and David. That she was in the same place as Daisy and Soraya, so why was Soraya having a breakdown?

After thirty-five years of *counting it all joy*, she just couldn't do it anymore. Apparently this came for everyone. This churning, black hole of cynicism.

She moved back to her spot against the wall and slid down, holding the cards in her hands as she pulled her knees up to her chest and sat there staring at the deck.

Daisy and Nora just stood there, looking at poor Soraya.

"I'm not crazy." Soraya wiped the tears off her cheeks that hadn't been on Nora's.

"I might be," said Nora. "Or homicidal. I did a love spell just a few hours ago, and now I find out that he's *cheating on me*."

"Maybe magic isn't real." Daisy adjusted her glasses.

"It's not about the magic." Nora slapped her hands against her thighs and turned in a slow circle, anger radiating off her in a palpable wave. "It's about what I believed. It's about me defending him to all of you. You knew. You knew, didn't you? That I was being delusional."

It was Soraya and Daisy's turn to exchange glances.

"I wouldn't say that I *knew*." Daisy adjusted her glasses again, this time clearly due to discomfort and not out of any need.

"You did." Nora's tone was almost accusing, and Soraya could see that if they weren't careful, they were going to catch some of the shrapnel from Nora's outrage.

"Nobody can tell you anything about your husband before you realize it," Soraya pointed out. "At least, nobody would've been able to tell me something bad about David. I wouldn't have believed them. Honestly, that text earlier with him telling me to get out of the house. Nothing has quite driven home the point of exactly who he is like that. But you can't know that before the moment is right for you to know it. Now you know it, and I'm really sorry that you had to know it that way."

"It's not any different than what you went through." Nora put her hand over her mouth, holding back a laugh. "I really thought I might be the only woman on earth whose husband was having a real existential crisis that wasn't actually about sleeping with a younger, hotter woman."

"She's younger," Soraya emphasized. "That doesn't make her hotter."

"Thousands of years of patriarchy would disagree."

"*Hex* the patriarchy." Soraya was hoping to make Nora laugh with the totally out-of-character comment, but she meant it a little more than she'd realized.

"I regret not putting the karma spell on Jonathan. Tonight, I . . . I might've cursed him. But I want to make another . . . another spell, and I want to put it in his truck. I want . . . I don't want him to get away with this. What if he was lying to me the whole time?"

That same fear echoed inside Soraya. She could see that it was a new fear for Nora.

"He tricked me." Nora was incandescent. "He made it sound like it had nothing to do with . . . with sex, with me. But it is about sex. He's off having sex with some woman who wants to do dentist role-play. It has nothing to do with finding himself. It has to do with losing his dick inside of another woman."

"I fear that's what motivates most men," Soraya said. "I spent so many years hearing all about that. I spent all of youth group being told I had to dress a certain way. That I had to be careful not to tempt any men with my . . . bare shoulders and front hugs."

"Front hugs?" Daisy asked.

"Yes. You can't hug a guy from the front because he'll feel your breasts."

"They said that to you in youth group?" Nora asked, her jaw slack.

"Yes."

"I mean, they were the ones sexualizing you. Just by thinking of it that way. Making you think of your own body that way."

Soraya sat and stared at a spot on the floor. "Well . . . oh."

"Like seriously, who says that to teenage girls?"

"Youth pastors. Then after you get told to cover up, never think about sex, never let yourself get turned on, don't be a temptation, don't be tempted, you get married. Then you get told to put out. To be a good wife who has sex with her husband whenever he wants it. I did that. I did it, and I still wasn't enough. I was pure and perfect for him, and it still wasn't enough." Soraya wiped angrily at her tears. "Maybe if I'd had more experience . . ."

"I was by no means pure or perfect for Ben," Nora said. "I give an awesome blow job. He still cheated on me. It has nothing to do with you, what you know, what you don't know, how many men you slept with, how many men you haven't slept with, or what size you are or how old you are. It isn't about anything but a man's own goddamn selfishness. No. It isn't you, Soraya. It's not me." Nora's voice broke. "It's just that you can't trust anyone. I was right, it turns out. I thought I could trust him. I thought that because I loved him it meant that he loved me."

"Exactly," Daisy said. "I thought that because he was the love of my life, I was the love of his."

"It isn't our fault." Nora was seething. "It's theirs." She looked down at the coffee table and sprang forward, grabbing the book of matches. She lit a candle, then took her phone out and started typing. "I wish I had the grimoire."

"What are you doing?" Soraya asked.

"I'm putting a spell on him. No. Not a spell. A hex." Nora's pupils were so large her eyes were black. "I don't want karma. I don't want balance. I want revenge."

She held her phone up, the light of the candle reflecting on her face, her goth makeup even more dramatic.

A chill went down Soraya's spine, but she didn't feel like she wanted or needed to turn away from this. Nora's anger was dark, but all of this was dark.

They'd been abandoned. Cast aside. Lied to. Lied about.

They had each other. And they had this. This one place where they'd found a way to reclaim their power. So far, it had been working. Except Nora had just wanted her husband to love her and she couldn't get that, so why not get payback?

Why not?

Soraya had spent all her life trying to be good in a very specific way.

She'd turned away from intuition. From power.

From rage.

Right now, she felt it all coursing through her like fire.

"What you did to me, be returned but times three," Nora said. "Head to toe. Skin and bone. It is time for fate to reverse. It is time to feel the pain you inflicted on me." Nora took off her wedding ring and dropped it so it encircled the flaming wick, the fire burning around it. "And so it is."

Daisy took her ring off and dropped it over the top of Nora's. "And so it is."

Soraya looked at them, her heart thundering hard.

Then she took her own wedding ring off, which she hadn't done since the separation. Because it had felt like something final. Because it had felt like giving up.

But this didn't feel like giving up. It felt like something else entirely.

She held it over the flame and dropped it over the wick, flame encircling all the rings. "And so it is."

Daisy reached out and took Nora's hand, Nora took Soraya's, and then she closed the circle and took Daisy's other hand, the rings around the flame, not melting, not scorching, just there. A symbol. A sacrifice.

Daisy closed her eyes. "I call my power back to me. I call my energy back to me. I call my magic back to me. I am shielded from anything that would take my power from me. Nothing can harm me or take my light. I am safe. I am protected. I am powerful. And so it is."

Nora nodded. "And so it is."

She leaned forward and blew out the candle. A rush went through Soraya, straight through the center of her chest. It was like everything had changed, even though everything was the same. She was shaking, and she dropped Daisy's and Nora's hands and put her palm against her chest.

She was afraid to speak. She was afraid to do anything.

Nora looked around the space. "This is beautiful. It's going to be a great place for you."

Soraya nodded, her throat dry. "What are you going to do?"

"I don't know. I don't know. I could call him. I could ask him what he's doing. I could move out without talking to him. I don't have kids to worry about. I . . ."

For a strange moment, Soraya envied Nora. She could just cut ties with Ben and be done with him. Except for all the emotional stuff. But she didn't have *this* . . .

These kids that she loved with every desperate part of her, tying her to the man who had betrayed her. Turned against her by the man who betrayed her.

"Why don't you give it a couple of days?" Soraya suggested. "Whatever he's been doing, he'll keep on doing it."

"Yeah." Nora shook her head. "Maybe he's never coming back. Maybe he's actually abandoning the house and the practice. He'll just quit paying for all of it, and maybe it'll get taken away by the bank."

"Maybe," Daisy said. "But I doubt it."

Soraya leaned down and picked up the candle, then she lifted it and put it on top of the mantel. "This is the symbol of the Discarded Wives Club."

"We're the First Wives Club." Nora looked intently at the flame. "Lord knows they may go on to have second wives. Maybe third wives."

Daisy laughed. "First *Witches* Club, remember?"

Nora grinned. "Yes. The First Witches Club. I have no idea what I want to do. Except I don't want to be with him. Sam said . . . earlier, Sam said I deserve better."

"Sam Reynolds?" Soraya asked.

"Yeah. He's my foster— Ugh, no, I don't like that label. We were in foster care together."

"He's right. You *do* deserve better," said Soraya. "We all deserve better."

She really meant that. She meant more than just what she deserved from her husband. She deserved better than friends who didn't believe her. Who didn't listen to her. Who didn't think it mattered that her husband was unfaithful. Who thought she should choose a concept of morality that her husband wasn't choosing. That she should be held to a different standard. She did want her family back. She wanted her sons back. On her terms. She wouldn't be blackmailed by her cheating husband.

"We'll help you get your things moved in tomorrow," Nora said. "Sam said he would help."

"I don't even know Sam." It was incredible to Soraya that someone outside the church would help her. For no reason. Which said a lot about what she'd been led to believe about people *outside*.

"It doesn't matter. He said he would help."

A door slammed out in the hall, and the three of them jumped. Then they heard heavy footsteps down the hallway.

"Are there other units up here?"

"Oh yeah," Soraya said, feeling breathless. "Aggie did mention that. There are two other units that go with the other stores on this strip."

"I just thought maybe we summoned a ghost." Nora put her hands up like claws, and there was still a slight tremble in her fingers, even as she tried to be funny.

Soraya pushed her shoulder. "Don't say that. I have to stay here."

She was still holding the tarot cards in her left hand. Nora took the pack out of her hand.

"You really are turning over a new leaf."

"I found them." Soraya's cheeks got warm.

"Do you want to draw a new card?"

Soraya shrank back. "I think I've dabbled enough for one night."

"You don't seem like you're freaked out."

"I feel like . . . I'm tired of letting everybody else tell me what I want or don't want. What's wrong and what's right. I feel . . . I feel like I'm okay."

She kept thinking about what Aggie had said, that this didn't require her to turn away from her whole belief system. It wasn't turning away from God. But of course she would have told Aggie that her beliefs were wrong.

Aggie was less judgmental than she was.

A shock to her, since she'd been told it was people like Aggie who wouldn't accept her.

"I'm doing it. I'm giving you a reading." Nora started to shuffle the deck in her hands. She cut it three times and then pulled a card off the top while looking at Daisy. "Six of Wands."

"What does that mean?"

"I'll have to look at the book." Nora set the cards down on the table and pulled out the guidebook. "Victory. Success. Bringing out the best in others."

"That's better than the Tower," Daisy said.

"No kidding." Nora cut the deck again three times, looking at Soraya. "Queen of Cups."

"I have no idea what that is," said Soraya.

"Romance." Nora raised her eyebrows. "Seduction. Focusing on what moves the soul. Slow and deliberate pleasure."

Soraya blinked. "Could not be me."

"I don't know. Maybe you're going to have a fling."

"Save me. I can't do witchcraft and fornication." She was sort of kidding, but just saying that made a zip of something go down her spine.

"Why not? Your husband was doing it."

"I'm not really worried about sex." After the explicit clip of Nora's husband, Soraya didn't think she'd be aroused for . . . a while.

"I kind of am," said Daisy. "I've been celibate for two months, and our sex life was garbage for a year before that. It sucks."

“Sorry.” Nora didn’t look sorry. “The Wands didn’t say anything about seduction.”

“What about *you*?” Daisy asked.

Nora took a breath. “Okay. Do me.”

Daisy frowned when she looked at the card. “Two of Wands.” She picked up the guidebook. “The choice between your comfort zone and new adventures.” She shut the book.

Nora scowled. “It doesn’t really feel like an adventure.”

“I don’t know. I’ve never really wanted to be adventurous,” Soraya said. “I feel like this is why. It’s kind of scary.”

“I didn’t think I was going to be doing a whole . . . new life.” Nora picked at her nail polish. “I thought I would get over this bump in the road.”

“Well,” Daisy began. “You are separated. Maybe he intended to come back and have whatever happened during the break be . . . not a thing.”

“The problem with that is we didn’t discuss sleeping with other people. I look like we might, but we don’t have an open marriage.”

“What do you mean you look like you *might*?”

Nora shrugged. “There’s a polyamory thing. They kind of have the look. I’m a septum piercing short. But that’s never been our thing. Maybe if he would’ve talked to me, I . . .” She swallowed hard. “I wanted something normal. I wanted it to last.”

“Well, it still could. If you want to forgive him.”

“Oh no. Forgiveness is not my thing.” Nora looked back up at the candle. “My thing is revenge.”

Soraya would have said forgiveness was her thing, that she didn’t want revenge. That was before she had been hurt. That was before her husband had tricked her. Before he had turned her own children against her. “You know, Nora, I think we have a lot more in common than I realized.”

They looked at each other for a moment, and Nora smiled.

Chapter Fifteen

Nora

Sometimes a spell sees the greater purpose, even when the witch can't.

—Rules for Witches

Nora really didn't want to have to tell Sam he was right. But they were moving Soraya into her apartment, and she was in Sam's truck, and the longer she didn't talk about last night, about all the revelations, about her total implosion, about the revenge spell she had cast . . .

It just started to feel silly. If not silly, then totally dishonest.

She already knew he'd just say that Ben was awful, and he'd known it all along. He wasn't going to be sympathetic. He would tell her how the institution of marriage was a lie, and she had been stupid to ever believe in it. Or maybe that she was stupid to have ever believed a Ouija board when it told her she would find love.

Oh, the love spell. It was *painful* now.

"So, Ben is cheating on me." She rubbed her knuckles against the passenger-side window, because for some reason she thought that might break some of the tension.

"What?"

Sam slammed the brakes and cranked the wheel sharply, pulling the truck over to the side of the road. He looked at her, an expression on his face that wasn't shock but was definitely fervent.

"Yeah, I did some digging around, starting from the Instagram you showed me." It felt like the whole sky was bearing down on her head, collapsing beneath the weight of the truth. "And I was pretty suspicious, but then he butt-dialed me during the act."

"What?"

She'd never seen Sam look so shocked before. If it weren't about something so hideous, she might have enjoyed it.

She shook her head and closed her eyes, just for a second. Like it might disrupt some of the intensity of the moment. Of him being so close. Looking at her. Seeing this humiliation.

"Yeah. It was awful. Thank God I didn't see anything, but . . ." Her throat tightened, and she swallowed hard in denial of the emotion. She didn't want to be sad about it. She was angry, and she deserved to be angry.

"That's really, really horrible, Nora. I'm sorry."

Sam looked helpless. She'd rarely, if ever, seen Sam look helpless. Kids like them couldn't afford helplessness, and even if they did feel lost, they rarely showed it. It was an inglorious honor to have a problem so big her friend seemed stumped by it.

He unbuckled his seat belt, and before she knew it, he was across the truck and had her pulled into his arms. It was more unexpected than the hug Soraya had given her last night. His arms held her tight, and she could feel his heart beating against her cheek, and she wanted to melt against him. They didn't touch like this on a normal day. They didn't touch at all. Nothing in their lives had added up to make them physically demonstrative people. He was doing this for her. To make her feel better. She took a deep breath that became more of a sob and turned her face against his neck, letting him hold her. Letting him take some of the pain away.

She couldn't remember the last time she had done that, if ever. The last time she had let someone comfort her. Maybe she was a wall. Maybe she was every bit as difficult as Ben had said she was. Except . . .

Sam was here with her. He had been here all this time. Soraya had given her a hug. Daisy was here for her.

She was letting them. She would continue to let them.

He was the one who shifted in the hug slightly, and then their faces were close.

She couldn't breathe. He was right there, so close she could see all the colors of blue in his eyes.

Sam and all the ways he was beautiful wasn't some truth she had just stumbled upon when she had walked into the bar and looked at his back muscles.

He always had been.

She'd tried not to linger on it. Never to think about it. Fantasize about him. He was too important for that.

Nora had, historically, enjoyed some bad decisions. Sometimes the guy was hot even if he was temporary. Sometimes the drink looked good and the idea of getting high sounded like a relief, even if it wasn't a great choice.

But Sam had never been one of her bad choices. He meant too much to her to be a mistake. That had been true since she was a teenager with no perspective, and it was even truer now.

She was married. He was her best friend. The person she needed more than anyone else to get through this.

It was just . . . It was a no. She took a shuddering breath and put distance between them.

"Poor Soraya," she said.

"Poor Soraya?"

"Yeah. Keep driving. We need to get to her house so we can help. She might be having a breakdown over which sourdough starter to bring. Though, she can probably bring as much of her sourdough starter as she wants."

"Right."

"You can start driving again."

"Nora, we were talking about *you*."

"But I'm not the only one going through this. Daisy's husband is marrying somebody else and . . . I'm not the only one going through this. It sucks. I'm not going to pretend it doesn't. But it's fine. I mean it. It's mostly fine."

"Your husband is cheating on you," he said.

"I know. There's nothing I can do about it. He's half a world away." She tried to take a breath, but it got stuck. "You're not even going to say you told me so?"

"No. What kind of dick do you think I am?"

"Are you going to pretend you're *not* one? That you've *never* been one?"

"No. But I'm also thirty-five, and I know how to choose my moments now. I'm not the same kid I was in high school."

"I know that."

"Do you?"

"Yes. I do. I do. Sam, you're one of the most important people in my life. You're the only person I've known for this long. Nobody else knows me like *you* do. You actually saw what it looked like when my mom didn't come. Or when my grandmother declined to take custody back. Don't ever think that I don't look at you and see the importance. There's a reason we're still in each other's lives."

"Yes, there is." He sighed heavily and pulled his truck back onto the road. "I'm not going to say I told you so, because in all honesty, Nora, I wanted this to work for you. Hell, I wanted to believe it was possible, you know? Forever. Even for someone like us. I didn't want you to get hurt."

"I know you didn't want me to get hurt."

"I *really* didn't," he said, something firm and certain in his voice. "I really, really didn't. I wanted it to be forever, so you could have that. I wanted the same thing you did. I wanted you to have normal and safe and good and . . ."

"But you didn't want it for yourself?"

"No. It mattered to you. I wanted you to have whatever you wanted."

"That doesn't make any sense. What about what *you* want?"

"It doesn't matter."

"That's bullshit. It does matter. You're so stable, you know? That's why it surprises me that you don't want a relationship or anything. I mean, you've got such a good job."

"I feel like I did as much *better* than my parents as I could. I'm not an addict, I support myself. I have friends. That's a good thing."

"Yeah. It's a good thing. But—"

"We weren't talking about me," he said. "You keep doing that. You keep making it about somebody else."

"I don't want to talk about it. It's just my own sadness. We can go over it and over it, but it isn't going to change anything." Her throat suddenly went tight. Grief was like an anvil pressing on her chest. "It won't make me understand it any better. I wanted to believe that this was happily ever after. I wanted to believe that I changed. But I'm stuck again. Just being a foster kid. Somebody who gets abandoned. You can't outrun it, I guess. It's always going to be waiting there in the shadows. Looking for a chance to swing on you."

"Or," he said, "and hear me out—Ben sucks."

It wasn't funny, but she laughed anyway. "This is getting dangerously close to *I told you so*."

"It isn't, though. Because what I'm telling you right now is you're wrong. There's nothing inherently wrong with you. Maybe there are certain blind spots that you have."

"Here we go," she said.

They were getting close to Soraya's house, though, so the conversation would have to end.

"What? You don't think you have any blind spots?"

"I think you were just taking the long road to do exactly what I thought you were going to do."

"Maybe," he said. "But maybe some things need to be said so you'll finally believe me when I tell you I don't think there's anything wrong with you."

"I don't think there's anything wrong with you, and you don't seem to believe that."

He snorted. "Waiting for empirical evidence."

"Same. Same."

They finished the rest of the drive in silence, and when they pulled up to the house, there was an actual moving truck Daisy was standing next to, looking perplexed.

"Oh." Nora slid out of the truck. "I thought we were doing this incrementally."

"So did I," Daisy said. "It's kind of a . . . It's a long story."

Then the cab of the truck opened, and Zach Woods, famous, hot as a house fire, got out.

"Oh. Hi."

"Hi." He stuck his hand out. "I don't believe we've met."

"No. I'm Nora. You're Zach Woods. Of course I know who you are."

"I don't need you to do that." He looked almost comedically uncomfortable for a man who must get recognized all the time. Nora wasn't one to be starstruck, but she also wasn't one to pretend to be deliberately unimpressed just to be cool, which was about the most try-hard thing a human could do.

"I'm not doing anything, I promise. I just thought it would be dumb if I pretended I didn't know who you were. This is Sam." She gestured to him.

Sam didn't look impressed or starstruck, and she knew him well enough to know that wasn't a bit. If anything, he looked irritated by the whole thing, though she couldn't imagine why. "Nice to meet you," he said, whatever irritation he felt locked down deep enough that probably only Nora could see it.

"I ran into Zach at the coffee shop this morning," Daisy said. "I told him what was happening, and then he just took charge, and before I knew it, he'd rented a truck."

Sam and Nora both swiveled their heads to look at Zach, who shrugged. "It just seems like basic courtesy. I could get the truck, and quick. She needed help."

The way he said it made it sound so practical.

"We were piecing together solutions." Daisy sounded arch and annoyed.

"Which is fine. But you could take the big, already-put-together solution." Zach's words were definitive.

"I did," Daisy countered, turning toward him, and Nora could practically feel the tension sparking between the two of them. Daisy hadn't mentioned that she had a preexisting thing with Zach. Yes, Nora knew he was a business partner to Daisy's husband, but she hadn't realized *they* had a thing.

Daisy was looking at Zach like she wanted to punch him, while Zach looked completely unbothered while somehow also conveying that he was a breath away from wrapping his arms around her and kissing her. It was clear to Nora that Daisy didn't see that.

If she did, she would probably look less angry and would be looking a lot more *flustered*.

Nora wasn't inexperienced, but that man was hot enough to make her stutter. If he had looked at her the way he was looking at Daisy, she might have combusted.

That made her feel eased slightly, which bothered her. Because she'd gotten a little bit prickly about Daisy's appreciation of Sam, and it was clear that was generic, and Zach was the one she had real, undeniable chemistry with.

Not that it should matter.

"Well. Let's get . . . going." Nora charged forward and knocked on the front door.

Soraya opened it a moment later, her face red and blotchy. "Sorry. Having a mental breakdown."

"Oh, that's completely allowed," Nora said.

Soraya looked past Nora and saw Zach standing next to Daisy. She shot Nora and Daisy weighted looks.

"We'll wait out here." Sam waved them away. "Go on."

Daisy and Nora went into the house, and Soraya closed the door behind them. "I didn't know Zach Woods was going to help with the move. I . . . I wish I didn't look like I had just cried my eyes out and ate my weight in bread and butter."

"You don't *look* like that," Daisy said.

"Oh." There was a hysterical giggle on Soraya's lips. "That's good. Because I just cried my eyes out and ate my weight in bread and butter."

"That's progress. Remember just a week ago, you couldn't eat your feelings." Nora practically did jazz hands—anything to lighten the mood.

Soraya laughed, but it sounded like a watery choke.

"I should have told you Zach was coming," Daisy said. "But I ran into him at the coffee shop, and I ended up telling him what we were doing today. I also told him that Amberly and Jonathan are getting married. *Anyway.* I think I must've looked sad and pathetic, and before I knew it, I had been hijacked, and he was renting a moving truck. I think he must feel like I'm his own personal charity at this point, between the sets and now this."

Did she actually think it was pity? Nora looked at Daisy, really looked at her. She was beautiful, and Nora had a feeling she had no idea. Maybe because she'd spent years with a man who hadn't told her, or maybe because of the way life had shaped her long before Jonathan had been in the picture.

Weren't they all a ragtag group of issues they'd collected through the years?

"Daisy." Nora grabbed Daisy's shoulders. "He likes you."

"I . . . What?" Daisy blinked furiously behind her large glasses.

"He *likes* you." Nora elongated each word. "Like, he thinks you're cute."

"He . . . he does not," Daisy said.

"Oh, he surely does," Nora countered. "I felt like I had walked in the middle of a good enemies-to-lovers romance out there."

"I'm *married to his friend*."

"I know," Nora said. "That wouldn't prevent him from being attracted to you, and also, you're not really married to him anymore, even if you are legally, given he moved in with another woman he's now marrying."

"That isn't the biggest barrier to Zach Woods liking me," Daisy said, her tone dry. "I'm . . ." She waved her hand over her body, and Nora searched for what on earth her friend could possibly be indicating.

"You're hot, Daisy."

"No. He's hot. I am . . . a thirty-five-year-old woman who carried and birthed three children and has all the stretch marks and baggy skin to prove it. He's physical perfection. He's the hottest man I've ever seen in real life. In fact, he was the hottest man I had ever seen on TV back in high school when . . . You remember."

"I obviously remember that, but what does that have to do with anything? What does that have to do with now?"

"He was the hot boy I was into when I was a girl, and he is definitely a hot man for the woman in me now, but, like, fantasy level. I'm only some woman he met a few years ago. Fantasies are all fine and good, but they're just fantasies."

"Why does it have to be a fantasy?"

"For all the reasons I said. He's Jonathan's friend and business partner." She looked at the back wall. "So I think you're crazy, just FYI."

"Noted," Nora said.

"But even if I didn't . . . I'm so tired. I spent all those years doing everything for Jonathan, and for what? If he was that costly, imagine how expensive a man like Zach would be to keep."

Soraya had been so quiet through the whole exchange that she surprised Nora by speaking. "I relate to that feeling. I gave David everything, and for what? I gave him my youth, my virginity, years and years of perfunctory sex that didn't blow my mind even half the time. I gave him my dreams. I let him reshape them around this house, around his business, his goals, his friends. That's why I lost my friends. They're all married to his friends. Everything in my life is his, and I get feeling so exhausted by all that. I just don't think we failed to hang on to them. They took us for granted. They didn't think we'd find a spine and tell them to go to . . . to go to hell. But we did. So if you're tired, I get that. I'm tired too. I'm sad. I'm . . . I'm so sad. But this isn't our failure."

It's not your failure.

Nora tried to cling to that. Maybe it felt more true if you hadn't been left by your mother, your grandmother. Your father, whoever the hell he was. Maybe for them it was more true.

"Thanks, Soraya." Daisy forced a small, quick smile. "God. I wouldn't know what to do with a man like him even if I had the energy to do it."

"Oh, don't let that stop you. Soraya and I could help you choreograph it."

Soraya barked a laugh. "I know how to give blow jobs that send your man straight into the DMs of other women."

The shock of Soraya saying *blow job* made Nora dissolve into laughter, and Daisy right along with her, until Soraya broke into a fit of giggles too. It wasn't that funny. None of this was funny, but laughing felt good.

Nora wiped her eyes. Tears of laughter or sadness, she really couldn't say. "Oh, we're a mess." She let out a breath. "Is Zach even still friends with Jonathan? He's here with you now, he's building your sets, he recruited Sam."

"He's . . . not happy with him, that's for sure."

"Because he *likes* you," Nora said, completely convinced of that truth.

"I don't even know what to say to that. I don't know what to say to that, and I wouldn't know what to do with him even if . . . I've been with Jonathan since I was sixteen."

"I know you're tired. I know you feel weird. But you were also just saying you were missing sex."

"That doesn't mean I can hook up with *Zach Woods*. Be serious." Daisy looked at Soraya. "Can you say something pure and pious now, please?"

Soraya smiled, or at least attempted it. "Sorry. I fear that I am all out of piety. It's gotten me nowhere. Here I am, moving out of this house that we had built for ourselves. By your husband, incidentally."

"Does your electricity go out all the time?" Nora asked.

"It does," Soraya said. "What made you think of that?"

"Mine does too. It's that electrician Jonathan uses."

"That doesn't really surprise me," Daisy scoffed. "He'd rather hire his friends than make sure he's getting the best. It's like a giant boys' club."

"Here's Zach. Breaking the terms of the boys' club. He's here for *you*."

Daisy's cheeks did turn a little pink then. "I think he's just nice."

"Except." Nora held up a finger. "Sam and Zach showed up to help a woman they don't even know move. I can tell you who wouldn't be here right now."

Daisy bit the inside of her cheek, and Soraya nodded slowly. "Isn't that a great point. The men who didn't think anything about betraying their wives wouldn't lift a finger to help someone in this situation. But you're right. I don't know Sam. Not really. I don't know Zach at all, except that he's rich and formerly famous. But they're here. Pretty amazing, honestly."

"Sam probably likes *you*," Daisy countered, looking at Nora.

Nora thought back to the way his arms had felt around her and pushed that thought away. "Sam and I have a trauma bond. That's its own whole thing. Besides, we're practically siblings."

The lie made her feel funny.

The truth was, Sam had never felt like a brother to her. Possibly because she didn't know what it felt like to have a brother, or any sort of intact family.

"Okay." Daisy clapped her hands like a punctuation mark. "We can't stand in here chatting about *boys* forever. Boys are what got us into this mess in the first place. We have moving to do."

Soraya nodded. "I don't feel like I can take anything that he could accuse me of stealing. But then . . . I didn't buy any of these things for myself. He made all the money. Everything is his."

Daisy gripped Soraya's shoulders and turned her to face her. "You had his kids. You raised his kids. You did that as a full-time job."

"Not really. I love my kids. They aren't a job, they're . . ."

"But you didn't work so he could. You kept his house and cooked his dinners and created this sanctuary. These things are yours too."

Soraya nodded slowly and took a long breath. "I have everything boxed up. It's just . . . It's been hard."

So they helped. They shared the burden. Lifted the boxes and brought them out to the truck. With Nora's insistence, they took the living room furniture. Took the table out of the breakfast nook, because they wouldn't need a whole dining table, and one wouldn't fit anyway. Took the pillows that Soraya liked best, her favorite blankets. Candles and pictures, clothes. All her kitchen supplies.

It fit into a pretty small corner of the moving truck.

Soraya wrinkled her nose. "Okay. Let's go."

Chapter Sixteen

Soraya

*Life will be hard whether you dance
or not. So dance anyway.*

—Rules for Witches

As they brought the last of the boxes into her apartment, Soraya was overwhelmed by gratitude. She'd been overwhelmed by the feeling that she had lost her entire safety net, her whole network, in one fell swoop, and here other people had rallied to help her.

It was humbling, honestly. Particularly because she had spent so many years being insular and not reaching out to anyone outside of the church.

Not that Nora had been nice to her back then, it was just . . . it was just she hadn't been any better.

Daisy was always nice to everybody. If anybody deserved to hook up with Zach Woods, it was Daisy.

For some reason, that thought made Soraya's heart beat faster.

Daisy was free to do what she wanted.

Soraya had never been free in that same way.

It's wrong anyway.

That thought, desperate and coming from deep within her, was the old version of herself clawing its way into her consciousness to try to find a foothold.

But it didn't have the impact it used to.

Well, life was complicated, which was something she had never given much credit to before, and people made the best choices they could in the middle of all of it. Maybe she would hook up with somebody. Maybe.

What would that be like? It was a weird thought to have, standing in this new apartment that had some of the pieces from her old life but also felt entirely new.

Much like her.

There were still a lot of old pieces inside her. Old feelings, old fears.

Yet there was this desperate need for something new. For something that felt good. Better. At least this felt powerful.

She'd been sad earlier, packing up all her things, but now that she thought about David coming into the house and finding half the stuff gone, she felt empowered.

She had taken control of a bad situation. He had been trying to force her hand, and she hadn't allowed it. So there was that.

"Dinner should be here soon," Nora said, popping in from the kitchen. They had decided to get delivery and christen the new apartment. Sam and Zach had helped move everything in, and then Nora had shooed them along, telling both of them not to worry, because they would find a way to get home.

"I'll just take an Uber," Nora had said.

Which was how they were getting food too.

Soraya *never* ordered delivery. Ever. She always did the cooking. It was part of her job, part of David's expectations. She couldn't retrofit it now and say that she hadn't wanted to do it, or that she'd found it unfair; she hadn't. She'd enjoyed her life as his wife, and she'd enjoyed keeping their house and cooking their meals. It was only she'd never realized that with the way their life was arranged, he was essentially her boss.

He could let her go and rescind every benefit she'd had from her job. Leave her with nothing, which was what he'd done.

She'd kept everything clean, and she'd done it for *him* in a way she hadn't fully realized. Because the house had always been his, when she'd thought it had been theirs.

This place would be hers. At least for a while. She could put what she wanted in it; she could leave it untidy if she felt like it.

She could order takeout.

It certainly wouldn't be anyone else's decision. That sent a thrill through her. She hadn't expected to get a thrill out of this.

She'd gone straight from her dad's house to her husband's house. No place had ever been hers. She had always lived according to the standards of the people around her.

This was about her.

The little space looked cute too. The couch and love seat fit, even if just barely, around the coffee table that had been there when she'd arrived. The mantel had the candles with all their wedding rings on it, and she had brought a hand-tatted rug that her grandmother had made, which made the space look cozy.

The kitchen was full to the brim with all her baking paraphernalia, and it was just hers.

Hers.

"Oh, the delivery's here," Nora said, looking at her phone.

"I'll get it," Soraya said.

Because this was her new place. It felt good to get delivery that she'd ordered just for herself. It was such a small, silly thing.

But she had been denied a whole lot of small, silly things in her life. She had jumped into adulthood with both feet and had never really done the young-adult thing. She wouldn't have chosen this. But here she was. She felt like the carefree early-twenties woman she had never been. Just for a moment. Just for a moment, totally unencumbered by anything.

She swept out the door and walked down the narrow hall, going down the staircase and opening the door. There was a person getting out of their car, who held up a bag of food. "Nora?"

"Yep," she said.

She didn't even feel the need to explain. It wasn't a lie, it was Nora's order. But in the past, she might've felt like she had to add a big, long description so it could all be strictly honest. But not now. Just not right now.

She took the bag of food and started back up the stairs, when she heard the door open a few feet away and stopped. It was the apartment across from hers. Probably the footsteps she had heard last night. A man stepped out, taller than she was by quite a bit, his dark hair pushed back off his forehead. His eyes were a startling blue, his jaw square, shoulders broad. He was maybe five years older than she was and . . . beautiful.

Stunning.

Yes, she had been around Zach Woods all day, who was Hollywood beautiful if ever that archetype existed. This guy was real-world glorious. That made him feel slightly more dangerous. Because Zach felt like he was on the other side of the silver screen even when he was standing right in front of you. This guy was like . . . there. There and gorgeous and . . .

"You must be the person who just moved in today?"

She blinked. He was talking to her.

"Yes." She was suddenly very aware of the fact that her left hand was bare. "Yes, I am. My name is . . . Soraya. Soraya Nichols. I work at Lady's Mantle."

"Nice," he said. "I'm Declan. I own Dice and Dragons, just downstairs."

"Oh. I've never . . . I've never been in there." That was a weird thing to say. Tell the guy she had never been to his business. "What kind of things do you have in the store?" She tightened her hold on the brown paper bag. She was practicing talking to him. Practicing talking to a new person. That was all. Was she flirting? No. She didn't even know how to flirt. She couldn't muster up any guilt over finding him hot even though she was still married. Not given all the issues with David.

David might not have been physically unfaithful to you . . .

No. Maybe not. But this wasn't being physically unfaithful either. She was just talking to her neighbor. The neighbor next to her place that was just hers. Part of her new life that was just hers.

"Board games," he said. "Tabletop."

"Tabletop?"

"Like *Dungeons & Dragons*. That's where the name of the store comes from."

She blinked. It was on the tip of her tongue to say she'd heard *Dungeons & Dragons* was demonic. Then she didn't.

She worked at Lady's Mantle, after all.

She'd also possibly put a hex on her husband.

Maybe, just maybe, she needed to stop labeling things when she didn't actually know anything about them, only knew what other people had said.

"I don't really know anything about that," she said.

"Come into the store sometime. I can tell you about it."

"Oh. My . . . my kids would probably like that."

Why had she brought her kids up? He didn't seem put off by it. "Kids *do* like the store."

"Well, they're teenagers."

His smile slipped just slightly, a line creasing between his brows. "You don't look old enough to have teenagers."

She wrinkled her nose. "I regret to inform you that I am. I'm . . . Sorry, you didn't ask for my biography, and I need to bring my takeout inside. But I'm getting divorced. So I'm here now. Maybe *Dungeons & Dragons* would get my kids to speak to me again."

He frowned. "Oh. That sounds . . . not great."

"It's not. I'm the bad guy in this scenario, I'm afraid."

"You don't look like the bad guy either."

"What if I am?" she asked.

"Somehow I doubt it. I'm pretty sure you didn't move into an apartment above a store you don't even own for fun. Or make your kids mad at you just for laughs. We just met, but I kind of get that vibe."

He was a stranger and giving her more credit, seeing her more clearly, than people who'd known her for years. People who could only see in black and white, in sets of rules. She'd been that person until she'd been shoved so firmly out of the black-and-white space she'd been forced to wade in the gray.

It felt good to have someone see her.

"Enjoy your dinner," he said.

She felt sorry to see him go.

"Thanks. I will. I'll definitely come into the store." She turned away from him, maybe a little bit too quickly. Then she walked into the apartment and closed the door behind her, putting her hand on her chest.

"What?" Nora asked.

"My across-the-hall neighbor is . . . *handsome*." That seemed insipid, but also safer than what she wanted to say.

"Oooh." Nora's eyes went round. "Handsome across-the-hall neighbor. How convenient."

"Well, I don't . . . I would have no idea what to . . . I don't . . . I can't think about that. I had a good conversation with him. I maybe even flirted with him a little bit. But that's all it's going to be."

"Oh, but you deserve to scratch that itch," Nora said.

"I didn't say *I* had an itch. Sex is *fine*." She sniffed.

"Sex is *fine*?" Daisy asked.

"Yeah," Soraya countered. "It's fine. I like it. Mostly. But this is part of what offends me, honestly. It's not good enough to go breaking a family up over."

"I completely agree," Daisy said slowly. "That sex with a stranger, or even sending nude pictures online or whatever, is not worth breaking a family up over. I will never justify what David did to you, or what Jonathan did to me. Or what Ben is doing to Nora. But sex can be pretty great."

"Yeah," Nora agreed. "It can make you do very stupid things."

"Not in my experience. In my experience, you . . . just wait until you're married, and then you have planned sex on your wedding night, and it's fine. I didn't have trouble resisting."

"Oh, Soraya." Nora pinched the bridge of her nose.

"Well. I've just never . . . I've never lost control."

"Maybe that should go on your list."

"I don't have a list. I already told you, I can't . . ."

"Listen." Nora paced into the room and touched the candle on the mantel, where their rings were still sitting on the wick, a reminder of the anger from the night of the spell. A reminder of why they were here. "If *you* feel like having sex with somebody you aren't married to is wrong, then I won't try to talk you into it. But if it's just a reaction to what other people are telling you? Then maybe I will."

"Are *you* going to have a fling with some other man?"

"I need to deal with Ben first," she said darkly.

"What about you?" Soraya asked Daisy.

"I might." Daisy looked away. "He's getting married to somebody else. I have weekends without the kids and . . . no reason not to. Except it's embarrassing to be my age and to only have been with one man."

"I'm in the same boat," Soraya said.

"At least you have a reason. Everyone will get it if you say you grew up in a purity-culture church. I just hooked up with Jonathan so early I never had the chance." She sighed. "I'm so *mad.* I was faithful to him. When I decided he was the one when we were teenagers, I gave up the idea of ever having other partners, and he didn't do the same. I'll never know if he was with other women the whole time or if it was just Amberly or . . ."

"You could ask," Soraya pointed out.

"Why?" Nora asked. "That sounds like borrowing heartache to me."

"I want to know," Soraya said. "While I was being a faithful wife, while I was getting the just-fine sex, what else was he giving other women?"

"We need to learn divination," Daisy said.

"I don't know about *that.*" Soraya's hands automatically retracted to her chest, like she was seeking out pearls to clutch.

"Too much Satan for Soraya."

Daisy rolled her eyes. "This has nothing to do with Satan. Or demons of any kind. Witchcraft is about tapping into your own intuition, your own power." She sighed. "Even if it isn't real. Even if the tarot cards aren't telling us anything, or if the spells don't do anything, I'd rather feel like I could change things than feel powerless."

Nora smiled, just slightly. "Maybe the real witchcraft was the friends we made along the way."

Daisy was right, though. The worst part about all this, under the betrayal and heartbreak and everything else, was feeling utterly and completely powerless.

"Poor Alexandra," Soraya said. "This is why she went . . . This is why she went crazy. This is why she was gambling and staying out late and engaging in all the destructive behavior that led to her accident. Because it makes you feel like everything is . . . fake. Like everything you believed in doesn't . . . mean anything." She let out a long, slow breath. "Part of me kind of wants to . . . self-destruct. Part of me wants to erase every part of myself that ever loved him. That gave so much time to him. Part of me wants to make that good, perfect wife into something else. A not-insubstantial part of me wants to sleep with the guy across the hall just to . . ." She sighed. "He's making everyone think I'm the villain, so maybe I should be."

"We're working on corrupting you," Nora said.

Soraya set the takeout on the table. They began to dish pad thai and pad see ew onto their plates, and it was Nora who retrieved a bottle of white wine and opened it.

"You said you didn't drink," Nora pointed out.

"Well, we didn't used to," Soraya hedged. "But we started to drink wine sometimes at home. But I . . . I've been embarrassed about it, because a lot of people in our church don't believe in drinking at all. But he said it was fine and . . ."

"And you like it," Nora pointed out.

"Yeah," Soraya said. "I enjoy a glass of wine."

"Then you should have it. Not because your husband said it was okay. Because you want some."

Soraya huffed a laugh. "I know I don't make sense to you, and I'm kind of pathetic. I'm starting to agree, by the way."

"I don't think you're pathetic." Nora got a corkscrew and opened the bottle. "I really don't. Not now, anyway. It was easy for me to feel like . . . I don't know, like you were just being mean to me, because I feel like I didn't understand how sincere your faith is, how deeply you believe what you do."

"I always have. What kind of ruined my life is realizing how little the people around me believe the things they say. Because they're not holding him to the standard they would hold me."

"I think some people have real, genuine faith," Daisy said. "I think you do, Soraya. I think other people like what a community like that gives them. Connections, power. A way to wield fear. I'm not even sure they know that's what they're doing. But there's a perfect set of rules for you to hold other people to while you don't hold yourself to the same."

"That's how it feels. Like the rules are just a convenience. But I never . . . I never looked at it that way. I've always really believed."

"You still can," Nora said. "They don't get to take that from you."

"No." Soraya snagged the bottle of wine from Nora's hand. "They don't get to take it from me. But also, I'm allowed to change." That was the scariest thing she had ever said. That she was allowed to change. Because change was something that was set up as a bad thing. "That's the problem. I was told that I knew all the secrets of life and of the world from moment one. So learning new concepts and ideas, integrating them, letting them change who you are is seen as an enemy. But I didn't know everything. I can see that now. I need to change. I can't just . . . dig in and learn nothing from this."

"Well, that's not what you're doing."

"So maybe I will have sex with somebody." She immediately felt a little bit bad even saying that. "Maybe, but not to prove something to anyone else. Just for me."

"Just for you," Nora agreed.

Daisy lifted her glass. "To Alexandra. Who isn't here, and should be. And to us, because we are going to help each other through this."

"To us." Nora lifted her glass.

Soraya was the last one to lift hers, and she clinked her glass against the others. "To us."

It was Nora who took her phone out and opened a music app. "Do you guys like Fleetwood Mac, because really nothing says spiteful breakup music like 'Silver Springs.'"

"I don't know it," Soraya said.

"I love that one."

The song started playing, a slow musical intro, and Nora backed away from the table into the most open part of the kitchen. "Stevie Nicks very famously sang this song right at the man who broke her heart. Imagine being stuck in a famous band with one of these jerks we were married to."

"Singing spitefully at them sounds good, though," Daisy said.

"Agreed." Nora spun in a circle as the tempo of the song picked up. She grabbed a broom from where it was wedged between the fridge and the wall and held the top end to her mouth like a microphone.

Even the song felt like a spell. A prayer. A promise.

That the man in the song who had left the woman in question would *never* escape, even though he was done with her.

Even though he betrayed her.

It did feel perfect for the moment.

Daisy stood and joined in, waving her hands in the air and moving her hips in time with the music, her voice clear and beautiful like it always had been. It had been way too long since Soraya had heard her sing. Daisy reached out to Soraya, and she took her hand, jumping into the dance.

As she did, tears slipped down her cheeks. Because this felt new and amazing and scary, all at the same time. But it was her life. There was pretty much no escaping it.

Just like she knew, somehow, that David wouldn't escape the consequences of this.

Because the three of them together were magic. If she was certain of one thing, it was that.

Chapter Seventeen

Daisy

I am the sun, the moon, the earth,
the stars,
I am all that is fierce and beautiful,
I am the divine feminine,
I am imbued with the power to give
and receive pleasure,
I am sensual magic waiting to be
unleashed.
And so it is.

—*A spell for reclaiming your sexuality*

By the time Daisy and Nora walked out of Soraya's apartment, they were hot and laughing. She was borderline wine drunk and felt better than she had in a long time. They'd danced to angry breakup anthems until they were sweaty and flushed, and even if she looked like a disaster, she felt great. Happy.

"I'm just going to get a car." Daisy started to search for the rideshare app on her phone.

"We can share one." Nora already had hers open and was ordering the ride. "He can do two stops. There's one just a couple minutes away."

"Okay."

They stood on the curb, and Daisy wrapped her arms around herself. Then she looked up and saw a man walk out of the bar across the street.

"Oh. That's Zach."

Then she realized he was looking right at her.

"Oh," Nora said. *"Shit."*

"What?"

"He's *waiting* for you."

A zip of excitement shot through Daisy's veins. It felt like high school, but in a good way. "No, he *isn't*."

Then he started to cross the street toward them.

"Yes, he is. Because he likes you," Nora hissed.

"I am in no position to have anyone like me," Daisy protested.

"You might not get to be in charge of that."

"What should I *do*?"

"There's nothing—"

"I can give both of you a ride home," he said. "Since I'm the reason you don't have a car here, Daisy."

"I ordered a car already." Nora waved her phone in the air. "If I cancel it, it's going to tank my rating."

"I'll just go . . ." Daisy started to say she was going to ride with Nora.

"You can take Daisy," Nora said.

"Nora . . ." Her heart thundered when she looked up at Zach. The truth was, he wasn't offering anything other than a ride. It was just that Nora had gotten in her head about it.

You're attracted to him.

Maybe. Okay. More than maybe. She was attracted to him. What woman wasn't attracted to him? He was . . . Zach Woods. It wasn't like he was her friend or anything. It's not like it would break anything if the two of them . . .

"Thank you," Daisy said.

Nora shoved her.

"Nora." She gritted her name out through her clenched teeth. The town square might as well have suddenly become a high school cafeteria.

Nora grinned, more than a little wine drunk herself. Daisy felt stone-cold sober.

And *alone*, as Nora's car pulled up and she waved, getting inside quickly.

"I'm just parked over here," he said.

"Okay. Okay."

"Are you okay?"

"I'm good. I . . . I'm very good. In spite of the fact my husband is marrying a woman who's ten years younger than us."

"He's an asshole." Zach was matter of fact. "I need you to know that. I also need to talk to you about something."

"What?" Her heart hammered. Was he going to say he liked her? Would he kiss her? She was getting way ahead of herself.

"What?" she said again, trying to sound a little bit less keen.

"I want to sell my portion of the business to you."

"What?" She was entirely sober now.

"I own the majority of it. So if you bought it from me, you would be the majority owner."

"But . . . but . . . I can't afford it," she sputtered.

She looked across the street, at the light on in Soraya's apartment window glowing above the apothecary. A reminder that she was in the real world and not having a delusional fantasy, because this didn't feel like it could possibly be real. It just didn't.

But Zach was looking at her in a way he never had before. No one had looked at her like this before. She wouldn't have been able to fantasize this if she wanted to. "I'd like to sell it to you for a penny."

"Zach, I can't let you do that. I can't . . . accept that. It was an investment for you, and there's no way . . ."

"I have plenty of money. I invested in this because I met him, and he had a young family, and he was trying to get this thing off the ground. I invested in it because . . . It's hard for me to explain it. The point is, I don't need the money. I also think what he's doing to you is shitty. I've seen some messy breakups. Entertainment is a small industry. People break up, and they still have to work together. It's not *unlike* a small town; it's not unlike what's happening to you. I hate what he did to you. I know everything you did for the business. I don't do much as far as the day-to-day running of it. I just . . . own the majority of it because I paid all the money to start it up, and I collect a percentage in repayment."

She was dizzy. "I get how it works. I did the books, remember?"

"I know you did. You did the majority of the organization. I want to make sure a fair percentage of that goes to you."

"You already arranged to have those sets built for the play, and they're so . . . beautiful—they must have cost a fortune."

"I have connections to set builders. It's not that big of a deal."

"It is, though. I just don't . . . I don't understand why you would do all this."

He lifted his head, and the streetlight caught his angles, just like it would have done on a well-lit set, making him look even more compelling. Even more beautiful. "Do you really not understand?"

She shook her head, her chest tight, her whole body shaking now. "I really don't. This is so much. It's a lot."

"I *want* you." The words were rough, fractured. As far removed from the actor version of him as it was possible to be. As far removed from her husband's friend and business partner as it was possible to be.

This was someone else. Someone she felt like she was seeing, really seeing, for the first time.

Oh. For some reason, it utterly shocked her now. Because it came from nowhere, came when she wasn't expecting it. "So is this . . . ? Are you . . . ? Are you *paying* me for . . . for sex, because I would've slept with you for free."

The words came out all jumbled up, broken, embarrassed and excited and angry all at once.

"*What?* Hell no. I'm not paying for sex. I'm not . . . I'm not paying you to . . . I did this wrong. I shouldn't have said that to you. I shouldn't have told you that I was attracted to you."

"You absolutely should've told me that. Because that's genuinely the best . . . nicest? I don't know, it's not *nice*, but . . ." *Get it together, Daisy.* "I'm not . . . You're Zach Woods. I'm just Daisy McNamara from Hemlock. I am a deeply average mother of three who doesn't have abs or any idea what the latest tips and tricks in sex are . . . I'm not your usual type."

"What do you know about my type?"

"Only what I've read on the internet."

He lifted a brow. "Do you read gossip about me?"

"Sometimes." She couldn't lie. Not now. Actually, she could have, but it would have seemed really stupid.

"I'm sorry. I screwed this up. One thing I decided recently, though, was that when you want your business partner's wife, there's never really a *right* time. Ever since he left you, I've been waiting. For the *right* moment. But there's not a right moment."

"You . . . you want me."

"I did say that." His gaze was steady. Unwavering. It made her stomach feel hollow.

"I know you did, but it . . . How is it that *you* feel like you're messing this up? I haven't been with anyone other than Jonathan ever, and I'm just me."

He moved closer to her then, and she could smell him. Which sounded weird, but he smelled amazing. "Let me show you."

She didn't really care about right and wrong. Didn't care if it was mixed up and messed up, or that there might be some potential consequence for it down the road.

She'd been everything for everyone else. She'd done everything for everyone else. This felt like something for her. It felt like something good and real and fun.

That horrible feeling she'd had the last time she saw Jonathan. The feeling of longing, of wanting to go home again knowing she never could, was unbearable.

Home didn't exist anymore. Maybe it never had.

She wanted that feeling to go away. She wanted to feel like Daisy, herself, whoever that was. She needed to make a home with herself. That started by making choices that had nothing to do with anyone but *her*.

She'd been with Jonathan since she was sixteen, so it was inevitable that she didn't quite know who she was standing on her own. Maybe sleeping with someone else wasn't the answer to that.

But what about her body? *Her* sexuality? What about her being desired not because she'd been there all along, not because she was a convenient, warm body? Not because of what she could do for someone, but just because she was wanted?

Maybe Zach only wanted her because she had been off-limits. Even *that* made her feel good. Even that made her feel like there was something sexy and exciting and illicit about her. She'd never felt like that in her life.

Not since the first time she'd had sex. Seventeen and trembling with delight and the fear of being caught.

It felt like that now, except more. There was a tangle of emotions inside her. She had the ridiculous inclination to tell Zach that she couldn't offer him anything more than a night. That everything was too complicated. That he shouldn't go getting his feelings hurt by her.

It was the silliest thing, because he was Zach Woods. He was sexy and singular, and famous, and could certainly have any woman he wanted. She didn't need to give him disclaimers, she assumed.

She just needed to decide whether or not she wanted this. It wasn't for the greater good; it wasn't for Jonathan; it wasn't for her kids, her mother, her grandmother. It wasn't for anyone.

It was hard to make herself move forward. Hard to make herself take the step. But then . . . he did it. He closed the distance between them. He lowered his head and kissed her.

It was like an explosion. Fireworks and bombs, some Molotov cocktails thrown in for good measure, homemade and sharp and unwieldy. She'd never kissed anyone other than her husband. The excitement of it, the intensity of it, nearly pushed her over the edge right away. Whether it was a rush of satisfied vengeance, a rush to her ego, or simply arousal, she couldn't say.

It was a baptism in the sweet water of justice as far as she was concerned.

Because while a younger woman had been stroking her husband and his ego, she had been sitting there frozen, feeling discarded and unwanted. She hadn't let herself marinate in that, not much.

There were kids to take care of and a play to direct and an aging mother and ailing grandmother and bills to pay and books to do and the general logistics of everyday life. She was constantly running here, there, and everywhere, and while she had been angry at Jonathan and grieved his presence in her life, in the kids' lives, like it had been before, she hadn't really examined all the ways in which this had made *her* feel. Rejected. Ugly, unwanted, undesirable.

She wasn't sure when she had last felt beautiful.

She felt it right now. With Zach Woods's mouth on hers, and his hands skimming over her curves. Like she was sexy, desirable, like she wasn't a woman who was easy to leave behind.

She moved her hands up to his broad shoulders and gasped. He was so tall. Muscular, like he was still working to be fit for Hollywood even though he hadn't been working there for five years.

She kissed him because she wanted it. There was something revolutionary about that.

It was also amazing to be *wanted*.

He moved his hands and cupped her cheeks, parting his lips and taking the kiss deeper, his tongue sliding against hers as she became very aware they were standing on the street making out like teenagers. Not like two grown adults who could be recognized at any moment. But did she care? She tried to imagine it. Rumors circulating around Hemlock that she'd been seen kissing Zach Woods.

It was a wonderful, dizzying thought.

It started with her, though. That realization nearly made her knees buckle. If she hadn't quit, if she hadn't taken the first step to cut Jonathan off, to stop him from being able to use passive-aggressive tactics against her, she might not be *here*.

She'd taken the job at the apothecary.

She'd asked for karma.

She'd thought of that as Jonathan getting something bad for all the hurt he'd caused. Maybe she was getting something exciting in exchange for being brave.

Zach lifted his mouth from hers and stood back, watching her, and she very nearly melted into a puddle at his feet.

"I want you," he said. "The offer of the business is a separate thing."

Oh, he wanted to talk. Which meant she had to remember how to do that. Easier said than done when her heart felt like it was going to pound through the front of her chest, and there were cars driving slowly by where they stood, casting them in a headlight glow, like an interrogation lamp. A demand that she answer the questions. That she know answers she didn't.

"It doesn't *feel* like it," she said.

Did she care? It was messed up, but the idea that he would trade half a business for the privilege of having her was flattering, even if it shouldn't be. Her self-worth had been trampled on, and the idea that she might be valued at *half a construction company* was flattery when the father of your children had left you and gotten engaged to a younger woman in record time.

"It's separate," he said. "I like you, Daisy. I increasingly do *not* like your husband. I regret being in business with him. For a variety of reasons, that's true, not only the way he comports himself in his personal life, but the way he does business. I'm also attracted to you."

The idea of *like* and *attraction* being two totally separate entities was one she'd never fully considered. She'd never had to. She'd been attracted to Jonathan in high school, and it had become the endgame relationship. Feelings didn't separate from it.

Maybe it was like the crush she'd had on Zach. He'd been on-screen, untouchable in most ways, but teenage Daisy still would have kissed him given half the chance. Maybe this was the adult version. Want, separate from everything else.

"I think I like you," she said slowly. "At least, everything you've done recently has given me reason to. But . . ." She wanted to tell herself not to do it, not give him the disclaimer. Because it was embarrassing. Because it would be assuming a whole lot. "I . . . I'm bruised. I'm messed up. I'm not even divorced yet."

"*He's* already engaged."

"Yes," she whispered. "He is. I don't know if I'm over him. We were together for nineteen years. I don't know if I'm over that. I wouldn't take him back. But I'm not done mourning the future I lost, and that's a complicated feeling. It's complicated."

"It doesn't have to be." He looked at her with all the confidence a man that beautiful deserved to have. "Do you want me?"

"Yes," she breathed.

She was shaking. She was so filled with need for him she was almost weak with it.

"That's not complicated, Daisy," he said. "Tonight, you can want me, and have me, and worry about the rest of it later."

It was like a burden had been lifted off her shoulders, one she'd been carrying for months now, or maybe years. Worry. About everything. About everyone. About what they needed, what would make them happy, what would contribute to the household, to the business. This stood alone. It wasn't about anything but feeling good now.

That was a revelation.

"I want you," she said.

It was all either of them needed to know.

"Your place or mine?"

"Yours," she said.

Because she wanted separation. From that house that her kids lived in, the place where she and Jonathan had slept together for all those years. She wanted her and Zach to be a separate thing, even though it really couldn't be. Even though it was always going to be colored by the fact that there was something satisfying about it being Zach who was coming to her rescue. Something satisfying about it being Zach who wanted her. Both because of who he was, and who he was to Jonathan.

But if she could just have this . . .

She would do her best not to compare, not to think about the reality of her life. She just wanted a fantasy. For once. She wanted to be swept away.

"Let's go."

His car was nice, of course it was, but that only occupied a fraction of her brain on the drive out of town toward his mountaintop home. She had been there before, but it had been a long while. Back when Zach had first partnered with Jonathan on the business.

It was beautiful. Wood and stained glass and glorious natural light that filtered through the windows, a profound view of the valley below.

It was like a church there, separate from everything, worshipping nature.

That was her memory of it, at least. Right now, everything felt contracted. Small. Like there was nothing beyond the car, nothing beyond the two of them. Nothing that mattered, anyway.

When he parked in the driveway, she hesitated, and then he rounded to her side of the car, opened the door for her, and took her hand. Even now, he was taking care of her.

The sound of their footsteps on the gravel heightened, the sensation of that rough hand closed around hers extreme.

She let him lead her inside, and the feeling of being outside her body was suddenly intense. An unfamiliar house, and an unfamiliar man. This wasn't her. But she wanted it to be. She slipped back inside herself and looked at him. Grounded herself in the moment.

She reached up and touched his face, tracing the angles of it. It was funny, because his face was so familiar. She had seen it a hundred times on her favorite TV series as a teenager before he'd moved to town. But that was different from the reality of him standing right in front of her. Different from this real version of him who had lines on his face and radiated heat.

It had been innocent back then. He'd made her heart beat faster, and he'd been hundreds of miles away. A stranger. A concept. He was real now. Her heart *was* beating faster, but her whole body ached along with it, and he was here. She could touch him. Taste him.

She wanted him.

More than she had ever wanted anything before. Or at least, that was how it felt. Because everything she had ever seen or done or wanted before was fuzzy in comparison to this.

This was all that was real.

If she had any magic within her whatsoever, she wanted to call all of it to the surface now so he could feel what she did. So that it would be as electrifying for him as it was for her.

Yes. She really wanted that.

"Don't overthink it," he whispered.

"I can't help it. I've spent my life overthinking all the details so I could be sure everything would work out according to plan."

"And has it?"

She laughed. Maybe this was a stupid time to laugh, but she couldn't help herself. She threw her head back and dissolved. "No. No. Nothing has worked out the way I expected it to, or the way I wanted it to. But right now it feels worth it."

She was about to have sex with Zach Woods. Teen Daisy would be elated, as long as she didn't look at the rest of the mess her life was in.

You don't need to look at it right now either.

"I hope you have condoms," she said. "Because I don't."

"I've got you covered." His voice was rough. Unfamiliar. He leaned in and kissed her again, but it was more intense than the kiss they had shared in the square. This time, there was intent. Intent to take her upstairs, to take her clothes off, to take her.

So she embraced it, embraced him, wrapped her arms around his neck, and arched against his body like she was trying to get closer to him, as if she could ever be close enough. Suddenly it felt like she was on fire.

This was Zach Woods. He was touching her. He wanted her.

She wanted to tell everybody.

She also wanted to tell no one, because while it felt like an insane, amazing fantasy, it was also real. Shocking and intimate, and as scary as it was liberating.

"I . . . I don't know if I . . . I don't really know . . ."

"Be quiet." His tone was firm but soft. "Just stop right there. Daisy McNamara, from the moment I met you, I thought you were one of the most beautiful women I've ever seen. But I was wrong. You're *the* most beautiful woman I've ever seen."

"That can't be true."

"Sure it is. Some people think the city is beautiful, and some people think the mountains are beautiful. Beauty takes all different shapes. What gets to be the most beautiful, that's in the eye of the beholder. To me, you are the pinnacle. This is my fantasy. You don't have to do anything to fulfill it. Nothing but just be here being you. I've never had a real relationship. I got chewed up and spit out by the machine, and it took me a long time to figure out who I was again."

"Is this the *I can't promise you anything* speech?"

His eyes glinted in the light and made her stomach drop. "Not exactly."

"It can be if you want. Because I can't . . . I can't see past tonight."

He held her face in his hands, comforting, electrifying. "That's okay. I don't need you to. But I also don't need you to worry or think that you're not going to please me. Because you already have."

Everything he said was exactly right, was the sexiest it could be. That she was *enough* just like she was, and she tried to believe it.

It was so hard when the man who was supposed to love you had gotten tired of you. But she wasn't going to think about him. She wasn't going to let him push away this moment.

Jonathan McNamara had taken enough moments in her life.

This was just her and Zach. Maybe it was the beginning of something. Maybe it was just tonight. But she wanted it to stand alone as something significant. She had done long term, and it had burned her badly. She knew better than to try to imagine happily ever after, because apparently twenty years didn't guarantee it was a happily ever after. So tonight might as well be happily ever after for the night. She might as well give everything to it. She might as well take everything from it.

He kissed her again, and this time he devoured her. She couldn't remember the last time she'd been kissed like this, if ever. Deep and slow, the friction created by their tongues maddening. He pulled her body against his, pressed her against the wall, let her feel how much he wanted her.

He wanted her. *He wanted her.*

He kissed her as he propelled her up the stairs, down the hall, to his bedroom. It was a huge room with a vaulted ceiling. A window on the back wall stretched from floor to ceiling, but there was no covering.

"There's an internal shade," he said. "But I just use that to block out the light. No one's out there to see."

So he could just walk around naked right in front of the windows. It was certainly an interesting mental image.

She was going to see him naked.

It was like getting hit by lightning. Because of course she understood what was going to happen, but the reality of it was sinking in deeper and deeper.

"Are you okay?"

"I'm so good," she said. "I'm not really spontaneous usually, so this is kind of extreme for me."

"We don't have to do this tonight." His brow furrowed with concern.

"No. I do. Because I want to. Because I *need* to."

"It's not going anywhere. It'll keep."

She shook her head. "No. No. Because life is . . . scary and unpredictable. Frankly, if life is going to fuck me like it has been, I'd rather have an orgasm."

It was his turn to laugh, and it did something to dissolve some of the tension in her chest. Then he closed the distance between them again and wrapped her in his arms as he pulled her shirt up over her head and cast it onto the floor.

He pressed his thumb to her lower lip, and her breath evaporated. "What if tonight you take a break from life, and let me fuck you instead?"

She could only nod.

He took her clothes off like it was a choreographed dance. Always keeping her in his arms as he separated fabric from her body, as he exposed her to his hungry gaze. She didn't feel embarrassed. Didn't feel awkward. Not when he looked at her like she was a revelation and he'd been badly in need of one.

A soft, tender part of her ached. Like a growing pain. Like something withered and ignored was beginning to come back to life. Expand.

She had never done a thing for Zach. She hadn't been particularly nice to him. She hadn't done him any favors. She hadn't done his laundry. She hadn't cooked him dinner. He was still treating her like she was special. He was looking at her. Really looking at her. It had been so long.

It had been so long since she felt like *her* just being there was good enough.

He lifted her gently and set her down at the end of the bed, and then he began to take off his own clothes. She dug her nails into her palms as she watched the expert strip show. Watched every inch of his muscular build reveal itself to her.

Her mouth went dry, and she shifted where she sat. He was more beautiful than any fantasy she could have ever had about him. He was a gift to every person who experienced attraction to men.

He was masculine beauty personified, and she wanted to worship at the altar of him. But before she could, he went to his knees in front of her and pushed her legs apart.

And she found herself as the object of worship.

She gasped, lifting her hips off the bed, but his iron grip kept her from moving away. He was a man with a mission, a man intent on doing exactly what he wanted, and God help her, she wasn't going to fight it.

He scooted her backward on the mattress, and she lay back as he vaulted up onto the bed, pleasuring her with intense focus with his lips and teeth and tongue. She forked her fingers through his hair and realized she wasn't even tempted to compare him to her one and only other lover, because this was already an experience that transcended everything she'd ever felt before.

This wasn't a perfunctory act of going down on her to pay her back for a blow job. He wanted her. He was tasting her, savoring her, luxuriating in her. She had never felt so beautiful, so filthy, so . . . cherished.

So she just let him.

When her orgasm crashed over her, she was shattered, broken into thousands of sparkling pieces of herself and put back together in another shape. Like he had rearranged parts of her and made her something else entirely.

She was recovering, while he went and got a condom, while he positioned himself between her legs, moving his hand behind her head and kissing her, intense and long as he thrust inside her. She clung to his shoulders as he began to move, their foreheads pressed together, the feel of him so deep within her, taking her, making her gasp.

This was like touching the sun.

It was almost too much, but it was not enough all at the same time.

When she came again, he followed her over the edge, the rough growl in the back of his throat sending aftershocks through her body.

She lay there for a moment, trying to catch her breath. Trying to breathe. Trying to think.

Would he want her to stay the night? Should she leave?

"I'll drive you home in the morning, as long as everything is good with your kids."

"Oh, you . . . you don't mind if I spend the night?"

"Do I mind? No," he said.

He sounded incredulous, but she didn't know what to think. "Well, I've never . . . I've never done this before."

"You did say Jonathan is the only man you've been with."

Her face went hot. "Yes. That."

"I'm still me. You're still you. Based on everything you know about me, do I seem like someone who would throw you out onto the street after that?"

"No. But I've heard people get weird after that. Need distance."

"Do you need distance?" His gaze was searching. Intense. Maybe she did need distance.

"Do you want a hot chocolate?" he asked, not waiting for her to answer the last question.

She blinked. "Do I . . . ?" The most beautiful naked man she had ever beheld was offering her a hot chocolate after giving her two screaming orgasms? What other dimension had she fallen into?

"Well, I . . . I would like one. But you don't have to . . ."

"Yes, I do. Get cozy. I'll bring it to you."

Get cozy.

A few minutes later, he returned with a tray that had two mugs on it and a plate of cookies.

She didn't want distance from this at all. She wanted to freeze time and just be here for as long as she possibly could.

"Do you do this a lot?"

"No," he said. "I assume you mean the hot chocolate and cookies. Not the rest."

Well, *that* was lowering. Not that she was entitled to a brief history of his sex life.

"I have sex, Daisy," he said, his tone firm. "But not usually here."

"*Usually* as in . . ."

"Never. Never at my house."

Her face felt warm. "Okay."

"Why? Would you be jealous?"

This made her feel inexperienced and silly. "I think so. But, in fairness to me, I've kind of had a rough run, what with my husband cheating on me and all. The idea of being one in a string of people feels kind of painful right now."

"Fair enough."

"This doesn't have to be anything. But I just want to know if it's not. I don't want it to be open-ended where we might do this again, but maybe you'll be with other people. I can't do that, not after everything. I feel like that's probably not very modern dating of me."

"I don't need to sleep with anyone else. Whether or not it continues is kind of up to you."

"Okay." She wasn't sure what she wanted. Not right now. Because that had been amazing, but this whole thing was also a little bit scary.

And she was just a girl.

"It feels weird to bring this up now, but the business . . ."

He sat on the edge of the bed, hot chocolate in hand. "I don't have a lot to do with daily operations—well, to be honest, I have nothing to do with them. I helped him get the business all set up, I invested a lot of capital in it, and I've been taking a cut of profits for years. I think he's let things slip, do you agree?"

"Yes. Not just because I'm mad at him. Though I'd guess some of it was the stress of trying to keep that double life going for a while."

"I hear those are tricky."

"You don't know?"

He shrugged. "I've never had the need for a double life. When I felt more and more like that was what being famous—and trying to *stay* famous—asked of me, well, that was when I decided to be done."

"I find that reassuring."

"Good. I want you to feel reassured. And I want you to accept my offer to take my fifty-one percent of the company."

She laughed. "Oh. That would be so . . . sweet. Marching into his office and telling him I'm technically the majority owner."

"Do it. You can do whatever you want. You can take ownership and just collect passive income, or you can really go in here and start messing with him."

She didn't think she was hallucinating the look of pure enjoyment in Zach's eyes when he mentioned her messing with Jonathan. And it was a good fantasy. But she just wasn't sure about any of this. It seemed like a no-brainer in many ways. She needed time to sit with all of this, though.

"I'll think about it."

"I didn't expect to have to talk you into it."

"It's probably good for you to have a woman who isn't a sure thing."

He shifted, his expression getting serious. "I don't want to cause you any stress. So if it stresses you out, we don't have to talk about it right now. But I'd like to do this again."

"So do I. But it feels like . . ." Too soon? Irresponsible? Like something she shouldn't be doing because it felt too good, because it felt too self-centered, because it felt . . . "Yes, I want to keep doing it. But I don't want Jonathan to know."

"Okay," he said, his expression neutral. "If he did, he'd think you were getting back at him."

Part of her couldn't deny that sounded a little bit satisfying.

You're also afraid of losing the high ground.

That was lowering. But it was true. Right now, even his mother was on her side because Jonathan was being so ridiculous. But if anyone knew she was sleeping with someone else?

You guys made out on the street, it might get around.

It might. But she wasn't going to announce it.

Whether he could pick up on her thoughts, he didn't say so. "It's whatever you need, Daisy."

She couldn't remember the last time anyone had said that to her. If nothing else, Zach Woods was a fantastic vacation from everything else happening in her life.

"Oh, shoot. I'm opening the apothecary tomorrow, and then I have practice and—"

"I'll drive you back in time."

"Really?"

"Yes. Really. You know, it's okay to let people do things for you."

When she finally fell asleep, warm and in his arms, she kept replaying those words.

She wanted them to be true.

Chapter Eighteen

Nora

A witch needs a coven.

—Rules for Witches

Nora felt like she had a storm cloud hanging over her head when she walked into the apothecary fifteen minutes late, but still before opening.

She immediately saw Daisy, who was sitting in front of the computer and was *glowing*.

"Oh my God!" Nora shouted across the empty store. "You slept with him."

Soraya's head popped out of the coffee bar area. "Excuse me?"

"Daisy slept with Zach!"

"Are you *psychic*?" Daisy asked, her whole face going red.

"No. But remember, I saw you after you lost your virginity to . . . he who shall not be named, and you had a very similar look about you. Except you also looked kind of guilty."

Daisy frowned. "Do I not look guilty now?"

"No. You don't."

"I don't understand." Soraya looked shell-shocked. Poor blossom. "What happened after you left?"

"Zach was waiting for her." Nora practically exploded with glee. "It was quite romantic."

"I don't know if *romantic* is the right word," Daisy mumbled.

"But I *need to know*," Nora said. "Because he is a hot teen idol from my youth. Was it everything my girlish heart needs it to be?"

"It was amazing," Daisy whispered. "But you're going to have to keep it down, because Aggie is going to be back in a few minutes, and she has a new employee coming in today, and I'm trying to keep this . . . quiet."

"You don't want to talk about your sex life? You're the only one of us with a sex life." Nora did her very best not to sound petulant.

"No, I don't want to talk about my sex life *here*. Later, though . . ."

"Excellent." Nora rubbed her hands together.

"Aren't you going to tell me that I did the wrong thing?" Daisy looked over at Soraya.

Soraya shook her head. "No. Not at all. I'm giving up judgment."

"Are you really?"

She wrinkled her nose. "Well, realistically no. But I don't feel judgmental about this."

"You know," Nora considered, "this would make a good article."

"An article?"

"Yes. 'My Husband Cheated on Me, and I Got Back at Him and Back in Touch with My Sexuality.' It's the kind of thing that gets a lot of clicks." She hadn't thought of anything to write for weeks, but she needed to get back on it.

"Oh," Daisy said.

"If you're interested in spilling the details, I could write it on your behalf, and we could get a little bit of money for it. Keeping your name out of it, of course. I don't want to let all of my writing go just because I'm working here."

"You could write about your own experience," Daisy pointed out.

Nora waved her hand. "I don't know. I feel like writing about myself is boring."

"You don't write about yourself?"

"Sometimes. But not . . . in depth. I prefer to write about other people's experiences."

"Why?"

Nora was about to answer, though she wasn't entirely sure what she was going to say, when the front door opened, jingling merrily, and Aggie walked in, followed by a young woman who had half of her head shaved and tattoos up both arms.

It was Alexandra's daughter, Madison, whom she had narrowly missed seeing at the hospital because she had been on a vape break.

"Good morning." Aggie was merry in spite of the early hour, which Nora was certain had to be witchcraft. "This is Madison. She's going to be the barista for the bakery area."

"Hi," Madison said. "I think . . ."

"We know your mom," Nora supplied. "I actually live across the street from . . . your parents' house."

"Oh." Madison nodded. "I thought you looked familiar."

"Yeah. How is your mom?"

"The same. The longer she stays out, the less chance they think she has of waking up. But . . . I don't know. She's a strong woman. I think she might make it."

"I think she might too." Nora wasn't sure she really believed it, but she wanted to, considering she related to Alexandra more and more.

"That's why I took the job. I used to work at Mix, but I quit when my parents got divorced because my mom needed so much extra help, but right now I can't . . . I can't keep sitting in the hospital while he comes in and out with his girlfriend."

"Your dad?" Daisy asked.

"Yes. He's such a dick."

Nora laughed. "Well. No argument."

Madison was herded to the coffee-bar area, and soon Aggie was doing her readings while Daisy continued to pore over the grimoire, Nora manned the counter, Madison and Soraya worked on setting out baked goods, and Madison showed Soraya how to make drinks.

"I don't know if I'm ever going to be able to memorize all this," Soraya said.

"That's silly," Nora called. "It's just a recipe. You're great at recipes."

"But I don't know how to do a job." Soraya chewed the edge of her perfect nail, which Nora was almost sure she'd never done before.

"You seem to be doing a job okay," Daisy commented.

"You never had a job before?" Madison looked incredulous. "Are you rich?"

"She was a tradwife." Nora smirked.

For a second, she felt a little bit guilty, but then Soraya caught her gaze and laughed. "Yes. I was."

"Oh. I didn't think you guys existed off the internet."

"Well, I don't really exist as one anymore. Because my husband left me, and you know what happens after that—you have to get a job."

"Wow. Shit. It's a lot like my mom, but they had a lot more money, and she did all the committees and boards and all that. But . . . I get it."

"How many jobs have you had?" Soraya asked.

Madison laughed. "Oh. I lost track. I have historically not been a great employee. Which I know isn't cool. But I don't know. I get distracted, I start looking for something new. I did, like, two years as an art major, and then I decided to check out science. I didn't last very long at that, and I dropped out. Then I worked at the quilting store, but I don't know how to quilt. Then I worked at the yarn store. Then I got a job at Mix, but then I quit to help my mom out after she found out about Dad's affair—not that I helped her much."

"And now you're here."

"Yeah."

Nora couldn't imagine choosing to have a life that was that haphazard. She had one she hadn't chosen, but she supposed that was what life could be like when you had financial stability for the entirety of it. You took for granted that you would land on your feet. But then, she supposed for Madison, life hadn't exactly been that stable. Her dad had turned out to be kind of terrible.

"Was your dad always a dick?" Nora asked.

Everybody looked at Madison. Maybe because it was the question they were all grappling with. Were there always signs, and did the people closest to the cheating men miss them? Did other people see it?

"I don't know. He was busy with work, but I can't say I'm surprised he cheated on my mom. I'm more surprised about the way he handled it. Because when she found out, he wasn't sorry. He didn't even act like he owed her an apology. He acted like she did the wrong thing for catching him. *That* surprised me."

"That's kind of how my husband has been," Daisy said softly. "He's acting like I did something wrong because I'm upset. It doesn't seem fair."

"Well, the problem is, all these men get told that they're good," Soraya said, speaking for the first time in a while. "At least, that's what I've seen. Like my husband, for example. Everybody thinks he's such a great guy, literally just because he goes to church all the time, so they assume he shares their values. But he doesn't. But he has this credit that's been given to him that he hasn't even earned, and it's like they think they're untouchable. No wonder billionaires and world leaders end up so corrupt. Our husbands are just mildly successful men in small-town America who haven't been told no enough, and look at how out of control they are."

"A good point," Nora said.

"They need to be taken down a peg or two." Madison spoke while taking inventory in the little kitchen area.

"We put spells on them." Nora could still feel all the rage, all the heartache, and all the triumph from that moment.

"Really? Like real witchcraft?" Madison asked.

"No," said Soraya at the same time Nora said, *"Yes."*

"Did it work?"

Nora thought about her failed love spell. About poor Soraya getting kicked out of her house. About Daisy having great sex.

"The jury is out," Nora said.

"I know I feel more powerful than when I started." Soraya studied her chewed nail. "That has to count for something."

Suddenly, Madison's eyes glistened with emotion. "You know, I came in the store the other day, and it just seemed right. But I've been so lonely since my mom . . . I have my partner, and my other partner, but I don't know. I've been missing something."

"Community," Nora said.

"Yes," Madison agreed. "Community."

Nora spent part of the day working on a sandwich board to go outside, harnessing some of her latent artistic talent to advertise tarot readings and their new café items. Madison was delightful, if terribly young, and Nora enjoyed watching her scandalize Soraya with commentary on her many polyamorous relationships and her casual approach to sex in general.

The day went by quickly, and when they closed up shop, Nora felt like lingering. Going back to her empty house felt . . . like a mess. She still hadn't dealt with Ben, and she was beginning to feel like a coward. But he wasn't here, which added a layer to all this that made it challenging. She was angry. A phone call or a text wouldn't adequately satisfy that. If she couldn't look him in the face when she was talking to him about . . .

She had never wanted to get married. But her deepest, darkest, most embarrassing fantasy was that she had always wanted a traditional life. Had always wanted a home and the kind of family she'd never had growing up. She hadn't believed she could have it, though. Hadn't believed she deserved it. Because something had always felt like it was fundamentally broken inside her. Falling in love with Ben, and him falling in love with her, marrying her, had made her feel like she had defeated that long-standing narrative.

This was cruel. It would've been better to have never had this love. To have never had that hope. Because it wasn't like he had been honest with her. It wasn't like it had been a relationship that wasn't working, a relationship where they had communicated honestly about that, and then worked together toward fixing it. He had let her believe they were happy.

Then he had blindsided her by going off on this trip, where he hadn't wanted to find himself at all but had wanted to find himself inside another woman. At least, that was the best she could assume based off what she'd seen. Fundamentally, even if it hadn't escalated to sex, it was a betrayal all the same. Because he was lying to her. About what he was doing, about why he was doing it.

"Have you read any new spells in the grimoire, Daisy?"

Daisy reached out and picked up the old book, sliding it toward her. "I've been reading more about revenge spells."

Nora smiled. "I'm all for that."

"We already did one," Soraya said.

"Yes," Nora agreed. "But nothing is happening yet."

"Much like prayer, I assume spells aren't always activated right away." Leave it to Soraya.

"I have to figure out how I'm going to handle Ben," Nora said. "I need him to come home."

"You could ask him to," Daisy pointed out.

"I think we're past cordial requests."

"Is there a reason you won't talk to him?" Daisy asked.

Nora scowled. "Because it doesn't change anything. At the end of the day, it doesn't change anything. It just is what it is, and I have to process it, and I have to deal with it, so I might as well deal with it on my own time. Without him here to watch me have a breakdown about the total and complete degradation of my life." She was breathing hard, so she sat down at Aggie's table and touched the top of the tarot cards. "I can think of nothing worse than having to make myself vulnerable to the man who's cheating on me."

"But at some point, don't you want to confront him?" Madison asked.

"Yes. When I can actually do that."

"You mean and not cry," Soraya said.

"There's nothing wrong with crying," Madison said. "Historically, the patriarchy has turned tears into a sign of weakness in order to invalidate women's emotions."

"Well," Nora said. "Fuck the patriarchy. But I still can't think of anything worse than crying."

"He's your husband," Soraya pointed out. "He cheated on you. You get to cry and scream and do whatever you want, short of murder."

"There's no point. You can do all of that. Cry and scream and whatever else, but it doesn't make people stay. You just end up debasing yourself for a man who's too detached from the marriage to even have an honest conversation. Uninterested, thank you." Nora shuffled the cards and laid out one. "Past." Then she laid out a second. "Present." Then a third. "Future."

She flipped over the first card, the Moon. She only had a little bit of experience with tarot at this point, but the Moon was a card that confused her, which was ironic and fitting because it was a card about confusion. But how was her past confused?

She turned over the next card. *Death.* Great. Her present was death.

But she already knew that. It was the slow, dying breath of her marriage. Of the life she'd imagined living. Of her safety and her belief in happily ever after.

She turned over the third card. The future. The Five of Cups. On the card was a man staring at three spilled cups with a look of despair on his face, while there were two upright behind them.

It was a card of ingratitude. Of not seeing everything you had.

Great. So her future was being an ungrateful bitch after experiencing death and confusion.

She blew out a breath and flipped the cards back over.

"What?" Daisy asked.

"I'm not connecting with the cards at the moment."

"Admittedly, that wasn't the most flattering reading, but you know you can always change the future card."

"I don't think that's how tarot works," Nora said.

"I don't mean just draw a different card." Daisy sounded lightly exasperated. "That reading was about what your future looks like now, based on your feelings. I'm not sure that tarot tells the future so much as reads the energy around you. Right now, your future looks like that because you won't be able to see what you have because you're focusing on what you lost."

"You do one." Nora was annoyed at Daisy's arch tone. She loved Daisy, she really did, but the problem with having a friend who did all that reading and research and crossed all her T's and dotted her I's was that she tended to be irritating in moments like this because she was too pragmatic.

Daisy sat down in front of the cards and shuffled them. "Past." She drew one out of the spread-out fan. "Present." She hesitated. "Future. The Ten of Wands. The Lovers." Her cheeks turned bright red. "The Two of Swords."

"See?" Nora said. "It's not fun when your future card is weird."

Daisy frowned. "It's about choices. A choice only I can make. I was overburdened, and now I'm . . ."

"Getting properly shagged?" Nora suggested.

"Yes. That." Daisy cleared her throat. "Then there's going to be a choice that no one can make for me."

"Swords tend to be sharp," Nora said. "So difficult choices, maybe."

Daisy glared at her. "You're only saying that because you're mad about your reading."

"I'm not mad."

Nora was, in fact, mad.

"I'll go." Soraya sounded tentative, but her offer to go at all was a shock. "Sometimes I've been . . . casually looking at the ones in my apartment. Daisy, I liked it when you said it was a reflection of your own energy. The depth of what you feel. I guess that's kind of how I think of it, and why it feels okay for me. I just hadn't articulated it before. I'm not asking a spirit to show me anything. I'm trying to make sense of what's happening around me and inside of me."

"*I* like to call to the spirits," Nora intoned.

"Yes, I know." Soraya furrowed her brow.

"Bonus points if the spirit is Satan." That earned Nora a steely glare from Soraya. "I'm kidding. I know Satan isn't a spirit. Plus, I prefer Hecate, if I'm honest."

"Past," said Soraya, putting one of the cards down. "Present." She took a deep breath. "Future." She turned the cards over slowly, like they might be a snake about to bite her. "The Hierophant. Well, that's what Aggie drew for me the first time we came in here. The Empress. The High Priestess."

"Trusting man-made structures, creating your own path, trusting your own intuition."

"Oh. I like that, I guess."

Nora felt personally victimized that Soraya's was so clear and unchallenging.

"Do you want to do one, Madison?"

Madison nodded, sat down at the table, and took the deck of cards. She shuffled them with ease and then fanned them out in front of her, repeating the same structure the rest of them had used.

"The Seven of Swords. The Tower. Justice." They looked at the reading, and goose bumps rose on Nora's arms.

Daisy frowned as she examined the cards. "Deception. Trying to get away with something. Then obviously . . ."

"Yeah. My mom being in the hospital and nearly being dead. That would be a tower."

"But there's justice." Soraya touched the card. "Justice for her."

"I don't even know what that could mean."

"Maybe something needs to come out," Daisy said.

"The cards don't tell the future." Madison stood up. "You all just said that."

"Daisy and Soraya said that." Nora pinched her brows together. "I don't know that I believe that." Of course, her past experiences with the metaphysical hadn't necessarily filled her with a great level of confidence about it. Because the Ouija board had told her she would find love, and she had done a love spell to no avail. She stared down at the Five of Cups and ignored the strange, aching feeling inside her. "I want to believe that, for you, that's a fortune."

It was far more comfortable to focus on Madison's reading than to marinate on her own.

"Thank you, guys," Madison said. "This is the first time I've felt . . . hope."

Nora wished she could feel the same. She didn't look at her reading and see a way forward. All she saw was more treading water. Three cups lying on the ground, poured out, and with two standing. That felt like her life right now. She had a lot of good in her life, but there was so much that was painful. She wanted to shut it off. She wanted to not deal with it. She wanted to embrace the anger that had driven her the night she had cast the karma spell. Because at least that had been clear. At least that had felt protected. Solid.

They said their goodbyes, and she reluctantly drove back to her house. She took a deep breath and decided that after dinner she was going to call Ben. Or text him. Something. But she was going to confront him.

While she ate, she pulled up that bitch's Instagram again. She scrolled through the newest carousels and let herself gag on the photographic evidence that there was something going on between her and Ben. In every picture he was in, they were touching. In the final photo, she was kissing his cheek.

She tasted something sour in her mouth and stopped eating her dinner. She was going to text him.

Then the lights went out.

"Agh!"

She picked her phone up, and instead of texting Ben, she texted Sam.

Can you come fix my lights?

You are a trial.

I know. Please. Rescue me?

What's in it for me?

Dinner. I have extra.

So she would put off texting Ben. She would have dinner with Sam, even though she'd already eaten. He would fix her lights.

And for a little while longer, she could live in this bubble. This bubble where she felt pain but hadn't pulled the trigger on anything.

This bubble where she had gently tugged the loose end of a thread, but it hadn't all unraveled yet. Maybe she was just focusing on her upright cups.

So there.

Chapter Nineteen

Soraya

Spells manifest when a witch's power meets divine opportunity.

—Rules for Witches

Something tapped Soraya on the shoulder early Sunday morning.

You have to go to church.

She hadn't been for the past couple of weeks because the kids were mad at her anyway, and David was demanding that she move out of the house. She hadn't spoken to him at all in the three days since she'd vacated the premises, and she knew he hadn't been over there to check, because if he had, she would've heard from him.

But it was an urgent, insistent feeling that overtook her, that she had to go to church.

Maybe to go without him.

While she got dressed, she checked in with herself. Was she doing this because he'd ordered her to, and she was still responding to that on some level?

No. This was coming from her. She had to trust that.

You have to go, the voice persisted inside her.

She argued with herself the entire time. What was the point of going to church and having everybody stare at her? Going and getting ignored by her own kids if she ran into them. Going and getting hit by a bolt of lightning on account of the light witchcraft she had been involved in.

She almost laughed at that as she looked at her reflection in the mirror while praying that her moisturizer would take away some of the new lines and creases on her face that were a gift of this particularly stressful time.

The truth was, she had never believed that God was only around in church. So going to church wouldn't reveal anything more than staying home would.

One of the strangest things was how she felt at peace spiritually while feeling at war with so many of the people she would've said she agreed with.

But that was what she had been grappling with this entire time. She didn't feel like she was out of step with God. She felt out of step with this particular community and their reaction to her marital breakdown.

Maybe she needed to go so she could . . . She wasn't even really sure. It was about dealing with the issues of lingering resentment. Maybe she was supposed to go so that somebody could say the offensive thing that finally drove her away. Or maybe there would be something healing. Maybe.

That felt a little bit optimistic.

She didn't feel optimistic. She felt driven. If there was one thing she had been taught all her life, it was that she was supposed to listen to the still, small voice.

She was listening. She was going, even if she didn't really want to.

She opened the door to her apartment and heard a door open across the hall at the same time.

Declan stepped out right as she did, and her heart jumped slightly.

He was just so . . .

Hot.

He was hot, and for the first time in her whole life, she felt free to do something about thinking a man was hot. That hadn't been the way it was with her and David. She'd found him attractive, yes, but she'd been young and innocent by design.

She was neither of those things now and more interested in Declan because of it.

Madison, who was a child, and it wasn't like Soraya could actually take serious advice from her, but she'd said mistakes were just mistakes.

He would be a glorious mistake.

"Hi," she said, because she was very aware she was standing there staring like a creeper. His blue eyes meeting hers made her feel like she was about to go up in flames.

What would happen if she moved toward him?

Are you insane? At least go out to dinner with him. You're going to go from Purity Culture Princess to dragging a man you barely know to bed?

When she put it like that, it didn't sound as crazy as she'd hoped it would. It sounded like maybe it was a Band-Aid that needed to be ripped off.

"Good morning," he said. "I'm just grabbing some coffee before work. I try to open the store in time to catch the rush of the after-church crowd."

"Ah. I'm the church crowd." Seemed like an ironic thing to call herself given the riot of illicit images in her head.

He looked at her, a very similar look to the one he had given her when she'd mentioned she had teenagers. Like she was defying his expectations, and she sort of liked that too. She was used to being in a group full of people who knew her. Who knew exactly what to expect from her, and who disapproved when she didn't do those things.

She had never, not once, felt like an enigma.

She sort of did right now.

"I hope you have a nice morning," he said.

She let out a breath, her face hot. "Me too."

She turned away from him and stuffed her hands into her coat pocket as she walked down the narrow stairs and toward her car. She felt awkward because she should have said she hoped he had a good morning, but she'd been thinking about her own nerves and that had just come out.

He was just so gorgeous. He made her want to jump into his arms, kiss him, or more. To embrace spontaneity in a way she never had.

That had felt . . . dangerous and fun and totally not like her. Even though she hadn't actually done anything.

Her life had been fixed for so long. Her path set. Her ideas of who she was, what she was capable of, what she would let herself do and what she wouldn't.

What had been a narrow path was now a wide-open field.

It was both terrifying and exhilarating.

But for now, she was going to church and not thinking about the wild impulse she'd had.

She took the short drive to the church, which was on the outskirts of town, a large building with a beautifully manicured facility. She had always loved the church grounds, but it struck her as being slightly unsettling now. Because it was so like the people. Perfectly manicured. Always with everything in place. Yet it concealed so much.

The emphasis on appearances wasn't doing anyone any favors. Not when the core was rotting.

She got out of the car and shut the door firmly behind her, taking a fortifying breath as she began to walk toward the main entrance to the sanctuary.

She was only about five minutes early, so there were very few people outside, but she saw him out of the corner of her eye. Saw him before he called her name.

"Soraya."

She looked over at David and felt like she was seeing him for the first time. The anger on his face was unguarded, naked. But there was something else along with that. Like he was looking at a lower life-form. Like she had no right to meet his gaze.

She had never realized before that her husband truly saw her as someone inferior to him. But she could see it now, with all his outrage written there plainly.

"I stopped at the house on the way here. How dare you?" he asked, the question low and angry.

Oh, David Nichols, from Nichols Realty, how dare she?

She wanted to laugh at him, except she was so mad.

"How dare I what? You said you wanted me to leave."

"I said I wanted you to be back with me," he said.

Pure, righteous fury filled her, a fire that had been kindling inside her for a while now igniting.

She didn't want to be beholden to this man anymore. He didn't own her. He didn't get to make choices for her.

She was going to be happier than David had allowed her to be.

She was going to have a whole life—goals, dreams, feelings, mistakes, and joy—that David hadn't allowed her to have.

She was going to stand apart from him and be her own person.

She'd been created to be whole, not to be his.

She'd never felt more certain of God's love for her, or of her own love for herself.

"That isn't acceptable to me," she said. "I'm not getting back with you. Not after—"

"Because of a *text*?" he asked.

"No. Because of so much more than a text. Because you don't respect me. Because you don't love me, not the way I deserve. And because you threw a giant, embarrassing tantrum at our sons' baseball game, which told me exactly who you really are. A selfish baby who claims to be the head of the household just because he's a man."

"We can talk about it," he said. "It isn't like I cheated on you. It was only a text."

"Was it?"

The discomfort and fury on his face told her it wasn't. It wouldn't have mattered, though. He'd exposed himself. He wasn't the man she'd believed him to be, and this wasn't the congregation she'd believed it to be. It wasn't the faith she had. Hers was leading her in a different direction, and they might think that meant she was abandoning it, but that wasn't true.

Perhaps most important of all, she wasn't the woman she'd thought she was.

She was stronger. She was clear on her own convictions. They wouldn't waver, even when her husband asked her to compromise them.

"David, what you did to me was wrong. But you can't even admit it. Instead, you're threatening me. Instead, you're sending people to talk to me, to emotionally manipulate me by questioning my faith. But *you* aren't talking to me. Not really. For weeks, we were separated and went to church together, but you didn't talk to me. You only sat with me to keep up appearances. It was about you, not about us. Our sons won't speak to me. That's because of you. But I'm not the one who betrayed our marriage vows."

His expression contorted, confusion, anger, and rejection warring on his face. He couldn't handle her changing his story. Couldn't handle her calling him out—rightly—as the villain, because he saw himself as the hero. As the wounded party.

Right then, she saw the fatal flaw in their marriage. In how it had been constructed from the beginning.

He saw himself as the one who mattered. Everyone else existed to support his view of himself, his own comfort, his own supremacy.

A lot of people went to this same church, had marriages that were structured like theirs, but crucially: The men wanted their wives to be happy.

They loved them.

David loved himself.

"You're going to pay for this," he said. "That car you drove here in, that's mine too. All of it is mine. You haven't earned a single cent the entire time we've been together."

"I got a job. I got a place to stay. So it seems like I'm doing okay."

He needed her to need him. Without it, he had no power.

She had taken his power. She had given it all to herself.

He took a step toward her but stopped as if he had encountered a wall. Maybe like he was suddenly aware that anyone could see him. "I'm helping with sound for worship today. I don't have time for this."

"I don't believe I called you over to talk."

His expression darkened. "You're cheating on me. That's what's happening, isn't it? How else would you have a place to stay?"

She jerked back in shock. He might as well have slapped her. "Excuse me? Maybe I have friends. Maybe there are people who want to help me because they care about me. Unlike you. And you were supposed to. You're supposed to be my husband. But you're so dedicated to not facing the fact you aren't perfect, that you're the one who messed up, that all you can do is accuse me of sins you committed. All you can do is be angry at me." She took a step closer to him. "Everything that is concealed will be brought to light and made known to all, David. That's a promise."

She turned away from him, her heart beating so hard it was all she could hear as she put her head down and walked into the sanctuary. People turned and looked at her, but nobody said hi. She walked straight up the middle of the aisle to sit in the front of the church. She wasn't ashamed. Not of anything. Not of *anything*.

She looked down the row of pews and saw Stephanie, the pastor's wife, blond and pretty and also not meeting her gaze. She took a breath and looked back toward the front, because if she found any of her close friends, and they did the same, she might lose her nerve. Might fail in her resolve to simply be here, unashamed and refusing to bend to this narrative of insanity.

Her boys were in youth group, so there was no chance of seeing them this morning, and it made her heart hurt. She missed them. Distant sightings at the baseball field weren't enough.

It was part of the torture from David.

On some level, he must know he wasn't enough all on his own. He had to take her kids, her house, her friends. That was what he thought might bring her back.

It was pathetic.

Pastor John came out onto the stage, a Bible in his hand, dressed in a collared shirt, but casually, his hair pushed off his forehead. He was a friendly, affable sort of man who made everyone who talked to him feel warm and accepted.

She wondered if she would still find that to be true or if he would close ranks on her also. If he would see it the same way everyone else seemed to.

She wondered if all the acceptance she had ever felt was something she had been paying for with compliance.

"All rise. Say hello to the person next to you."

She turned, and the person to her left turned away. She turned to her right, and her gaze connected with a woman she didn't know very well. Jennifer, she thought her name was.

"Hi," the woman said softly. "It's good to see you."

Soraya was very aware she didn't have her wedding ring on, but it was good to know not everyone was going to treat her like she didn't exist.

She sat down when Pastor John gave the directive to do so, and he made some announcements, and then the worship team came out. She looked behind her, up into the sound booth, where her husband was manning the projector that put the words to the worship song, along with video clips behind it. Rushing streams and mountaintops and other natural wonders, all curated to create maximum feeling during the service.

Just another service David provided that made everyone think he was *just so good*.

She shouldn't think of him as her husband anymore. Legally, he might be. In her heart, that was over. He'd broken their vows.

He'd released her. Set her free.

Two songs in, all the small children were dismissed to go to their classes.

"All right, everyone!" The worship pastor's peppy tone felt so at odds with her internal monologue, it was jarring. "Stand up for this one." He put his hands up over his head, clapping, before returning to the guitar and strumming rhythmically while he turned away from the mic and then back again to begin the song.

It was about trading your sorrows for joy. Even in this moment, she felt it. It didn't matter what it meant to David. It didn't matter if everyone here couldn't understand her decisions. The song still resonated with her.

So she would sing it.

A choir filtered out from backstage, came to stand behind the worship team, all in red robes, swaying and clapping, singing a choral arrangement of a Madonna song that had been recently appropriated by church spaces, though even Soraya knew that, when Madonna sang about being on her knees in the song, she was not in fact singing about literal prayer.

She did her best to push that to the side and just listen to the song, which was being beautifully sung. She looked up at the lyrics on the screen and tried to sing along. A rushing river moved behind the words, the water swelling in time with the music.

Then the movie behind the words changed. It was dark and shaky. Then suddenly it was . . .

Her jaw dropped, and she put her hand over her mouth as the reality of what she was seeing washed over her. As a man's naked rear was suddenly projected across the whole screen, a few short screams rose over the music and the clapping faltered. When a naked woman bounced into view and onto the couch in the frame, the crowd fractured. Some were moving, turning away; others were frozen, mouths open and staring.

The lyrics were still rolling over the top of what was now a pornographic scene. What was now the literal, original interpretation of the prayer in the song.

Oh. God.

She knew the ass on-screen. And she knew it well.

David. It was David. *Naked.* With . . . with Pastor John's wife.

At . . . That was the pastor's house. She'd been there. She had seen the painting of Jesus on the cross behind the purple velvet couch where her husband was filming himself getting . . . *taken there* by the pastor's wife.

Everything that is concealed will be brought to light and made known to all.

Everything.

This was the text but sent to everyone. This was the secret of who he was, playing out in full color in front of all the people who had told her how good he was.

The screen went dark.

But everyone had already seen it. Everything seemed to slow down as she looked around her, at the shocked reactions of all the congregants, at the swell of outrage. Some people were yelling. Some were laughing uncomfortably. Some, she realized, had no idea it was more than random internet porn.

John came rushing out onto the stage, his face red, frozen in shock. She knew a moment of real sympathy for him. Because she'd felt that shock, right in these pews only a few weeks ago.

But no one had cared when it was her.

Would they care now?

Soraya looked over at Stephanie, who was frozen in place while chaos swirled around her.

Then Soraya turned back to look at David, who was standing in the sound booth looking down at the chaos below, his shock, his rage, palpable even from down there.

Then he found her, their eyes making direct contact.

Good luck playing the hero now.

She smiled. Slowly. Deliberately.

She smiled, because she knew.

The noise around her had reached deafening proportions. The growing chaos mirrored a slow-motion action sequence in a war movie.

Soraya turned away from all of it and began to walk toward the back of the sanctuary. The crowd parted for her like the Red Sea as she moved with ease through the uproar.

Vindicated. Smiling.

She felt a hand on her arm, and she stopped, looking directly into Kristi's eyes. Her Bible study leader was clinging to her shirtsleeve, her gaze apologetic.

Soraya didn't say anything. She just pulled away from her and continued to walk out, with that same chorus that had signaled his downfall playing in her head.

He was cheating on her with the pastor's wife.

Now everybody knew. Everybody.

They might have all told her that what David had done to her was something she should forgive, but no one would *ever* tell Pastor John he needed to forgive *that.*

Maybe she should feel bad that he'd been dragged into all of this. But she didn't. They'd all made their own beds. Including her. She had been married to, lived with, a man she didn't really know for years. This was the consequence. This whole mess.

But it was all out in the open now.

What are spells but prayers men don't like?

Of course, her husband would not like this spell. This prayer. But it had come home to roost either way.

Karma. Justice. Revenge.

Right now, it all felt the same.

She walked back to the parking lot and right past her car. Well. His car. He could . . . he could have it.

She laughed. She laughed, and she simply continued on by it. She would head back to town on foot, and she would do it with her head held high. He could have all his stuff back. Everything. As long as she didn't have to deal with him anymore.

About a mile into the walk, her resolve started to falter slightly. But it was a grand gesture, so she was doing it.

"Soraya!"

Her head whipped around, and she saw Nora stopped in the middle of the road in her navy-blue Camry, looking at her incredulously. "What are you doing?"

"I'm walking away from an explosion. Triumphantly."

"Where's your car? Do you mean a literal explosion?"

"No. Better. Better." She ran into the middle of the road and leaned into Nora's window. "David is . . . He was *fucking the pastor's wife*. Everyone just saw it."

She could scarcely remember having ever said that word in her life, but it was fitting to her now.

"*Oh my God*, get in the car," Nora said. "I need the whole story." Soraya rounded to the passenger side and got in. "I'm working this morning, you weirdo. What would you have done if I hadn't driven by?"

"I would've walked all the way back to town. Angrily. But I would've done it."

"Okay. Explain to me about the car later. First, I need to hear about how everyone saw your husband and the pastor's wife."

She recounted the entire story in great detail, and by the time she was finished, Nora was crying with laughter.

"I'm so sorry. I sadly, unbelievably, know how traumatizing it is to have seen a video of your husband having sex with another woman."

Soraya blinked. "It . . . it wasn't? I think because I knew. I knew he was doing this. Well, not with her, and I certainly didn't know he was taking a video of it, but he took pictures of his . . . his junk, so it makes sense. He sabotaged himself. He did it to himself. And he's been so angry at me. So bitter at me. But I didn't do this. He did. I just feel . . . It was magic, Nora. I saw him before the service, and I told him: *Everything that is concealed will be brought to light and made known to all.* The scripture from my spell."

They were silent for a few minutes. "Nothing came of mine."

"Have you talked to him?" she asked. Meaning Ben.

Nora shook her head. "I don't have anything to say that isn't an incoherent ramble about betrayal and bad dirty talk. If he saw that he called me on accident, he hasn't acknowledged it." She let out a slow breath. "My marriage is over. I really didn't want it to be."

"I get it. But I don't want to be married to that man either. I suspect you don't want to be married to a man who treats you this way."

"No. It's an illusion, I think. That anyone is actually decent."

"Maybe it is. But I feel . . . a lot more powerful than I ever have before."

"You probably shouldn't have given him your car, though."

"He said he was going to take it back. He was trying to take everything from me. Everything, so that he was my only option. He lost everything today." Her heart twisted, just slightly. Because their sons were going to hear about this, and thank God, thank God they hadn't been in there. Not for that. Hearing about it would be bad enough. But actually seeing their own father . . .

At least they'd see him clearly.

She wasn't on the schedule to work today, but she opted to go into the apothecary for a while. Alexandra's daughter was cheerfully making coffee, and Daisy was sitting there with an old-fashioned ledger in front of her.

Aggie was sitting at her table where she did her readings, and Soraya approached, even though she had typically kept her distance from this part of the store.

"Just so you know," Soraya said, "it worked."

Aggie looked at her, her clear blue gaze sharp. "Of course it did. We're all magic, Soraya. It just needs to be claimed."

She stayed until the evening, and when she finally walked back up to the apartment, there was a vase sitting outside the door with flowers in it. She paused and bent down, picking it up and looking at the card.

I'm sorry. Let's have coffee sometime. Kristi.

She didn't know if she was warmed by the gesture or not. It had taken that—it had taken a man being betrayed by David—for Kristi to see that he was not, in fact, a good man. It had taken video evidence. But it was better than nothing.

She heard the door across the hall open, and she turned. Declan was standing there, his dark hair slightly disheveled, looking no less gorgeous for it. The little leap in her chest from earlier was . . . subdued. Today had been a lot, and hope was a strange beast at the moment. She was vindicated, but she had also been forced to look directly at the truth of all of this. She supposed that was the flip side of pure, unvarnished truth. There was an ugliness to it.

"I was going to ask you to dinner sometime," he said.

Well. That successfully got a leap out of her beleaguered heart.

"Am I too late?"

She looked down at the card. And then back up at him. "No. You're right on time."

Chapter Twenty

Daisy

Mischief is best enjoyed in the
company of friends.

—Rules for Witches

"What is the emergency coffee meeting for?" Nora asked as she and Daisy walked into Soraya's apartment at far too early an hour.

"I have a date!" Soraya's exclamation was halfway between a shriek of delight and a wail of despair, which, frankly, Daisy could understand.

Zach, and sex with Zach, was great and wonderful, but also the newness was weird, and in the midst of a whole bunch of other newness, it was a lot.

"With hot across-the-hall neighbor?" Nora was bright eyed and swept past them into the kitchen, where Daisy could hear her clattering around looking for a mug, then helping herself to coffee. She'd taken a seat at the small corner table by the time Daisy and Soraya joined her.

"Yes," Soraya confirmed. "Declan."

"Oooh." Nora rubbed her hands together.

Daisy spotted a tarot deck at the center of Soraya's table. "Getting more comfortable?"

Soraya huffed a laugh. "*Comfortable* might be the wrong word? Desperate, maybe."

Nora took hold of the deck and opened the box, shuffling the cards in her hand. "Here, I'll do a pull for you." She laid a card out on the table. The Tower, with fire coming out the windows and men falling down to earth. "The Tower means he likes you," Nora said sagely before tucking the card back into the deck and stuffing the whole deck quickly back into the box like she was trying to hit erase on that draw.

Soraya was fussing with her coffee maker. Clearly, a tarot card didn't have the power to make her more anxious than she already was.

"I don't have anything to wear!" She whirled away from the coffee maker. "All I have are church-mom outfits."

"Your outfits are pretty," Daisy said.

Soraya took a breath. "They're outfits I chose to fit in with a certain group and a certain image, and they don't fit anymore. They fit physically, but . . ."

"You want an outfit that doesn't say 'going to a potluck.' You want one that says 'would like to get railed.'" Nora's words were succinct and undeniable.

Soraya's cheeks went red. "Honestly? Yes."

"Then we need to go shopping. We were going to hang out today, and now we have a mission!" Nora was triumphant.

They started with iced coffee—because the coffeepot split three ways in Soraya's apartment wasn't enough—and trooped up the sidewalk of Hemlock, the flowers in full bloom, the breeze fluttering through the trees, casting a golden-green glow everywhere around them.

This was the kind of tourist stuff that Daisy never did. She was too busy organizing the house, taking care of the kids, basically too busy living here to actually enjoy being here. It was surprising to her that there were shops up on this end of town that she hadn't even known were there. A brand-new potted-plant store with immaculate vibes, and a shop that had locally made candles and handcrafted soaps.

The first boutique was decidedly for people in a different stage of life, and part of Daisy longed to wear the trendy styles, even though they were ephemeral and for bodies that hadn't birthed humans.

"I just don't understand who would want to wear this." Nora pulled out a dress that had multiple holes in the bodice area. "If I put this on, it would look like a Play-Doh fun factory."

It was a descriptive image. And one Daisy felt strongly applied to her too.

"My boobs would hang out of this." Soraya stuck her finger through a cutout on a bright-orange dress that was likely to hit right at the rib cage.

Weirdly, Daisy felt like she might actually consider wearing it. To bed, with Zach. He made her feel hot in a way that she just hadn't. Maybe ever. He was a magician like that, but it wasn't ladylike to brag about wonderful men and multiple orgasms when your friends were still in the trenches.

Not that she wasn't in a trench, still. There were all kinds of nonsense yet to deal with. There was still the fact that Amberly and Jonathan were getting married, which felt like it was stuck right underneath her ribs, and every time she took a breath, she could feel it.

"Okay," Daisy said. "Something a little bit more demure."

"I am demure," Soraya said. "Just demure and hoping to also seem sexy."

She looked deeply embarrassed to have even said the word.

"Okay. You've got to own your sexuality." Nora tapped Soraya on the forehead.

"I don't know *how* to own my sexuality. I was told my sexuality belonged to David."

"No," Nora said. "Your sexuality does not belong to that man. It belongs to you. Your vagina, your rules."

"Thank you. I don't know that I need to think of my vagina in those terms." The work Soraya was putting in to not flinching was admirable.

"Look at you, saying *vagina* on a city street." Nora clasped her hands in front of her chest like she was a proud mother.

"Strange times," Soraya said dryly.

They walked into the next boutique, which boasted some lovely floral dresses in a 1950s style, and Nora shooed Soraya away from them. "That is too much like things you already have."

"What about this?" Soraya asked, pulling out a powder-blue bodycon dress.

"That is acceptable."

Daisy pulled a lavender dress off the rack and held it up, examining the silhouette. Then she lowered the hanger just slightly and gasped. Because there she was. Amberly herself, swanning into the boutique with that big engagement ring on her finger.

She almost swallowed her tongue.

"What?" Soraya asked.

"Is that . . . ?" Nora followed Daisy's gaze. "It is. I'm going to go—"

"No," Daisy said. "Nobody do anything. It's not her fault anyway. She's twenty-five. Her prefrontal cortex isn't even fully developed, and my husband is . . ."

"That is very girl's girl of you," Nora said. "And I agree, blame must be allocated to the appropriate parties. But she's not *blameless*."

"We're not going to get in a fistfight with my husband's fiancée in a boutique."

"We can just go," Soraya whispered.

"Absolutely not," Daisy snapped. "I am not going to sacrifice your amazing dress on the altar of Jonathan's nonsense. You go try your dress on."

"Daisy!"

Daisy looked over, and to her horror, Amberly was charging toward them with a smile on her face. "Are you trying that dress on?"

Amberly had said Daisy's name and still, Daisy couldn't internalize that Amberly was actually talking to her. Directly.

This was the first time she'd ever seen her without Jonathan around. The very weird thing was that Amberly always acted like she was happy to see Daisy. She waved, she smiled, she pissed Daisy off because she was sparkly and pretty and cheerful.

Because she wasn't bitter and sad and jilted.

It made Daisy feel weird and small right then.

"I . . . was thinking about it."

"You should! It's your color. Oh my God! Do you ever wear emerald? You should." Amberly plucked a very short emerald dress off the rack and handed it to Daisy. "I used to work here. I love this store. This dress looks so good on everyone."

Daisy looked at Nora and Soraya for help, but they were just standing there, staring.

"Try it on! You have the play coming up. The kids are so excited!"

"Yeah. True. I . . . I do."

What did this bright, sparkly woman see in Jonathan? It had been easy for Daisy to make Amberly a caricature in her head the few times they'd seen each other, but this interaction was nothing like she'd ever imagined.

"I'm Amberly," she said, looking at Soraya and Nora.

Soraya smiled. "Nice to meet you."

Nora said nothing. Her disapproval was rock steady, and no amount of smiling from Amberly would fix it. Daisy did like that about Nora.

Though Amberly didn't notice it.

"Oh, Daisy, they have a green skirt I think you should try. Or they used to always keep it in stock. Come here."

Daisy could tell Amberly no, but this was the kind of out-of-body experience not even drugs could provide, so she gestured to Soraya and Nora to keep shopping while she went to the opposite side of the boutique with Amberly.

Amberly's smile faltered. "Um. I'm . . . I do want to show you a skirt. But I also just wanted to say, I know things are weird between us."

Daisy blinked but said nothing.

"I don't want them to be," Amberly continued. "Your kids are so great. They love you so much. Whenever Jonathan says negative things about you, I shut it down. I know you guys weren't happy together, but I can tell that you're really great because of how the kids talk about you."

Daisy's head was spinning. For the first time, she wondered if Amberly didn't know she was the reason their marriage had broken up.

Is she? The marriage was really over when he was open to having an affair. You finding out about her was the catalyst. But it isn't her fault.

That thought seemed so reasonable while she stood there looking at Amberly.

Who was a person and not a symbol of anything.

"Well. Thanks."

"Women need to lift up other women." Amberly took a skirt off the rack and handed it to Daisy.

Daisy cleared her throat. "Yeah. They do."

As she walked to the fitting room, Soraya was just coming out in the powder-blue dress. "Damn," Nora said. "You are built like a brick shit-chapel, my friend."

Soraya looked both embarrassed and pleased. "You think he'll like it?"

"I think it will look amazing on his bedroom floor."

"I'm not going to sleep with him on the first date."

"Sure," Nora said. "But you could."

Soraya looked at herself in the mirror, and her lips twitched. "Well. Yeah. I could."

"You can do whatever you want."

Daisy looked behind her and saw Amberly ducking out of the store, giving her one final wave.

Soraya could do whatever she wanted.

So could Daisy.

Amberly couldn't, though. Amberly, who was too sweet for Jonathan and was now engaged to him.

Daisy suddenly felt pity for a woman she would have called her nemesis only ten minutes ago.

It was helpful to remember who the real enemy was. It certainly wasn't the twenty-five-year-old saddled with Jonathan and all his nonsense.

"I want to go try on that orange dress after I try these on," Daisy said.

"In the nightmare store?" Nora asked.

Daisy smiled. "Yes."

"Why, are you feeling too good and you need to make yourself cry?"

She laughed at Nora's drama. "No. Because I can do whatever I want."

Chapter Twenty-One

Nora

Your power is waiting for you. You have to be ready to meet it.

—Rules for Witches

On the night of Daisy's play, the air was filled with electricity. The mural outside the Holly was three-quarters of the way finished and looked great, if Nora said so herself. It was fun to stand outside the theater and watch people's reactions to it as they filed in.

Though she knew a lot of the electricity in town was still happening in response to what had happened Sunday.

A few days later, the buzz of what had happened at church with Soraya's husband hadn't worn off. It was hard to believe his karma had been quite so public. Intense and obvious.

It was magic. Or at least it seemed that way. It was hard to attribute it to anything else. It felt like karma was a golden thread unspooling before them, winding itself around them.

Soraya seemed to be handling the whole thing well. Nora had a feeling that if she'd been confronted with an actual pornographic movie of Ben having sex with that Instagram girl, she would've had a total meltdown.

Soraya was already inside saving seats for her and Sam, and Nora just had to wait for Sam to arrive. Daisy had been at the theater all day doing rehearsal, and Zach had been with her every step of the way making sure the set was immaculate. It looked so much more professional than anything Nora had ever seen in their small town, and she had a feeling Zach had gone way over the reasonable budget for a community children's theater production.

A testament to his feelings for Daisy. Maybe Zach was Daisy's karma.

Nora was still waiting for hers.

She saw Sam walking down the sidewalk then, taller than the crowd around him. She waved. He tilted his head upward.

"It was nice of you to come," she said.

"Of course. I have to see my electrical work in action." He stood next to her and looked up at the mural—at the mountains, trees, and flowers she had painted. "It looks really good."

"Thank you," she said.

"Doesn't it start in five minutes?"

"Yeah. We'd better go in."

She walked next to him, her knuckles brushing against his, and she ignored the zip of electricity inside her. She became very aware that people were looking at them. If people knew who they were, then they knew that she and Sam were friends. Or maybe they didn't. People who knew her from the art center and as Ben Clarke's wife might not know Sam was her best friend and that by being with him in a public space like this—at a place where many people would probably bring a date—well, maybe it seemed like an announcement.

She swallowed hard, suddenly uncertain of what to do. Whether to lean in or lean away. Maybe somebody would text Ben. Maybe somebody would start a rumor about it. Maybe that would be her karma.

It felt strange and sat uncomfortably in her stomach, but she couldn't say she was repulsed by the thought. There was something invigorating about the idea of being a surprise. Of being a rebel again. She had been squished into this box she had made for herself for so many years now. She had wanted that. She would never have pushed out of it on purpose, but now . . .

Ben had broken something in her. He had broken them.

She wanted to get back at him.

She and Sam walked into the theater, and she saw the back of Soraya's head, her blond bun unmistakable.

"Over there." Nora grabbed his hand, not in an intimate way, but a familiar one, and dragged him toward the seats. She ignored the way the contact with his skin made her feel. It was just this moment. This moment that felt wild and reckless and like anything was possible.

The feeling of imminent magic in the midst of triumph that had been lingering around them all for days.

This strange excitement that had covered what had been the worst couple of months for the three of them and had turned it all into something brilliant.

Nora met Soraya's gaze and saw a question in her eyes she ignored.

Soraya looked back down quickly, and Nora noticed there were messages flashing on her phone in rapid succession.

"What's that?"

Soraya made an exasperated sound. "It's getting kind of insane. Pastor John got my number, probably from Kristi. He's been calling me since Sunday. And now he's texting. Nonstop. He's supposed to be here tonight. His and Stephanie's kids are in the play. Of course, they're not together right now."

"Why is he trying to get in touch with you?"

"I don't know. I haven't wanted to talk to them. It's all . . . I don't have anything to do with it."

"Except I heard your magic created the situation." Sam didn't sound skeptical, exactly, but he also didn't sound fully sincere.

Nora elbowed him, and he made a gruff sound. "Don't make fun of it. I'll hex you."

"I wasn't making fun," he said.

Soraya looked uncomfortable. "You told him?"

"She tells me everything."

Nora's stomach did another uncomfortable flip. "He doesn't believe us anyway."

"It's pretty undeniable." Soraya looked more woeful than excited about that. "I mean, it would be awfully coincidental for that particular video to play at that time without something behind it."

"Agreed." Sam clearly saw no point in arguing.

Soraya looked up, and Nora followed her gaze. She vaguely recognized Pastor John Pruitt standing in the aisles, scanning the crowd.

"I'll go talk to him," Soraya muttered, and got up out of her seat and scooted past Sam and Nora.

"I think we're making waves," Nora said, looking around.

Sam frowned. "Really?"

"Hey." She took her phone out, holding it in front of them, and flipped the camera around to face them. "Smile."

He looked handsome and uncomfortable in the photo, giving her side-eye that could never have been called affectionate. She rolled her eyes. And then, without overthinking it, she opened her text chain with Ben. Going to Daisy's play tonight. Then she popped the photo in the text and sent it.

"What the hell are you doing?" Sam asked.

"Nothing." She tried to sound innocent, but she wasn't innocent, so that made it tough.

Sam frowned, a deep groove between his brows. "Are you . . . are you trying to make him jealous?"

"He has a problem with you." Her voice was small, the confidence she felt a moment ago drained away by his anger.

"Yeah, I know." Sam looked legitimately disgruntled. "Jesus, at least ask me before you bring me into your drama."

"Sam, you're my best friend. You're permanently in my drama."

Her phone rang. Ben.

"Oh, look at that. He called your bluff," Sam said.

"I'm not answering it. He said he didn't want to speak to me. And anyway, he's cheating on me. Last time he called, it was to give me an audio-erotic experience that made me want to die. Let him wonder."

"Yeah. Great. Let him wonder."

Soraya

"John, hi," she whispered. "Is Stephanie here?"

She looked around and didn't like the fact that she had an audience for this interaction.

"Somewhere," he said. "I need to know what you know."

"I didn't know anything about their affair. I didn't leave him because of Stephanie."

She had issues with John.

He'd been one of the people who had absolutely thought she needed to go back to David.

He hadn't been on her side.

But if she'd known his wife was cheating on him with David, regardless of how he'd treated her, she would've made sure he knew.

She was glad David had been embarrassed on the level he'd been. She didn't feel as triumphant about other people being dragged into it. She knew her husband wasn't faithful. She genuinely felt bad that John had discovered his wife wasn't in a room full of his congregants.

Her own baggage with the church aside.

"He's your husband," he said.

The words made it clear he didn't truly believe she hadn't known. Made it clear he still felt she was responsible in some way.

Anger spiked inside her, hot and fast. It didn't matter that he was the senior pastor of the church she'd gone to for years. It didn't matter that she'd once seen him as a spiritual leader.

She didn't need him to tell her what was right and wrong, not now. Not anymore.

"I didn't know. But I did know he wasn't faithful to me, and I knew I couldn't stand to be with a man who didn't honor me the way I did him." She took a deep breath. "You didn't support me. No one in the church did. I already knew he wasn't a good man. Now you see it, but only now that it affects you. And you're *still* trying to blame me. *Still.* Why don't you lay blame on the person who deserves it for once? Because it isn't me. I am not taking the weight of his sins."

She felt alive. Filled with righteous fury. Filled with certainty. "He's not my problem anymore. I left him. I'm not going to be your example of sacrificial love. I'm not going to be at fault for all his transgressions. How does any of this make sense? That women are at fault for everything and yet in charge of nothing. That women are expected to have the greater ability to forgive, to carry the weight of men's sins, and yet we're supposed to be weaker than them. I feel sorry for you right now, but you are *part* of this. Put the blame where it belongs. Not on me."

She turned and walked away, shaking. She'd really done it now. She had blown up at her pastor. She would never be welcome back again.

The truly wonderful thing she realized as she walked back to Sam and Nora was that she didn't care.

Daisy

The play felt like a triumph.

For the past couple of months, Daisy had felt like she'd been treading water wearing a life jacket made of lead. Like she was going to sink to the bottom completely, and there would be no way she could do it all.

But she had.

The kids had been amazing, including her own. The sets were fantastic. And when the play closed and the curtain dropped, Marjorie, the director of the theater board, called her up to take a bow.

She saw Jonathan, mainly because Amberly was standing and clapping and hopping. She pointed at Daisy's dress—she had worn the emerald one—and gave her a thumbs-up. Jonathan, meanwhile, didn't seem to notice at all.

Daisy scanned the crowd for Zach.

Marjorie handed her a giant bouquet of flowers, and she looked down at them, then up at Zach. Because she knew they were actually from him, and he wasn't giving them to her in public out of respect.

But she knew they were from him all the same.

She felt like she was standing on top of a summit. It wasn't *everything*. Her whole life wasn't sorted out. But she had managed to do this. For the kids. For Alexandra, who should've been there helping, but was still in the hospital, unable to.

She'd done it. She wasn't defeated by this. By the hideous, awful thing she'd gone through.

She was still standing.

Then she looked and saw her friends. Soraya was standing up and clapping, with Nora next to her, and Sam on the other side of Nora.

It meant so much to have friends.

She'd been so sure her life was over when Jonathan walked out the door. Her life had shrunk down to him. Him and the kids and their house.

Over the years, she hadn't kept up with all her friendships, hadn't kept up with herself. And yet, there were all these people here for her. And she felt like herself. Her friends had waited for her, and so had Daisy. The girl she'd been. The one she'd lost touch with all that time ago.

Who used to sing but didn't now.

But had, in Soraya's kitchen.

Who had been desperately in love with Zachary Woods on the TV screen, and who now got to go to bed with him pretty much every night. Her dreams weren't over. Her dreams were just starting.

Daisy felt magic. Right then, she felt absolutely magic.

Chapter Twenty-Two

Nora

Love bleeds life on all it touches.
Revenge is a poison that withers the
weeds and spares not the flowers.

—*Rules for Witches*

Sam had left quickly after the play the night before, and Nora felt weird about the whole night.

She wished she hadn't taken the picture. That she hadn't used him to be petty. It wasn't fair to him. She just hadn't been . . . She'd been thinking about the way Soraya's husband had gotten some comeuppance. The way that Daisy would be able to pop up in Jonathan's face one of these days bragging about how she was banging Zach, and Nora felt like she had nothing. But she had a weird feeling that she'd hurt Sam, and she really didn't like that.

"What's wrong?" Soraya asked when they were midway through their shift, Nora hanging out over the counter of the coffee nook, Madison and Soraya working diligently in their little space.

"I'm a bad friend," Nora wailed.

"No, you aren't." Soraya was gentle but firm.

How far they'd come.

"Why?" Madison asked.

"It's a long story. Actually, it's a really short story. My husband is in Chile, and he's cheating on me."

"Ouch." Madison winced.

"He doesn't know that I know, because I'm waiting to confront him in person. If I do it on the phone, he can just block my number. Or hang up on me. I don't want him to be able to get away with that. But . . . I have a friend, who is a man . . ."

"Oh," said Soraya, clearly picking up on where Nora was going.

"I took a picture with him last night and sent it to my husband, because I knew it would get under his skin. Because he has a little bit of an issue with Sam."

"Why?" Madison asked.

"Because he's a man and I'm a woman."

"Yeah," she said.

"I mean, that's how I feel, Madison," said Nora. "He and I have been platonic friends since we were kids."

The words felt dishonest on her tongue, and she couldn't say why. Maybe because when she had touched his hand last night, she had felt something more. Something different. Maybe because the fact she knew she could use him the way she had to get at Ben spoke to something she wasn't ready to admit.

"Your husband sounds like a throwback. In a bad way."

"Agreed."

"Did Sam say he was mad at you?" Soraya asked.

"No. But I feel like garbage."

"Don't worry about it!" Daisy shouted from across the room.

"Eavesdropping," Nora shot back.

"You talk loud. Anyway, I'm sure he understands. You're in a weird place."

"Yes. But that isn't an excuse to be petty at the expense of my best friend."

"I'd let you do it with me." Daisy's offer was both sincere and unhelpful.

"Thank you, Daisy. Somehow, I don't think that would have the same effect on him."

"I don't really understand these men. Why not ask for an open relationship?" Madison sounded sincerely dumbfounded.

"Because I don't think they want polyamory. I think they want to inflate their egos."

"Ethical nonmonogamy seems like the better choice to me," Madison said.

Of course it did. Because she was in her twenties and had lived the sort of privileged life where she was only just now beginning to see the complications that existed in being human.

"I don't think that would be for me." Soraya took muffins out of a tin she had brought down from her apartment and put them into the display case.

"How do you know if you don't try it?" Madison asked.

"Well, you can't just . . . you can't just try something like that?"

She shrugged. "Why *not*? How do you know what you like if you don't try it? If you don't like it, then it's just a mistake."

"Just a mistake?" Soraya laughed. "There is no such thing as just a mistake."

"Oh no, there definitely is." Madison tapped her fingers on a mug just before she put it up on the shelf. "I can list mine if you want, but it's long. And I don't know all their names."

Of course, Soraya wouldn't feel that way. Because for her, it was all heaven or hell.

Nora would've said she saw things in a totally different way. But it hit her right then that she didn't. Everything felt like high stakes to her because when she'd been a child, doing the wrong thing could get her thrown out of her mother's house. Out of any of the houses she'd lived in. It could cost her safety and survival. She had internalized that. Doing the wrong thing could have very real consequences, and nothing about the current situation made her feel differently.

Sam was another person she could never make a mistake with, and she was very worried that last night she had.

They closed the store for the night, and Daisy had to leave quickly to get her kids, while Soraya seemed antsy to get up to her apartment. Nora said goodbye to Madison, which left only herself and Aggie, who had been in and out all day seeing to various errands.

"Can I trouble you with some help getting these herb bundles down, Nora?"

Nora looked up at all the herbs hanging above the counter, drying so they could be made into teas and tinctures and spells. "Of course."

She hoisted herself up onto the counter.

"I do have a ladder," Aggie said.

"Oh, I don't need that."

Aggie's laughter was deep and loud. "Oh, Nora, you like to take the difficult path."

Nora made a scoffing sound as she reached up and freed a bundle of rosemary. "Or the difficult path likes to choose me." She tucked the bundle under her arm as she moved to the next.

"When there is a ladder and you choose to climb onto the counter, I think it can be argued you chose the difficulty, my dear."

"Metaphorically, though." Nora snagged a bundle of lavender.

"Yes," Aggie said, without elaborating.

Nora frowned as she moved on to the wormwood.

"Do you know what wormwood is used for?" Aggie asked.

"I wouldn't even know what it was if you hadn't told me the day you put it up."

"It's for breaking hexes and banishing evil. There are certain challenges that come to us, and we have no control over them. There are certain painful events visited on us that we can only try to ward off. One thing I love about herbal magic is it's active. You have to touch the herbs, choose them, smell them. You have to touch your magic. You have to claim it."

Nora took the rest of the herbs down and refused to admit that squatting back down on the counter to try to lower herself to the floor with full hands was in fact the harder path.

She spread the bundles out in front of Aggie, who smiled at her and picked up a small satchel. "What was that love spell of yours, Nora? 'I have the love I deserve'?" She picked some leaves from one of the bundles. "Mint. For cleansing. Cinnamon for luck and prosperity." She added a stick of cinnamon to the bag. "Basil, which many use for wealth, but what is love but the most precious thing beyond price?" She pulled petals off a dried pink rose. "Roses for romance." She reached into a bin beneath the counter and took out a small pink-and-gray stone. "Rhodochrosite. It's for self-love. Because all great loves start from within." She pushed the bag to Nora. "You have to choose each ingredient. Just like you have to choose to have anything you seek."

There was a lump in Nora's throat she couldn't explain. One of the side effects of not having her mom, her grandma, in her life was she'd never been able to benefit from the wisdom of women who were older than her. Who cared about her and wanted her to succeed. Even though she was being lectured and Nora hated to be told what to do, she hadn't realized how much she might want to be told what to do like this.

This was the kind of vulnerability she usually wanted to run from.

Instead, she took the bag and put it in her purse. "Thank you."

"You don't have to take the hardest road." Aggie reached out and squeezed Nora's hand. "Good night, my dear."

Nora sucked in a sharp breath. "Good night."

She turned away, the spell in her purse, and paused when her phone buzzed.

Do you want to come to my place and watch the Thursday night game, and eat chicken wings?

Sam.

The relief she felt that he wasn't angry. That he wanted to see her.

Yes.

They didn't usually hang out at his house; they normally chose neutral ground somewhere.

She wanted to see Sam because she wanted to feel connected to somebody. She had just been thinking about how high stakes every single relationship in her life felt. And it felt . . . affirming but also frightening to go and be with him now.

She was going anyway. When she pulled up to the house, she viciously banished any reservations that she had, because it was Sam who she had known her entire life.

But the scary thing was, she had become a version of herself she didn't know at all. But that was a problem for another time. She just needed her friend. Her stability. Her comfort.

"That was quick." He grinned at her. "You must be hungry."

A heavy weight shifted in her chest, like a well was uncovered inside her.

He was so familiar, and yet in that moment, he also felt like something new. Or maybe it was that she was looking at him in a way she had never truly let herself do before.

Every time she had started down that path, she had put a stop to it. Because certain traumas were survivable. Like losing her mom, losing her grandma, even losing Ben felt surmountable. But life didn't feel particularly possible without Sam.

Sam was her prized possession. Once she had realized how much he mattered, she had put him in a glass case, trying to preserve their feelings for each other in that exact same place. That safe spot. So they would never wear out or get tired. So that they would never become something unmanageable. So that they would never change.

He was a collectible. She wanted him, their relationship, to stay in this mint condition forever.

But the longing inside her didn't allow for that.

"Yeah," she said. "Just really want some chicken."

"And to watch sweaty men tackle each other."

"Naturally."

As she always did when she went to Sam's house, she felt a swelling of pride as she walked through the neat entryway and into his living room. There was a tray of chicken wings and bowls of chips, along with two opened beers. "I love that you have this house," she said. "It's miraculous. All things considered."

"Yeah. It is."

She grabbed a plate and piled it high before sitting at the farthest end of the couch from him. Keeping distance between their bodies seemed like the best practice.

This wasn't usually a problem, but everything just felt unstable. And with all the instability, she worried, she really worried, she would do something to jostle this mint-condition friendship in its glass case. Because she was a ruiner. If one thing was true, it was that.

She drove everyone away from her. Eventually.

She took a breath, ready to apologize for last night. She owed him that, even though he wasn't acting mad about it.

"My dad died."

All her problems and her apology were momentarily forgotten. She stared at him, her heart squeezing tight. "Oh, I'm so sorry. When . . . when?"

"A month or so ago, apparently, but the word just got back to me. Some half brother sent me a message. He was in jail."

"Your half brother or your dad?"

"Both. But . . . yeah. Anyway."

"Are you . . . okay?"

"Not really. But that's true of anything concerning my dad. My family."

"My whole shitty family is still alive," she said. "At least as far as I know."

The one thing she knew about Sam's dad was that he had once gotten angry at Sam for drinking one of his beers and had beaten him with a shoe. Also that he was a drug dealer, and so he was often in and out of jail.

His mom was a sex worker who was hooked on the drugs his dad was dealing. She also knew he loved his parents.

That was the awful, complicated truth they both knew. Drugs and neglect didn't stop you from wishing your parents would magically transform into a happy sitcom mom and dad. Betrayal, abuse, didn't knock the affection out of you instantly.

"It's just so . . . bland. He never changed. He never reached out. He's dead at sixty-five because he was a hard man who lived a hard life, and now that's it. It's never going to be fixed. It's never even going to be better. Or worse. I'm never going to go yell at him for making my childhood terrible or . . . for hurting my mother." He paused. "I don't know where she is anyway."

She and Sam had spent their childhoods being alone. But this was a different kind of alone. There was a finality to it. Maybe nobody else would be able to understand, but she did. "Fuck him, and I'm sorry. I'm really sorry."

She didn't move to hug him, which seemed like a crappy thing to do because he had hugged her when she found out about Ben. But she was afraid to touch him. Moments like this underscored why. She knew everything about him. She knew why this hurt him, and how it hurt him. That it was a complex grief made of anger and sorrow and words that would now be left unsaid forever. Someday, when she lost her grandmother and her mom, she'd need this. The kind of knowing that came from years and didn't require a big explanation.

"Thanks, Nora. I knew you were the one I needed to see."

There was a heaviness to that, and it only increased the ache inside her. She was the one Sam needed. Because they were both so messed up, they understood each other's brand of it.

Then it just seemed absurd for her to sit over on her side of the couch. To not offer comfort. To not give him physical affection when who else would? Who had ever hugged either of them?

She'd had Ben for a while, but it wasn't the same. He didn't know all the parts of her. And yes, he touched her, kissed her. They had sex, but how could you comfort somebody when you didn't really know what all their demons were?

She and Sam needed each other. She moved to him and wrapped her arms around him, bringing his head down against her chest as she rested her head on his.

Her heart was beating fast, her whole body felt warm, but she had just gone ahead and grabbed hold of him without overthinking it. Now they were touching in so many places, he was hot against her, and . . .

He lifted his head, and it was very close to hers. She touched his face, dragging her fingertips along his cheekbone, down to the sculpted line of his jaw, and he moved, pushing her back slightly on the couch, bringing himself over top of her, his thumb and forefinger gripping her chin, and there was no way to interpret the hold as platonic.

I have the love I deserve.

She thought about that spell in her purse. It was almost like she could feel the heat from it.

Her heart was beating so hard, she thought she might die. She couldn't tell if she wanted to move closer or move away. But she was scared.

She was so damn scared.

"Sam," she said, her voice pleading. "Sam I . . . Please don't. Please." But her breathing was labored, and she ached between her legs, which made lies out of her pleas.

He listened immediately, because he was Sam. Because he was the most trustworthy man she'd ever known. He moved away from her, and then there was distance between them. Profound distance. She reached out and put her hand on his shoulder. "Sam . . ."

Her phone started to ring.

"Shit. Let me just . . ." She didn't recognize the number. She frowned. Then she answered. "Hello?"

"This is Sandy at Mercy Hospital. You're listed as Ben Clarke's emergency contact."

"What?"

"Is this Nora Clarke?"

"Yes. Yes, it is. I . . . Was Ben in an accident?"

"He's being airlifted here in serious condition from a hospital in Chile."

"Oh. When . . . when will he be there? What happened . . . ?"

"He should be here in forty minutes or so. The doctor can give you details when you arrive."

"I'll be there." She hung the phone up, her heart in her throat. "They're bringing Ben to Mercy Hospital. They airlifted him from a hospital in Chile . . . He . . . he had an accident."

"Shit," said Sam. "Let's . . . let's go to the hospital."

It was that quick. They'd been about to kiss, maybe, and now he was springing right into action to help her deal with Ben. Her chest was sore, a churning sensation in her midsection making breathing almost impossible.

What if Ben died?

What if he died and she never got any clarity in their relationship or what was happening or why he'd cheated on her or . . . ?

Maybe that wasn't what should matter, but it felt like what mattered.

"You don't have to take me," she said, even as she got into Sam's truck.

"You're not driving yourself. You look like hell."

"Gee, thanks."

"Do you want to hear that you look totally normal after finding out your husband was in a terrible accident?"

"No. No, I . . ." A tear slid down her cheek. "I don't know what's happening."

It was a drive to the next town to get to the hospital, and Ben was there when they arrived, but she couldn't go in to see him yet.

Sam hung back in the waiting room when they finally did let her go back.

"You're the patient's wife?" the doctor asked, her expression creased with sympathy.

"Yes. What happened?"

"From the notes we got from the other hospital, he slipped during a hike and fell down a mountain. They got him stabilized and thought it would be best if we got him back home."

"So he's stable." Relief washed through her.

The doctor nodded. "Yes. He's not awake right now, but that's due to the heavy amount of painkillers he's on. He has severe lacerations and broken bones."

"But he's not going to die?"

"If he was critical, they wouldn't have flown him back to the States, though I haven't had a chance to make a thorough evaluation."

Nora nodded and braced herself to walk into the hospital room. He wasn't going to die. He had to talk to her.

"Can I see him?"

"Of course."

She pushed down on the door handle and walked in, sweeping the curtain aside. Ben. She hadn't seen him for over a month now, and she hadn't expected to see him like this. All his belongings were in clear plastic bags next to the bed. Including his phone. She could see it lighting up inside the bag, texts and missed calls flashing over the screen.

She moved to the bedside and looked down at him. His limbs were in traction, his neck in a brace. His face was familiar, undamaged. He looked like he was sleeping peacefully, just as he'd done for years beside her before he'd bounced off to Chile to find himself.

"What did you find?" she whispered, leaning in and letting her hand hover over him. She was tempted to touch him. To push his hair back off his face. Did she have the right to do that anymore?

His mustache had grown into a beard.

When she'd met him, he'd been clean shaven. Through most of their marriage, it had been the mustache. Maybe it was good she couldn't look at him now and see back into the past. See the man she'd met, who'd gotten past her barriers and convinced her that love was something she wanted to try.

She'd wanted this to work so very, very badly.

She just stood there, hovering, not sure if she should touch his hand or his face or not at all. His phone lit up again, and she turned her focus to the bag. To the phone.

Her answers were on the phone.

She'd never been one to snoop in Ben's business. She'd let him go off to South America without questioning him too deeply. Because she'd wanted to trust him. She'd always wanted this to be the thing she'd dreamed about, and she'd let herself believe it was because it felt good to believe it.

Whether he was hers or not, whether she should touch him or not, the answer was in his phone.

She moved to the bag, hesitating before she picked it up and opened it, the ziplock making a loud noise over the top of all the beeping in the room. Announcing to the world: *I can't trust my husband.*

But she couldn't.

He'd put them in this position. He'd abandoned her. As Sam had said, he'd left her alone while he'd dealt with his issues, but he hadn't done a thing to include her. She'd been trying to be . . . open minded or cool.

No.

She'd been trying to not be a bother.

The realization stopped her in place. She'd have never said that was her. She'd been so sure she was herself—her brash, bold self—all the time. But not with him. She'd left her personality confined to her office. She hadn't told him it hurt her that he was leaving. She hadn't even let herself feel the hurt. She'd told herself she had to be okay with it. She'd prioritized his feelings, his needs, over her own because she'd convinced herself she was too damaged to be allowed to have the final say in anything. That he was the one who knew how life, marriage, and relationships were supposed to be because he'd grown up in a situation that was functional and she hadn't.

She'd convinced herself that he was whole, and she was half.

That she would always have to follow him because he knew how to walk on a road that wasn't broken.

But she hadn't listened to herself. To her own needs. To her own intuition.

She'd buried it.

Heart in her throat, she took the phone out of the bag and held it in her palm. It saw her face and tried to unlock, shivering because it didn't recognize her and asking for a pin.

She entered it—his mom's birthday, it had always been that.

It unlocked, and she looked at the screen. At the bright-red notifications on his messages numbering in the hundreds now. At the apps and icons. His D&D app. His bird-watching app. The little weird things that made him *him*.

Then she opened the messages.

Tara.

That was the top name, the most messages.

That was her name. *Examine meee* Tara.

With her heart in her throat, Nora clicked on the name and looked at the messages.

I just need to know if you're okay.

I know you said not to message you but I'm so worried.

They won't tell me anything because I'm not on any of your paperwork. They just took you away and I have no idea if you're even alive.

Divorced from the context of all this, Tara's messages were sort of sad. But she wasn't on any of his papers because Nora was on them. Because Nora was his wife, and Tara was a woman he'd met only a month or so ago. Because Nora had given Ben years of her time, her love, her body.

She scrolled up blindly until she hit a photo. Not explicit. Just the two of them. Tara was holding on to him and gazing at him with adoration. Love ya!

The accompanying message was enough. She didn't need to see any more.

She stared at the picture, trying to see what Ben was thinking, feeling. She didn't see the same level of adoration in his eyes that she saw in Tara's. He looked like Ben. It made her feel sick. Was she Tara? Gazing at him in utter, total adoration while he looked . . . fine?

While he looked like he was just . . . going through the motions of their relationship?

Even the affair didn't make him look adoring or giddy.

It was a weird thing to be upset about. But God, if he was going to sleep with another woman, shouldn't he be beyond control? Enraptured? Enchanted? Something?

Instead, he just looked like some guy. Standing there with any woman.

It was maybe worse than seeing a video of them screwing.

Seeing him look at Tara like he'd been married to her for ten years. Seeing the disparity between her adoration and his, like she was looking in a mirror of her own life.

She'd been so happy. Was she rewriting the truth now to make it hurt less? Or had she really been with a man who just didn't see her or love her the way she'd loved him?

She scrolled up just one more screen length and could see that he'd . . .

Sent Tara a picture of his dick.

She threw the phone down on the bed. *God.* Why were they all the same? Why? Why were they all like this? Soraya's good-Christian husband and her hipster-atheist husband and Daisy's blue-collar construction-worker husband. Why? Why had they given so much for so long to these assholes who took more pictures of their junk than they'd ever taken of the women who loved them?

She sat in a chair near the bed, head in her hands. She wasn't crying. She was just . . .

Ben groaned, and she jerked her head upward in time to see him fidgeting beneath his blanket. She stood and moved to the bed, his eyelids fluttering as she stared down at him. Every movement he made pissed her off even more. Because it was evidence he wasn't dying, which cleared the field for her fury.

His eyes fluttered more and then opened.

That was when her fury exploded. "Good morning, sunshine," she said. "It's time to wake up. Our marriage is over."

Chapter Twenty-Three

Soraya

To know your body is to know your magic.

—Rules for Witches

Soraya rushed downstairs to the apothecary to see if she'd left her purse there. She'd put in for a grocery order and was going to need her ID to get the wine and hadn't been able to find it anywhere.

Thankfully, Aggie was still inside with one light on, standing at the counter arranging herbs.

Soraya went to the door and knocked. The lack of surprise on Aggie's face when she looked up and saw Soraya could have easily been attributed to the fact that Soraya's purse was in there.

But it felt like something more.

Aggie left her post at the counter and crossed the expanse of the shop to open the door.

"Oh, thank you, Aggie," she said.

"You're very welcome."

"I left my purse, I think. I walked right out with my phone and keys in my pocket and didn't realize I didn't have my bag. I'll just check the back."

"Of course. Are you in a hurry?"

Soraya opened her phone app and looked at the grocery delivery. The shopper was still only halfway through her order.

"No." She poked her head in the back, saw her purse on the peg and grabbed it, and went back out to the front of the shop.

It was so cozy in here to her now. All the little shelves with their crystals, tinctures, and tonics. The teas and herbs, tarot cards, and beautiful objects meant for altars or just to be used as talismans.

How strange that she'd felt so differently about it only a couple weeks ago.

"I was wondering if you had a moment to talk about tea."

"Oh?"

"I think you're the perfect person to handle tea blends when I'm not in the shop."

"Oh, but I . . ." She knew that for Aggie, tea was a source of magic. The blends weren't just about how they tasted, but what they could do.

Madison wasn't even allowed to make these kinds of teas. Aggie did blends and also made single cups for customers.

"Soraya, you're my kitchen witch. You're the one who can make these magical."

A witch.

She'd been doing a lot of research on this, and she knew there were many people who considered themselves adherents to their faith while being witches. Witches didn't have to have gods associated with the craft. They could worship whatever god they wanted, or none at all.

It made her feel more comfortable with the label. Aggie, of course, only meant it with the utmost kindness.

"These are all the new teas we have, and here are some of the activators for different spells. We have teas for positivity: chamomile, honey, and lemon. Healing tea: black tea, vanilla, cinnamon, and honey." She waved her hand over three other bins. "There are rosemary and rosehips, and elderberries are other good additives. Now, the most common teas we get asked for here promote women's sexuality."

If it had been Nora, Soraya might have thought Aggie was testing her. Trying to see if she could get a reaction out of her.

"Let's practice making a cup."

"Are you going to drink it?" Soraya asked.

Aggie looked at her, her eyes sparkling as she pushed the lever on her electric kettle and started the water warming. "Do you think that's amusing because I'm a crone?"

"Not at all!" Soraya said, feeling instantly awful. "I didn't mean it like that. I just didn't realize you were . . . or that you had . . ."

"It isn't for me. I don't need it." Aggie smiled mischievously. "You, on the other hand . . ."

It was like Aggie could read her mind. Like she knew about the date and all of Soraya's associated worries and fears and desires.

"I'm tired of men," she lied.

"Who said it had to be men?"

"I'm not into women." She frowned. "I don't think."

"You know you can just have sexuality all on your own. It doesn't have to be for anyone else. You can feel beautiful, you can feel desire, and you can let yourself express that desire just for you, just with you."

Soraya blinked. "Well, isn't that . . . I know it's not evil or anything, I *do* know that. But it just seems like if you don't have someone with you . . ."

"It's not wrong to feel good."

That was revelatory in a way she felt it shouldn't be at thirty-five.

"Follow my instructions." Aggie took her electric kettle and poured steaming water into a teapot. "Rose, hibiscus, and calendula."

Soraya took a pinch of each and added them to the pot.

"Red clover, elderberries, cinnamon, lemon balm."

Soraya added those slowly to the steaming water.

"Then add black tea leaves and a bit of dried apple."

She did, and put the lid on the teapot.

"Now we let it steep." Aggie looked at her. "It's rare I've ever met a woman so afraid of her own power, her own body, her own feelings.

Soraya, what you want matters. God did not create you with all this love, creativity, and magic to hide it forever. Tell me, is the shame you feel from a divine source or from the people around you?"

Soraya glanced down. "It's from the people around me."

"They needed you to feel fear and shame, to be sure you would ignore the beating of your own heart, the burning of your own conscience. You were taught to ignore it, and told you had to fall in line. Isn't it written in your Bible that God would often raise someone up to speak against the ones in power? Didn't Deborah speak prophecy and lead her people to victory? Wasn't it up to Jael to kill her enemy? Women must stand in their power, in their conviction, just as much as any man. So should you, as much as any leader in any church. Those around you who are styled as leaders can be wrong."

Soraya took a breath. "I am afraid. I was always told that I needed a leader. That women were the weaker ones. I went from my father being my leader to my husband, and I've never been my own."

"You are your own already. You just need to embrace it."

Aggie picked up the teapot and put a tea strainer on top of a small purple teacup with a crooked gold handle, and poured the tea into it, all the leaves and petals collecting in the strainer. She took it off the top of the cup and pushed it toward Soraya.

She lifted it and took a sip, the spiced, floral notes a shock to her senses.

She let it wash over her as she sat and drank it in silence. Did she feel more beautiful, or did she just want to? Did she feel more confident, or was that just wishful thinking?

"Magic is all about taking the energy around you, the deep desires of your soul, the beautiful, sparkling crackle of desire, and making it into something you can touch, something you can hold," Aggie said, like she could read Soraya's thoughts. "It's about taking hold of feelings and transforming them into something that serves you."

Soraya's phone buzzed, letting her know her delivery was on the way. She took pleasure in her last few sips of tea, then she went to rinse the cup.

"Oh, don't worry about that," Aggie said. "I'll clean up."

"Thanks, Aggie. For everything."

She carried her purse out to the curb and waited until the delivery arrived. She showed her ID, then took the wine bottle and other bags, and as best she could, she walked to the stairwell door and managed to wrench it open.

In her infinite freedom, she'd gotten a whole bunch of things David and the boys would never eat, along with a ten-pound bag of flour because she had burned through what she had baking for the apothecary. An enjoyable aspect of the job, as was learning how to make drinks, along with her newfound permission to do the special tea blends.

She was trying to embrace and enjoy the novelty of living by herself too. It was different. It was something she had never experienced, and the ability to please herself was fun, even if she would have traded it immediately to have the boys back.

Not that she had a choice. All her texts went unanswered, as did her phone calls.

Even after everything. But then, knowing David like she did, he was doubling down. How could he admit he had done wrong after all that? After the way he had looked her in the eye and tried to blame *her*?

Bracing her arm against the apartment door as she dug in her purse for her keys, she lost her grip on the bag and grabbed the top of it quickly, growling when it tore and the bag of flour and her bell peppers, cilantro, and noodles all went crashing to the floor. The door across the hall opened, and it was like a Pavlovian response. Her whole body took notice.

She was starving, then, but not for a sweet treat.

She turned, pushing her hair out of her face as she tried to smile. "Just a minor grocery accident."

They had a date. But she hadn't talked to him since, really. They had made a plan to have dinner in three days, and she didn't know if it was weird to see her date before the date, or if that was only seeing the bride before a wedding.

She felt warm suddenly. Flushed.

Aroused.

The tea.

No. There was no way that tea was this powerful. Or maybe it was, when combined with Declan's raw masculine beauty.

"Let me help you," he said.

"Oh, thank you."

He bent down, and the scent of his cologne made her stomach swoop. He smelled amazing. Unfamiliar. It was like having a crush. Something she could barely remember because she'd been with David for so long, and their relationship hadn't felt like that since before they were married.

He scooped up all the items and stood. He was close. So close. She curled her fingers into fists, dug her nails into her palms. "I'll just . . . unlock the door."

He was going to come into her house. Before the date. Because he was holding her groceries, and not for any other reason. It wasn't for any other reason.

She swallowed hard. Then she fitted her key into the lock and turned it, pushing the door open. "Come in," she said.

He did, walking through the living room and into the kitchen, putting the groceries on the table.

"That was my fault. I trusted the paper bag too much."

"Thwarted by too much trust." He smiled, and she tried to ignore how hard her heart was beating. He was dangerously attractive. There was an interesting energy around him. He was authoritative, comfortable with himself, and if she would've been asked what she thought he did, owning a store that specialized in tabletop games wouldn't have been her answer. He didn't have a geeky vibe to him at all. He was tall and muscular, broad chested. His dark hair was long, pushed back out of his face. He wore glasses, which did make him look slightly studious, but it was kind of Clark Kent–ish in nature.

Like the glasses were a costume, and if he tore his shirt open, it would reveal the superhero underneath.

Well. There was a *thought*.

There was no reason for him to linger in the apartment. There was no reason for her to ask him to stay. There was definitely no reason for her to move closer to him. But she was.

She was in her magic.

His expression went deadly serious, the grooves by his mouth deepening as he looked down at her. She was so much shorter than he was—she was only one or two inches shorter than David—and Declan was tall. She just came to his shoulder, and it made her feel small and pretty. She reached up and touched his face before she could think better of it. Before she could second-guess herself.

He made a short, masculine sound and gripped her wrist, wrapping his fingers tightly around her. "Be careful," he murmured.

"I'm kind of tired of being careful, actually."

Before she could think better of it, she stretched up on her toes and wrapped her arms around his neck. He bent quickly, kissing her, hard and fast and deep.

She was dizzy.

When was the last time she had been kissed like this? Maybe never. Because when they had been dating, she and David had tried not to kiss like this, lest they fall into temptation, and then after they'd been married, he was so excited to get her naked, to get inside her, that kissing wasn't really the point.

But right now, kissing felt like the point.

His lips and teeth and tongue were hungry as he wrapped his arms around her, enveloping her completely. She clung to his shoulders, her toes lifting off the floor as he took the kiss even deeper.

She didn't want to think. She didn't want to overthink it, she didn't want to moralize it. She didn't want to decide if it was a mistake or growth or a step toward a future. She just wanted it to be. Not right or wrong, but just something that felt indescribably incredible.

She was the one who started tearing his clothes off. As she propelled them both through the living room, she stripped his shirt up off his body, gasping when her palm made contact with his muscular chest. Yes. Yes. Yes.

She wasn't sure if she was saying that out loud or if she was only saying it in her head. If it was just a chorus playing over and over inside her or if it was overflowing into the moment. It didn't really matter. She was beyond shame.

She couldn't remember the last time she had wanted something because it felt good. That she had surrendered to pleasure.

Maybe never. Just like these deep, long kisses, maybe the answer was never. Maybe this was the first.

She was only dimly aware of him taking her shirt off, undoing her bra and leaving it somewhere in the hall as they stumbled to her bedroom. He growled, curses on his lips as he drew back and looked at her body, as he lowered his head and started to kiss his way down her breasts.

She pushed her fingers through his hair as he sucked one tightened bud into his mouth, and pleasure exploded in her midsection.

This was losing control. This was giving in to temptation. This was that fast and furious roller coaster of desire straight to hell.

But she wasn't afraid. This was it. She finally knew. She finally understood. What it was to be reckless. What it was to want beyond the limits of your own propriety.

What a gift.

She had been wandering in the desert for way too long.

She had thought everything was okay. She had thought that the number of days she and David had sex a week spoke to the health of their marriage. That lying down and giving him what he wanted was the secret to a happy life, but she hadn't been enough. It hadn't been enough.

This felt like more than enough. It wasn't about sacrifice or duty or doing what she was supposed to. It was just about desire. Her desire. It rocked her world; it remade her into something new.

There was no sound in the room but their breathing, rustling clothes, his belt being whipped through the loops on his pants. The zipper came down, but she only managed to push his pants partway down his hips. He had her lying on her back, totally naked, his hands between her legs as he teased and tormented her, heightening her arousal to near-untold proportions.

Then he replaced his hand with his mouth, and she went up in flames, his hold on her bruising as he forced her hips down onto the mattress, forced her to surrender to the never-ending pleasure he was showing her.

It was about her, this moment, and yet it was clear he was enjoying it. It wasn't a sacrifice. It wasn't something he was doing to just try to get her off easily, a once-a-very-special-occasion act that existed only to trade for the reverse.

No, he was acting like this was the journey and the destination all rolled into one.

She came on a harsh cry, and he kissed his way up her body, draping her leg over his hip as he thrust into her, and she clung to his shoulders as he carried them both to the finish line. As he brought her to the peak yet again just as he cried out his own release.

"Oh, dammit," he said, his voice rough. "I didn't use a . . . a condom. I'm sorry . . ."

"I'm on the pill." She felt slightly dizzy. There were other considerations to think about when you hooked up with people you didn't know. Considerations that had never been a part of her life, never been a part of her reality except . . . Well, she had been sleeping with a man who was sleeping with other partners, so the truth of the matter was, if David hadn't been practicing safe sex . . .

She swallowed hard. "I'm fine, I think. My husband . . . He was cheating. But I saw a video of him screwing somebody else, and he was wearing a condom, so at least there's that."

"Oh, Soraya . . ."

"Yeah. So, as long as you don't do this all the time . . ."

"I don't," he said. "That's why I didn't even think of it."

They looked at each other for a long moment, and she wondered. She wondered if he was like her. If he had come out of a long-term relationship. But he didn't offer the information, and she didn't feel like she could ask.

"I never really did the irresponsible-teenage-behavior thing, so I guess this was my moment." She had expected to feel more embarrassed. But she wasn't.

He smiled just slightly, lifted his hand, and touched her face. He didn't run away.

"Are we still on for dinner?" she asked.

"Oh, definitely."

She looked away. "We did this backwards."

"I hope not, because that implies that this won't happen after dinner too."

She bit her lip and waited for an avalanche of guilt to drop on top of her, but it wasn't there. It wasn't there.

"I would like it to. As long as you do."

"I definitely do, Soraya, make no mistake."

"Good. Me too. I . . . I've never really dated. So I'm sorry if I'm bad at this."

"What exactly do you think you're bad at, because that was great." He actually looked like he'd been hit over the head, and she couldn't have received a nicer compliment.

"I was the good girl in high school. Boys weren't really knocking down the door to get to me because they knew I wasn't easy. Though it turns out I kind of am. All they would've had to do was carry a bag of groceries for me."

"Here I was hoping I was a little bit special." That made her chest feel tight. Did he want this to be something other than just sex? She had been so conditioned to believe that men who wanted sex like this, early and without strings, didn't want a relationship. That they didn't want anything more than an orgasm and to forget your name.

"Well, you are," she said. "I made my husband wait until he married me."

He laughed, and she couldn't tell if it was a shocked sound or an amused one. Maybe both.

"I should let you get to dinner," he said.

"Yeah." She was glad he didn't want to stay. Because she didn't want him to spend the night, oddly. She wanted her own space. She couldn't . . . The idea of spending the night with him made her feel claustrophobic. She was just now figuring out living on her own. She was figuring out sex for the sake of it. It had been *great* sex. She was glad they were going out. But it didn't need to be more than that.

Not right now.

"Okay. I'll see you in a couple of days." He said it affirmatively, not like a question.

"Yes. See you then. If I don't run into you in the hall first."

Just thinking about that made her heart rate pick up. Because if they ran into each other in the hall, maybe they would kiss each other. Maybe they would end up back in bed.

The excitement, the open-ended nature of it, the spontaneity, all of that was so foreign to her, and it really excited her.

They both got dressed, and he kissed her before he walked out the front door. She shut it and leaned against it for a moment, looking wistfully up at the ceiling. She waited for the guilt to descend, and eventually it did, while she was cooking, along with a healthy dose of fear. There were consequences for behavior like this. She'd always been told there were, and she believed it.

It's okay. You had sex. The world isn't going to end. It's not like you were a virgin.

No. She hadn't been a virgin. But until tonight, she'd only ever been with David.

He was with other people.

If a video of her with Declan were to be played somewhere? Well, he wasn't anyone's husband. She wasn't anyone's wife. It might be embarrassing, but it wouldn't break anything.

She'd wanted him. She had him.

If David got to behave that way, why didn't she?

Well. She had.

Whatever the consequences were, they would be hers.

Whatever the consequences were, she would gladly accept them.

They would be a small price to pay for the best sex of her life.

Chapter Twenty-Four

Daisy

The universe listens.

—Rules for Witches

She wasn't wearing a bra.

That was a stupid thing to realize right when she ran into the emergency room, but then the whole situation was very weird and very stupid. She'd been half naked and kissing Zach on his couch when she'd gotten a frantic call from Jonathan's mother that she needed to go to the ER to get the kids because they were there with Amberly and she was out of town.

Daisy's heart had stopped for a few seconds before she'd realized it wasn't the kids being admitted to the ER.

Jonathan had had an accident working on something in the garage and had been rushed to the hospital, and Amberly was there with all three kids.

So she'd gotten dressed as quickly as possible and driven down to the ER while Zach protested about her driving herself. But she had to have her car, because she had to have a car seat for Alden. Also, she was avoiding rolling into the ER with Zach. But her bra was at his house, so there was that.

She rushed across the room where Amberly was sitting, pouting, and staring at the kids who were in their pajamas. Avery was stoic. Wren was crying. Alden was down on his knees playing with a toy truck and looking unconcerned.

"Oh, Daisy!" Amberly flung her arms around Daisy's neck.

"Oh . . ." She patted the younger woman on the middle of her back. "It's . . . it's okay."

"Oh, God! It was awful." Amberly's face was streaked with tears, and there was blood on her pink shirt, which read, in glitter: Bonus Mom.

Irritation. Anger. Pity. Solidarity. Fear. Compassion. They hit Daisy one by one, so fast she could hardly decode one before the next hit.

"He's . . . okay?"

"I had to put his finger in a ziplock bag!"

"Oh!" She hadn't expected a detached finger.

"I've never seen anything so awful."

"But he's okay? I mean, they can put it back on, right?"

Amberly sniffed. "That's what they said, that they could reattach it."

"That's promising."

"It was bloody!" Alden shrieked.

Daisy knelt in front of him "Are you okay?"

Alden nodded. "Yes. I didn't cut my finger off."

She nodded, feeling somewhat shocked. "No. You didn't."

"Daddy cut his hand really bad," Wren said, her cheeks tearstained.

Daisy wiped one of the tears away. "I'm so sorry, sweetie. I'm sorry Daddy got hurt."

"Daddy said you'd probably laugh about it," Avery said.

Daisy worked to keep her face neutral. "Daddy was wrong about that. I don't think it's funny he got hurt." Though clearly if he had the breath in his lungs to talk shit about her in front of their kids while he was en route to the ER, he was fine enough. "I don't think it's funny that you're scared for him."

The ER doors opened, and she turned to look, right as Zach walked in. Her heart slammed against her breastbone. He was disheveled and sexy.

Did he have her bra with him?

He crossed quickly to where she and Amberly were and moved to stand next to Daisy, protective intensity radiating off him.

Amberly looked at Zach and . . . turned pink. "Zach Woods."

"Yeah," said Zach, looking between her and Daisy.

"I mean, I know you're, like, Jonathan's business partner, but we haven't met yet, and I binge-watched *Second Chance City* on streaming like three months ago, because I was five when it was on, so I didn't see it then, but you are amazing."

Zach shot Daisy a look, then he looked back at Amberly. "Thank you. I'm glad you enjoyed it."

"Jonathan hasn't seen it yet. I should make him watch it while he's recovering."

"That's . . . uh . . . nice." It was rare that Daisy had ever seen Zach lost for words, but Amberly had done it.

She noticed Amberly had blood on her hands too. She had been there for Jonathan when he was hurt. And she'd been there for the kids.

Those mixed feelings were even more intense now.

"You can go, Amberly," Daisy said. "I've got the kids."

"Are you sure?"

"Yeah. Of course. They need to get to bed, and you can go and be with him."

"Thank you." She walked quickly toward the counter and filled out a badge, and for some reason Daisy found herself standing there watching her. It was an out-of-body experience. If this had happened a few months ago, that would have been her worrying about Jonathan. It would have been her going back to see how he was doing.

Worrying about his hand and the future of the business.

"Are you okay?"

She turned to Zach, who was looking at her. "I don't know. But I need to get the kids home."

"I'll go with you."

She could protest. But she didn't want to.

The doors to the ER opened, and right as Amberly started to go in, Nora came rushing out, her eyes round. She looked past Daisy, over her shoulder, and Daisy noticed Sam for the first time since she'd come into the crowded room.

"Nora!" Daisy called out to her, and the two of them stood there staring at each other. As if this could get any weirder or more reminiscent of that moment they'd reconnected in Alexandra's hospital room what felt like a whole lifetime ago.

"What are you doing here?" Nora asked. "Is something wrong with your mom? Your grandma?"

Daisy shook her head. "Jonathan had an accident."

Nora didn't react, her expression flat for a full second before she blinked rapidly like she was trying to wake herself up. "What?"

"He . . ." Daisy shook her head, trying to get her thoughts together. "Power tools. He's going to be fine." Well, he might lose a finger, but he wouldn't die. "I had to come get the kids, they were with him and . . . well." She frowned. "Why are you here?"

"Ben. He had an accident while he was hiking."

Goose bumps rose on Daisy's arms, and right then she could see why Nora had paused like that. Why she'd looked shell shocked.

This couldn't be a coincidence. It couldn't be. There was karma. David getting caught being a cheater, that was karma. Dramatic karma, but karma all the same. Ben falling down a mountain? Unless he was getting a blow job at the time, that wasn't karma. That was something more.

"Is he . . . ?"

"He's going to be okay." Nora's eyes were glassy, her voice distant. "He'll be okay."

Sam didn't say anything, but he moved closer to Nora and put his arm around her. It was a possessive gesture, one that spoke volumes about them. Volumes Nora herself had never spoken, but that were becoming more and more apparent.

"Take care of your kids," Nora said. "I'll see you at work tomorrow."

"If I make it in."

"You know Aggie would let the kids come in."

It's true, she would.

She felt reluctant to leave Nora, but she knew she was taken care of as long as she was with Sam. "You can come over later if you want to," Daisy said.

"I . . . I think I'm okay."

Daisy nodded and gathered the kids.

She got the kids loaded into her car, and Zach followed in his outrageously expensive vehicle, adding to the out-of-body of it all.

Two of the three cheating husbands were in the hospital after having spells put on them. It would seem like a coincidence even without the magic. Now it seemed . . . Well, it seemed like much more than a coincidence.

She pulled into the driveway, and Zach pulled in behind her. Her chest went tight, and she got out of the car, opening the back door and starting to work on Alden's seat belt.

Avery and Wren were out of the car like a shot.

"I can unlock the door, Daisy."

She looked over her shoulder at Zach. "Um. Sure. My key is in my purse on the front seat."

She heard Zach getting the keys. "Come on, guys. Have you had dinner?" Zach was actually talking to the kids.

"No," Avery said, sniffing. "I'm hungry."

"Of course you are, it's getting really late. What's your favorite restaurant?"

Daisy's movements slowed, and she was basically just standing there hovering over Alden's car seat as Zach and the kids moved out of earshot.

"Mama." Alden tapped her on the nose, and she laughed.

"Sorry!"

"Are you sleepy?" Alden asked.

"Yeah," Daisy said, unbuckling the belt. "I am sleepy."

She lifted her little boy out of the seat, then set him down and watched him walk into the house. Zach appeared in the doorway and smiled at her.

Seeing him in her house like that . . .

Was it her house?

She wasn't sure about anything anymore. Except that seeing him here felt better than it did worse, that was for sure.

She collected her purse and closed the car door, walking into the house.

"We ordered Olive Garden," Zach said.

"You what?"

"Avery said he likes Olive Garden, so we ordered. They said you always get the alfredo, and I didn't know which one, so I got one with chicken and one without."

"Zach . . ."

"Sit down," he said, his voice authoritative.

God. He could tell her what to do all day every day and she would be okay with it.

When Zach told her what to do, she didn't feel powerless. If she did, she wouldn't like it. Zach had things taken care of. His orders made her feel safe. Made her feel like she wasn't carrying every single burden all on her own.

"I'm hungraaaaaay." Alden growled, and stamped around the kitchen like a tiny, inconvenienced T. rex.

"We ordered you spaghetti and meatballs," Zach said.

"Oh good!" Alden looked cheerful and much less like a dinosaur.

Daisy decided to busy herself getting plates out of the cabinet.

Zach took the stack from her hands, and their fingertips touched. What did this man even know about being domestic? And why was he so damned good at it?

"Thank you," she whispered.

"Dad got blood everywhere." Wren sat down at the table and rested her head on her forearms. "And he was swearing and shouting, and Amberly was crying."

Imagining the scene made Daisy's stomach wrench tight. "I'm sorry, Wrenny. That must have been really scary."

"Everything is bad now." Wren's voice was small.

This was a stark contrast to when they'd come home wild and sugared up the other night. They'd seemed in high spirits and seemingly unaffected by being shuffled back and forth between two households.

But then, seeing your father after he cut his finger off and having to go to the hospital and being kept hungry would tend to put kids in a low mood.

"Not everything, surely," Daisy said.

"Amberly has weird snacks like seaweed chips and cuts our cheese into stars with cookie cutters," Avery said.

"That sounds cute," Daisy said.

"It's dumb," said Avery. "She's not our mom. And Dad is either always at the gym or playing Xbox, and everything is bad."

Amberly was trying; Jonathan wasn't. The finger thing felt pretty karmic. "It was an upsetting day. It's probably not fair deciding that everything is bad the day someone cuts their finger off." She took a breath. "Okay, let's go do bath time while we wait for food. We have, what, forty minutes, Zach?"

"About that," he responded.

"I think when someone cuts their finger off, no one should have to take baths," Avery said sagely.

"Incorrect," Daisy replied. "Off you go."

There were two bathrooms with bathtubs, but it still took time to rotate everyone through. They were old enough now to do it themselves, which meant Daisy spent bath time lying face down on her bed trying to recover from the day, which she decided was a futile task around the time Wren was done and ready to have her hair brushed.

Alden scrambled up onto the bed while Daisy brushed his sister's hair, and he sat down on his knees, chin in his hands, jostling both of them with his movements.

"When are you and Dad moving back in together?" Wren asked.

Daisy paused. "What?"

"You aren't going to live apart forever, are you?"

She'd made a lot of assumptions about what the kids had seen and observed that seemed stupid now.

Why would kids this age be able to pick up adult dynamics from context? It seemed outrageous that she hadn't made it clear to them before.

Daisy took a sharp breath. "Dad is with Amberly now. Not me. So he's going to live with her because she's . . . she's going to be his wife."

Had he not even told them that? He didn't do anything, not a damned thing except cut his own finger off. What a useless asshole.

"They're getting married?" Avery popped around the corner and into the room.

"Did you even wash anything, A?" Daisy asked.

"Are Dad and Amberly getting married?" He looked at her seriously.

Daisy looked away. "Yes."

"That means she's going to be a stepmother!" Alden shouted, with all the horror a child was taught to feel about wicked and evil stepmothers. In this case, Daisy couldn't ease his concerns.

"*Not* mine." Wren's expression was angry and vicious.

"Unfortunately, that's not up to you or me." Daisy heard the doorbell downstairs. "Hey, come on, that's dinner."

"I don't want a stepmom!" Alden said as he hopped off the bed.

Daisy closed her eyes. "If you have to have one, she seems pretty nice." That was costly to say, but it also seemed true. Amberly didn't allow Jonathan to talk smack about her, and she would return the favor by defending her now.

Besides, the kids didn't need to descend into hysterics.

"But what does it mean?" Alden asked.

"Don't worry about it right now." Daisy realized you couldn't tell kids that, though knowing Alden, he would forget as soon as he got his spaghetti. "There are a lot of things that have to happen before then, and who knows what might change."

Wren was sullen as she went down the stairs behind her brothers, and Daisy paused, pulling her back for a hug. "Wrenny, it's going to be okay."

"I don't want divorced parents." She looked up at Daisy with big tear-filled eyes.

"I didn't want to be a divorced parent." Daisy couldn't protect Jonathan from how the kids felt about this. She wasn't going to pretend everything was fine. "But whatever I am, I'm your mom. That won't change."

Wren nodded, and Daisy hugged her again while they walked down the stairs just as Zach walked through with takeout, and Alden jumped out from behind a potted plant and nearly collided with him.

"Are you going to be our stepdad?" Alden asked, hopping around Zach's feet.

Daisy's heart went into a full-on spiral, but Zach didn't even seem ruffled. "Right now, I'm the guy who got you dinner."

She could see that put him light-years ahead of Amberly, at least in the present moment.

The kids dug into the food, though Wren especially seemed glum. She took her meal and sat down at the table, and Zach did the same.

They ate with only minimal shenanigans, though Alden managed to get a piece of spaghetti stuck to the ceiling, which Zach retrieved. Daisy thought her heart might actually burst.

"Okay," Daisy said. "Go up and brush your teeth. Then I'll come in to read you your stories and tuck you in."

The kids scampered off with only mild complaints. She attributed their good nature to the pasta and breadsticks.

"You didn't have to do all this." She touched his arm, his body, warm and solid beneath her hand, a comfort she was afraid of getting used to.

"I know," Zach responded.

"Do you . . . do you have nieces and nephews? Because you seem like you're really good with kids."

"I do. But I always figure you just treat kids the way you wish you got treated. I personally would love it if someone got me pasta when I was hungry. So I followed that instinct."

"I know I loved it," she said.

"Then settle down, and don't act like you're about to throw me out the front door." His gaze was serious, so much it made her chest hurt.

"I'm not throwing you out, I promise. But you really don't have to stay."

"I haven't done a damned thing I haven't wanted to do all day."

She smiled slowly. "Do you have my bra?"

"What?"

"I left my bra at your house."

"I don't have your bra. Does that mean you aren't wearing one?"

"Yes. Thankfully sort of hidden by the sweatshirt."

"That's all I'm going to be thinking about for the rest of tonight."

For the rest of tonight. Would he spend the night? Did she want him to? It seemed like such a big, dangerous thing to have him in her house, with her kids, like they were a couple when they were very much not labeling it at the moment for obvious reasons.

Dangerous because it made her want things she couldn't want right now. Because it would be foolish to rush right into something permanent, and Zach . . .

Zach was looking at her like he would stay as long as she wanted him to.

"I have to do story time," she said.

"I'll wait."

She read the kids their stories, but they weren't as bright and happy as they often were. Of course, the kids were mourning that all of this was different. That Jonathan wasn't part of bedtime, bath time, story time. She'd mourned it too.

But he'd made his choice.

She needed to make hers. To stand firm in hers.

She tucked Wren in, then followed the boys to their rooms, where she tucked them in too. As she closed Alden's door behind her, she saw Zach at the top of the stairs. She reached her hand out toward him, and he came to her.

She led him down the hallway, toward the room she'd shared with Jonathan for all those years. "Do you want to spend the night?" she whispered.

"I thought you'd never ask, Daisy."

At least now she was grateful she wasn't wearing a bra. Everything would go that much faster. She was desperate for him.

Desperate for this thing between them to carry her away to a better moment in time.

He kissed her, and she let him lay her down in bed. Let him tuck her in.

Let him make her grateful that he was the man she was with today.

She didn't miss Jonathan at all.

Chapter Twenty-Five

Soraya

There is no such thing as too much power.

—Rules for Witches

Mom someone is trying to get into the house.

Soraya sat up and looked at her phone. It was late, and she'd been reading a book that was in no way edifying, after having eaten excessive amounts of Chinese takeout while still trying to recover from the best sex of her life.

Seeing her oldest son's name on her phone screen was jarring, even if it was welcome.

The message he'd sent, however, wasn't welcome.

She was up and moving around the apartment immediately, looking for shoes, for socks, for keys, for *something*.

Then she stopped.

Which house?

The one we're staying in. On Candle St.

Where's Dad?

He's sleeping.

She doubted that. He was probably sexting someone. Or maybe he had a woman in his room for a prayer session that was actually him bending her over and . . .

I'm calling 911.

Why hadn't Levi done that? Why had he texted her? Like he thought she could still fix his emergencies. Like she still mattered, which was a weird thing to think as she dialed 911, her hands shaking.

"911, what's the location of your emergency?" The woman's voice on the other end sounded like it was in a tin can far away.

"111 Candle Street. I'm not there, my son texted me and said that someone is trying to break in."

"Your son heard someone trying to enter the house?"

"As far as I know. He didn't give me a lot of details. He's seventeen. But he doesn't make things up."

"We can do a welfare check."

"Someone is trying to break into the house." They weren't taking her seriously because her son was a teenager, and she wasn't there.

"We can have a police officer drive by, okay?"

"All right. All right."

"What's your name and phone number for a callback?"

She gave it. Resentfully. Because this wasn't enough. Something was wrong. It was wrong.

She was halfway out the door before she had her coat all the way on. Because if her son was going to text her like she was the one who could save them, then she would damn well be the one to save them.

She got halfway down the stairs when she remembered she didn't have a car.

Should she knock on Declan's door? Should she tell him what was happening? Everything in her rejected that. She couldn't show up to whatever was happening with him. She couldn't involve him in this.

It wasn't just because she was embarrassed about the sex. That after a lifetime of being puritanical and judgmental, she'd folded like a house of cards because a hot guy had given her a smoldering look within one hundred feet of a bed.

Though that was one reason.

She called Nora.

"Nora! Someone is trying to break into David's house, and Levi texted me about it, and emergency services aren't taking it seriously, and I have to go!"

"I'll come get you." Nora sounded stretched thin.

"Are you okay?"

"I'm . . . Ben is in the hospital. I'll come over and get you and explain everything on the way."

Ben was in the hospital?

Someone was trying to break into the house. She was having difficulty wrapping her head around all of this.

She paced the hall until Nora texted: I'm here. Then she ran down the stairs and out to the street and jumped into the passenger seat.

"Did you text Daisy?" Nora asked.

"I thought she was probably busy with . . . well, either her kids or Zach."

"She was." Nora pulled away from the curb. "Well, she was with Zach. Now she's with the kids because Jonathan is also in the hospital."

"What!?" Any worries she had about Nora looking at her and seeing *harlot* stamped on her forehead were gone now.

There were much bigger issues at play.

"Ben had a hiking accident. Jonathan had a construction accident."

Soraya pulled her phone out and fired off a text to Daisy to ask if everything was okay. "How's Ben?"

"Fine. For a cheating liar."

"I'm sorry, Nora." Soraya scrubbed her hands over her face. She felt cold. Like she was a hundred miles away from her own body. She felt like nothing was real.

"I'm not. It's better that I know. It's better that I see him for exactly what he is. Better that all of this came out, and if he had to fall down a mountain for me to see it all, then that's what had to happen." Nora sounded grim but resigned. Almost bloodthirsty.

She thought of the Tower card Nora had drawn that day at her apartment, that she'd quickly put back in the deck. Fire and men falling to their doom.

"This is the magic, isn't it?"

Nora was silent for a moment. "I don't know what else it could be."

"My kids might be in danger."

"But it's David's fault," Nora said. "Whatever is happening is David's fault."

"Maybe." Soraya wrung her hands together. "But if something happens to them because we messed with power and spirits and whatever else that we weren't supposed to, it doesn't matter. It doesn't matter." Her throat went tight, fear making it hard for her to speak.

"If magic is real, it won't do that."

"Of course it would," Soraya said. "*Everything* has a cost. You can't just cast a spell and get everything you want. You can't just make everything work the way you want it to and not have any . . . side effects. You can't."

By trying to get revenge, they'd done damage.

Soraya had known they were messing with real power, and she'd let herself get sucked into it anyway because she was so angry. Because she was so . . . so . . .

"Holy shit."

She looked up when Nora swore and saw an orange glow in the distance. Her heart stalled, and when they rounded the corner, she could see for sure that the glow was flames. And that those flames were enveloping David's house.

Nora stopped the car in the middle of the road, and Soraya scrambled to undo her seat belt, then ran down the street toward the fire. There was a police car in the driveway with the lights on, red and blue, but no fire trucks yet. It took her a moment to register that the kids were standing on the front lawn, and David was sitting there, holding something against his arm. The cops had someone in handcuffs.

"What's happening?" she shouted, running to the scene.

The world was on fire. Hell was on earth.

She'd had sex with someone she wasn't married to. It couldn't be a coincidence.

It couldn't all be a coincidence.

"Ma'am, stay back." An officer held her hand out, trying to stop Soraya's forward motion.

"Those are my kids!" Soraya said.

That made the officer relax, just a fraction, and Soraya went past her to grab both boys, holding them tight.

"Mom, oh my gosh. Pastor John lost his mind. He lit the house on fire, and he tried to shoot Dad."

"What?" She whipped around to see that Levi was right. John was, in fact, the man in handcuffs being pushed into the back of the police car.

She could hear sirens in the distance, coming toward the house. Everything was a blur, and they were herded away from the residence and out into the street, just as the flames burst through the windows. She clung to her sons, David standing distant from them.

"Look what you did." She turned to look at David, who had an expression of horror on his face. She'd been talking to herself, but she knew she couldn't take all the blame. He was the one who'd slept with John's wife.

"I know I . . ."

She moved closer to him. "You're bleeding."

"I was shot," he said.

"David, this . . . this is not okay. All of this. It's not okay. You need help."

"I know I do."

He sounded genuinely contrite. Was it the house burning down? His kids being in danger? His own life being in danger?

Was it having his facade go up in flames along with everything else? He couldn't hide anymore. Everyone knew.

Was that the reason he was finally admitting it?

The neighbors were out on the streets now, too, watching the house burn. They were on a stage. They had been ever since David's video had played at church, and now it was all crashing down on them.

"I'm sorry, Mom." Levi held on to her more tightly. Jaden didn't say anything. He just let her hug him.

"I forgive you," she said. It was easy to forgive her kids.

She'd been part of raising them in the place that had taught them to make her the villain for what she'd done. She'd made other women in her situation the villain in their hearing.

She knew better now.

So she would do better.

She would help them do better.

A prayer, a promise, and a spell all rolled into one.

An ambulance drove onto the street, and she moved to David on instinct. "Come on, you need them to look at this." She walked him over to the paramedics and then moved back to the boys. "Do you want to spend the night with me tonight?"

"What about Dad?" Jaden asked.

"He might have to go to the hospital." She thought about Ben and Jonathan. Would all their husbands be in the hospital tonight? She felt sick.

"Yeah. I want to stay with you." Jaden's shoulders shook. "All our stuff is gone."

It was. But not the most precious possessions, because they'd been at the other house, and she'd taken them with her. "I have our pictures," she said. "I have your birth certificates and your passports. I have your stuffed animals."

"You do?" Levi asked.

"Yes. I had to bring what was most important to me."

"But you left us," Levi said.

"I left Dad. I'm sorry that it didn't make sense to you."

"I know that he . . ." Levi looked down. "I'm sorry I acted like I did. I didn't believe he did anything really bad because he said he didn't. He said you were . . ."

"I know what he said." Or at least she knew a variation of it. She was doing her own thing. Walking away from what they knew. From the faith. Walking away from her marriage was that terrible. "It doesn't matter now."

The female police officer approached them. "I'm sorry, I know the timing is bad, but I need to get some witness statements from the boys while everything is fresh in their memory."

"Oh . . ."

"It won't take very long." The woman gathered the boys to her as she started to ask them questions.

Nora came running up a moment later, and so did Daisy, wearing a bathrobe and slippers. "Soraya, are you okay?" Daisy's eyes were wide with fear.

"No," Soraya said. "No, I'm not okay. I can't . . . I can't do any of this anymore. I need to leave the apothecary. I need . . . I have to stop this."

Guilt gnawed at her. Guilt and rage and so many other emotions.

But guilt was her friend. Guilt was the one she knew best.

Daisy grabbed hold of Soraya's shoulder. "Soraya, you don't want to leave the apothecary. We . . . we're doing good there. You're doing good. And Aggie . . ."

"I'll figure it out." Fear and regret were tearing Soraya apart, her whole body aching, shaking like she'd just been chased by a lion. "My kids could have died. Maybe you can believe we didn't do this with our spells, but I can't escape the feeling that it's a punishment for meddling with what we shouldn't have. I almost let darkness consume me, and look what happened."

"Soraya . . ." Nora tried to walk after her.

"I'm taking my boys home. Back to my apartment, and I'm not . . . I can't do this."

Her car that she'd left for David was in the driveway, and she still had her set of keys in her purse. David was in the ambulance, and she went to check in on him one last time.

"We'll take him and make sure there isn't any other trauma. Would anyone like to come with him?"

"No." Soraya didn't listen as David protested her simple answer. She went back to the boys in the car and started the engine. She had her kids back.

But she'd almost lost them. Nothing was worth that. Nothing.

They got into the car, Levi in the front, Jaden in the back, his knees folded up against his chest. They were both so tall. But when she looked at them, she still saw them as little boys, and being separated from them like she had been was so painful. Tonight had been terrible. But they were with her.

"You should have seen him," Levi said. "He was unhinged. Yelling at Dad about taking his wife and humiliating him and . . ." There was a short pause. "Dad made us get purity rings."

Soraya couldn't help it. She laughed. She laughed and laughed until tears were streaming down her face. Until she was just crying, clutching the steering wheel, the streetlights going blurry until they were like stars.

She slowed the car and eased into the space she used across from the apothecary.

"I know," she said, wiping the tears away. "Oh. I know, it's all so absurd. I'm sorry." She hiccupped. "I'm so sorry about all of this."

They went upstairs to the apartment, and she made beds for them, then sat in her own, unable to sleep for a long time.

She felt so lost.

She'd known who she was once. What she believed. What she wanted. She'd known how the whole world worked, and she could see that now for what it was. That arrogance that was actually masking fear. Because if everything was black and white, you never had to question anything.

Now she questioned everything, and she constantly felt like she was about to slip and fall.

Tonight, she had.

She felt like she'd done the wrong thing. Had gotten lost in a quest for vengeance and potentially caused serious harm.

But she didn't like what she'd said to Nora and Daisy.

Didn't like the idea of leaving all of it behind.

Partly because she couldn't go back to who she'd been before.

Even standing there with David in front of the burning house, that was clear.

She couldn't go back.

But she didn't know how to go forward.

For now, her boys were sleeping down the hall from her. Maybe that had to be enough. Maybe there couldn't be anything else.

She picked up her phone and opened the text chat for Declan.

I'm sorry. I can't do dinner.

There. It was done. Over. She was ending it.

Pulling herself back from the edge.

She had to.

Chapter Twenty-Six

Nora

The sun will rise. The tide will flow.
Seasons change. If one thing is sure,
nothing stays the same.

—*Rules for Witches*

She felt gritty and nearly demolished by the time she left the site of the fire. Soraya had completely melted down, and who could blame her? Her kids had been in danger, the entire church community was now going to be decimated, and even though Nora didn't personally care about that, she . . . she understood Soraya better now. She respected that it was genuine for her. That even if that community had treated Soraya badly, she cared about them. Nora also knew how complicated it was when your husband was a cheating dickbag but also still your husband.

Though she could genuinely say that looking at Ben in the hospital bed, she hadn't felt bad. Yeah, the spell was out of control. Building. But it was karma. She hadn't put him up on that mountain. He had put himself there.

Don't start shit, and there won't be shit.

Don't climb a mountain, and you won't fall down it.

Karma couldn't work unless you deserved what rebounded on you.

That was how she felt about Jonathan and David.

Yes, it was terrible he cut his finger off. Kind of. But he was a jerk.

If David didn't want men attacking him, then perhaps he shouldn't sleep with their wives. And film it. And keep the film on his phone, which he then hooked up to the church's projection system. It really wasn't . . .

Yes, the spell might have gained momentum as it rolled downhill, an avalanche of karma, but it was still rooted in the men's actions. Their own behavior was being doled out to them by the universe. That was exactly what she asked for. That they would feel the same pain they inflicted.

She drove past her house. She just wasn't feeling like being by herself. Sam had driven her home earlier, and she wanted to see him again. He was the only thing that felt steady and stable in the middle of all this. She ignored what had happened at his place before she got the call.

Pushed that out of her mind. She had stopped it. So . . . that was all that mattered.

She got out of the car and walked up to his door, knocking on it. Then she waited. It opened, and he was there, shirtless, wearing nothing but gray sweatpants. Something inside her shifted, and she felt . . . afraid. That she had made a very serious miscalculation. She kept her eyes on his face, very deliberately didn't look at his sculpted chest and abs, because she just didn't need to focus on that. He was Sam. The familiar shape of his features, the comforting sensation she felt when she looked into his eyes.

"I just didn't want to be by myself."

"Yeah." He stepped away from the door.

"David's house burned down. They arrested the pastor from their church. The one who . . . you know, the one whose wife he was banging."

"Is everyone okay?"

"Yeah. Everyone's fine. Soraya is catatonic. She thinks the spell we did caused all of this."

"The spell?"

"Yes. It's entirely possible that we did a little spell for justice and karma when Ben's affair came out."

"Right."

"I just . . . They deserved it. You know?"

"No argument from me."

He walked into the kitchen, and she followed him. He went to stand behind the island, his palms braced on it. The overhead light cast a dark shadow in the hard-cut groove of his biceps, drawing her focus more intently to his shoulders, his muscles.

"Do you want anything?" he asked.

"A drink, maybe. I might . . . I might need to crash on your couch."

His eyes clashed with hers and held. He didn't have to say it. She could read it in his eyes. His couch?

What about his bed?

"Sam. Please . . . I don't want to do this." She took a step back. "I can't."

"I didn't say anything."

"But before . . ." She didn't really want to address it, and in fact, she would much rather ignore it, but there was this tension between them, and she needed it to go away. She just couldn't have everything with him changing on top of her marriage collapsing. She needed him to be Sam. Stable, easy Sam.

"Before the phone call, I was going to kiss you," he said.

God. Dammit.

She swallowed hard. "Okay. But I just need to table that right now. Please."

"What if I don't want to?"

The spike of fury that lanced her was almost a shock. She was never this angry at Sam. But how dare he? Why was he doing this now?

"But I need you to. Because . . . this is absurd. The timing of all of this is absurd. We've been friends forever. *Forever.* We've never even almost kissed."

"That *you* know of," he said.

Her whole mind went blank, and she chose not to entertain that. Chose not to go deeper with it. "My marriage is dissolving. It's a ridiculous time to try and introduce physical attraction to our relationship."

He lifted his hands and scrubbed his face. "Introduce it. *Introduce it?* Are you for real, Nora?"

"Yes, Sam, I'm for real. We've had a wonderful, platonic relationship—"

"Get over yourself. We *don't*. We never have. I'm your goddamned husband with no benefits. Because who fixes your electricity? Who do you go to when you need to talk about something you feel is just a little bit too intimate for anyone else? It's me. It's not him. It never has been. You play a character for him." He let out a hard breath. "I've never understood it. I have never understood it. Why do you think I didn't go to your wedding? Because I couldn't stand that. You were trying to be some quirky Stepford wife. For *that* guy. For what? What did he ever give you?"

"Ben gave me love," she said. "A beautiful life. He gave me—"

"He gave you a script to his play. The one you've been so devoted to ever since you met him. Because you had this idea in your head that you wanted something normal, and you had an idea of what that was, of what it meant. But it has always required you to pretend you were something you're not, Nora. Whenever you needed a break from that, you came to me. Whenever you needed something real, you came to me. You're here now because you need someone to listen to you. Because you need somebody to make you feel like it's going to be okay, so you're here with me. You're not with your fucking husband."

"Well, I'm divorcing him." She sounded small, she felt small. And angry. Sam was supposed to be safe. He was taking that from her at the worst possible time. "It's just not fair of you to do this right now because—"

"The hell it's not," he growled. "I've been there for you. Endlessly. I haven't asked for a goddamn thing, but you *use* me." His voice was rough, fractured. Pained, and she hated it. "You use me as a security blanket, and it never gives me anything back. You're not a safe space for me, Nora Clarke, you are hell. You are constantly teasing me with a look into a future that we could have, but you won't give it to us because you would rather have a spineless dentist just because he has two parents and grew up in a cul-de-sac. I'm not walking you through a divorce. I hit my limit."

"Sam . . ."

"No. I can't do it. You know it's not him. You know that's not real. You know he sucks, and you still don't see *this*. I can't wait for you anymore. You looked at me, and you asked me why I haven't had a relationship, and I . . ." He shook his head. "Get out."

"Are you *throwing me out*?"

"Yes. I am. Because you won't even listen."

"I . . . I'm listening," she said. "I'm listening, but you have to admit that the timing is psychotic."

"It isn't to me, it's all the same. I have been living in the hell of not having you for all this time. And I'm . . . facing the fact I'm still not going to have you. Because you are never going to—"

"So you're going to cut off our friendship because I won't fuck you? Is that it? We've known each other our whole lives and you'll just end this because I won't sleep with you right now?"

"That's unfair," he said. "It doesn't even surprise me, because that's you. Backed into a corner and you try your damnedest to hurt someone so you don't get wounded."

"Like you don't do that."

"You're right. I do. With pretty much everyone but you, but you can't even give me that. I've known all this time I couldn't tell you how I feel. Not ever. You compartmentalize your feelings into these little pieces, so you never have to be honest. Because it is never going to be a good time for me to talk about mine because you want to use me as a crutch rather than see me as a person. Ben told you that you were emotionally unavailable, and he was right, Nora. You aren't honest with any one person, including yourself. He got the housewife, he got to sleep with you, he got your marriage vows. I get your trauma. I'm over it."

What you did to me, be returned but times three. Head to toe. Skin and bone. It is time for fate to reverse. It is time to feel the pain you inflicted on me.

He wasn't going to be there for her anymore. He was abandoning her. Taking this shelter away from her. This thing she needed so, so badly.

Pain wrenched her.

She had tried, all this time, not to disturb her relationship with Sam. He was breaking it apart now. Even though she had never given in to temptation. Even though she had never . . .

"I never said anything, I never did anything." She knew it didn't make sense to him. But it did to her. She had kept it the same. He wasn't honoring that. He wasn't . . .

"I'm not a security blanket."

She wasn't entirely sure how she walked out of Sam's house. She didn't fully come back to herself until she was in her driveway, holding the steering wheel of the car. Her heart was thundering hard. It hurt. Had she really been using him all this time? She hadn't meant to. She loved him. She loved Sam, but she needed to keep herself safe and . . .

His words were like poison darts, and everywhere they'd hit, she felt stung. She was . . .

Selfish.

And he was right.

She didn't like talking about herself, not because she cared about other people so much, but because she never wanted to be vulnerable. She hadn't called Ben when she found out he was cheating on her because she couldn't stand the idea of crying in front of the man who cheated on her, and as Soraya had pointed out, if you couldn't even cry then, when could you?

Was her relationship with Sam really a one-way friendship?

She thought of all the times he had come over and turned her lights on. Dropped everything and been there for her.

She got out of the car and went upstairs and lay down in bed in the room that probably wouldn't be hers for much longer. In the house she would have to leave.

She couldn't sleep. So she started making a plan instead.

Chapter Twenty-Seven

Nora

Nothing withers magic faster than selfishness.

—Rules for Witches

"Good morning. Whore."

Daisy gave Nora an extremely unamused look as Nora pushed her way into Daisy's house, holding a bag of pastries that she had a feeling would lighten Daisy's mood.

"You sound jealous." Daisy crossed her arms and wrinkled her nose, trying to meet Nora's gaze without flinching, clearly.

"Hey. That was whore, *affectionate*, if you couldn't tell."

"I assumed." Daisy pushed her hair out of her face. It was disheveled. More than just a side effect of sleeping.

Good for her. Genuinely. Nora wasn't bitter or jealous at all.

"What's going on?" Daisy asked.

"I haven't heard from Soraya. She's not answering her phone."

"It *is* pretty early."

"Yes," Nora said. "But of course I'd be checking in on her this morning, and of course after she said she . . . Do you really think she's going to quit? Do you think she'll go back to that church and all those people who are so awful to her—or worse, to David—because she feels guilty?"

Daisy sighed. "*I* feel a little bit guilty."

"Why?" Nora asked.

"Because it feels like it all got out of hand. It feels like everything went too far. I wanted karma, sure, but this is . . ."

"You're assuming what we did actually had an effect."

Daisy looked at Nora, unwavering. "We wanted it to happen, Nora. We wanted to ruin them, to hurt them. There was a point where that felt good and like it was enough, but now other people are in the cross fire."

Nora turned away, walked into the dining room, and set the bag of pastries down on Daisy's table. "Are your kids still in bed?"

"Yeah," she said. "So is Zach."

"Ooh. He spent the night?"

"Yeah. He stayed with the kids while I went over to the fire last night. And then . . . well. You know." She smiled.

"Yeah. I know."

"What about Sam?"

Nora ignored the discomfort in her stomach. "What about him? He drove me back home and dropped me off."

"That's all?"

"Yep. That's all." She edited out that she'd gone back. That she hadn't stayed away from him after the fire, and everything was now ruined. Why talk about that?

You're emotionally unavailable . . .

Daisy sighed. "He's in love with you, Nora."

Nora bit the inside of her cheek. She didn't want to hear it. That it was so obvious to everyone else when she'd missed it. "I love Sam. With all my heart. But it's not like that." They'd almost kissed. They'd almost changed everything. They'd almost unraveled the carefully knit together relationship that had sustained them all this time.

It was one of the most terrifying moments of her life, *improved* by the fact that she'd discovered her husband had been rushed to the hospital because he had fallen down a mountain.

"Why not?"

"I'm dealing with the fallout of my marriage."

"So am I." Daisy wrinkled her nose. "Though it is deeply improved by the amazing sex."

"Zach doesn't mean anything to you. Sam is everything to me, and if I mess up what we have, I don't know what I'd do."

"Zach is not *nothing* to me," Daisy said. "I don't know what he is but . . . he's not nothing."

Nora looked down at her hands. "That's not what I meant. I didn't mean he meant nothing to you now. But I mean, you don't have this preexisting *thing* with him." She never talked about this stuff. She was very good at deflecting from the reality of her life in foster care. In fact, she was good at it on purpose. But everything felt so . . . undone.

Like her life and the whole world was falling apart around her, and the idea of preserving the facade that she'd kept in place all this time seemed silly.

When even Sam was gone.

Of all the people left in her life, other than Sam, Daisy was the closest to a lifelong friend, but even back then, she had kept a lot of her deep, dark personal stuff to herself.

"Sam has seen everything," Nora said. "He's met my mom. The whole thing with my family is ugly. It's not something I like revisiting or talking about, so I have this one person in my life who knows. He knows and he understands everything. It's the closest thing to acceptance I've ever had. To security. To . . . family, I guess."

"You don't like talking about your past. That doesn't mean other people wouldn't accept you."

"I know. I do know that. I know that you would. I know Soraya would. But I would have to talk about it. I would have to talk about the times when my grandmother slapped me across the face for being disrespectful and told me I was too much of a burden. Or all the times my mom lied to me and said she was going to get clean, said she was going to give up the men in her life so she could be with me. She never did. She chose them every single time. I can't even talk about my dad letting me down because I've never seen him. I don't know who he is. God knows he's not flinging himself onto DNA databases, either because he's a criminal or because he knows he has an illegitimate kid out there somewhere. I never had people who stuck with me. Ben is just another one in a long line. But Sam has been there. From the beginning. I've never wanted to jeopardize that."

She thought of the way he'd looked at her last night. All hurt and fury.

She'd jeopardized it, and she knew it.

"He's mad at me," she said, her voice sounding small.

It reminded her of being a child. Of the way disappointment had sounded in her voice all those years ago.

My mom didn't show up, did she?

"What do you mean?" Daisy asked.

"Last night, I went back to his house. I said something about sleeping on the couch, and it got really tense. Because we did almost kiss last night. I wanted to pretend it didn't happen, but it was impossible."

"Oh dear."

"I just don't get why he couldn't leave it. We were fine." Her heart clenched tight when she thought about his face. His anger. His hurt.

He wasn't fine.

Daisy opened the pastry bag and plucked a croissant out of it, examining it for a moment. Then she looked around the kitchen, her gaze drifting to the ceiling. "Nothing stays the same. Nothing. I didn't want my marriage to end, but it did. I tried to hang on, but I couldn't. I'm in this house, and there's a different man upstairs in my bed, and if you'd have asked me what I wanted six months ago, I would have told you I wanted my same life. My same marriage." She took a bite of the croissant. "I don't have it. I'm happier, Nora. I'm happier with all the change I wouldn't have chosen, even though there were parts of it that hurt. That still hurt. I've seen you and Sam together over the years, and of course you were married for some of those years. I can feel things changing between the two of you. That relationship is changing, no matter how hard you try to keep it the same."

Nora sighed and sat down at the table. "I can't deal with this right now. Soraya's life is in shambles, and even though she's pulling away, we have to be there for her. We can't let her lose all this . . . progress she's made."

"*Your* problems matter." Daisy took another bite of croissant.

"I know. But I'm tired of them. I would rather talk about Soraya. Or you. I would rather talk about anything else but my own issues because I'm just so desperately bored of being a dysfunctional wreck."

She'd tried so hard to change that. She'd tried to get married and make all her problems go away. To wave a magic wand and become healed, secure, and normal, and it hadn't worked.

"All right. What are we going to do? About all of this."

"I don't know," said Daisy. "But at least we can talk to each other about it."

Nora sighed. "That is true. The problem is, these things happen, and you end up feeling isolated. You feel like you're the only person who's going through something like this—"

"Successfully cursing your ex?"

"No. The divorce. Being left, being cheated on. We banded together. That was a lot better than being isolated and alone. But we've been thinking too small. Too angry. We got work at the apothecary, and we learned about magic. I would've said none of it was true. But it is. We made all that happen. It was karma meeting our intention. Some of that has backfired." Nora thought about how hurt Sam was. "I know it did. On Soraya's kids, on me. But I think that's what came from using all our power for revenge. We have to do something else with this. Because there are other women out there who feel like they're by themselves. Who have lost their friends, their kids, their husbands, who feel powerless. We know that we are not powerless. We're powerful. Profoundly. Dangerously, even."

Nora's heart was beating faster. "The apothecary is the perfect space. For more women to get together. Women who need a community. That's why we found each other, because we needed a community. It's why Alexandra lost herself. Because she needed a community, but she didn't have one. So what if we could stop even one woman from ending up like Alexandra? From losing everything just because your husband cast you aside. Revenge isn't enough. That's what we've been focusing on. Saving ourselves and getting revenge. Don't get me wrong, I don't feel bad. I'm pretty happy with my revenge. I'm kind of glad he fell down a mountain."

"Nora . . ."

"Well, I am. But I get that you aren't loving this. Hell, I don't like that the karma spell grabbed me and made me hurt too. I know Soraya is upset. I know her kids were in danger last night, and that scared her. But she isn't going to lose her community over this. We're not going to allow other women to feel isolated. Not the way that we did."

"So, what exactly are you suggesting?"

"We use our power for good. We think bigger. Better."

"Is this all so you can avoid self-reflection?"

Nora shook her head emphatically. "No. No. Maybe a little. But think about Soraya. How she didn't have a place to stay. You and I and how we needed to do something to make money so that our husbands couldn't take everything from us. We're not the only ones in the same situation. And what helps? A network of women. So we need to make the network bigger."

"I like that idea," Daisy said.

"We should have an open house at the apothecary, if Aggie wants to. We can invite anyone who needs a community. Anyone who's feeling lost. We know that we're powerful together."

"That's true."

"So let's make it happen. But we need Soraya."

"Maybe we give Soraya the day." Daisy was as pragmatic as ever.

"Maybe. Although, the next thing I need is to find a lawyer."

Nora heard footsteps on the stairs. "A lawyer?" Her jaw almost dropped when Zach came around the corner shirtless, and good God, so sexy. "I can help with that."

"Zach, you don't have to do everything," Daisy said.

"Why not? I have resources. I might as well do something with them."

Nora looked at Daisy, who was staring at Zach like he was the Second Coming. Fair enough. A man who wanted to help. What a novel concept.

Daisy smiled overly sweet at him. "We might be wanting to use your resources as our new idea gets off the ground."

"What idea is that?" Zach walked over to the coffee maker and began to make a new pot.

"Can you clone him?" Nora asked Daisy.

"Back off." Daisy made a mock-fighting stance, and the very idea of Daisy fighting Nora was enough to make her laugh.

Then she explained everything to Zach, who listened intently, though paused partway through the conversation to go upstairs and put on a shirt. By the end of the discussion, Nora could see why Daisy had been quick to say she had feelings for Zach. Who wouldn't have feelings for Zach?

"Now all we have to do is get Aggie on board," Daisy said.

That proved easy. Aggie was more than happy to celebrate Beltane by having a tarot and spell night at the store, and was even happy to donate her services for the evening, doing readings free of charge and offering certain spells.

By late afternoon, Daisy had started making a poster, while Nora went straight to the lawyer's office that Zach had set her up with. "I need a divorce."

The lawyer was a young woman with a quick wit, a lot of opinions, and a forearm covered in tattoos. Nora liked her instantly. The conversation was bracing. Really digging into the reality of separating hers and Ben's lives was sad, but it was also clarifying, and now that she had a more concrete plan, she felt better.

She also knew her lawyer was the exact sort of person she'd love to have at the open house. "You wouldn't happen to be interested in coming to an apothecary open house this week?"

She furrowed her brow. "An apothecary?"

"Yes. I work there. In addition to writing and painting. At the apothecary, we do spells. Tarot readings. There are tea blends and coffee, baked goods. Everything and anything that might be good for the soul.

But also, I'm hoping that some women might come who could use some help."

"I'll see if I have time."

She and Daisy spent the next couple of days talking to small-business owners and spreading the word about the open house.

The next thing was getting Soraya on board. They waited until Tuesday afternoon, and after she still didn't respond to their texts, they ambushed her in person.

Soraya opened the door partway after they knocked, her hair back up in that ridiculous blond bun. "Can I help you?"

"Yes, you can." Nora reached out and took Soraya's hand. "Because we need you."

"We really need you," Daisy emphasized.

Soraya drew back. "Well, I'm done with all of this."

"So are we." Daisy took a step forward.

"You are?"

"Well. Not with the apothecary. But with . . . the petty stuff. The vengeance stuff."

"We're expanding," Nora said. "We want to help people. Women like us. It's not enough to just get revenge on the men. We need to do something more. Better."

"We've done enough." Soraya moved to shut the door.

Nora stopped her. "No. We haven't. We haven't even come close to doing enough. We proved that we're powerful. And you know, maybe that's the thing men don't want us to know. You got told to ignore your instincts. To not listen to your intuition, and to listen to a man instead. I spent my whole childhood being told that everything I did was too much. That I was too much work. That I was someone who had to be put up with. I carried that into my marriage. Daisy always feels like she has to do everything for everyone."

"Thank you, Nora," Daisy said.

"Well, it's true. We're amazing. We came together at the worst time in our lives, and look what we made happen. Maybe it backfired. But what if we channeled that power into something good? You can hide it, Soraya, and pretend that you never discovered it. You can go right back to how you were before. But then what's the point of any of it? Isn't that part of your faith? That you're not supposed to hide your light? Now that you found it, don't cover it up again."

"The boys are in their rooms. Probably on their phones."

"Then we'll be quiet," Nora said.

Soraya moved to the side and let them come in.

"What happened the other night was . . . devastating." She crossed her arms. "And I just . . . I'm scared."

"Listen," Nora said. "It backfired on me too. It backfired on Daisy. The man cut his finger off, and how is he going to work and support their kids? My whole relationship with Sam is a complete wreck. That's what happens when you invest in revenge. It's not enough. It's not enough. We have to get justice. Not just for us, but for every woman in town who feels this way. Think about how different it would've been for you if instead of judging you, people had rallied around you. What if we can be that for other people?"

"I think that would be good." Soraya looked away. "It isn't just a rebounding spell, though. I think I was being punished."

"Why?" Nora asked.

"I . . . I slept with Declan."

Nora and Daisy were completely silent. Nora had assumed Soraya would sleep with someone eventually, but she'd expected it would take multiple dinner dates and an emotional connection, not . . . a couple encounters in a hallway.

"So, you know, having the house go up in literal flames right after felt like a plague. A punishment."

"Oh, Soraya." Daisy reached out and put her hand over hers. "Sex didn't cause it. Okay, sex *did* cause it, but that was on David, not you."

"That seems logical, but what about any of this has been logical? We're playing with all this power, and who knows what all it can do?"

"Yes. Yes, that is true. We have power," Daisy said. "And yes, it can hurt people. If all we're channeling is anger."

"So how do we channel something else?" Soraya asked.

"I'm trying to figure that out," Nora responded. She had a couple of things she had to deal with that she wasn't especially excited to confront. She needed to have it out with Ben, and at some point she was going to have to handle Sam. Sam. Just thinking about him hurt. "Am I emotionally unavailable?"

Soraya and Daisy looked at her. "Yes." Their answer was in unison.

"Well, that . . . I don't like that. I thought it was just a shitty thing that had been said to me to manipulate me."

"It might've been a shitty thing that Ben said to you," Daisy said. "Because he wasn't trying to work your issues out. He was just looking for an excuse to leave you and not talk to you. Having said that, I can't say that you're the most open person."

Nora huffed. "I just . . . I . . ."

"It's not actually a character flaw," Daisy said. "I think it's trauma. Has anyone ever actually attempted to communicate with you, or have they just weaponized your own issues against you?"

"Sam," Nora said. "I think he tried. I blew it up by generally being closed off."

"Well, I am sorry about that."

"It's a bad combination of things. Because I want to work on myself but also be less self-obsessed. Focusing only on my own issues is what caused a lot of this."

"Maybe that's the thing." Soraya rubbed her arms. "Maybe the more we reach out to other people, the more we help other people heal, the more we heal ourselves."

"That's kind of profound," Nora said. "Thank you. I think you're right. Isolation is the enemy. It makes you feel like you're crazy and making all of it up. That's what makes you feel like everything is hopeless. When you get cut off from your community and your kids and everything else, that's what makes it unbearable, and then you're sort of focusing on all your own issues at the exclusion of everything else, and you can't ever catch your breath."

Daisy put her hand on Nora's. "I think this is the right thing. I think it's the way forward."

"Also," Soraya said, "Sam is your best friend. It's okay to be hurt by what happened, but don't you think you need to go talk to him?"

"But if I do, then . . ."

"What are you actually afraid is going to happen?" Daisy pressed.

Nora buried her face in her hands. "I'm going to kiss him. Then I'm going to sleep with him. Because I want him."

The stark truth, coming out of her own mouth, so unambiguously, was not quite what she expected. But it was true.

"I have wanted him. I . . . But it's so scary. At every stage of my life, it's been so scary. I've been playing this game where I try to prove to myself it's not that. Especially since I married Ben. He's my husband. If I was married to somebody else, if I *loved* somebody else, then I couldn't love Sam. He was safer, because he was off-limits."

"He wasn't *safer*," Soraya said. "Because you love him, with or without Ben in your life."

"But just talking about it is breaking us into pieces."

"No, because you didn't talk about it. He threw all of that at you, and you didn't tell him how you felt."

"Because I want to protect it."

"But it's not protecting it," Soraya pointed out.

"You know what." Nora put her hands on her hips. "If you could just stop being right, that would be great."

"Sorry. I'm wrong a lot. I've been wrong a lot with you, so it's nice to be right for a change."

"Wow," Daisy said. "Soraya admitted she's wrong sometimes."

Soraya shot her a look. "I've been wrong about a lot of things for a very long time. Being able to admit that is really freeing. Maybe I'm wrong about everything now too. Maybe." She sighed heavily. "I told Declan I can't have dinner with him."

"Why?" Daisy asked.

"Because of the apocalyptic sex."

"Oh, for heaven's sake, Soraya, your sex did not burn the house down!" Nora said. "You just spoke a hard truth to me, so I'm going to speak one to you. The way you're thinking about God feels narcissistic. I think—if God is up there—that he isn't obsessing over every little thing you do every day. It makes sense to me that he would want you to love others and not be a hypocrite, not do harm, to be honest and to lift other people up. I really hope he hates it when people like your husband preach about him and then do all this awful, awful stuff to the people around them. But the only people who benefit from you being scared of every little thing are the ones who are invested in controlling you."

Soraya looked away from her. "It didn't feel like the wrong thing. Mostly. I got worried about it afterward, and then the fire happened."

"I will grant you, I think we dabbled a little too darkly. I think there was definitely power at play in all of this. Our spell worked too well. But that has nothing to do with you and Declan."

"You say that very confidently. Like you know the rules to all of this, and I don't see how you can."

"That's what I do. I talk confidently and loudly to hide that I'm an insecure wreck, okay? But one of us has to pretend they know what's happening, and neither of you are going to do it."

"True," Daisy said.

"Yeah," Soraya agreed.

"We need to sort our shit out," Nora said. "Because we can't be afraid. We can't be afraid of ourselves. We can't be afraid of the future. Not anymore. We didn't want any of this to change, but it did. So when the universe gives you a chance at a new life, you have to take it."

She was just talking confidently, though. Because when she tried to imagine a new life, the only thing she could see clearly was the image of losing yet another person she loved.

Chapter Twenty-Eight

Nora

I call forth my wild,
From the earth,
From the sky,
From the trees,
I call forth the sparrow song,
The song of the flowing stream,
So that they might flow through me,
I am in the wild,
The wild is in me.

—A spell for reclaiming your wild heart

Aggie was especially pleased that their inaugural tarot night would fall on Beltane. But that meant Nora, Soraya, and Daisy had some extra errands to run. Not that Nora minded. She needed distraction right now more than anything. Was it weird that not having Sam in her life was a bigger heartbreak than losing Ben? It made sense in a lot of ways. It definitely reinforced her instinct to keep Sam in that box.

Being sent on an errand up into the woods to forage flowers, sticks, and greenery for flower crowns and homemade witch's brooms was a gift. As was the burgeoning warmth in the air, following a couple of false starts to spring that had happened already. That, at least, made her feel a little bit less grim. A little bit less dark.

Soraya was the one who suggested they all wear dresses.

"It's a cute adventure," she'd said.

She wasn't wrong, really, though Nora only had a black dress that fell to mid-calf, which did look quite witchy but was a bit out of place with Soraya's white and Daisy's green.

As the sun washed over her and the breeze caught her hair, she had to acknowledge that perhaps she had underestimated the healing power of nature. It was tempting to squirrel herself away at her house, to binge-watch TV shows or reorganize her closet, anything to disassociate from the present moment. She hadn't realized that the present moment might be the key to healing.

The sun on her skin, the sound of the birds around them, the scent of pine and warm earth.

Daisy had taken them to a hiking trail that she liked to walk with her kids, which Nora did her best not to take personally, but the implication was clearly that Nora was best suited to a trail that was friendly to children.

She could take that on the chin, because it was true.

Soraya was in the front and spun in a circle, looking up at the trees.

"You seem improved," Nora said.

"Well, I've been thinking a lot about the state of my life. Not like I wasn't thinking about it before, but since I had a total breakdown after David's house burned down, I've been thinking about it in a different way."

"Sure." Nora shrugged.

"One of the things they always said in our church was that you had to be a fruit inspector. Because every action has a consequence. It's like the branch of a tree. Our pastor used to ask us if someone's actions were bearing fruit." She turned to look at them, a confidence in her eyes Nora hadn't seen before. "David's fruit is rotten. There's a lot of rotten fruit at our church. I had a feeling about that far longer ago than this past year. But I had also been taught that all the answers were in that church. I don't mean the faith, but the physical church. I'm looking at the fruit, and it's rotten. I'm doing exactly what I was told, and I'm seeing clearly. I agree that the three of us need to turn our focus to helping rather than hurting, even if these men deserve it. Their actions will catch up with them; their fruit will remain rotten, whether we curse them or not."

"Amen." Daisy lifted her fist.

"True," Nora agreed.

"I'm also paying attention to what's growing in my own life." Soraya reached up and lowered a branch filled with blossoms toward herself. She inhaled the scent and smiled before releasing it again. "I'm happier. I have a different relationship with my kids, and it might even be better than it was before. One where I can be honest, and not a hypocrite. Aggie said something to me, too, that made me think. She said it was okay for me to do things because they felt good. I realized I don't actually know how to do that. I have attached guilt and worry to just about everything. I don't want to do that anymore. Not because I don't care about being right. I do. I care so much about doing the right thing and not hurting other people or inconveniencing them. But somewhere in there, I lost myself. Or maybe I've never even found myself before."

Daisy stopped walking for a moment. "She asked me when the last time was that I was wild. What happened to the girl I was, who used to scream and growl and howl at the moon whenever she wanted to. Spin in wild circles. It's weird, because one day you do stop doing that. It's not a decision, but you get some kind of awareness—shame, I guess. That thing that tells you what you're supposed to want, supposed to do."

"And look where it got us," Nora said. "All that civility, all that shame, for what? All that need to fit inside a box. I don't think I was ever carefree. I always felt like my passion, my feelings, were a burden, and I alternated between embracing it, being that burden, angry and difficult to deal with, and then trying so hard to be normal. To be the wife Ben needed. I'm so tired of it. Maybe I'm difficult. A lot of people are. Don't I deserve to be?"

"Not difficult," Soraya said. "You've been through a lot, but you are a deeply passionate person. Creative and kind. You were there for me when I needed you, even though you didn't like me, and for good reason."

"*Daisy* was there for you. I was just kind of along for the ride."

"That's not true." Daisy was vehement.

"It's a little bit true," Nora said. "But also, Soraya, even though I had some complicated feelings about you from high school, there's a reason that we stopped for you. Because you are the kind of person who cares deeply about doing right by others. Because even when you hurt my feelings in high school, I know you meant well."

"Yeah, I guess so. But you know, so much of a belief system that rigid is wanting to believe that you're protected. I wanted to believe that as long as I did good things, nothing bad would happen to me. But you can't control the world that way. At a certain point, you have to surrender. I'm working on that."

"I think we're all working on that," Nora said. Control and desire were definitely at the root of her issues with Sam. Hell, it was probably the root of all the issues in her marriage.

Her inability to let go. To put herself in harm's way. To make herself vulnerable.

They came around a curve in the path, and there were wildflowers growing in bright-green patches of grass beneath the trees. They took their baskets and walked off the path, picking bunches of flowers, finding leaves, twigs, and grass to make the brooms. Aggie had explained to them that a witch's broom was used to clear negative energy out of the house, and by making one out of local grasses and flowers, it could be infused with extra magic.

They wandered farther and farther from the path, the sun beginning to beat down on them. Daisy stopped and suddenly flung her arms wide, threw her head back, and screamed. Then she started to run, her basket flying behind her, her other hand holding her skirt up, trying to keep herself from tripping. Soraya and Nora exchanged looks and then ran after Daisy. Soraya shrieked, and Nora kept quiet, concentrating on not falling on her face as they careened over the uneven ground. When they reached Daisy, she was standing on the edge of a body of water.

"Swimming hole," she shouted on the breeze. "I've taken my kids here before."

"Daisy," Soraya said. "It's the end of April. That water has to be freezing."

Daisy set the basket down, took her glasses off and placed them in the basket, and gathered her skirt in her hands. "I don't care. I stopped singing. I stopped dancing and acting and being silly. I stopped screaming and running. I lost myself. Never again." She flung herself off the bank and into the water.

For a moment, she was gone. Completely disappeared beneath the surface. She popped back up a breath later, sputtering and shrieking. "Oh my *God.*"

"How is it?"

"Terrible!" she shouted, swimming farther away from the shore. "You have to jump in."

"I've never given in to peer pressure in my life," said Soraya.

"First time for everything," Daisy shouted back.

It was Soraya's turn to set her basket down, though she muttered the entire time she did it about *caving* and *compromising*. She took a deep breath and scrunched up her whole face, along with a handful of her dress, and ran toward the shore, screaming the entire way until she flung herself into the water.

"You've lost your goddamned minds!" Nora yelled from the relative warmth and safety of the shore.

"Be free!" Daisy shouted.

"Be *freezing*, more like," Nora said.

"Be in nature." Soraya moved a little closer to the shore and spun with her arms hitting the surface of the water.

"You all look silly."

"We don't care."

Nora couldn't argue with that. She set her basket down, gathered up her skirt, and went to the very edge of the swimming hole. Before she could think better of it, she leaped off the ground and plunged into the water, the impact of it so intense she got an immediate brain freeze when her head went under the surface. When she came up, she was screaming. "This is awful!"

"And brilliant," Daisy said.

This was something they might've done in high school. Maybe that was why it felt brave. Maybe that was why it felt revolutionary. Because life had intervened and made them afraid. Because it had taken the things they loved and turned them into trials, it had taken joy and sharpened it into a fine point, a weapon rather than a gift.

She couldn't remember when she'd stopped being able to act without worrying that it exposed her as a feral foster child. She'd married Ben and had been so beset by the feeling she didn't belong with him or in his life that she'd done everything she could to make herself seem normal. This day wasn't normal. Maybe none of them were.

Maybe they were better than normal.

She rolled onto her back and floated there, looking up at the sky, looking up at the sun, letting herself feel everything. The parts that were too cold, the parts that were just right.

They only lasted a few minutes in the frigid water before they got out, their dresses sodden, and stood there on the bank wringing out their skirts as they gathered their baskets. They were laughing, out of breath.

"That was dumb." Daisy laughed as she stumbled back down the path toward the car.

"You were the ringleader," Nora said.

Daisy smiled. "I was. I didn't plan it, and it wasn't for anyone else. I didn't care about looking stupid."

Maybe that shouldn't have been revolutionary. It was, though. They skipped back through the field, soggy now. Nora howled as they got into her car soaking wet. Everyone had parked at her house, with the idea that they would go back there and make some of their flower crowns over charcuterie boards and wine. Nora had a firepit in the backyard, and it was the perfect time of year to fire it up.

If she was honest, *Ben* had a firepit in the backyard, and once he got out of the hospital, she was going to have to deal with the fact that it wasn't going to be her firepit anymore, or her house.

She was in the process of making the very difficult decision to not pursue any kind of support from him. She would miss the house, but she would rather disconnect from him. Not have any kind of tie to him anymore. Including his money.

She didn't need to think about that right now. It was a vacation rental, in many ways. But then, it had been for quite some time. A place where he was represented, but not her.

She did love the firepit, though.

They turned the heater on high in the car, and when they got back to Nora's house, she got blankets down from the closet and then pulled the meat and cheese boards out of the fridge and brought them outside to the lovely backyard area, where she lit a fire.

The flames exploded, reached up for the sky, and cast a halo of warmth on them as they sat in the Adirondack chairs placed around the firepit. They began to weave twigs together to make the bases of the flower crowns.

They added blossoms and ribbons, little things Aggie had given them for the project.

"Zach is offering to sell me his part of the construction business," Daisy blurted as she wound a ribbon around her crown.

"Seriously?" Nora asked.

"Yes. But I've been hesitant to say yes because it feels . . . wrong. He's the one who invested his money into the company."

"But you spent years helping to keep it running," Soraya pointed out.

"True." Daisy started to weave in a second ribbon.

"You have to take it," Nora said. "You just have to."

Daisy looked into the fire, and a slow smile crossed her face. "Okay. As soon as he's out of the hospital and back in the office, I'll let Jonathan know. *If* you'll help me with my hostile takeover."

Nora clapped her hands together. "Oh, Daisy, I was born for hostile takeovers."

When Soraya completed her first crown, she put it on her head and stood up, twirling in a circle, her damp dress and ribbons swirling around. Nora finished hers and stood up, joining Soraya, spinning and twirling in front of the flames. They were shortly followed by Daisy. They grabbed each other's hands and spun in a circle, the flame serving as a backdrop, until they separated and flung their arms up in the air. Nora felt exhilarated. She felt brave. She felt like she had shed twenty years' worth of baggage today. She could still laugh. She could still be a fool. Maybe for the first time, she could believe she was magic.

I have the love I deserve.

She felt it. Coming from the earth, coming from the flames, coming from her friends.

There was love all around her.

She wasn't alone.

With Ben out of her life, she wasn't alone.

With Sam angry at her, she wasn't alone.

She was surrounded by friends. By their strength.

Their support.

Their joy.

They collapsed into their chairs, laughing, breathless, and Daisy picked up her glass of wine and held it up. "The next time Aggie asks when we were wild, we can tell her it was today."

Chapter Twenty-Nine

Daisy

Men cling to false power, money, and status. It is not the highest power. But it can be used against them.

—Rules for Witches

The morning that she signed the papers to buy out Zach's 51 percent of the business, she slid a penny across the table, and he slid the contract back toward her.

"This is the hottest thing that's ever happened." She stared at the paperwork.

Though, truthfully, it was much more than hot. It was something that felt dangerously like a partnership.

She wasn't supposed to want more from him. But he was so good. Something she really hadn't expected out of her gorgeous, ill-advised fling.

Shouldn't the hot actor from your teenage fantasies be good for nothing other than multiple orgasms? He was good for that. Last night, he'd joined her in the shower and covered her mouth so her screams wouldn't frighten the children while he did things to her she'd never even imagined were possible. Then he'd gotten up early and made pancakes for everybody.

It was intoxicating, and far too tempting to believe that it could be something.

But it was silly to fall for somebody this soon after splitting up from the man she'd been with all her life. The responsible thing to do would be to be single for a good long while.

The responsible thing. The idea of being single didn't particularly make her feel *responsible*. It made her feel sad, not because she couldn't be alone. If she had to choose between Jonathan and being alone, she'd choose alone every time.

Zach had nothing to do with a fear of being single.

He made her feel wild. He made her feel beautiful. He made her feel like she didn't have to perform endless chores and tasks to keep him happy or satisfied. He just seemed happy and satisfied to be with her. He was funny, which she hadn't really expected, because she had been led to believe that when men were handsome, they often didn't hone their personalities to go along with it. But he certainly had.

"Do you want me to go with you?" he asked.

Her face must have given away her obvious hesitance.

The look he gave her was hard, and she couldn't quite parse the meaning of it. "You *still* want to keep this a secret?"

"I . . ." It wasn't so much about the moral high ground anymore. It felt like unnecessary chaos for her to have him show up in Jonathan's driveway. "It's not a secret. The kids know that you're here."

"It's not like you've kissed me in front of them."

"I know. But they might say that Mommy had a friend spend the night. They might not know what that means, but Jonathan will. I mean, he'd have to actually pay attention, but I think at a certain point even he'll put it together."

"Fair."

"I am willing to risk that. He's moved on. I'm not pretending I'm not capable of having other relationships."

"Other relationships." He frowned.

"You know what I mean."

"I think you're trying to minimize this, Daisy."

"I'm not," she said, a little bit of panic making her heart beat faster. "I'm really not. But you know, when I storm the office and tell him you sold me the business, I didn't think you'd want to be with me, standing right there."

"Wrong, actually. I would love nothing more than to watch and then let him know that I'm fucking you better than he ever did."

Her mouth went dry. It was true, but it was cruel, and Zach seemed to delight in that. She could see why he would, and frankly that was one of the things she was avoiding. Flaunting her extremely hot lover seemed like a petty move. Maybe part of her was avoiding turning him into something petty. Because he didn't feel insubstantial, and he certainly didn't feel like revenge.

"I get why I would want to do that. But why do you?"

"Because he didn't appreciate you. He had you, Daisy, and he cheated on you. I don't know Amberly, but she's young. I can't imagine she's even half as interesting as you are."

"I'm not sure if you know this, but generally speaking, when men cheat on their wives with younger women, it's not because those younger women are more interesting."

"Daisy, maybe it's because I had an experience where I could have any woman I wanted."

"This is weird." She moved away from him.

"I'm not going to pretend that didn't happen. I'm not going to pretend I handled that differently than I did. When the show was popular, it was whatever I wanted, whenever I wanted. You can gorge yourself on sex, but the thing is, it's like anything else. You're just hungry again when it's over, and just like when you're indulging in too many things that are bad for you, you kind of feel sick. It doesn't satisfy you. It doesn't fill the ache inside of you. It's been twenty years, and until I met you, I didn't understand what the drive was. What I was actually looking for."

"You can't mean that," she said.

"I do. The problem was, you were married. And now you're not."

"I'm still not divorced."

"Doesn't matter. You're in my bed and not his. Yes, I wanted you, so it's perverse that I'm mad he fumbled you. But I'm mad that he did that because he hurt you, and you didn't deserve that. You deserve to be treated like something precious, because that's what you are. I watched the way you cared for everybody. Everybody who ever came into contact with you. Whether it was me, him, other random guys on the construction crew. His parents, your parents, your grandmother. Your kids."

"If that's what you like about me, then that might be a problem, because I'm kind of tired."

"You don't get it. I didn't look at you and think I wanted you to do that for me. I thought it was amazing how many people you were there for, and I felt like no one was doing the same for you. Not with that same amount of energy. I just wanted to take care of you. And be inside you. I can't say it was all chivalrous."

"That's good, because I can't say I want all chivalry all the time."

"Well, I don't want to be a secret. I'm going to need you to tell him, if you don't want me to do it."

She scoffed. "You're infuriating, do you know that?"

"Why? Because I don't let you control everything?"

"Yes, actually."

"It's a trade-off. You got to control a lot of things in your marriage, but he made you do the heavy lifting. He wasn't honest, he wasn't proactive. That's not what I want. But that means you aren't in charge of everything."

Her cheeks heated. Damn him. His bossy streak was hot, even if it shouldn't be. But he was right. She had been that woman who had taken care of all the details. Who had been married to somebody so passive that he'd let her find the things he'd been buying his mistress rather than have a conversation with her.

"Are you telling me this is a partnership, and I don't get to be in charge of everything?"

"I'm afraid so." He kissed her forehead. "But you also don't have to do everything by yourself." He pulled away from her and smiled. "Now, give 'em hell."

She kissed Zach, then walked out to the driveway and put Soraya and Nora on a group call after.

"How would you both like to earn a little bit of extra money?"

"Money?" Nora asked.

"Yes. I'm letting Jonathan know about the change in business ownership today."

"Oh!" Nora crowed.

"And there's going to need to be some overhauling," she continued. "I might want a mural. And I love the way your house was decorated, Soraya. Perhaps you might like to do a little bit of design work."

"But I've never done that," Soraya said.

"It seems like the right day to learn. I'm about to storm the office, and you agreed to help with storming."

"*Yes.*" Nora sounded ecstatic.

"Should I swing by and pick you guys up?"

"Hell yeah!"

"Yes," Soraya added.

When they arrived at the offices, Daisy pushed open the double doors, went right past reception, and straight into the open-plan workspace. Jonathan's office was at the end of the room. There was a slight ripple throughout the five or so desks in the space when she came in.

Veronica, one of Jonathan's coworkers, stood up. "Daisy. Jonathan is actually in a meeting."

"Well, he's about to be in another one."

"No, I . . . You don't understand, he's busy."

"He's not too busy to talk to the new majority owner of the company."

With that, Veronica backed way off.

With Nora and Soraya flanking her, Daisy strode straight through the office building. "I think we need a lovely sitting area over there," she said. "Don't you think so, Soraya?"

"Oh yes." Soraya walked quickly to keep pace.

"And there." Daisy pointed at the big blank wall at the back. "A mural, I think, Nora. To really express the mission statement of this company. The natural beauty of the surroundings. Family. This is a family business, after all."

The door to Jonathan's office opened, and he emerged a moment later, looking somewhat wild eyed, and Daisy smiled, suspecting Veronica had messaged him.

"Hi," she said, as bright as could be.

"What are you doing here?" he asked, looking from her to Nora to Soraya.

"Oh." She did her best to look innocent. "I'm looking at my office."

"Your office?"

"Well, not *only* mine. But majority mine. Fifty-one percent of it, I think."

"What the hell are you talking about, Daisy?" he asked.

"Oh, that's right, Zach probably didn't tell you. He's unhappy with the trajectory of the company, Jonathan. He doesn't want to be involved anymore, and so he sold it to me."

"He what?"

"He sold it to me."

She waited. Waited for the accusation that she was screwing Zach, or whatever, but it didn't come.

Because he didn't see her that way. He didn't see her at all. He saw her as a housewife. As an attachment to him. And not as a whole human being. He couldn't fathom her having goals, ambitions, skills, a life outside of him. It was almost hilarious.

"You can't do this," he said.

"Yes, I can, and I did. Things are going to change around here. Immediately. Starting with the fact that you're going to be paid a salary. You can no longer spend indiscriminately out of business funds."

"I don't—"

"You do. I saw all the jewelry you bought for your girlfriend from the company account."

The employees shifted all around. They didn't like that. And why would they? They were probably being denied raises to help support the lifestyle Jonathan wanted to cultivate.

"Any excess will go back into the company or will be evaluated for disbursement at the end of the year. To be split among business partners, and staff, of course. Also, you need to do something about your subcontractors. Effective immediately, you will be using Sam Reynolds for your electrical. I'll get referrals for your other subcontractors, but there have been complaints."

"You're not in construction. You don't get to make these decisions."

"I get to make these decisions because we are now business partners. You can divorce me, but you can't get rid of me entirely." She looked around the room. "I'm thinking pink accent pillows."

"This is insane," he said.

As she turned to face him, with Nora and Soraya on either side of her, she'd never felt more powerful. More like a coven.

"No. Insane is cheating on your high school sweetheart, not even trying to work out any problems you were having, just cheating like a coward. Insane is lying to your new girlfriend about the state of your marriage and bringing her into a mess she wouldn't have brought herself into if she'd known." That was a Hail Mary, based on her recent chats with Amberly, but she could tell by the look on his face she was right. "Insane is being a father who acts like he doesn't know his kids' meal schedule or what their teachers' names are. *This* is just a little light revenge."

"I'll buy you out." His tone was desperate, and the feeling of being in charge right now? She'd been the one who felt so powerless. She'd be lying if she said she didn't enjoy this. Watching him sweat. Watching him wonder what his life was going to look like in the next month, the next year.

He'd taken all her certainty away. Now she was taking his.

"I'd make you pay," she said.

"This is petty." He took a step toward her.

Nora, Soraya, and Daisy exchanged glances. And they laughed.

"Petty? Hell yeah, it's petty. It turns out I'm very, very petty, Jonathan." She smiled. "To think, you could've lived your entire life without ever experiencing just how petty I am. What a treat."

Chapter Thirty

Soraya

I am allowed to have joy.
I am allowed to have pleasure.
I am allowed to live.
I am the embodiment of all that is
beautiful.
And so it is.

—*A spell for claiming your confidence*

Soraya thought she could do one better than texting Declan. Instead, she decided to bring both boys down to the store.

Maybe the newfound confidence was from the tea, or from the night she'd spent with Daisy and Nora, screaming and jumping into freezing water and dancing in front of the fire like pagans. Or just like women who had no one to impress, no more shame and nothing to lose.

Maybe it was having the kids back.

Maybe it was everything.

She felt grounded in who she was now. In what she wanted.

"This is cool," Jaden said as he touched a large sword mounted in a display. "I thought you didn't like *Dungeons & Dragons*."

"Well, I'm changing my mind about some things. I don't think there's anything wrong with you playing a game. Even if it does have magic in it."

"Are you trying to be the cool parent?" Levi asked.

"Excuse me?"

"I just mean, because we were . . . because we weren't being nice to you, are you trying to be cooler than Dad?"

"No. I'm trying to be myself. I'm still figuring out what that looks like." She looked around, glad that, for the moment, Declan wasn't in the front of the store. "I'm trying to unlearn some beliefs I don't think are good anymore." She took a deep breath. "I was really hurt that you sided with Dad, but I helped teach you the rules that made me into the bad guy in all this. I don't believe it anymore. I don't believe that a woman has to do everything her husband says, that she has to forgive everything, and endure everything, for the sake of the marriage."

She put a hand on her son's shoulder. "I don't want *you* to believe it. I want you to be able to be a better partner for whoever you end up with. I want you to respect them more. I'm not trying to say anything awful about your father, but you know what happened. Everyone does. He was never honest with me about who he was. Or what he wanted. There was nothing I could do better if he didn't talk to me. But all that, him, what he wants, that's up to him to figure out now. I don't want to be married to him anymore. I think I've changed too much. I can't forgive him. I hope that you do. I don't want you to hate either of us. He's your dad."

"But you're supposed to just know everything," Levi said.

"Why?" she asked.

"Because you're an adult."

"You're in for a disappointing time if you think that's how it works, my love. I'm sorry. In fact, I feel like I know less now than I did when I was your age."

"Can I help you find anything?"

Her heart hit her breastbone so hard she thought she might faint.

She'd seen that man naked, and now he was simply standing there behind the counter, looking at her like she was a normal, everyday customer he hadn't been inside of.

"We're just looking around." Her throat was dry and scratchy. "I don't know anything about games like this."

"We do run monthly *Dungeons & Dragons* campaigns. If they want to sign up."

"I might." Jaden looked a little shamefaced, but obviously not shamed enough to let the opportunity pass him up.

"I don't know about that." Levi pulled a face.

She cleared her throat. "Jaden, Levi, this is Declan. He lives across the hall."

The boys looked at each other, and then at her, like they didn't understand why they were supposed to care.

Fair enough.

"Cool," Levi said, because he was old enough that he was at least trying to be polite.

The door opened, and a group of teenagers came in, kids from the boys' school, and they started talking, sufficiently distracted from her, which made it the perfect time for her to approach Declan.

"I'm sorry that I canceled." Her heart was fluttering rapidly, so much so she felt like he could probably tell.

"That's okay. I wondered if I did something wrong."

"No. You didn't." She closed her eyes. "It was me having baggage and religious trauma and not knowing how to deal with myself and my feelings."

"That's a lot of things."

"It is." She laughed, because if she didn't, she might cry.

"But your kids are with you." He gestured toward them. "Speaking to you."

"Yeah. You probably heard about the pastor who burned the house down by now."

"Yes," he said.

"That was my ex's house."

"Oh wow."

"Yeah. Well. He kind of earned it. He . . . Well, that's a story I'd like to tell you, maybe over dinner."

"You want to uncancel the date."

"I do. I got freaked out for a minute."

"Of all the reasons you had, I didn't imagine *that* one. Feels kind of understandable."

She laughed. "Good. I . . . I'm really bad at this. Because I don't have any experience. I literally didn't even date my husband. I just married him. When I was eighteen." She winced. "I'm going to do things like that. I'm going to tell you things you didn't ask. Probably scare you a little bit."

"I'm not scared."

"Okay. So that's good. It's a good start."

"It is."

"So as long as you're okay with me being weird and awkward, we should be all right."

"Soraya," he said slowly. "I own a store that focuses on role-playing games. Awkward is definitely something I'm used to."

"But *you* don't seem awkward."

"Again, I'm very good at role-playing. I'll tell you more about me at dinner."

"Great."

"I'll text you details," he said.

"Okay."

The boys' friends walked out of the store, and Jaden and Levi drifted back to her side.

Declan waved, and Soraya smiled before leading the boys back out of the store onto the sidewalk. "Burritos?" she asked, gesturing toward the little walk-up window down the street.

"Sure," Levi said.

She started walking, and they followed. "I'm going to dinner with Declan this weekend."

They both stopped right where they were on the sidewalk, their expressions filled with shock and horror.

"Well. Better that you know. I just don't want to go back to not talking. I don't want to do secrets."

"But . . ." Levi looked pained. "You're actually dating?"

"I guess so." She started walking again. "I'm doing my best to not be a liar or a hypocrite." Best practice would be to not talk smack about their dad, but she also wasn't going to take on fault for the sake of being the bigger person.

The martyrish wife. No. She was done with that.

He'd put their kids in terrible danger. He'd lied to everyone. Like Levi said, he'd made *them* get purity rings, for God's sake.

"You really need to date?" Jaden asked.

"No. I don't need to. But I'm not just your mom, you know. I'm a whole person, and I want to be happy and meet someone. I want romance and to have someone with me."

"But not Dad," Jaden confirmed.

"No." She looked at him. "Do you blame me?"

"No," Levi mumbled.

"No." Jaden seemed surprised at his own answer.

"Good. Then I'll keep you posted." She put her arm around Jaden, and Levi dodged her, smiling just slightly, but it felt teenage and normal, and not like he hated her.

She could breathe.

She felt like she was coming out of it. Felt like she was coming into the light, after walking in the darkness for way too long.

Chapter Thirty-One

Nora

I release what holds me back,
I release what no longer fits,
I honor the ending of the cycle,
I am at peace,
I am free.

—A spell for moving on

Nora needed to deal with Sam. The night around the bonfire had given her clarity. It had made her feel new. It had given her a much clearer view of herself, not just as she had been, but how she wanted to be.

She spent the day working on the mural and came to a very important conclusion.

Before she did anything else, she needed to talk to Ben. She needed to rip that Band-Aid off, because it was a wound she was protecting. Because if she had gone to Sam first, it would have felt wrong. Like she had decided to beta test how things were going with him before she pulled the plug on her marriage. She didn't want to put Sam in that position. She didn't want to put herself in that position.

So she had to do it. Maybe it was the right move. Because she needed to practice. Being honest. Being vulnerable.

She just needed to do it.

She took a deep breath and walked into the hospital room. She didn't even know if he remembered the one interaction they'd had when he'd regained consciousness. He had been totally hopped up on pain meds, and mainly delirious.

"Nora." He looked completely shocked.

"Yeah. Me."

"It's good to see you." His tone was warm and calm, and she hated it.

"Maybe don't be too emphatic about that until I tell you what I have to say. I want a divorce."

"Nora . . ."

"I know you cheated on me." She wasn't even going to get into how she'd found out.

"I was on a trip to try and reevaluate life. I wasn't cheating, I . . ."

"Oh, were we on a break?"

"I thought it was implied that, during the separation, we could explore the things we need to explore."

"That's weird how you didn't say that explicitly," she said. "Almost like you didn't actually want me to take you up on that."

"Nora, I'm sorry. I'm sorry I didn't communicate more clearly with you. But you know I love you. I got a little bit lost. But I have clarity now."

"She loves you, by the way. I read all her frantic texts."

Ben looked distressed. Genuinely. It would have been funny if it weren't so pathetic. "But she's not who I want with me right now. She's not who I want to care for me while I recover."

"That's . . . You have to be kidding. That's how you're looking at this? That's your lens? You want to have me take care of you? Suddenly you realize maybe the twenty-year-old bohemian chick you banged up on a mountain isn't the one. You didn't say we were on a break. You're just a liar. You are so good at packaging it into something palatable. Pretending you're so rational and cool, and I am . . . a mess. You're the one who ran away from our marriage. You're the one who couldn't have a conversation. You're childish. Because you've never experienced a struggle in your goddamn life, and mine terrify you. That's it, isn't it? I make you feel breakable and fragile. Because I've actually lived through things. I'll live through this too. But we aren't going to make it."

She turned away from him.

"This is rich, Nora," he said, his voice suddenly hard, his entire demeanor different. "You taking this moral high ground when getting you to share anything is an uphill battle. When you have Sam loitering around constantly. Are you going to tell me that you never slept with him?"

She closed her eyes. "No, Ben, I never did. You're right. I do have him. He means a lot to me. But I've never cheated on you. I thought we were happy. I can see now all the ways in which we weren't. I can see now that I had blind spots, but if you had tried to work on our marriage, if you had talked to me, I would've done whatever I could to fix it. But you didn't. You lied to me instead, and now you're trying to turn it around and make it seem like it's my fault. I'm not going to say I didn't make mistakes. That I didn't freeze you out sometimes. That I didn't . . . have emotional intimacy with a friend that may have kept us from being closer, but I thought it worked for you. I would've changed for you. So thank God that you left. That you lied to me. That you didn't stay. Because if I'm going to change, it needs to be for me. I think if you hadn't done this, I wouldn't have realized that."

She turned and walked out of the room, and she wasn't sure quite what she had been expecting. For him to try to bargain with her. For him to yell that she wasn't going to get anything. She didn't want anything. She just wanted to start over.

She didn't cry because she could see the reality of their relationship too clearly now. She'd needed him to make her feel normal, safe, like she was okay.

But not now.

Now she finally felt powerful. She wasn't going to hang on to a broken marriage just for the sake of having a marriage. Not when she could have everything. Even if everything felt like a risk.

Chapter Thirty-Two

Soraya

Your heart is your North Star, your compass, and your truth.

—Rules for Witches

The lavender dress had seemed perfectly reasonable in that shop, and she'd felt pretty in it. She still did. She just had this concern that it was too much.

That she was too much in it.

No. No, she wasn't going to do this. She'd bought this dress in a moment of total empowerment, and she wasn't going to backslide now.

She looked hot. She was owning it.

The boys had gone back to their old family home to stay with David for a couple of days, and she couldn't say she blamed them. The apartment was tiny, and it didn't really have an excess of room. But things with them felt so much more okay now. So much less precarious. Even with the date.

They knew about it. There was no other shoe she was waiting to have dropped. No big secret waiting to come out. At least not on her end.

Maybe David had a hundred more secrets. Who could say?

When they actually sorted out the legal part of the divorce, she might fight him for the house, depending on how she felt at the time.

But probably not.

Which meant she would always have the house that wasn't as nice. But she would have herself. So even if she couldn't give the boys the best material possessions, she was going to try to be the honest parent. The one who showed them that they could fail and get back up again. That they could be wrong. That they could make mistakes and it wouldn't undo them completely.

She'd spent so much of her life afraid to do the wrong thing. Here she was, sitting in the consequences of her husband's wrong thing. So maybe she would make a mistake. Maybe Declan would be a mistake.

She needed to find a way to be okay with that. Doing what she wanted. Going with what felt right to her at the moment, even if it wasn't right forever. It was so categorically not the way she had ever done anything before. Following her own intuition . . .

That would be a new experience.

The knock on the door nearly made her jump out of her skin, and she checked herself in the mirror one more time before opening it up. His gaze flickered over her, down her legs, and she was glad she'd gone with the short dress. It hadn't felt like her when she put it on, but the pleasure she felt about being admired was very real and made it feel like the right choice. The choice that fit her now.

"We can just walk down the street. I thought Indonesian food sounded good."

"Yeah. It sounds great." She drifted nearer to him, their shoulders bumping. Her heart jumped. "I don't know if we're supposed to hold hands or not."

He looked at her. "Do you want to?"

"Yeah. I would."

He took her hand, like it didn't require any thought at all. "So, you got married very young," he said as they walked down the hall together, down the stairs. He didn't waste any time.

"Yes, I did. And it ended very badly."

"I gathered that. You said you were going to tell me the story."

So she did. The whole thing. Which wasn't cool, reserved, or socially appropriate for how well she knew him. She kept on talking all while they got seated for dinner and while they ordered. She didn't finish her story until they were halfway through their order of corn fritters.

"So, that's me," she said. "What about you?"

"Are we going to stick with the theme of just putting it all out there?"

"I think we should."

"My son died. Five years ago."

"Oh." She put her hand against her heart. "I'm sorry . . ."

He cleared his throat and looked down. "Yeah. He loved board games. We used to play together. That's how I ended up starting the store. I was an ER doctor before that. But I couldn't do emergencies anymore. Not after that. Marriage ended, and I moved here."

"How old was he?"

"Fifteen. About the same age as your younger boy."

Soraya's eyes filled with tears. "That's awful. I'm so . . . I'm so sorry."

"I can talk about it. Much easier than I used to be able to. But one of the good things about moving to a place like this, where nobody knows you, is that you can choose who you talk about it with. I think that was what ended my marriage, honestly. We couldn't escape it. Our grief, each other's grief. For some people, it brings you together. It just drove us apart."

She was on a completely different date than she had imagined she would be on. "I'm so sorry. I feel like that's not enough."

"The good news is, nothing makes that okay. So there's actually nothing you can say to make it worse or better. Just don't freak out and not want to date me anymore."

"Why would I do that?"

"My sadness usually makes other people uncomfortable."

"Not me." She wasn't entirely sure that was true. She didn't think it was discomfort making her breathing labored. It was something else. Yeah. It was something else.

Just sadness for him. Curiosity about the man he'd once been. Before the loss. Because it had clearly changed him profoundly. It made so much sense that he was a doctor. She had thought he had that sort of controlled manner about him, a confidence. The kind of guy who would be great in an emergency.

"So when you said you didn't do this all the time after we . . ."

"I really don't. Not since my divorce, honestly."

"Really?"

"I was never big on hooking up. Everything in the years since have been so heavy. It's one of those things—you either keep it to yourself or you have to tell the other person. And the minute you tell someone something like this, it's a lot more serious."

"Yeah. I understand that. I haven't *experienced* that. But I'm sort of dysfunctional and traumatized by the way my marriage ended, and also by the way my church treated me. So I'm probably the exact wrong sort of woman for you."

He laughed. "I don't know about that. I saw you, and I was instantly . . . I want you."

"Well, that is nice. Maybe we can be mutually dysfunctional until we figure something out."

"I'd like that."

"Do you want to talk about him?"

It must be a terrible thing to be in a town where no one knew who his son was. Where he couldn't easily share memories about him.

"I'd like that," he said.

They finished their meal and took a walk, and he told her all about Brody. About the games he liked to play, and how he was great at drawing and Xbox. That his birthday was in October, and he really liked ice cream. About the *Dungeons & Dragons* campaigns they'd done together. Which led into a long story about how *Dungeons & Dragons* had gotten Declan through high school.

"Are you actually a geek?" she asked.

"Guilty," he said. "I was horrendously awkward for all of my teenage years."

"You're just too attractive for me to believe that."

"It got me into a lot of trouble—please forgive me for not having false modesty here—because I could get a girl to go out with me, but she didn't necessarily want to hear about *Star Trek*."

She laughed. His stories wove in and out of his loss, sad memories and happy ones, and by the time they finished and found themselves back at the apartment, she was afraid she was enchanted by him.

"I'm glad you decided to go out with me again," he said.

"Me too." She sighed. "I was kind of afraid that God was punishing me for having sex with you."

To his credit, he didn't turn and run away. "I see. What do you think now?"

"I'm willing to risk it. But if another building burns down after we do it this time, we might have to rethink some things."

He laughed. "Are you serious?"

"I don't actually know."

"I'm willing to risk it if you are."

"I am," she said.

"How about we do it at my place this time?"

"Okay."

She let him lead her into his apartment and left worries about Judgment Day for another time.

Chapter Thirty-Three

Daisy

I heal my body,
I heal my mind,
I draw on the power of those who
stand with me,
I heal the sacred within me,
I heal the ones who stand with me,
I am whole.
And so it is.

—*A spell for healing*

Daisy couldn't have been happier with the way that the tarot night came together. They'd had twenty-five women sign up for the event since they'd first posted it. Soraya had made cream cakes with Maibowle wine, topped with strawberry slices and sweet woodruff sprigs, lemon honey cakes with candied citrus slices on top, and savory scones with herbs from Aggie's garden.

The shop was decorated with bunches of flowers, swaths of flowing fabric, and woven ribbon that mirrored the look of a maypole. They put three folding tables together to make a long banquet table, with a brightly patterned cloth covering the whole thing. Candles in golden holders were placed down the length of it, and malachite and rose quartz were scattered in a line like glimmering stardust.

"Daisy, I'd like for you to give readings tonight." With only two hours until the event, it was a surprising request for Aggie to make.

"I don't know if I can give a reading," Daisy said.

"Why not? You've become very familiar with the cards."

"But I don't know if I . . . I'm not like you." Daisy looked over at the deck of cards just to her left, a strange, burning sensation in her chest.

"It's intuition," Aggie said. "Everyone has intuition. Everyone has magic. All you have to do is tap into that voice inside of you. You can do it for yourself, and you can do it for others."

"You think I can?"

"Daisy, I know you can. The way you have always planned for everyone, cared for them, that's been you using your intuition to discover what they need. This is something you already know how to do."

Daisy had never thought of any of that as intuition, but it made some sense. "Okay. I'll do it."

Soraya was busy behind the counter, fussing with baked goods, and even though Nora had seemed a little bit off ever since her fight with Sam, she was better than she had been before their bonfire night. Soraya, for her part, seemed cheerful.

"How was your date?" Daisy asked.

Soraya smiled. "It was very good."

"Oh, I recognize that face," Daisy said. "It's the exact same face I made after Zach absolutely rocked my body for the first time."

Soraya shrugged. "Well, it wasn't the first time, but I'm growing. And changing. And enjoying the incredibly handsome man who likes me."

"Good for you," Daisy said. "You." She turned to Nora. "What are you going to do about Sam?"

"I just need to fully let go of all my terror at changing things with him and screwing us up."

"I think you're in just the right place to get the energy you need." Daisy squeezed her shoulder.

Nora sighed, and they stood in the back while the room slowly filled up. There were several groups of young women, girls that none of them knew, and then, much to Daisy's surprise, a group of moms from the school. But the real shock came when one of the women from Soraya's church came in. She looked a little bit intimidated but made a beeline for Soraya.

"Kristi?"

"Well." Kristi was looking around a bit nervously, like Soraya had that first day. "Since you work here, I thought I would see what it's all about. Also, since the church is . . . I don't think it's going to make it. There's been a big divide over everything, over David and how John handled it and all of those things, and it's just . . . It's never going to be the same."

"I know how hard it is to lose your community," Soraya said.

"I know." Kristi was almost whispering, like shame had stolen half her voice. "I'm really sorry. I was so . . . prideful. I just thought I knew the way everything worked. I thought I knew who was good. Who wasn't. I thought I was being kind by coming to your house and telling you all of that. I thought it was tough love. But it wasn't. I didn't listen to you. That's what I keep feeling so upset about. How uncurious I've been for so long. So I'm here. Being curious."

"I can relate," Soraya remarked. "But I'm glad you're here. Maybe we can have coffee sometime."

"I'd like that," said Kristi.

The room was filled with laughter and conversation, and everyone took their seats around the table. Aggie was at the head, and she stood, her long white hair hanging freely, her eyes sparkling. "Welcome to our first tarot night. This is the night for all of us to explore our intuition. To tap into our needs, physical and spiritual, and to offer help to one another in whatever form it might take."

A woman wearing a blue blazer and a pencil skirt slipped into the room and sat down at the table.

"That's my lawyer," Nora whispered.

"All are welcome here. All your hopes are welcome here. All your fears. Tonight, we are filling this space with good energy and sharing it with one another. But that doesn't mean there won't be tears or there won't be difficult conversations. But we are making this place safe for all of that."

Aggie picked up a piece of palo santo, the slender chunk of wood glowing bright as she touched it to a candle at the center of the table, a stream of smoke that smelled sweet and fragrant filling the air.

"I banish all negative energy. I call all good energy to us. That we may give and share and hope. I ask that only truths come into this place. That all lies be expelled. I ask for protection from any energy that seeks to do us harm, I ask for only good to be done here tonight. I ask for peace. And so we begin."

Aggie had a small station set up for making flower crowns, and Soraya had a space where she could talk to people about tea blends and remedies. Nora was helping with simple spell bags.

Daisy pulled a deck of tarot cards to her, and soon there were different groups rotating through her space, taking readings. She was nervous at first, afraid she was going to say the wrong thing. Tarot was interesting, because you couldn't control it. While she was well studied in the cards, she didn't know what would come up, how it might relate to the person across from her, or if what she was saying was completely wrong or not.

But she surrendered to it. To her intuition, rather than a detailed plan. To the idea that she did have magic within her. It had to be true, didn't it?

Zach had fallen in love with her from the first moment he'd seen her.

That thought made her stomach feel hollow. Zach. He loved her. He hadn't said it, but right then, with her hands hovering on the tarot cards and all the shared wisdom in the room, she felt it.

She felt a voice in the air telling her to accept it. Not to push it away. Because life was strange and miraculous, and there was so much that couldn't be understood, including the timing of all this. Except maybe it was the path she had to be on to get here.

Jonathan was an integral part of her story. They had created the three most wonderful kids she could have asked for. He had helped her at different points in her life. And he had given her baggage. It had all come together to make her who she was. To make her into the woman Zach admired.

The woman who appreciated him so much.

She could never regret it, or wish that things had unfolded differently, because if even one thing had changed, would she be who she was now?

Sitting here, in the full knowledge of her own magic, with Soraya and Nora and this wonderful apothecary, she smiled as she finished her reading.

The woman who sat across from her next looked like she was near tears.

"I'm Daisy. What's your name?"

"Angela."

"What do you need help with?"

Tears slid down her cheeks. "Everything."

"I'm sorry," Daisy said. "Do you have a question for the cards? I can suggest a simple past, present, future spread."

"Is there . . . any way to know how to . . . fix my life? What am I supposed to do?"

Daisy's heart thundered as she started trying to think of a spread. "Okay . . . the problem, the action, the outcome."

She laid out her first card, the Devil, then the Three of Cups, followed by the Star. "Your problem is that you're being kept down by something. Someone."

"My husband," Angela whispered.

Daisy nodded. "The solution is to seek help." She looked at the art on the card, at the women dancing together. "To seek friendship and a community." Goose bumps broke out on her arms. "The Star is the outcome. It's hope. In the major arcana, the Star comes after the Tower. The Tower is a period of disruption and sometimes destruction. The Star is the clarity and the goals reached afterward."

"I need help," Angela said. "He's . . . It's not safe for me to be with him, but I don't have anywhere to go, and I can't afford a lawyer."

Daisy looked back where the woman in blue had sat, Nora's lawyer. Nora was looking at her too. Then she stood and made her way to Daisy and Angela.

"I'm Elisa Patrick. I overheard. If you need my services, I'm happy to help you. Pro bono."

"But . . . no, you can't do that." Angela looked genuinely shocked. "It's your job, you need to get paid."

"I do get paid," she said. "Enough that when there's a situation like this, I can afford to help."

"It's so embarrassing." Angela's face crumpled.

Daisy put her hand on Angela's. "There's no shame in this, not for you. He's the only one who should be ashamed."

Elisa wrapped her arm around Angela. "Come over here, we can talk."

This was basically Nora's prophecy being fulfilled. That if they did this gathering, people who needed help would come. If they filled a room with women, there would be those who needed help, and the helpers who were ready to give it.

Daisy did more readings, heard more stories, and found more ways to meet needs. By the end of the night, people had found caregivers for ailing family members, jobs, tenants, and more.

As the evening was winding down, Madison looked at her phone and gasped. "Oh God. I have to go."

"What happened?" Daisy asked.

"My mom had a brain aneurysm. They're rushing her in for surgery to try to stop the bleeding."

Daisy's blood went cold, her heart thundering sickly in her chest.

"Ladies," Aggie said, standing at the head of the table. "Tonight, we've made magic in this place, and now we need to make more. Because Alexandra needs us. She needs us all to use our magic."

There was a rumble in the room, and Daisy could see some women shift in discomfort, doubt. Disbelief.

Aggie continued. "You all came here because you want this to be possible. Because you want to believe in your own magic. In your intuition. Because you want to tap into your power. Use it now. Use it now for Alexandra."

Daisy stood up, grabbed a candle, and set it at the center of the table. She lit the flame, burning conviction guiding her. Intuition.

She closed her eyes. "May healing descend upon Alexandra Stone. May all the darkness that attempts to bind her be locked away. May it be bound. I call forth healing from all who have the power to will it to her. She must survive. She must wake up."

Daisy felt pressure in her head, and she touched her forehead. Nora moved to her and took her hand. Then Soraya came to her other side and held on to her. All the other women around the table joined hands.

"The truth must be revealed," Daisy said. "Only through healing will the truth be revealed." She was going off book, deviating from the healing spell exactly as it had been written. But it was like truth was flowing through her. Vision. Insight and intuition. She hadn't ever imagined such a thing was possible, but she couldn't doubt it now.

She had been there the night they'd cast the revenge spell. She knew what it felt like when magic was in the room. It was like that now. "Everyone say this with me. We call for healing on Alexandra Stone."

"We call for healing on Alexandra Stone," the women repeated in a chorus, the sound of their voices unified leaving goose bumps on Daisy's arms.

"Only if she wakes can the truth be revealed," Daisy said.

"Only if she wakes can the truth be revealed."

"Healing will be given."

"Healing will be given."

"The truth will be known."

"The truth will be known."

"And so it is."

She picked up the candle and blew it out.

The silence that followed was heavy, weighted by the profound sense of what had just happened.

There was power here. There was power in this group of women. They had all gathered tonight because they needed something. Desperately.

They needed to know that this power lived inside them. That they were magic. No matter what their parents, their partners, their teachers, their friends had told them. That search had brought them together for this. Daisy had to believe that it was true. That when they came together, women were powerful. That this was the greater good they had been searching for all this time.

She turned and looked at Nora.

"I have to go," Nora said.

"I understand."

She did, without Nora having to tell her. It was like real, true clarity had descended on everyone here. The moment she realized Zach loved her, things had become sharp. She could see it was true now for Nora.

She knew exactly what Nora had to do.

"Let me know if you hear anything about Alexandra?" Nora asked.

"Of course I will."

Chapter Thirty-Four

Nora

Protection can be power. But protection can also be prison.

—Rules for Witches

Nora had been shaking ever since they cast the spell. Maybe it was wrong to have any epiphanies beyond the healing spell, but something had happened with all that magic moving through the room. Moving through her. Something had shifted and changed inside her.

She couldn't wait anymore.

She drove to Sam's house, unseeing. She was being fueled by the burning conviction in her heart, and nothing more.

She tumbled out of the car and went to the door, knocking ferociously until he jerked it open.

"Nora," he said. "What are you doing here?"

"I . . . Sam."

There was so much she wanted to say. So much she needed to say. But they had been talking, even if they'd been talking around the truth, for twenty fucking years. She was done.

She launched herself at him, wrapping her arms around his neck and pressing her lips to his.

He cupped the back of her head, angling his head and deepening the kiss, and for the first time, she felt like she was breathing. Like part of her had come home, like she was restored.

Will I find love?

I have the love I deserve.

Will I find love?

I have the love I deserve.

It had been here all this time. He had been there all that time. She had been too broken to see it. She had been casting love spells and asking for what had already been delivered to her.

Sam.

She had thought she was running toward love all her life, but she had been running from it. From something that felt too big, too risky, too dangerous. From something that felt dangerous in ways she hadn't been able to face.

Because the truth was, she had chosen Ben because she knew she could survive this.

She'd run from Sam because she'd known that if she ever lost him, she would have to make serious changes. She would have to remake herself.

He had forced her to do that.

Maybe the magic had forced him to do that.

She had thought it was karma, but it was love all along.

The only way she could get that love, the only way she could have it, was by dismantling every barrier she had ever put in place.

"Sam," she whispered against his mouth.

"Tell me this has nothing to do with him," he said.

"It has nothing to do with him." She touched his face, looked into his eyes. "Nothing. I told him I wanted a divorce days ago. I made that choice. I . . . I can live without him. I can't live without you."

"Is this pity? Is this what you're doing to keep me?"

"No. No. It's not. I swear to God, Sam, I . . . It's not."

Then they were kissing again, and she was sure his face was wet, but she didn't stop kissing him, because then he would look and see that so was hers. That she was right there with him. Dissolving as they finally, finally tore this mint-condition relationship all to hell.

This was risky. This was a change.

But it was either be burned alive in this house on fire or take a risk and jump.

She was a whole goddamn burning house. That was the problem.

She had to jump outside herself, outside all these issues, in order to have a hope of being saved.

She just wanted some hope.

She just wanted him.

She'd kissed her share of men. She'd been so convinced that the reason it had never lit her on fire in the way she fantasized it might when she'd been a teenage girl was because fantasy was always going to be more potent than reality. But it clicked now, this obvious truth. The fantasy had always been Sam. No one had ever been him, so the others had fallen short of all she had ever wanted.

Of all she ever needed.

It was Sam.

She just needed him.

"I need to see you," she said. "Naked. I need . . . Oh God. Oh, Sam . . ." She thought she was on the verge of having a panic attack, or maybe a heart attack. Maybe both.

"We can slow it down." His words said *slow down*, but his voice sounded like it was pained.

"No. This has been a twenty-year slow burn. We just have to let it happen."

He stripped his shirt off, and she was overwhelmed by her desire for him. When the rest of his clothes came off, she lost the ability to think. The ability to speak.

He was so perfect. So utterly and completely perfect. And Sam. Precious to her in ways no one else had ever been. Her lifeline. Her sanity. The only one who knew her. When he began to take her clothes off, she felt truly exposed for the first time in her life. Like he was taking off not just her clothes, but all her defenses, every bit of protection she'd ever had.

Because he knew she wasn't tough. He knew she was that girl who had gotten on her knees in the dirt and asked a Ouija board if anyone would ever love her. He knew she was broken. He was kissing her anyway. He was looking at her like she was something beautiful and precious anyway.

He took her bra off, cupped her breasts, and looked up. "Jesus Christ."

It might've been a prayer, it might've been a curse. It was impossible for her to know. He moved his thumbs over her nipples, pleasure arcing through her.

He kissed her like she might be fragile, then picked her up and pressed her against the wall like she was unbreakable. His fingers dug into her hips as he lifted her off the floor and wrapped her legs around his waist. She was topless, only wearing jeans, while he was naked and glorious, and she didn't think they were going to make it to a bedroom. And that was just fine.

They had already done the crazy thing. The thing that terrified her. They had admitted that it had never really been only friendship.

He had been right. He was the most intimate relationship she had, and she had convinced herself that as long as she kept sex out of it, she was never going to have to expose herself. She was never going to have to take the risk.

But now she was risking it all. A gamble. Betting it all to try to have it all.

He laid her down on the couch, and she scrabbled up onto her knees, kissing his stomach, hard and well muscled, moving down to take the head of his arousal into her mouth. He was so hot. Gorgeous. She wanted all of him. Wanted him to touch the back of her throat, claim her, make her his. He gripped the back of her hair and thrust his hips forward, her name a growl on his lips as she continued to pleasure him.

Because she knew him, she knew just what to do. Because he knew her, he didn't take it slow or gentle.

Because life had been rough with them, so this might as well be rough in the best way possible.

"Fuck," he said, jerking away from her suddenly. "I can't . . . Not like that."

"One of these times it's going to have to be like that. Because I want you. All of you."

He pushed her down onto her back, leaned in, and bit her neck. "I want it too. But I wanted to be inside of you for as long as I've known such a thing was possible. You are my sexual awakening, my darkest fantasy. And I need it. Now."

She moaned as he wrapped his arm around her and lifted her hips up off the couch.

"Do I need to get a condom?" he asked.

She shook her head. "I have an IUD."

"Perfect."

He thrust into her, and it was like everything made sense. Like all the pieces of her were finally together. Not sporadic. Fractured. Like she was a little creature hoarding bits of treasure in different places so that she was never in danger of losing it all. He was the entire treasure. Her best friend. Her lover. The love of her life. It was risky. So risky.

But she didn't want anything else. Couldn't stand to have anything else. Not when she needed him.

Oh, she desperately needed him.

He moved deep inside her, her desire ruthless and uncompromising. This wasn't pleasure like she'd known it before. This was something new. Something different. Sharp and glorious and dangerous all at once.

She wondered if the roof would cave in. If the very delicate ecosystem that was her life would suddenly be out of balance, out of control in a way she could see or feel. If the whole world would end.

Because that was what this had always felt like. Like it would be world ending. Like it would be the kind of catastrophe neither of them would ever be able to come back from.

Instead, Sam was holding her, touching her face, whispering her name as he kissed her lips, and it wasn't strange or wrong. It was like things were right for the first time ever.

It was like what had been out of place before was suddenly locked in, and it just felt good. She had spent so many years not touching him. Not knowing what it was like to taste him. Not knowing what it would be like to have him inside her.

It was a waste. But then, maybe she wouldn't have been able to appreciate it then. Maybe back then they would have blown it all to hell. Maybe they would've sabotaged it. Themselves, each other. But not now. Not now that they were thirty-five. Not now that she'd had other relationships, had been in a marriage that hadn't worked. Not now that they had done some important healing from childhoods full of trauma. Most of all, not now that she knew they would both do anything for each other.

The way he moved inside her was a revelation, and all the words in her brain evaporated as she clung to his shoulders and surrendered to the moment. To the deep strokes of his cock and the intense, sharp desire that grabbed her by the throat and held her there. Not docile or submissive but enjoying full surrender.

She looked into his eyes as he lost control. He was always so stoic, his features hard as granite, but now they trembled just a bit. As tears filled his eyes and tears spilled from hers in response. As her orgasm gripped her along with sobs, and she dissolved completely. A mass of need and clinical destruction utterly reduced and remade in his arms.

"I didn't cry for Ben," she whispered in his ear.

She needed him to know that. That this was different for her in every way. That he wasn't second place. He'd been the first, the deepest, and she hadn't been able to handle it when she was younger. She could handle it now.

He collapsed beside her, touching her cheekbone, drawing his thumb down to her lips. It was Sam who was touching her. Sam who was naked beside her. Sam.

"I've never cried for anyone, Nora. Not anyone but you."

"I was really afraid of this. Like people are scared of the plague or plane crashes."

"Are people scared of the plague?"

"Prairie dogs carry plague. It's not eradicated."

"Okay," he said, his hand on her face. "You're very you."

"What does that mean?"

"I don't know. Except that I wanted you for most of my life. I've loved you for most of my life, but . . . I was afraid that if it happened, you would turn into someone else. It would be like every other relationship I've ever tried to have, which wasn't good."

"I have to wonder if maybe our relationships haven't worked out because we were waiting for this one." She took a deep, shaking breath. "You've always been a nonnegotiable. The most important person in my life. I made sure Ben knew you were a package deal with me. I know that when I married him, it compromised us."

"I couldn't go to your wedding because I couldn't watch you marry somebody else. I could watch you date other guys. Sleep with them, whatever you needed to do. But not marry them. I knew what you wanted. You wanted somebody normal. You wanted somebody who understood family. I wanted to want that for you. I wanted to be okay with it, because I knew I couldn't be that. But I wasn't. I was so pissed off, Nora. I wanted you to marry me."

Sorrow cracked her chest open. She'd hurt him. This man she loved with all her heart, she'd hurt him because she'd been trying so hard to protect herself.

"I've seen myself as nothing other than an agent of destruction for most of my life. The kind of person who alienates everyone around them. What you and I had worked. It worked, and so I didn't want to change it. I didn't want to disturb it. I was attracted to you, but that seemed unimportant in the face of what we were. You were everything to me. You're right. I've been a coward."

"I was too. I should've said something before you married Ben. I let that happen."

"I wouldn't have been able to do it then." She shook her head. "I'm too stubborn. Ben was like a trophy. A trophy that said I won at keeping our friendship safe. That I never gave in to any of the moments of tension between us. I never let myself fantasize about you even though I wanted to. But I kept it formless, hovering at the edges of my consciousness rather than ever really admitting I wanted you. I wanted to keep myself safe. But wouldn't you know it, life is just one endless gauntlet of danger. One after the other. When you choose yourself, you just become like my mother. Like my grandmother. I choose you. I would love to say that it should've happened a long time ago, but I think it had to be now, because I've never felt stronger or more sure of what I want. I'm sorry it had to take this long to get here, but that really is a testament to all the absolute shit we went through."

He wrapped his arms around her and held her close. "I know I wouldn't have known how to make things good with us. Not without time and therapy and the years I've spent figuring out what a stable life looks like. I do know that. But you know that day you got out the Ouija board and asked if you would find love? I was mad because you already had it. But I couldn't say that, so I was an asshole to you, and I hurt your feelings. That was the only way I knew how to express anything back then. So I guess you're right."

"Really? You didn't think I was dumb?"

"I thought you were dumb because I thought it was pretty fucking obvious that I loved you."

"We were kids."

He nodded. "Yeah. We were. Can you imagine the kind of disaster we would've been then?"

"We would've just repeated some of the same cycles."

"Yeah. We would have." He paused for a moment. "Or not. I didn't manipulate the answer, Nora. That was all you. I think you might have been magic all the way back then."

Magic.

She'd been magic all along.

She'd never felt magic even once, though she did right now.

Time could be an enemy. It stole a lot of things. It would be easy to look at time as a thief in their relationship, but she was pretty sure it was actually the ultimate gift giver.

They'd become who they needed to be to meet this moment. To know what to do with a love the size and intensity of theirs.

"I was just so afraid," she said. "I didn't feel like I was good enough. Not for you, not for anyone. I didn't want to be with someone who knew everything about me. But now it feels like a gift. You know why I'm . . . me. You're the only one who really knows how hurt I was by everything, how much I just wanted somebody to love me."

"You've had it. All these years. You never had to earn it. I took one look at you, and I fell. I could never be in another relationship because they weren't you. Everything I did was to try and become a man that you could see yourself with."

"But I married somebody else."

"I was going to reach my end point one way or the other. No apologies to Ben, but I would've kissed you when I felt like it was right whether he was in the picture or not. He made things a little easier for me."

"I think I should be offended by this, by the fact you were basically lying in wait . . ."

"There was no lying in wait. None of this was secretive. I have loved you from that first moment till now, and I've never wavered on it. We couldn't be together for some of it for a lot of reasons. But I want to be now. I know you're still married. I know it's fast. But it's not. If you think about it."

She shook her head. "It's not. I was emotionally unavailable to him because you had most of my heart. You were right. I was dividing it up so I could never lose everything. Well, now I can, Sam. If I lose you, I lose everything. You're the only person I trust with my heart. With my tears."

"Same goes, Nora." He looked at her for a long moment. "I'm in love with you."

"I'm in love with you too."

Her phone started to buzz from somewhere on the floor. It must've been in her pocket. "I have to get that." She scrambled off the bed and got onto her knees, pulling her phone out of her jeans and answering it when she saw Daisy's name on the screen. "Hello?"

"Alexandra is awake."

"Really?"

"She got out of surgery, and she . . . she's awake. Madison says that we need to go to the hospital."

"Okay. See you soon." She hung up. "Alexandra is awake," she said, looking at Sam.

"I'll drive you."

"Thank you, Sam." She leaned in and kissed him, then paused. "Sam, I did a love spell when I first started working at the apothecary."

"What?"

"I did a love spell."

"Well, if you're going to try and claim this isn't real because you did a love spell a month ago, I have some news for you."

"No. It's just . . . I thought I wanted Ben back. But my mantra was that I have the love I deserve, and when I said it, I saw your face." She looked at him in awe. "You were it all along."

He leaned in and kissed her. "Nora, I know."

"Am I the love you deserve, Sam?"

"No, Nora, I don't deserve you at all. But I'm damn glad I have you."

Chapter Thirty-Five

Alexandra

Revenge is a sweet treat; justice is the whole feast.

—Rules for Witches

I thought he was too much of a coward to do anything half as dramatic as try to kill me.

Then he loaded me into the car and drove it out onto the road I would normally take to get home from a trip, and pushed it off the edge of the embankment.

I watched it all, hovering over my body.

Just like I've been hovering over my body since I was found and taken to the hospital. Watching who came to visit, including Christopher and his mistress. If he would've had the chance to pull the plug on me, he'd have done it.

I found out he was engaging in fraud. Tax fraud, wire fraud, you name the fraud, he was doing it, and I planned to use it to get a just settlement in the divorce. He decided he'd rather I was dead.

That was my fault. I thought he was just a scammer.

Bad news for him.

I'm alive.

Which might have been the first words out of my mouth when I woke up. I'm not surprised to see my daughter standing vigil. But it is a surprise when Daisy McNamara, Nora Clarke, and Soraya Nichols come into the hospital room. I saw them here before, when I was floating above myself. I wouldn't have said I knew them well, but they came.

"I have to tell you everything," I say.

He might try to come for me again, but he can't get them all.

Daisy leans in and takes my hand. "You have a coven looking after you now, and we're going to keep you safe."

Chapter Thirty-Six

Daisy

A witch's greatest strength is found
when she loves herself.

—Rules for Witches

The details about what happened to Alexandra were pieced together slowly by both Alexandra and law enforcement over the next few weeks, culminating in charges being brought against her husband.

The surgeon had said there was no logical explanation for why she'd woken up afterward. Why she'd been able to speak and remember.

But Daisy knew. It was the coven. The power of that group of women who had come together to demand justice. It was the promise of the cards. Of their magic.

"I was the Five of Cups, you know," Nora said. They were closing up the store and working on new plans for their next gathering, which would happen around Litha, the summer festival that followed Beltane.

Daisy wanted to have it outside, a massive feast that could fit even more people, and they had been turning over the logistics of that. "In what way?"

"I had Sam the whole time. I was so busy looking at all my spilled cups, I didn't realize that I'd had what I wanted all along. Right there. The entire time. I wanted love, but I didn't want to give all of myself.

Conversely, though, I wanted all of the other person. It was right there. I couldn't see it."

"Eagerly awaiting my Two of Swords moment," Daisy muttered. "Though maybe it has to do with planning this monstrosity."

"It's not a monstrosity," Soraya said. "It's going to be amazing. I'm going to make the cutest cakes with little edible flowers."

"You're just chipper because your reading was so good."

"To be fair, I had that whole house-burning-down incident, which the cards did not predict."

"I suppose."

"The divorce is moving right along, though."

"I am very happy for you about that," Nora said.

"As am I."

When they finished closing up, it was time for Daisy to pick the kids up from Jonathan's. They were no closer to getting their divorce going, which seemed ridiculous. But at least sharing custody had become amicable, even if he was still disgruntled about the company.

But she'd thought he would push to get the legal side of it together so he and Amberly could get married.

She got out of the car, and Jonathan met her out in the driveway. "Hey," he said.

"Hi."

"I saw the news about Alexandra's husband getting charged for what happened."

"Yeah. It's . . . crazy. Thanks for not trying to kill me."

He laughed. Sort of. "I never wanted to kill you, Daisy."

"It's all the rage with men who want to get rid of their wives, so even though that's a low bar, I feel like it has to be said."

"I have something I want to talk to you about," he said.

"What?"

A million possibilities swam through her mind. He was unpredictable. The man she'd known all those years wasn't that man anymore, and she couldn't begin to guess what he might say.

"I want you back, Daisy."

She felt like she'd been punched in the stomach. She would have been less shocked if he'd punched her.

And when that shock settled, all she could think was . . . he didn't even want her. He wanted his company back. Everything Jonathan wanted was about Jonathan.

Maybe she did know him. Maybe she knew him now better than she ever had.

"What?"

"I know I don't deserve it. But all of this, my injury, my recovery . . . it's made me realize what's actually important. I got lost in my ego. It was dumb. I thought that a new partner would make me feel excitement again. Make me feel young. But that's you. You knew me back in high school. You're the only one who really gets me. You were the one, Daisy. And I want that back. I want our family back. Our home. Our life with the kids. I don't want to be a part-time dad."

If she didn't know him so well, she might have believed he meant he wanted to change. That he wanted to try again because he fully understood the ways in which he had fallen short, and what he would have to do to fix it.

But knowing him like she did, she knew he wasn't seized with love or regret so much as wishing his life could go back to how it had been. With her doing everything for him. With his life going the way he wanted it to. But even if he didn't mean that . . .

"No," she said.

"What?"

"I don't want you back, Jonathan."

He looked astonished. Honest-to-God astonished.

"But we . . . we have a family," he said.

"Yes, we do. And we're doing a pretty decent job of making it work while not being together. No, it's not what I would've chosen a few months ago if a survey had been taken, but it's what I want now."

"Daisy. You can't be serious. You can't . . . This is crazy. We can have our lives back."

"You have Amberly! You asked her to marry you. This is about me having the business. This isn't about us, and what are you going to tell her?"

"It's not about the business, it's about our life."

"I don't want that life."

It was almost worth going through all the pain, the betrayal, just to see the shock on his face now. Just to live in this moment. Where this man could not believe he didn't own her anymore. Her heart, her body, any part of her.

"There's somebody else, isn't there?"

Of course he was that oblivious, even still. Of course he hadn't put together that she was with Zach, probably because he didn't think she could get Zach.

Zach, who had been instrumental in making her see that she didn't have to be the caregiver in the relationship who never got anything in return. In making her understand what she actually wanted out of life and a partnership.

But the honest truth was, she would be making this decision even without Zach.

Because she was a woman who remembered how to run wild, how to howl at the moon just because it was there.

She was a woman who wanted a wild and fierce life, and a love that went with it.

She had that with Zach.

But she had it with herself too.

"Yes," she said. "There is someone else."

"I knew it, I—"

"It's me. I'm choosing me."

Chapter Thirty-Seven

Soraya

It's never too late to break a cycle
and begin anew.

—Rules for Witches

Declan went with Soraya to her divorce proceedings and then helped her clear out her apartment, once she got the finances in order, and ended up with enough money from the settlement to get herself a house that would be big enough for her and the boys.

Their relationship with David was rocky now. She was trying to facilitate inroads, but they felt betrayed by his lies, and fair enough. She couldn't say they were entirely comfortable with her relationship with Declan, but when David had tried a last-gasp form of manipulation by saying she was a sinner for sleeping with him and exposing the boys to her lifestyle, they had pretty much told him to go to hell. "It's not Mom that starred in the church's first and only sex tape."

She loved Levi for that one. And the old version of her would've been slightly appalled by her decisions, it was true, but she was aiming for honesty when it came to the kids. Because she did feel like lies had harmed them so much.

Declan also helped her get moved into the new house. As she stood there, gazing wistfully at the living room, now entirely full of furniture, she looked at him and felt a pang in her chest. She cared about him. A lot. She knew everything about him. His life growing up, his journey to becoming a doctor. How he'd met his wife and fallen in love with her. How much he loved his son. How badly it had hurt to lose him. He talked about him with ease. She was so glad that he could. It was a real relationship. He was patient with her, with her baggage, with the things she was still struggling with.

"Declan," she said. "I . . . I really care about you. This is my first house. The apartment was my first apartment that was just mine. I love my work at the apothecary. I love all these things I'm finding out about myself, and you helped me with some of it. But I'm afraid of what this means. I'm afraid of what I'll lose if we keep getting more and more serious. I just don't—"

"I'm going to stop you right there. Soraya, I'm falling in love with you. I know the timing is terrible. I also know that your experience of relationships is meeting and getting married, and that it forced you to give up a lot. I don't need that from you. I love spending time with you. Talking to you. Being with you. I love watching you figure out who you want to be. I'm still doing that too. Because I'm a different person than the man I was before I lost my son. I'm still figuring out what it looks like to be a dad who doesn't have a kid in this world. I really like spending time with your kids, but I know I'm not their father. I appreciate all that about you. That it gives me space for myself too. I'm never going to ask you to give something up to be with me. Now, if you don't want to be together because it's not working for you, that's just fine. But if you're scared of losing yourself, don't be. I'm never going to ask you to give up your independence. I'm never going to ask you to cut off pieces of yourself to make me happy."

He paused for a moment. "I know you never got to date, though. So if you feel like you need to go sleep with other people . . ."

"I don't," she said. "And you're right. I don't know what a relationship looks like when it's not a rush down the aisle. I don't know what it's like to just let one be."

"Let's let it be."

The very idea filled her with hope and a sense of freedom she'd never known was possible. With her, everything had always needed to be planned. Certain. Done with a rigid set of boundaries and guidelines.

The idea of just living for a while, just loving for a while . . . it was a revelation. One she was happy to embrace.

Chapter Thirty-Eight

Nora

To see yourself clearly is to see the world clearly.

—Rules for Witches

It was a whole lot of moving. Between getting the apartment cleaned out and then refurnished as they got it set up to be temporary housing for women in situations like theirs, women who no longer had a place to stay because of a divorce, a death, a separation, or any other circumstance that left them in the lurch, Nora was vacating her house. And moving in with Sam.

While she hoped that her move wouldn't intersect with Ben, it did. He ended up getting discharged right as she was getting the last of her boxes loaded into her car.

"Jesus, Nora. Can't we talk about this?" Ben said.

"No. There's nothing to talk about. I'm moving in with Sam."

"What?"

"I'm in love with Sam. Thank you for the time apart, which helped me finally see that."

"Oh, I knew it. I knew you were screwing him behind my back."

"I wasn't, actually. If I were sleeping with him, I would've married him in the first place, Ben." She took a deep breath. "The one thing I'll say is that I'm sorry. I'm sorry, and I'm not trying to be hurtful when I tell you this, but . . . you didn't have all of me. And I'm sorry for that. I'm sorry that the way I grew up made it hard for me to recognize that. I'm sorry that it made it so I married you when I shouldn't have. I swear I didn't do it on purpose. I didn't know at the time I wasn't giving you everything."

"My mom said you weren't good enough for me. She was right. She was right. You're just trailer trash. You can't help yourself. Water seeks its own level."

What he was saying was deeply messed up. Deeply hurtful. At least, the way he meant it. But the truth was, he was right, even if he wasn't right in the way he meant to be.

For her, it had to be Sam. For her, it had to be a man who truly understood her. Who saw her. It had been what she was running from. Because she hadn't wanted that. She had wanted to paste over it, to make herself into something new. She had thought she could outrun her trauma and not have to deal with it. Not have to process it. But the chickens were always going to come home to roost, and there was no running away from what had happened. From the pain she experienced in her life. She understood that now.

"You were never good enough for me," she said. "You never actually loved me. You love the woman I dressed up as, and some of that is my own fault. But you were never strong enough to handle me. To take on everything I went through. Everything I am. Sam is. I had to get good enough for him. I had to get strong enough for him. But I'm there now. I think the way you handled ending our marriage was terrible. I deserved better. But I'm glad that it's over. I've never been happier."

With that, she walked out of the house for the last time. The house that had a playroom devoted to her and nothing more. That house that had never, ever felt like hers.

It was like finally closing the door on something she'd needed to get rid of for a very long time.

Their first night together in Sam's house, which was now their house, Sam looked up at her over dinner. "So, when are you going to write your book, Nora?"

Because Sam actually knew. Knew her. Knew it was one of the things she'd been holding herself back from all this time.

"Maybe it's time."

"Do you have an idea?"

"Yes, I do. I think I want to write a book about women finally figuring out who they are. Finding their magic."

"It'll be a bestseller."

"I love you," she said.

"I love you too."

And when he said that, she knew he meant he loved all of her. Because he was the only person who had ever known her like that.

To realize she'd had it all this time wasn't sad. It was wonderful. She had spent her life being so cynical. Believing in very little.

Now she believed in everything.

Her own magic most of all.

Chapter Thirty-Nine

Nora

The best revenge is living well. The best living is making sure those around you live well too.

—Rules for Witches

The dinner could not have been more beautiful. They staged it in the park across the street from the apothecary. Long tables were set out on the wide green lawn, with bright, cheery sunflowers all over the tables, and orange and yellow candles set between them. Soraya had indeed made the most beautiful cakes for the event, and there was other food catered by local female-owned businesses. Nora, Soraya, and Daisy were all dressed in white dresses, glitter on their cheeks, which Nora had pronounced deeply uncool, and Daisy and Soraya had paid no attention to whatsoever.

Soraya had also supplied them with summery witch hats. Pointed and dramatic, but white with pink flowers.

"For cute adventures!" she'd said.

"And what would the leaders of your new church have to say?" Nora asked, looking in the mirror in the shop one final time before they stepped outside with baskets full of the last little bit they needed to bring over to the feast.

"Half of them are coming," she said cheerfully.

Nora smiled.

Watching Soraya stay fiercely true to herself and her beliefs was inspiring. She had changed, but it was following her own conscience, never acting out of anger or bitterness toward the people who had manipulated her. She had kept it, as she had expanded herself.

Their guest of honor was Alexandra, who had just been discharged from the hospital and was already sitting at the head of one of the tables, with Madison to her left.

So many items had been donated for the silent auction that would happen after the feast, a fundraiser to help women in their area who had been victims of domestic violence. In honor of Alexandra.

They had already decided that Lady's Mantle would have this event every year, for the Alexandra Stone Fund. Which Alexandra was more than capable of organizing and overseeing, as the queen of committees. When someone in their community found themselves pushed out of their lives, found themselves in the same position that any of them had been in, where they were forced to remake each other, relearn what living meant, there would be a whole network of people waiting for them. A coven, waiting to help them unlock their magic. To unlock their joy.

Because sometimes the end was only a beginning.

That was the real lesson of the Death card, after all, loath though Nora was to admit it, since she had been bitter about that reading of hers for weeks.

It hadn't only been about the ending. It had been about the new beginning. What better time to celebrate that?

There were quilts and baked goods, ceramics and crystals. A hand-drawn tarot deck, and so many other beautiful baked goods, crafts, handknits, and paintings in the auction, made by hand by the women in the community who raised an extraordinary amount of money for the cause.

It would help Angela, who was their first resident at the Lady's Mantle Sanctuary. Well, the second. Soraya had been the first.

Now Soraya had a whole new life.

Nora looked around at all the women gathered together, and then at her two best friends. The friends who had walked her through the darkness right into this new light. Who had walked her into her magic.

She'd been doing finishing touches on her mural, and there was something that wasn't quite right about it yet.

She suddenly knew just what it was.

It needed the three of them.

The mural was about community, after all.

They were her community. Her support.

Her coven.

The dinner was bright and glorious, and the spectacle of it being in the park brought other people to come and watch. Men and women who hadn't heard about it before. Children. And yes, there were some who looked at it and decided it was evil. But most everybody could see the magic, all its beauty.

"Where's Aggie?" Soraya said, looking around about midway through dinner, not seeing their mentor anywhere.

But Aggie did everything on her own time and on her own terms, so Nora couldn't say she was alarmed.

The three of them left while there were still some diners lingering—the city had agreed to let them leave the tables out on the lawn for the night. Madison and Amberly had been sitting together talking about polycules. Amberly had broken off her engagement with Jonathan a few weeks ago.

"I need to get home. Zach has the kids tonight. Not that I'm worried but . . ."

"You just want to go jump him," Nora said.

"Maybe." Daisy smiled, touching the ring on her finger.

It was fast. But Nora understood. When it was right, it was right.

Right now, their lives were more than right. They were magical.

What Nora really wanted to do was go home and kiss Sam. Tell him everything. About how well the evening had gone and how much money they had raised.

"I'm staying with Declan tonight," said Soraya. "The boys are having some big Xbox thing at our house, and they're going to be up all night drinking Mountain Dew and generally being menaces. Anyway, I'm two minutes away if they need anything. But they won't." Soraya paused for a moment. "I think I'm in love with him. Like *really* in love with him. That doesn't seem . . . Does it seem weird, that we all found love again so quickly?"

Daisy looked thoughtful. "What's the point of being magic if you can't have everything?"

Nora smiled.

She walked through the dark, empty apothecary, and stopped when she noticed a white sheet of paper on the table, with three tarot cards underneath.

"What's this?" She picked it up and saw it was a letter written in Aggie's handwriting. *"My three beautiful witches, my work here is done. This apothecary belongs to you now, where I know you will continue this work. To help others, to harness your own magic, and to bring joy and community to those who need it."* Nora's eyes filled with tears. "She left us the apothecary."

"What?" Daisy grabbed the paper out of Nora's hand. *"Daisy, I know you'll do a great job with the finances. Soraya, your baking magic will be exactly what this place needs. Nora, your creativity will always keep it alive."*

Soraya took the sheet of paper and read the rest. *"I left you each a card, to show you how far you've come. The queens are the highest form of feminine energy in their suit, as you have all changed, evolved, and gone on this journey, and emerged stronger, more powerful. Nora, my Queen of Swords. You are a sharp communicator, using words with precision and clarity. The Queen of Swords is the author of the deck, as are you. Soraya, Queen of Pentacles, my kitchen witch who knows how to balance her responsibilities with life's pleasures, one who takes joy in creating beauty wherever she goes, sensual and nurturing, all in harmony. Daisy, my Queen of Cups. Compassion, intuition, and love are her strengths, and they are yours too. You see the divine in everyone and recognize it in yourself. You remember to first treat yourself with compassion, so you can let it flow out to others. My three queens, my dear witches, your time is just beginning."*

"I can't believe she's just . . . gone." Nora looked around the shop, which contained the same amount of things it always had but felt emptier somehow.

"I can," Soraya said. "Because it's just exactly what she would do."

Nora couldn't argue with that.

"She's not gone, though," Daisy said. "Because she changed us. She'll always be here. Her and her magic."

Nora took the letter and folded it, tucking it away, and they each took their cards. Then they walked outside onto the street, and Daisy locked the door of the apothecary, and they all stood there for a moment together, looking at this place, which was now theirs.

Then the three of them linked arms and walked down the sidewalk toward where they had parked.

Daisy tugged Nora's hand, and they twirled underneath the streetlights, Soraya joining in. Daisy howled, shaking her hair and looking up at the sky.

"I call my power back to me!" Daisy proclaimed.

"I call my energy back to me," Nora said.

"I call my magic back to me," Soraya added.

Then they chanted together. "I am shielded from anything that would take my power from me. Nothing can harm me or take my light. I am safe. I am protected. I am powerful."

"And," Soraya added, "I get to have every beautiful and wonderful thing the universe has to offer."

One thing Nora knew for sure was that if your life was going to implode over a guy, you needed to have friends, you needed to be brave, and you needed to find your magic.

She'd found hers.

Nora smiled. "And so it is."

Acknowledgments

A very special acknowledgment to Megan Crane, who once asked a question that has stuck with me ever since: What are spells but prayers men don't like?

And who also supplied me with the very helpful perspective: The Tower means he likes you.

Megan, you are magic.

About the Author

Photo © 2023 Kerry Shroy

Maisey Yates is the *New York Times* bestselling author of over one hundred romance novels, including *Happy After All*, *Cruel Summer*, and the Four Corners Ranch series. Whether she's writing strong, hardworking cowboys, dissolute princes, or multigenerational family stories, she loves getting lost in fictional worlds. An avid knitter with a dangerous yarn addiction and an aversion to housework, Maisey lives with her husband and three kids in rural Oregon. For more information, visit www.maiseyyates.com.